THE STARS WITHIN

by

STEFAN PETRUCHA

Published by

GUNGNIR

GUNGNIR

· TALES FROM THE ALL-FATHER ·

Original Title: The Stars Within
First edition: 10 December, 2025
Written by: Stefan Petrucha
Edited By Jim Krueger
Designer: Mohamed Samah
Published by: Matthew Medney
First print run: 1000 Units
© 2024, Stefan Petrucha
© 2024, GUNGNIR

CONTENT WARNING
- Discussions and descriptions of death and dying
- Anxiety and panic
-Violence against children and elderly
-Graphic, detailed descriptions of injury and/ or bodily harm
- Suicidal ideation

Printed in China
ISBN: 978-1-962594-17-2
Published by Gungnir

"Let us treat men and women well; treat them as if they were real; perhaps they are."

– Ralph Waldo Emerson (1844)

"We're so invested in thinking highly of what we believe we are, we prevent ourselves from thinking highly of what we may actually be."

– Seiðr Ludi (10,687)

CHAPTER

0

Calico, who would one day be known as the Mother of All That is to Come, was right there at the supposed end of the world. Her thin hands held ratty cardboard pictures out towards passersby, wordlessly asking the soon-to-be-dead for help in the form of money or a meal.

Before it all shattered, the Grayborn picked her up. They explained things, asked her to help, then sent her on ahead to meet the World Soul and decide, well... everything.

CHAPTER

1

White. Everything in the Chamber was white, so white that not a footprint, let alone a history, could be left behind. Were it not for the occasional crack from poor maintenance, the white would render everything in the Archosian prison meaningless, save for the whiteness of its white.

"Go on."

The boy didn't want to start a whole conversation about it, not with their armed escort listening, but being a boy, he also didn't want to stand in line forever, so he said, for the second time:

"Go on, already. Move! Seriously, what are you looking at?" He glared at his distracted companion. "It's all white, like every prison in the galaxy, to enhance the photonic shielding."

Everyone knows that. Why doesn't she?

He growled in his not-yet-deep voice: "If you have to stare, at least look at the people."

Their color, the color of everyone waiting in a hundred lines, varied like madness—umber, russet, gold, ochre, rubicund and alabaster, rosy and taupe, dull bluish-gray, olive. His father told him skin color used to be an indicator of geographic origin, but a few generations of Archosian free migration made it all guesswork. His skin, for instance, was ecru, the grayish-yellow once native to Archosia itself, but now too common to place.

Luckily.

Calico, his companion, had skin somewhere between gold and copper. Not metallic, like some fringe system natives. Hers was soft, like one of the thousands of ill-defined hues he'd seen in Archosia's sunset. The sight of it filled him with a longing, a longing for more than home – one of the reasons he'd fallen in love with her at first sight.

No, not love. And not exactly at first sight. When he woke in the dark bunk of the patroller that brought them here, he expected to be alone. Seeing her, sitting on a bench, long frayed hair covering her face, too still to be alive, he thought she was a nightmare, that at any moment, she'd snarl and scream like a hungry ghost, ready to devour him like all lost boys.

But now, not too much later, if it wasn't love, it wasn't far from it.

He didn't want to feel anything for her. He didn't know her. The age difference was embarrassing. He had other things, far more important things, to worry about. Still, he felt the urge to protect and guide her, two very odd instincts for the boy. Maybe he was naturally heroic. His mother always told him he was special, more than special, and this could be that. But his mother was supposed to think the world of him – or think of him as the world. Still, Calico must think he was special, too. Why else would she trust some filthy kid stowaway?

Maybe because she was crazy. She certainly looked and acted that way. Maybe she reminded him of his mother, but his mind didn't want to go there at all.

"Go on," he said, for the third time. "What are you doing?"

"Judging," she said softly.

"Judging? What could you possibly be judging here?"

She blinked a thin half-smile to her face. "Everything."

But she also, at last, obeyed and stepped forward.

The boy instantly told himself his irritation had been fake, strategic, a way to protect them both. Beyond the moment's annoyance, something about her undeniably, unequivocally, put him at ease. The only things about her that didn't were the dark, old bruises he glimpsed beneath her threadbare tunic.

Who would…? Stop. Stop it. She probably got them from flailing around in that old survival pod the patroller found her in. I'm better off thinking she's hopeless. It'll make it easier to ditch her, or even use her as a human shield if it comes to it.

While he would have to move on alone, he doubted there'd be weapon fire here. The guards kept their aged gyrojets holstered. Subject to reloading, they weren't nearly as dangerous as the new breed using Stifler's Plasma, making them more symbols than threats.

It made sense. All they needed was a symbol. No one escaped the Chamber.

The intake kiosk admin they waited for didn't bother wearing any protective gear at all, probably to make it easier to sigh and type. Which is all he seemed to do. No doubt the man considered himself powerful. His father would have called him an apparatchik.

Finally, the admin waved Calico closer. He spoke as if saying it for the third, not the first, time, and she was hard of hearing.

"Just Calico, huh? Like Calico the Mother of All?" He chortled like a good Archosian atheist.

She nodded absently.

"You were in some sort of survival pod way out there? Crazy luck they found you at all. No missing ships in that sector. For the record, do you remember anything other than your first name"

Like a child on her first trip, Calico smiled, looked up and around, then shook her head, no.

The admin clucked. "That patroller captain entered a debris field to save you. He didn't have to do that, you know."

"Yes," she said. "I owe him a great deal. He made that clear."

And he was rude about it, too, like he expected her to pay for the damage. True, the little patroller, the same that found the boy stowing away on a freighter, was now badly in need of repair. The Chamber close by, the captain decided to let the prison deal with them both while he tried to get their shop mechanics to cut him a deal.

More sighing, more keying. "You'll be taken to the block H1420 infirmary for a med and psych workup. You're not a prisoner, but I strongly recommend you stick to the green areas. This is not the sort of place you want to wander."

He thumbed an icy smooth arch to his left.

Puzzled by it, Calico looked to the boy.

He nodded her forward. "Go on. It's okay. It's a scanner."

Understanding or not, she entered, then studied the lines of light that struck the sides of her body with the same curiosity she brought to the white walls.

Beyond the arch, two guards waited at the head of a narrow corridor. More severe, their body armor was thick, and their gyrojets held at the ready. When they approached

Calico, she turned back, worried she'd be taken away and lose track of the boy. Instead, they waited for him.

And here he'd been hoping to talk his way out of being scanned. The more eyes on him, the lower his odds.

The admin focused on his screen. "And you, stowaway… don't even have a first name?"

"Of course, I do, but I'd… rather not say."

"Hrm. Freighter's not pursuing charges and your biometrics don't match any fugitives."

"So, I can go?"

The apparatchik produced his loudest sigh yet. He almost seemed proud of it. "Wouldn't that be nice? Unfortunately, ever since we released an unregistered hish dealer who turned out to be a genocider, anyone found in the commission of any crime stays put until their identity's confirmed."

The boy aimed his nose at Calico. "How do you know she's not a genocider?"

She smiled and waved.

"I don't. Could've bumped off a dozen worlds single-handedly for all I know. It's the quiet ones you need to look out for. But she wasn't caught committing a crime."

"But… there must be millions of unregistered."

"Maybe a trillion. Half the sentients in the galaxy aren't in Archosia's database. But they also weren't picked up in the commission of a crime. You, on the other hand, are a stowaway. End of story. Want to give me a name?"

He had to give the man something, just not the truth. He never had to wonder who to be before. The boy had always been told. There was a name he'd answer to instinctively, but he hated it more than anything. It wouldn't show up as registered, and there was no way the admin thought he might actually be a criminal. He just wanted to tick his boxes. So…

"Wyrm."

The admin laughed. "No wonder you don't want to tell anyone…"

"I'm an orphan. My parents were eaten by Kardun."

The admin laughed harder. "Were they now?"

Wyrm wanted to crawl inside himself. *Ack. Old Ludi was right. I never know when to shut up. Eaten by Kardun. Could I come up with a more stupid...*

"Accent's Archosian, assuming you're not smart enough to fake that." The apparatchik, annoyed now at having to think about what to put in his boxes, turned back to his keystrokes. "That freighter was headed for the fringes. What's out there for you?"

Out of options, Wyrm tried some of the truth. "Earth. I was heading for the Earth."

Believing that less than the lies, the man leaned forward, jacket buttons clicking the kiosk. "Right. Let me tell you about myself. If they paid a decent wage, someone much better than me would have this job. Why? Because I'm lazy and forgetful. Running your biometrics through all the independent databanks will take up to six cycles. By then, I'll have forgotten you exist. And incompetent little me is the only one of any import who knows you're here. That means now is the time to ask yourself if whoever or whatever you're hiding from, is worse than going through puberty and possibly adulthood with what's waiting inside."

The boy gulped. That was it, then. He might die in prison.

Still, he met the glare head-on. "I told you. My name is Wyrm."

"Fine." He turned to the guards waiting beyond the arch. "Take Wyrm here to H5676. I'll notify the block ward."

He nodded the boy toward the scanner. Wyrm, out of options, fought to reassure himself.

Oh, it'll be fine. If the patroller didn't find it, how much better can these scanners be?

He stepped through.

I can make it. I can make it. Once I'm inside, the rest will be easy.

A buzzer buzzed. A red light glowed.

"Contraband," the system announced.

As Calico watched, ever-curious, the two outer guards aimed their weapons at the boy, while one of the inner guards pinned his arms behind his back. Pointing at the too-large lump between the boy's legs that was now painfully visible, the admin put his hand out.

"Unless you want me to go fishing for it?"

It's still fine. They won't know what it is. They can't know what it is. No one does. If I play it right, maybe they'll let me keep it.

Trying to keep his hands steady, Wyrm undid the belt and withdrew a clear, fist-sized sphere. Reflected in it, the Chamber's white surfaces acquired a rainbow edge.

A rare moment of interest in his otherwise dull life prodded the apparatchik to give it a closer look. "Whatever it is, I'm sure the owner's reported it stolen. Probably a reward for returning it."

Wyrm mustered his indignation. "It's mine. A keepsake, from my father."

"Before or after the Kardun ate him?"

The guards laughed.

Calico did, too, but when she figured out the joke was directed at Wyrm, she stopped.

"I was lying about that," Wyrm said. "But he is dead, and I don't think it's worth much to anyone, except me."

The admin narrowed his eyes. "What's your father's name?"

"I never knew. My mother gave it to me before she died. She said it was his."

Unmoved, the apparatchik reached across his little desk to take it.

Despite knowing it was useless, Wyrm protested. "I'm not supposed to let anyone touch it!"

Calico moved as if she wanted to help, but one of the guards blocked her path.

Holding the sphere, the admin turned it this way and that, fascinated by the indentations and subtle undersurface reflections.

As Wyrm squirmed in the guard's grip, he panicked, and when he panicked, he began to sweat.

No, no, no! Not now! They'll recognize me!

The others enchanted by the glistening ball, Calico was first to notice that Wyrm's sweat wasn't normal. Not at all. Viscous, copious, opaque, it rolled more than dripped down his forehead.

"Give it back!"

His plea barely earned a sideways glance. "I'm doing you a favor, son. Just last week a man was killed for his socks. Do you think they won't find this? It's better for you if I keep it to remind me that you're in there. If I do manage to identify you, and it's as worthless as you say, you'll have it back."

Noting how the guards eyed the sphere, the admin slipped it into his pocket.

No!

Meanwhile, Calico had drawn close enough to place a hand on Wyrm's wet cheek. When she withdrew it, strands of the sweat briefly clung to her palm.

That, they all noticed.

The admin leaped back. "By Abraxas! What the fuck?"

Realizing that even the boy's wrists were moist and sticky, the outer guard released his grip and stared at the slime on his gloves. "Is it contagious?"

Wyrm considered lying again, saying that it was, that they'd all die just from touching it, but then they'd probably shoot him to prevent the spread. "No. It's not contagious. It's an allergic stress reaction, triggered by things like having my sphere stolen."

If the admin was worried, he hid it. "Everyone relax. The scanner would've identified any known pathogens. But to be sure, let's take a closer look. Back in the arch, boy."

Through the thick drops obscuring his face and eyes, Wyrm managed a defiant stare. "Only if you give me back my sphere."

"It wasn't a request."

The admin nodded at the guards.

In no hurry to touch the boy and his odd secretions, they didn't budge. Not used to being disobeyed, the admin hissed and snarled, trying to decide what to do. Noticing Calico's gooey palm, he grabbed and pulled her toward the arch. When her body stumbled into his, she let out a little yelp.

He spoke to her as if trying to calm an animal. "Easy. It's for your own protection."

Damn stupid sweat. They'll figure it out now. Sooner rather than later.

When the terminal flashed green, he let her go. "See? He wasn't lying for a change. It's just mucus. On the lighter side, between that and the sphere, it won't take long to identify him. Take him to the infirmary, too. See if they can calm him enough so the prisoners don't think we're trying to infect them and decide to incinerate him as a precaution."

Panting, Wyrm entered the endless white of the inner corridors.

One guard leading, the other at their back, they marched along a series of similar, and similarly disorienting passages. The Chamber's maze of halls was said to be more effective than the photonic shielding in keeping prisoners inside. Even the guards had to check their wrist locators when making turns.

Wyrm's heart sank. *Even if I could get out of my cell, I'd never find a way out of this.*

Dry air from the unseen ventilation evaporated the moisture on his skin, but, as usual, the crackly residue left him covered in hives. Hard as it was to deal with the itching, Calico made it worse, sidling so close there was barely any space between them. "Go on, move ahead of me."

The words not having any effect, he scowled at her, hoping she'd take the hint. When she didn't, he shouted: "Stop! Just stop!"

The lead guard paused, but not because of his outburst. Something was wrong with his locator. When his partner came up to see what the problem was, Calico elbowed Wyrm hard, in the ribs. Between the hives and what felt like it would become a bruise, he nearly screamed.

Instead, he made a face that asked her: *What?!*

Her eyes dipped toward her belly, where her hands were cupped as if holding a small animal. When she parted her fingers, he saw she held the sphere.

Eyes wide, he mouthed, *How?*

She mimed the moment she fell into the admin.

Stunned she'd help him, stunned she could help him, Wyrm mouthed, *Why?*

Her fingers played against her cheek, indicating his sweat. An exaggerated sad face told him she'd felt bad for him. He wanted to hug her, but imagining it would be painful, he grabbed the sphere and shoved it back under his tunic.

The cool, smooth surface felt good against the hives, already making them shrink, until he realized that at any moment, the admin would notice it was missing. The guards still busy with their locators, he dared a low whisper.

"Calico, could you do one more thing for me?"

"What?"

"Run!"

With that same thin half-smile she used while judging the world, she obeyed.

As he sprinted beside her, Wyrm thought that so far, he hadn't done badly after all.

Mother always said I was special. Hell, maybe I really am the World Soul.

CHAPTER

2

Neiman Os' shower guard shifted about, uncertain where to stand. He was clearly uncomfortable, a fact which pleased Os.

"If you'd like to watch, I don't mind."

"No."

It was always a different guard, and always only one, their schedules shifted randomly to prevent any possible collusion. Otherwise, it was feared Os would turn them against each other.

This clumsy fellow seems new. I can't have gone through them all already, can I? Well, why not? The only thing about this place that still surprises me is how so much white can be so filthy – all those smells hanging naked in the air.

Os smiled at him. "Are you sure? It is a unique opportunity. I am the only sentient alien humanity knows about. No harm in looking. Toujours gai."

The poor man frowned, highlighting the lines in his reddening face.

"Toujours gai. It's a phrase I came across in an ancient story databank, poems written by a cockroach. Means something like, always happy. More a request than a statement, really. Always did have a fondness for pre-Calician Earth culture. Even got the idea for creating my own nonhuman pronoun from a 1920 novel, back when they counted the years since they killed the child of their god." Os stretched. "So, what do you say? Have a look?"

"No," the guard said. After a beat, he added, "Thank you."

Definitely new. What sad turn brought you to this crappy job? Archosia's new plasma swallow up your home world?

Thanks to the elite naturalist panel tasked with studying ƶher, Os was required to shower alone. Having bedded everyone on that panel, Os thought their report was rife with sour grapes. After all, the convicted con artist chose prison over remaining their laboratory plaything.

But… of course, they were right to be careful. If they weren't, Os would be long gone. Homo sapiens were constantly in heat, and zher ability to generate targeted pheromones could easily exert a problematic influence on other inmates, or most anyone for that matter, with an accent on mate.

More than problematic. An outsider able to excite and manipulate human mating and bonding urges could start their own army, control a nation, or a world.

Wish I'd thought of that before they caught me. But… toujours gai.

Os gave the newbie a wink before disappearing behind the privacy screen. Undressing, zhe considered "accidentally" pushing the screen aside, just for fun. All thought of personal amusement vanished, though, when the incredibly unusual, and incredibly contraband, communicator hidden deep in zher ear canal squawked to life.

"Small change in plans."

Though Dr. Warland's device was the size of a triticale kernel, the audio was crisp and clear. It was Alek Fray, the soldier. Former soldier since he assassinated somebody or other. Now he was a convict, just like Os.

Half-dressed, Os started the shower and waited for the hissing steam to better cover zher response. "Do go on, soldier boy."

"We're escaping now. Right now."

"A small change? Fray, what the fuck? My things are back in my cell."

Running, Fray panted. "Not my call. Charnel overheard that two new arrivals decided to make a run for it in the maze. He figures admin will blame them for anything unusual, giving us cover, so he had Warland bring down their coms."

Os stared at the streaming water. "A pity, but he's right. Most of the guards won't even notice until they check their wrists. Then they'll get terribly lost. This is our best shot."

"Yeah, well, I'm on my way, aren't I? Warland said her blocker will burn out in about five minutes, along with our chances."

"I'll need at least two to seduce the guard."

"I'll be there in one, and I'm not into three ways."

"Spoilsport."

Fray was an easy read, Warland reliably insane, but Charnel had secrets, and the smells sociopaths gave off didn't always match their intent. Charnel also, wisely, insisted they meet with Os only when they were all present, so there was never a moment to voice those doubts one-on-one. They did all need each other to escape, so there was that.

No going back, then. Free or... dead. Toujours gai.

Soaked and steaming, zhe yanked away the privacy screen. The guard couldn't help but gape. Not that the black, far-set eyes, neatly divided by a strong, aquiline nose, were particularly attractive to humans. Neither was the zaffre skin, or the cloud-white feathery tufts atop zher narrow skull.

What was appealing was the accompanying symphony of pheromones zher glands produced. Carried by the steam, the chemicals not only engendered desire, but they also promised a satisfactory release. A rare few did manage to defer acting on this desire – little puzzles Os stored for future rumination – zhe hoped the guard wasn't one.

He wasn't. He was already lowering his weapon.

"Wh-what are you doing?"

Lacking time, Os dared a few barefoot steps forward. "Exploring."

"I can't..."

"Of course, you can. Everyone does. Every guard in the Chamber. Ask around. If I never see you again, and I won't, admin doesn't care. Consider it compensation for the shitty pay."

The latest hires were largely from fallen Pantheon worlds. Their home economies in shambles, displaced workers were forced to take any pay available. That included the low wages here, which had been further reduced under High Warden Swope. That sort of resentment always helped loosen the chains on base desire. He worked hard. Why shouldn't he have some fun?

"Are you even a...?"

Zhe caught a whiff of the man's expectations. Heteronormative. Zhe was a she then.

"Yes. Whatever you're thinking, whatever you want. It's me."

Os took the guard's hand and pressed it to zher chest so he could feel, as well as see, the curves swelling along zher slender form.

"There are limits to what I can change, but I've never had any complaints."

Os ran an index finger through the man's hair, pressing hard, careful not to scratch, but promising zhe would, if he liked.

"If they catch us…"

It was the only opening Os needed. Being from the Pantheon, he must believe in some deity or other. Some sects were wonderfully inventive, but those that maintained order tended to be prudish on principle, none worse than the followers of Lau. That, of course, made them easy, but boring.

In this case, a lucky kind of boring.

Zhe cooed, "Isn't it a waste to devote all that imagination to the punishment, and none to the crime?"

That did it. He pulled zher in for an open-mouthed kiss. As Os roughly slid zher tongue against his, zhe provided the promised scratch. Rather than a fingernail, it came from a tiny, needlelike protrusion, courtesy of Dr. Ema Warland. As expected, the guard didn't notice anything wrong until his eyes rolled up into his head.

Os was pleased to think it had been considerably less than a minute, but a second later, Fray arrived. Soldier-boy didn't reek of fear, that much was tamed by his Archosian training, but it was still there – a subtle, background note.

Seeing that the guard was out, he wasted no time spinning back to the exit, moving with a precision that made his monochrome prison outfit almost look like a military uniform.

"Good. Okay, let's go."

"In a moment."

After slipping back into the prison overalls, Os gave the guard's crotch a good last squeeze and took his sidearm.

"Must you?"

"I may not have scruples," Os explained, "but I do have an aesthetic."

When his disapproving look remained, Os worried about being mistaken for a liability. Fray wasn't the type for an outright betrayal, he was the only one of them who showed any form of kindness, but he was a soldier, used to making sacrifices. And while the Pantheon might believe in an afterlife, Os did not.

In any case, I'm told it's only for humans and their pets. I suppose I might get in as a pet, but then I may as well have stayed with those naturalists.

Just outside the showers, two custodial staff lay on the white floor, rendered unconscious by Fray through less enjoyable means. Ahead lay four thousand courtyards surrounded by blocks of five hundred cells, each in turn encircled by labyrinths of disorienting corridors complete with kitchens, showers, service docks, and other support areas.

Fray sized things up as he moved. "With the coms out, the guards will automatically redeploy to trouble spots and choke points. Only a few will stay in the maze itself."

"Assuming they've realized what's wrong yet," Os responded, trying to be helpful.

The narrow stretch of hall was their last easy landmark. Leaving it behind, they sped through the ever-white, hunting for any hint of movement other than their own. Fray's eyes darted raptor-like. Os relied on smell.

Fortunately, the soldier had memorized the first five turns, and the con artist was pleased to remember the sixth. At the next four-way intersection, though, both paused.

Fray's head snapped east, north, south. "The mark. It must be here. Cleaning isn't scheduled until…"

They'd spent weeks placing them, weeks more replacing them whenever maintenance washed them away. Losing one would leave them hopelessly lost.

Os pointed to a nearly invisible smear of grain mash. "There."

"Where? I don't see any…"

Os tapped zher nose. "Smells like the cafeteria."

After a rare complimentary nod, they barreled ahead.

Having shown soldier-boy zhe had value beyond "acquiring" a launch code, Os realized this would be their only opportunity to chat about their partners.

"I'm sorry we've never had a chance to get to know each other better."

"No, thanks."

"Not what I mean. Fray, can we chat? Just chat? I can do that, you know. One wants to trust their companions even during a jailbreak. Has it bothered you that General Charnel made sure we were never without him?"

"You blame him? He may be a better pilot, but I can fly, too."

"Speaking of which, what was the last you heard from Charnel and the good doctor?"

"They were at the edge of the dead zone. By now they're either dead or close enough to the docks for the photonic shielding to block her organic communicators. Not that it makes growing audio components from prison food any less impressive."

"Here's another question then. Why are we meeting in the main cargo hold? Why not head straight to the dock?"

Fray picked up speed. "A little busy right now."

His tone betrayed no opinion—but Os caught a whiff of doubt, and more than a little sympathy toward the question. "You've been wondering the same thing, haven't you?"

"So what? I only know what they told us both, that it shares a wall with the service dock, and they want to avoid the guards at the entrance."

Os used a compliment to state the obvious. "You know there are just as many guards outside the cargo hold as there are outside the dock, and one fewer wall."

Fray didn't slow. "If you're asking whether I trust two genociders, the answer's no. Charnel especially. I'd never work with that scum if I didn't know he was dying."

"Warland's crime troubles you less?"

He frowned. "She created a race of sentient microscopic beings, then destroyed them. Was it a nice thing to do? No. Is it the same as wiping out the population of an entire planet? Honestly…. I... I'm… not sure, okay? What are you fishing around for? Do you know something?"

"Only that…"

Before Os could finish, a high-pitched keening flooded their ears, a sound painful enough to make them stop short.

Wincing, Fray forced himself to listen for a pattern. "It's an old contingency alarm. Probably hasn't been used in so long the newer guards won't know what it means, and the rest won't remember. The sub-chiefs will position more security at the docks—

meaning we'll have company soon." He motioned for the weapon Os had taken. "Hand it over."

"I'd rather keep it."

Fray made a face. "That's not the deal. I'm the one with the training."

"I have my reasons."

"Like what?"

Os could tell he was considering taking it by force, but also that he wouldn't, not yet.

The explanation had to be quick. "You've heard the rumors about that cargo hold?"

"That ghost story? So what? It was probably spread by a bunch of Pantheon refugees who still think the universe was created when Beast Father fucked Mother Sky and his seed spurted through the void, and all the gods are their children."

Os released some pheromones, but only to offset his anger. "I never met a lie that didn't contain a kernel of truth."

Rushed, and not wanting to listen, the soldier grunted and took to running again, speaking only when Os caught up. "Do you honestly believe there's a prisoner so dangerous they had to build a cell around them right there in the cargo hold?"

"Yes, but not until a lower warden confirmed it. And before you ask, yes, it was while she was fucking me and yes, she exaggerated to impress me, but she wasn't lying. Think about it. The service dock in our block is half the size of the others."

Fray slowed a little.

At least he doesn't *not* believe me.

"Even if that's true, how does it translate into me not holding the only gun?"

"Simple math. The scow we're stealing will barely hold four. If they plan to break someone else out, I don't intend to be the one giving up my seat."

Tramping boots, distinctly nearby, cut the conversation short.

Reeking of impatience, Fray hurried to take the next turn. "Suit yourself."

Os grabbed his shoulder just in time, right before he could be spotted by six guards crossing the adjacent hall.

The alien let go. "If I save you a few more times, will you help hold my seat?" Placated, Fray gave Os a more grudging nod. "Maybe."

As predicted, the closer they got to the main cargo hold, the more boots they heard. By the time they hesitated at another uncertain turn, some were headed their way.

Os aimed the weapon toward the rising sound while a crouching Fray scoured the corners for the food smear. Too many seconds passed.

Os whispered. "Problem?"

Fray squinted. "There are two marks! I think it's this one, but it could be a boot-scuff. Can you... smell this?"

"Thought you'd never ask. I'll have to kneel."

A gyrojet projectile zipped by Fray's head, a scorch mark marring the white wall. Os fired back, wide, but the guards dove for cover.

As they took up firing positions, Fray put his hand out for the gun. "Give it to me! You have to smell the thing. I'll cover you."

"No. I'll cover you." Os fired again, zher aim no better. "Lick it!"

"What?"

"You know what prison mash tastes like. Lick the wall!"

Fray's eyes flared but, already crouching, he put his tongue out and, a moment later, pointed. "This way!"

After a few sprinting steps, they felt a blast of heat at their backs and watched a fiery black line race along the wall beside them.

Twisting gracelessly, Os fired twice more and nearly fell. One shot hit the ceiling, the other the floor.

"This is ridiculous. You're wasting ammo!"

Fed up, Fray grabbed the gun and fired so quickly, that it was hard for Os to believe he'd aimed at more than one target. Two of the guards dropped. The two running behind them stumbled over the bodies.

"That's why nobody gets my seat."

"Toujours gai," Os replied.

CHAPTER

3

Where are they? I swear, if I'd made humanity, I'd have killed them all long ago.

Thin and forever steely straight, turquoise sack in one hand, a gnarled oatmeal-gray device in the other, Dr. Ema Warland waited by the open door to the cargo hold. Her beehive mind could hold a million things, but patience wasn't one of them.

The stifling body armor, stripped from a dead guard, did nothing to placate her, but, if seen from a distance, it might keep her alive for a few valuable seconds.

When Os and an armed Fray rounded the corner, rather than gratitude, she felt terror.

What if they take me for a guard?

She yanked off the helmet and threw up her hands. "Don't shoot!"

Once sure she'd been recognized, she calculated their speed against that of the automatic door. The lavender green of her eyes whirled like the lifeless oceans of her world, a lavender green she shared with her father, or at least many of the men who claimed the role. Genuinely having the title would bring much in the way of social cache and sexual partnering.

Satisfied she was giving them enough of a chance, she hopped into the cargo hold and hit the control.

The thick portal dropped. Warland's estimate off, Fray and Os had to dive in to avoid being crushed.

So what? I'm not a mathematician.

Fray was upset, but he never seemed to like her anyway. "You could've killed us."

"Yes, I could have, but I didn't, did I? So… you're welcome. Were you followed?"

The out-of-breath alien responded. "No."

Not yet fully understanding the creature, fearing Os might somehow read her mind if she made eye contact, Warland focused on the former soldier. "Anything else I should know?"

Rather than answer, Fray picked among the dead guards, collecting ammo and a better weapon.

I asked out loud, didn't I?

Beyond the spite in his silence, which Warland knew she could be imagining, his efforts seemed pragmatic, predictable—until he handed Os a sidearm and pointed out the scope.

Did Os get to him? They've only had minutes. Surely there wasn't enough time to…?

She imagined them coupling, in the shower, in the hall, among the dead. The image dangerously enticing, she had to pull herself away.

The moment she dared look directly at the alien, Fray finally decided to answer. "We took out half a squad and lost two others. Without locators or a line of sight, I doubt they followed us here. Hell, I'm not sure how we got here."

The delay fueled her suspicions. *My creatures did similar things to distract me from their little revolution, but it didn't get them far, did it?*

Still, her mind produced such dazzling patterns, Warland always had to be wary of confusing those patterns with an often-inferior reality. More so since Charnel's call hadn't given her time to properly prepare. Her biology had certain requirements she'd been too hurried to see to properly.

It could be nothing. It could be everything. The distance between the two is so hard.

She studied his eyes as Fray scanned the flat, seamless eastern wall, then compared it to its western mate, a rough, pockmarked slab held in place by two vertical lines of sealant. It was obvious that the space behind it had been hurriedly closed off.

He knows! Or he suspects.

She wished there was some discrete way to communicate her concerns to their fourth member, but the aged General Charnel had his scrawny back to all of them, his only interest, the border of the inelegant, pockmarked slab.

Fray zeroed in on him. "Wrong way, old man. Dock's through the other wall."

"Oh, dear!" the old man croaked. "Have I gotten the wrong wall again? No wait, that's right. I'm a fucking genius, not some grunt lucky to be along for the ride. How's your com blocker holding, Dr. Warland?"

She set the sack between her legs to better examine the gray device. "We've got about forty seconds before burnout."

"Twenty before a whole lot of guards arrive," Fray added.

"An excellent reason not to waste time telling me what I already know." The general's twig-like fingers ran along the coarse slab. "This alloy could withstand a railgun blast. It must have been taken from the Chamber's outer wall. The sealant holding it is five times the required thickness. After three applications, it wouldn't provide any additional structural integrity, so, clearly, it was a decision made from fear."

The alien fingered its new weapon. "Fear of... what? Ghosts?"

Warland tensed.

Charnel ignored the question. "The technicians knew it was a waste. That's why the last two applications, are so sloppy..." Fingering a point along the sealant midway to the ceiling, he withdrew a vial from his loose-fitting prison garb. "...providing exactly the rutted space a catalyst would need."

Pulling the stopper free with his yellowed teeth, he poured a clear liquid over the fingered spot. "Much as I'd like to take credit, we have Dr. Warland to thank for what we're about to see. It's miraculous what she can accomplish with prison food."

Warland gave Os and Fray a tight smile.

That's it, then. Too late for any little rebellions now.

As he continued pouring along three of the four welded sides, a wet foaming stretched up and down along the seams. The sealant bubbled and started to drip away.

Charnel walked briskly into a corner beyond the far column. "Join me. Now. Quickly."

Warland grabbed her sack and strode to his side.

Os was enroute when Fray hesitated. "I don't want to be stuck in a corner if the guards come in."

"Then you'll die," Charnel said. "Normally, I'd be fine with that, but at the moment, it would be terribly inconsis..."

A loud thud made them all jump. Something was banging, not on the door, but on the other side of the slab. Taking advantage of the surprise, the general pulled Fray into the crowded corner.

"We needn't stand like old friends posing for posterity, but you should stay roughly here, so if that slab were to, say, fly open, held by the remaining sealant as if it were the hinge on a large door, we'd be protected and hidden." Satisfied with their arrangement, Charnel crossed his arms. "There. Was that so hard?"

Warland felt like she was in a crowded turbo-lift, staring at the display as the floor numbers rose. The only thing missing was insipid music.

The odd image shattered when the device she held did likewise.

"So much for the blocker," Fray said. When the alarm's high-pitched keen was suddenly replaced by an urgent beeping, he added, "And now all the guards in the Chamber are back online."

Idiot. Warland barely kept from screaming. "When the sun rises every morning, do you feel compelled to announce that, too?"

He gave her a look. "You're angry."

At least the sudden blaring wail, which she, of course, expected, confounded him. "What the hell is that?"

His confusion made her giggle. Not a good sign. She was losing it.

Hold on. Stay clear. Not yet.

Charnel explained. "The priority alert. And please, Fray, don't tell us that means they'll be here any second. Trust that we know."

There was more pounding from behind the slab.

The worried expressions from Os and Fray made Warland face away—lest her giggling become laughter. An instant later, she felt like sobbing, the quick mood shift trumpeting her fading clarity. The yustick in her bag could restore her balance, but that required privacy.

Nothing to do but hold on for the bumpy ride.

Hugging the sack to her chest, she forced her eyes to the entrance and tried counting.

At six, the catalyst hadn't quite finished melting the sealant, but the entry door began to rise.

Fray raised his weapon. "They've found us!"

Warland howled. "Does saying it somehow make you more certain it happened?"

Charnel put a hand on the barrel of Fray's gyrojet. "No. It's not us they're here for."

A final, massive bang came from the slab. Pivoting on the remaining line of sealant, it flew open like a door, stopping at the adjacent wall with a terrible boom, hiding them behind it. The constant white-on-white vanished, plunging the convicts into shadow.

As loud as the explosion was, it was nothing compared to what came next.

Knowing Warland had never experienced war, General Charnel had tried to prepare her. Vivid and precise as his descriptions were, especially about how her chest, ears, and jaw would feel, they paled against the way her whole body vibrated at the whine of enormous actuators, the crunch of mechanics rattling like an earthquake on treads—and the unforgettable roar that laid waste to the boundary between the living and the machine.

Briefly, it stopped her from thinking.

There was more—repeated explosions, falling rubble, dying screams, but they all came so quickly they folded into one another. Even that din was shortly overwhelmed by a terrific, rapid chopping as if the wall containing the doorway to the hold was being shredded.

When that stopped, the cries and explosions came again, softer, not as imposing, allowing Warland to attend to her other senses. Heat emanated from the protective slab. She smelled smoke, then saw it curling in from the sides.

Charnel gingerly touched the surface. Satisfied his palm wouldn't burn, he pressed hard and commanded, "Push."

Warland obeyed instantly. Their junior partners were sluggish, but together, they moved the slab a few yards before the remaining sealant gave. The slab teetered and fell.

Her faith in Charnel hadn't been misplaced. As he predicted, once released, the thing's first objective was to fire and pursue what lay before it. Its initial blast, aside from mutilating a dozen guards or so had also, by dint of its direction, drilled a molten tunnel through the eastern wall and into the service dock.

Blithely, the general stepped across the bloody mess toward the new passage. "Was this the wall you were talking about, Fray? Don't look back. There isn't time."
A rattled Os and Fray followed him. Warland, close behind, nearly tripped over a disembodied arm, its charred hand still holding a weapon. She thought of retrieving it, then decided reaching the dock was more important.

Things looked good, good enough, until Fray disregarded Charnel's advice and did look back, through the shredded door and down the corridor. His eyes widened as he took in a raging, one-sided battle.

He can see it. Worse, I think he's recognized it. Will he collapse in terror or....?

"Gog," he said.

Fray moved on the general so fast, he seemed to leave the name hanging in the air. He grabbed the brittle shoulders so hard they looked as if they might snap.

"It was supposed to be destroyed! You knew it was in there and you released it?"

Charnel responded with a rattling wheeze. "Still... stating... the obvious?"

Though the situation had grown even more desperate, Warland had to stifle a giggle. *Fray might kill him whether he means to or not. The sedative I gave Os for the shower guard would stop him. I packed the remainder in my sack. Just have to slip it out.*

With a little gasp, she realized the sack was gone. It must still be in the other room. She whirled back and there it was, hanging from a jagged corner of the fallen slab, torn and smoldering.

When she moved to retrieve it, Os blocked her path.

"Let's let the boys sort it out among themselves, shall we?"

"It's all right, doctor," Charnel said weakly. "I'm sure Fray is no longer quite so damaged from his earlier encounter with our ghost. I'm sure he'll see reason." Head trembling, gaze steady, he met the soldier's eyes. "The Chamber is the most secure facility in the galaxy. Did you really think we'd any hope of escape without a distraction?"

Fray shook with rage. "It'll kill everyone on the planet!"

Charnel tsked. "Lay with a dog and got up with fleas, did you? Sadly, even if you kill the dog now, you'll still have the fleas. What good will it—urk."

Fray squeezed harder. The general went limp.

As if his soul left his body. As if there were such a thing. Heh.

Losing it or not, in a surprisingly deft move, the memory of which would later please her, Warland snatched the gun she'd spotted earlier in the disembodied hand and aimed it at Fray.

"Can we continue this discussion once we're off-planet?"

Did I do that correctly? Did I say it right?

Apparently, she did. Os didn't try to stop her.

"Fray, he is our pilot."

Still shaking but looking as disgusted with himself as he was with the general, Fray let go. Charnel, kept aloft only by Fray's grip, fell. Ignoring him, Fray joined Os by the new tunnel.

Warland knelt by Charnel. A tiny rose of blood marred the white of his upper lip. Fascinated, she wasted long seconds watching it flower. When she finally helped him to his feet, the cracking of his bones snapping roughly back into place likewise transfixed her.

By the time he managed a few shuffling steps toward the tunneled hole, she snapped out of it and raced for her dangling sack. Most of the contents were a loss, but the yustick was thankfully intact.

Charnel's tongue clicked like sandpaper on skin. "Do you need that toy so badly, doctor?"

She secured it in her waistband. "Yes. Without it, in hours, I'll be completely useless. Feral would be a kind word. Why do you think our jailers let me keep it? Bad enough our rushed schedule change left me with a quarter charge and no adaptors."

Charnel managed a coughing laugh. "We all have our vices."

Ema wasn't offended, at least she didn't think so, but semantics had become a sort of lifeboat in her swirling mind. "It's not a vice. It's a genetic psycho-sexual need, endemic to my world, part of our culture and our strength."

"Apologies, doctor," Charnel said as if remembering what it was like to be alive.

CHAPTER

4

It was Fray's turn to try to keep himself together.

Easy, easy. Use that training, soldier. What did the mesmerist say? Think of the woman you love, think of how she loves you.

With the tumult at their backs, the four climbed through the tunnel and into the service dock.

Focus on what's ahead.

Crouching, he peered through the flickering light and settling smoke. Shattered containers littered the floor, mixing dried foodstuff and foaming beverages with machine lubricant and gore.

After boring the hole, smashing the cargo, and killing the two mechanics, the blast retained enough force to travel the length of the dock and produce a sizeable dent in the thick outer wall.

Shaky, Fray lowered his gun and nodded for Os to do the same. "Any block guards that aren't dead yet will be busy."

"Dealing with Gog, I assume. Gog being?" Os asked. "Other than a ghost story, I mean?"

"Yeah, you were right, okay? I couldn't imagine anyone was stupid enough to keep that thing in one piece, let alone here, let alone... it's... if I tell you the rest, I'll end up trying to kill Charnel again."

Zhe seemed to be smelling him. "Alright. I'll put a pin in it."

"Good. For now, let's just hope that pilot gave you the right access code."

"Don't worry. He did."

An exhaust deflector blocking their view of the ship bay, Os strode ahead.

Zher face dropped. "But he didn't leave the ship…."

Fray rushed up. "That's not it?"

"No! It was a service scow. I don't know what *that* is."

A dual-engine craft sat in the bay, its pulse drives barely held in place by damaged struts, its hull littered with deep indentations.

Warland and Charnel caught up in time to hear the alien groan.

"The scow will be here in two cycles when we were *supposed* to escape!"

Charnel looked like the rules to a puzzle he'd already solved had been unfairly changed. "No. It was here this morning. The doctor checked the logs."

Still wanting to kill him, Fray snapped, "Maybe Gog *ate* it?"

Muttering, Warland made her way to the only intact terminal. After a few keystrokes, she froze. Fray couldn't tell whether she'd laugh or scream.

"It was moved an hour ago, to make space for that damaged patroller."

Os gave the patroller another look. "Well, it is bigger."

Fray shook his head. "It could be a luxury cruiser, it's useless without a code."

"Maybe not," Os said. "The scow's code gives us the format and the bay ID. I know a dozen people who could hack the rest, and seeing as how we have our own mad momma scientist…."

Warland backed away from the terminal. "No, no, no. Can't. I can't"

Os' head cocked. "Fray's not the only one with issues. You're giving off some very powerful odors."

"Stop… smelling me! It's not happening. I can't handle it, right now."

"Then that's it," Fray said. "We're dead."

I'll think of the woman I love and how I never got to say goodbye.

With a clap of his hands, he took to stacking undamaged crates.

Warland stared at him. "Is that meant to act as cover? Are you planning to get into a firefight with the Chamber's entire security force?"

"Yep. A very, very short one. Why not? High Commander Mordent's been sending assassins since I got here. Not because I murdered a man, mind you, because I fell in love with his wife. A failed escape and they'll execute me legally. Not to mention releasing Gog."

"Was she worth it?" Os asked. Zher nostrils flared again, lips curling in an approving smile. "She was, wasn't she? The smell on you runs deep, and I mean that as a compliment."

"Is he right?" Warland asked. "Is this it?"

"It is," Charnel said. "Fray, you may kill me now."

Still working on the crates, he said, "I'd rather use you as a body shield. You and I are staying here. Os and Warland can crawl back through that hole and try to pretend they had nothing to…"

"I can start the ship."

Fray pivoted, ready to shoot. The voice, so sudden, so near, so young, made the others jump.

A scraggly youth stepped from behind the deflector. His face was smeared with oily gunk. "If you have a pilot, I can start the ship."

A woman appeared at his side. Her skin reminded Fray of Archosia's sunset. More than that, something about this woman, not her wan face or thin form, reminded him of her. Still, he aimed between them so he could take out whoever moved first.

"Who the hell are you?"

Ema blinked rapidly as if she'd suddenly acquired a tic. "The two the fringe patroller found. Their escape is what got us here."

They were unarmed, so Fray pointed the barrel up. "Why'd you run?"

"And what's that gunk the boy's covered with?" Os added. "Is it contagious?"

The woman spoke first. "They took something from Wyrm and I took it back. Now they're chasing us."

They all frowned, but Fray said, "Wyrm?"

"That's me," the boy said. "That's Calico." His rubbed fingers made a few dried goo-flakes tumble. "And this is how I sweat… sometimes. When I'm stressed."

Charnel crept closer, as if they were small animals he planned to snatch. "Well, then, Wyrm, let's try not to add to your stress. You said you could start the ship. Do you have the code?"

"Not exactly."

"Then how….?"

"Like this. Birefringe, access the patroller, and open the hatch."

They hadn't noticed the orb in his palm until it glowed. The patroller hatch slid open. The unoiled entry ramp squeaked until it reached the ground.

Warland's gaze snapped to the globe. "Crystalline AI? Either very advanced or very ancient. Grayborn tech if you believe in that sort of thing."

Calico placed a protective arm around him. "It's his. Leave it alone."

The tightening of Charnel's thin lips made for a poor imitation of a smile. "Wyrm, if you knew who we are, you'd realize you're far, far better off simply giving us that device."

As far as Fray had seen, the old man wasn't easily phased, but Wyrm's smug response surprised him. "You're General Charnel, butcher of Hydrokos, that's Dr. Ema Warland, the child-eater." He looked toward Os. "You're that alien who stole state secrets."

Os bowed. "Do we ever really own anything?"

Lastly, he turned to Fray. "I don't know you, but from the way you're holding that old model 6, you're Archosian military, or used to be."

Fray gave him a slight nod. "Special operations. Marksman. Used to be."

"I can't stay here," Wyrm said. "I don't have a choice. Neither do you. Birefringe is keyed to my biometrics, so it's useless without me. But with it, I can override ship security and mess with the scanners to evade the orbital patrol. No one touches it aside from me, understand? You only have to take me with you." Almost as an afterthought, he indicated the woman. "Calico, too."

A low rumble from the not-so-distant battle sent sparks from the fixtures above.

Os headed for the ramp. "That's settled, then. Toujours gai. Are there private beds, or will we be sharing?"

"It's not settled." Fray spoke to Wyrm but looked at Calico. "Unless being hunted down and killed is how you want to pay her back, let her stay. She can say she was kidnapped."

Wyrm was ready to agree when a giggling Warland said, "Don't be ridiculous. They'll assume she was involved from the start and torture her. I know *I* would."

Os was halfway up the ramp. "I hope *someone's* coming with me."

A reluctant Fray gave in. As they entered, Calico touched the soldier's arm, steadying him. *Why, how do you remind me of Vee?*

"Thank you, but I'll be fine. I'm supposed to stay with Wyrm."

Familiar with the ship, the boy led them to the wide cockpit where he again spoke to the sphere. "Birefringe, seal the hatch and prep for launch."

The panels lit. The power whined.

Warland helped the general into the pilot's seat. He flipped a few switches. After a hesitant cough, the engines thrummed.

"Second chair, doctor. The rest of you, strap in."

Calico struggled with her harness. Wyrm moved to help her, but Fray got there first. "I've got her."

Noticing, Warland whispered to Charnel. Fray overhead but said nothing.

"I think soldier-boy is falling in love again. Os was right. He's a romantic."

"His history makes that obvious." Head motionless, his eyes turned her way. "It's your compassion I find surprising."

She fell to blinking again. "Seeing you to your seat was pragmatism."

"Not for me, for Calico. Your warning that she'd be tortured saddled us with an extra passenger. Are you looking for a human substitute when your yustick batteries fail?"

"Under duress, I answered reflexively. Wrong gender in any event. Heh." As prelaunch executed automatically, the readouts tightened her brow.

"Do you see the hull condition?"
Fray strained to look.

The general shrugged. "I knew we'd likely die on launch the second I saw this ship, but why spoil it for everyone?" Leaning back, he raised his voice. "Wyrm? Do I open the bay doors from here or do you…"

"Birefringe, open the hangar bay. And lower the photonic shields."

Obedient, the twin doors spread – and color returned to the world, the first natural light the prisoners had seen in a long while. So long, Fray gave off an involuntary, uncharacteristic, sigh.

I guess I am a romantic.

The muted sounds of conflict were drowned by the engine's sputtering roar. With a lurch, the patroller left the incessant white-on-white for a blue-green-sky. The brief relief was shattered when it took to rattling as if it might fall apart.

"Is this normal?" Calico asked.

Wyrm, Fray, and Os answered simultaneously. "No."

Torso held steady by the seat, Charnel's already shaky hands vibrated furiously. "Maybe you should tell me about the hull status."

Warland ran her fingers along the readouts twice before answering. "Surprisingly within tolerance parameters. We're doing much better than I would have…"

There was a crunk – as if a large part of the ship had fallen off.

Disturbing as it was, Fray was equally surprised to see Wyrm's skin oozing again. The boy closed his eyes. Unphased, Calico patted his hand.

"The worst will be over soon," Warland announced. "Leaving atmosphere in five… four… hold on. Is that another launch?"

"Shouldn't you be telling us?" Fray said.

The image on the rear mech-camera made the Chamber seem small. Even so, the tiny yellow arc streaking up from it was hard to miss.

Charnel eyed it with a frown. "It's too soon for them to be worried about us."

Ahead, a thousand stars poked through yielding wisps of sky. But as the haze receded, three grew brighter, larger than the rest. Despite twisting wildly, they kept a steady triangular formation.

Warland threw up her hands. "Well, that's ridiculous."

The launch thrusters cut, and the ship no longer rattled. Fray unbuckled and moved behind the pilot's seat for a better look. "The orbital patrol? That's…"

"As I said, ridiculous! They shouldn't be anywhere near here."

"And yet! We can still put up a fight. Any gyro-canons on this thing?"

"No!" Warland shouted. "There aren't! Unless you plan to hurl yourself out an airlock and take them down with your sidearm, get back in your seat."

"Wyrm," Fray said, "you said you could scramble their scanners?"

The boy stared into the sphere. "As soon as they're close enough."

Warland's eyes flared. "How fucking close do they have to be?"

"Birefringe…"

His sentence unfinished, the three ships abruptly veered off.

"They're… ignoring us?" Fray said.

Warland dug her fingers into the side of her head. "Am I dreaming? Is this even… real?"

"Let's pretend it is," Os said, "And get us out of here!"

"Agreed." Charnel reached for the burn switch, but before he could engage the drive, a lime-green flash pulsed through the ship. The already damaged patroller nosed fiercely up, then down.

Fray nearly fell into Warland's lap. "Shit! What kind of weaponry does the orbital patrol have?"

Her eyes moved shakily along the readouts. "It wasn't the patrol. The patrol is… gone."

Fray pulled closer. "What do you mean, gone?"

"What does gone mean to you?" the doctor shrieked. "Destroyed, dead, atomized! No longer extant!"

Covering his ears to protect them from her shouts, the soldier was readying a response when Os warned, "Don't try her. Just, don't. Think of her as a boobytrap, and any wire you touch will set her off."

Warland ground her fingers into the controls. "You're just like every sniveling being I've ever created. You'll get your answers when I have them…if I let you live that long…"

"Doctor?" Charnel said. "Focus, please. Analysis. Quickly."

"Yes. Yes. Okay. The attack originated from whatever launched from the surface. It's still sub-orbital, too far for visual ID, but picking up speed."

"Maybe," Fray said, "some other prisoners took advantage of the chaos and stole a better ship?"

Charnel ignored him. "Call up the energy signature."

Warland obeyed, but a moment later said, "I know that can't be real."

"It is," Charnel assured her. His usually impassive death mask of a face grew exceedingly grim. "I've miscalculated. Apparently, like many convicts, Gog spent its prison time improving itself. It's… following us."

Staring at the monster outside, feeling it crawl into his mind, Fray realized he couldn't remember his lover's face.

CHAPTER

5

The sky burned sweetly. The Archosian artisans boasted their fireworks would put the stars to shame. The stars in no position to argue, the cheering crowds agreed. Having absorbed ten more systems, the empire that refused to call itself an empire now controlled enough ironwood, a key ingredient in Stifler's Plasma, to free the galaxy from superstition, whether anyone wanted that freedom or not.

Along the miles of mega-city streets, rich and poor alike were riveted by the celestial display. No one so much as glanced at the dancers twirling beneath the new statue of High Commander Sebe Mordent, the emperor who refused to call himself an emperor.

Except for Haden Primble.

From a high open window, the round-faced older man studied the lithe bodies. From Danvo, they were the first Pantheon system to watch Stifler's Plasma shred their armies. Some were happy to have been conquered, pleased the war was quick, with few civilian casualties. Others, no doubt, were sickened at having to prostrate themselves before an atheist's image.

But how many of each? That was the question. Who to watch? With so many new worlds, and so many newly liberated citizens, it was impossible to keep track. And yet the impossible had to be done.

Beneath the pong of people, spice, and smoke, Primble imagined he caught a slight, oily whiff of something terrible, and profound, of a world-wheel grinding, what believers might call the Beast Father rousing to a bone-deep tug.

It made him shiver.

"Break's over, Primble. Come look."

Relieved to close the window and seal out the world, the servant sighed. "This one lasted nearly a minute."

"I'm spoiling you," the gravelly voice said, its tone a mix of arrogant humor and stifled fondness.

The vast room once served as a temple, Archosia's youngest High Commander standing roughly where a divinity had been worshipped. Delighted with himself, he strummed the surface of his ironwood desk while sucking a clot of meat from his teeth.

"Pick up some plates, so it looks as if you're cleaning. If Rais arrives early and decides to barge in, I don't want him knowing I value your opinion over his."

"As if?" Primble eyed the mess. "If he asks how you stay so trim, can I explain it's because you never take a second bite from the same meal?"

Two maps were projected above the clutter. One was an astrograph of known systems that included the Pantheon, the ever-encroaching edge of Archosian territory, the uninhabited barrens beyond its fringe, and past them, the distant remains of the Kardun empire. The second displayed the surface of Mordent's next target; a ravaged, abject husk of poverty and ruins, the Land of Birth and Sorrow, Earth.

Primble frowned as he lifted dishes. "You haven't placed your pride and joy?"

"The new orbital artillery?" Mordent shook his head. "We'll bring it, but the naturalists insist the eco-system is so fragile even a small bombardment could leave the planet incapable of supporting life. Our invasion must be quick and land-based. We'll overwhelm them with numbers even if we only use gyrojets. Just as well, I want it clear to the indigenous Budari that we're displacing their overlords, not replacing them, that we are liberators, not new masters."

As Primble reached for another plate, Mordent slapped his hand. "Haven't finished that."

"My mistake. I thought you'd rather the maggots be eradicated lest they evolve into a more rebellious form. What is it you want me to see? The occupying Kardun are minimal, their forces scattered among rival warlords, and their tactics are primitive. Less than half give nominal fealty to that quasi-religious figure called the Pushka."

"It's not the war I worry about, it's the peace. There is one influential Kardun warlord, Bodspah, who's no fan of the Pushka's excesses. He might be swayed to our cause, and some others with him, but that's a long shot. The Budari are key. If they don't welcome us, the Kardun could hole up in the wastelands long enough for their fellow Slave-kings to arrive. And I've no maps of those damned nooks and crannies. The only Archosian to have traveled there in over five hundred years was my dear friend Anacharsis Stifler. If this fails, it won't be my fault, it will be his."

"Not to speak too highly of the loathsome cur, but he did procure, in your name, the formula for the plasma weapon that made the current expansion, and your meteoric rise, possible."

42

"Yes. but what has Chari done for me lately? Or should I say, to me lately?" He grabbed a goblet from Primble's pile, filled his mouth with its dregs, and swallowed joylessly. "The lovesick fool headed back to find a cure for a madwoman and disappeared, making this whole damn invasion necessary. I can't let anyone else find those secrets, can I? "

"How rude to risk his life for his wife's health, rather than your ambitions."

"It's beyond rude, it's treason. If Chari were alive, I'd have him executed. Forget the plasma, he was our greatest naturalist, and he knew it. Now who am I left with? Ludi, that addled god-appeaser? I'd execute him, too, if I weren't sure he'd die of old age before the Directorate approved the paperwork."

Mordent's fingers trilled the wasteland, magnifying the last spot Stifler's expedition had been seen. "Primble, is it possible he is still alive?"

Primble took an appropriately somber tone. "Highly doubtful, but anything is possible. After all, I still hold out hope for your humanity."

"Hrr. Does feeling abandoned by my best friend make me a savage? Maybe I'd have a higher opinion of monogamy if Vita weren't so intent on cuckolding me with such... gleeful repetition. Speaking of which, I want her followed again."

"Are you sure? It's not as if you don't indulge your own passions."

"Not since we were married."

"Less often since, but…"

Mordent hurled the goblet so quickly, Primble barely dodged it. "Defend Chari all you like, but not her! Are you afraid of what I'll do to her?"

Primble remained in a crouch. "More about what the loss of your remaining emotional ties might do to you."

"Oh, get up. I'd have hit you if I'd wanted. And relax. I wouldn't harm her if she mounted every man in my army, which seems to be her goal. It's about legacy, Primble. Once she bears me children, she can do as she pleases, but I won't bequeath the galaxy to another man's seed. Why do you think so many Pantheon sects burn adulteresses?"

"The recognition and fear of feminine power. The same reason others make them high priestesses."

"Peh. The only true purpose of religion is to keep the poor from killing the rich." Mordent gave the map a wry smile. "The Kardun women abort all their pregnancies. They kidnap children to groom as heirs. The Budari, they say, cut off the woman's nose."

"Which is why you fight to free them. So that women everywhere may die thanking you for their noses."

Primble moved to clean the broken goblet.

"Leave it," Mordent snapped.

"You don't mean that. Rais will be here soon." The servant walked toward a small chest and removed a suitable rag. "I have an agent in mind, but you'll have to promise not to throw him in the Chamber like you did Alek Fray. He was a good man and loyal soldier."

"Before he slept with my wife! And he did kill someone."

"On *your* orders because you *suspected* Dr. Beckles of bedding Vita. And, speaking of loyalty, Fray didn't once mention your name during his rather lopsided murder trial."

"Because he knew *that* would've been a death sentence, eh?" Mordent tugged his bejeweled wedding ring. "Oh, fine. Don't even tell me who it is. I'll leave it entirely to you. I swear, Primble, I'd make you a general if it didn't mean I could never trust you again."

"Thank you?"

A knock came at the door.

"Rais." Mordent wiped his mouth, then his hands on the sides of his pants. "Go. Get it."

Disposing of the rag, Primble pulled open the tall twin doors.

"General Gil Rais, Cohor Dagus, please do…"

Rather than await the end of the sentence, the rotund, hirsute Rais strode to the window and opened it, again filling the room with the sights, sounds, and smells of celebration. Utterly delighted, he pointed into the distance.

"Did you see, Sebe? Did you notice?"

Mordent's practiced smile reminded Primble of his new statue. "With our fleet currently obscured by the fireworks, I assume you mean the skyline's more subtle change."

"You know I do! For ages, the remaining temple to Abraxas was the tallest structure by law! Today, the Athenaeum's new expansion edged higher. Knowledge surpasses superstition at last!"

A grinning Mordent stepped beside him. "At least metaphorically, Gil."

Rais' new Cohor, Dagus, took up a guard's position by the doors. He was sleek-headed and lean, any outward sign of personality drowned by discipline. Primble distrusted him at once.

Arm on Rais' shoulder, Mordent drew the general nearer the maps. "How is your young son and namesake? Excited to join my flagship crew?"

"Of course! All of sixteen and Gilby's more full of himself than his father." He winked. "I think he's planning to sneak a girl aboard."

The twitch of Mordent's lip only hinted at his disapproval. "Well… we must ensure he's not caught breaking the rules that hundreds of thousands are expected to obey."

Rais harrumphed. "The heart wants what it wants."

Primble saw his master's face twitch. He knew what he was thinking – *Yes, the heart wants what it wants. That's why we have laws."*

Harrumphing again, Rais poked at one of the forces to be deployed on Earth. It was humanoid, but gigantic, and not merely as a symbol.

"And what are your rules regarding Colossus?" He rubbed his fingers as if the hologram had somehow left them dirty. "Bad enough we were strong-armed into bringing Wintour's new contraption along, don't tell me you mean to use it."

Mordent shrugged. "Family, eh?"

Rais lowered his voice. "Family, yes. My son may be randy, but your father-in-law should be in prison for creating Gog."

"You'd have both been tried. You know that. Keeping his career was his price for not publicly blaming Axton on you. Lies, I know, but…"

"Worked out for you, didn't it? Wintour and I used to be your competition. Too late, in any case. Turn on him now, and he'll bring you down, family or not. The inventor of the pulse drive still has a lot of support among the people and in the Directorate."

Mordent's head bobbed. "Which is why I want to raise a somewhat delicate…"

A knocking shattered the moment.

Mordent was furious. "Primble!"

Before the last syllable sounded, the servant was at the entrance, speaking to the newcomer in a soft, but firm voice. "The High Commander does not wish to be disturbed."

Their response was loud. "Stand aside. I'm here on official Directorate business."

Primble stood his ground. "Be that as it may, the High Commander does not wish…"

Shoving Primble was no great feat, but the speed with which the thin, older man flew back and hit the floor was so startling, that Cohor Dagus' hand snapped toward his sidearm.

The officious intruder bowed deeply, the feather atop his blue and yellow cap scraping the floor. "High Commander, the Directorate requires your presence within the hour. I am to make it clear this is not a request."

Already angry, Mordent's face reddened. He flew across the room and slammed the toe of his boot into the man's lowered cheek. As he reeled, Mordent yanked him to his feet for a fierce back-handed slap. "I don't care if the god Abraxas sent you! If my assistant says I'm not to be disturbed, I'm not to be disturbed! How dare you lay a hand on him!" He clenched his fists. "Defend yourself!"

The messenger's hands rose in surrender. "You know, I cannot. The law forbids…"

"So now you respect protocol?" Mordent sneered. "Come, stand on your hind legs, and pretend you're a man. I assure you there'll be no charges brought. Will there, Gil?"

Rais' eyes lit. "Not from me!"

For a moment, the messenger's eyes flashed defiance. Then he offered his bleeding cheek. "I took an oath, sir. As did you."

Mordent pointed at the hall. "Get out. Tell your masters I'll come when it pleases me."

With a half-bow, the messenger exited.

"Leave the doors as you found them!" Mordent barked.

Briefly, the man stumbled back to pull them shut.

Rais clapped like a giddy child. "You've committed treason!"

Primble still on the floor, Mordent extended a hand and helped him up. His lip cracked and bleeding, Mordent handed him a handkerchief. "True Archosians wouldn't see it that way."

Rais' amusement ran deep. "Are you that confident in your popularity? You *will* answer the summons, won't you?"

Mordent again bobbed his head. "That depends… on you. The Directorate wants me to publicly acknowledge the target of our next invasion. It's their way of forcing me to heel, to show they still have control. You know I don't want to do that. True, the Pantheon can't defend against the plasma, let alone stage an attack on us, but they have spies who'd happily warn the Kardun that we're coming. The Directorate's request is foolhardy showmanship, "

The general shrugged with doubt. "Some Seneschals say any invasion so soon is ill-advised."

Primble could tell he was hiding his interest, and that his interest in what Mordent would say next was keen.

"Some still believe in gods and wet themselves at the sound of thunder. Earth was ignored until Stifler brought back the plasma formula. Now all our foes will seek similar secrets there. If they succeed, we'll be bracing for invasion. The time is now—we win or lose everything. And, as I was saying before the interruption… that's why I asked you here."

Rais' eyes narrowed. "If you're planning a coup and you want my help, you'll have to come out and say it."

"Then I will. The Directorate once led our reform. Now they're as foolish as the kings, queens, and dictators they replaced, conspiring to increase their own wealth at the expense of progress. They've not only outlived their usefulness to the Archosian dream, they've put it at risk."

Rais indicated the image of Colossus. "And if I have only one doubt?"

Mordent sighed. "Here on Archosia, my hands are tied. In the field, I'm free to act as I see fit. Once we're orbiting Earth, I will side with the better argument, regardless of family ties."

Rais grinned. "Then I'll follow you to the Land of Birth and Sorrow, to the Pantheon realms, and beyond!"

Mordent cupped his hands around the general's. "Thank you, my wise friend."
As Primble escorted a cheerful Rais and his Cohor out, he noted that Dagus' expression
had darkened. Once they were gone, he put his back to the closed doors.

"Speaking of Pantheon spies, that new Cohor was listening more intently than he should."

"Was he? Send Rais a secure note expressing your concerns as my own." Mordent
adjusted his shirt. "I think that went well. Knowing the timing of the Directorate's messenger certainly helped. How much did we pay the poor fellow to let me beat him up?"

"More than you pay me," Primble said, tapping a handkerchief to his still-bloodied lip.

CHAPTER

6

A futile desire is a shadow on the soul.

Ansen Gui, Pantheon Temple Lord, and Arbiter of Lau, stared sullenly out the porthole, robes black as the void, save for the symbols of the gods, hair gray as the Earth's cloud cover, argyriac skin slightly bluer than its seas. Tall as a child, towering as an adult, he stood in the cog's cramped hold feeling trapped, as bolted into place as the support beams.

But Lau preserve me, how I want that man.

At least their long, close-quarter journey together was over. The four Pantheon emissaries had reached the edge of the Kardun Empire, nearly sixty years after the Hollow Wars drove the Slave-kings beyond the fringes of civilized space.

Gui longed to take their safe arrival as a sign from his god, but after so many compromises, the notion that he still served Lau was more plea than belief. Accepting the title of Temple Lord meant allying with the very heretics he, as Arbiter, once tortured and condemned to death. What lay ahead made those differences quaint.

The Slave-kings considered holy Lau a demon.

Not even a demon lord. Just a demon. And I'm here to offer them help.

Was that why lust chose to betray him? To tear his thoughts from his blasphemous mission and drag them to the praying figure at the far end of the hold – to his bare feet pressing scarred toes into the hard metal floor?

Futile, futile, shadow on my soul. Why does the heart want what it wants?

Their little gold-bought captain appeared in the quarter hall and waved for Gui's attention. Cap in hand, he spoke softly. "Temple Lord, they say the Budari will lop off a man's hand for so much as wearing a woman's ring. I've already risked my life, crew, and ship, but to land in Qus with… *him*… dressed that way, would be suicide."

They looked toward the kneeling man they'd both been thinking about, his sheer

Udlean silk pressed tightly against his muscled form, his delicate bracelets glinting in the porthole cone of earthlight. A cruel quirk of the air circulation system carried his musk-laden perfume directly to Gui's nostrils.

Why Lau? Why? Why now? Why Harek?

He straightened, to better look down on the captain. "Must I repeat myself? The Bannonites decreed that Acolyte Harek dress as a woman as penance for his sins, which include fathering two score children through rape, so he may learn to see through his victims' eyes."

The captain worried his cap. "I've no ill will toward him. I just don't want to be a victim. Qus isn't the worldly port we left behind, and our own people attacked him there. My fists are still bruised from getting him on board in one piece. Can't you... ask him to cover up until he's clear of the ship? Not completely, just..."

His hands ran along his short body, indicating which parts might best be kept concealed.

"No. I can't. The Pantheon forbids any interference with his vow..." The heady scent strong in Gui's nostrils, he muttered, "...even from a priest of Lau."

The captain took a knee so quickly, Gui was startled. "Sovereign of law! I was told it would be an affront to ask which gods you served. My apologies, Arbiter."

Gui eyed him with new appreciation. *A fellow worshipper. Is this a sign?*

"No. I should not have said. It was my... error. You have a family?"

"Six children and a wife, all of whom I'd like to see again."

"Do you teach them Lau's ways?"

"As my parents taught me."

In a flash, Gui decided. "Prepare a survival pod with our belongings. We'll land down the coast, alone. You and your crew will proceed to Qus to await our return."

Grateful, and wordless, the captain bowed and disappeared.

Though now the only one in the hold, Gui did not feel alone. For a moment, he hoped he was sensing what he'd long missed, the serene, powerful presence he associated with Lau. But it was something else.

"Ahem."

His head snapped toward the sound. To better conceal the ship's arrival, the interior was kept so dark he barely made out the open hatch. Rigdon, their mission's cowled scrivener stood in the gap, barely a silhouette. Normally, the gnomish man couldn't intimidate a child. Being reduced to a voice somehow made him more menacing.

"Did I startle you, Temple Lord Gui?"

"The hatch usually creaks."

"It did." Rigdon moved it back and forth to illustrate. "Perhaps you were lost… in contemplation?"

He stepped into the dim earthlight, revealing a ritually-shaven head, bald save for a row of chestnut hair running from the scalp to the chin, circling his lemur-eyed face. "May I make a confession, Lord Gui?"

"It would be uncharacteristic but go on."

"I find it a *relief* that the cog's blackout negates my duty to record your every word. It's a refreshing break, however brief, that I hope we might both enjoy. If mutual respect might extend to trust, we might even speak off the record."

Gui loathed the man, but his audacity was intriguing. "If it doesn't, you flirt with a death sentence."

Rigdon sucked in a worried breath. "Then let me add that were the situation reversed, I'd never consider reporting a harmless fixation so trivial its nature would be lost without context, without, for instance, understanding that wanting is not getting."

He glanced pointedly toward Harek.

Gui felt his insides twist.

He knows. Of course, he does. The toad has nothing to do but study me.

Rigdon's hand waved as if to conjure a soothing breeze. "Peace be with you; peace be with us. Perhaps a different example would seem less threatening? The Pantheon might misinterpret your mention of Lau and conclude that the faith you share with the captain unduly influenced your decision to separate us from the ship. For instance."

The clever shift to a lesser crime only put Gui more on guard. "Blackmail remains blackmail. Do you really want to test my reputation against yours?"

The scribe laughed lightly at himself. "Apologies. *Apologies*. Not having spoken plainly for so long, I've lost the knack. To be clear, I agree with your decision to use a survival pod. I only hoped we might discover where else we agree."

Crooking a finger, the scribe disappeared into the quarters the three emissaries shared. At this point, it would be dangerous not to follow, so Gui did, surprised to find the space otherwise empty. "Is Palchus still sick?"

Rigdon nodded. "Say what you like about the captain, but he warned him not to keep staring into that meteor swarm, then offered his own bunk and bucket as comfort. Shows a generosity of spirit, don't you think? And, like him, while I'm willing to sacrifice, I want to be sure the sacrifice is worthwhile."

He closed the hatch without a sound, let alone a creak, plunging them into complete darkness.

Gui felt vulnerable – and annoyed. "What do you want? You know I needed Bannonite support to break the deadlock, that Harek and his wardrobe was their price. You were there when I made sure they were aware of the rumors regarding the Budari customs. But they believe Bannon decides our fates before we're born. Bannonites handed an entire world to the Archosians without lifting a weapon, accepting their slaughter as a matter of faith. They don't merely tempt death, they invite it. To celebrate our mission here, they danced with venomous *pitohui*. Sixteen dead, counting the unborn child one carried. All *meant* to be. It's a wonder there are any Bannonites left."

Rigdon's response came slow and soft. "I *agree*. I can only imagine how an Arbiter of Lau feels about bringing a transvestite to deal with devil-worshippers."

"Even Lau's followers abandoned judging gender mores ages ago." Gui sneered. "But you've no need to imagine how I feel about this. You heard me speak to the captain. If the rumors are right about what the Budari believe, they'll flay him, and us, alive, destroy any chance of beginning, let alone completing, our mission. I don't fear my death, not anymore, but I do fear the death of all I've lived for. Peh, it's not as if poor Harek believes he has a choice. You can tell by the horrified look in his eyes. But there he is, painted like a whore, trying to rid himself of pride. It's... untenable."

"The Pantheon itself is untenable, no?" Rigdon asked without asking. "Keeping some thirty-odd faiths together, even if all our divinities, from the Lost God on, are children of the Beast Father and Sky? The Pantheon justifies itself spiritually by arguing that the universe is driven by contradictory forces and that the worship of the gods rightly reflects that. But no sect actually believes it. The Pantheon is not in any sense holy to your god, mine, or any other. But it serves a purpose, to fight Archosia. And when it comes to politics, isn't it better to serve the Pantheon's actual purpose, rather than honor its façade? To not treat the Pantheon like you would a church?"

Gui laughed. "Going from gossip to heresy, are you? Even if I do agree, it's not as if I can simply send Harek back."

"Not back, but perhaps *ahead*. Your decision to spare the captain and crew inspired a related idea in me. Our liaison awaits in Qus, but the pod will now deposit us outside the city. Why not simply… send Harek ahead of us?"

Having presided over the torture and execution of scores as an Arbiter, Gui thought he was beyond being surprised by cruelty. "To his death?"

"Who knows the future? I don't, do you? We're all simply spirits caked in mud, plopping about based on our beliefs. Harek and the Bannonites believe if he's meant to live, Bannon will save him. I'd call it *respectful* of their faith."

Gui scoffed. "You've reached the limit of your nominal skills, Rigdon. There are lines I won't cross."

Rigdon's voice lost its sweetness. "Then perhaps there are other lines we should revisit. I've seen how Harek tasks you. Celibacy is still part of Lau's oath, isn't it? Chastity of body and mind? If I made note of it, you'd lose your Temple Lordship and your title as Arbiter."

Gui only pretended to rally. "If I report half what you've said, our destruction would be mutual."

"If Harek stays with us, it's already assured. If you've some other idea, I'll happily embrace it. Do you?"

If he weren't exhausted from wrestling his passions, Gui might've. Instead, he felt an uneasy gratitude. At least he found something in himself stronger than his lust: self-loathing.

"How did I become such a vile thing?"

Rigdon's voice somehow shrugged. "By surviving. Even to worry how Lau will judge you is shortsighted. If the Archosians wipe all worship from the galaxy, what's to keep the gods from doing to us what they did to the Land of Birth and Sorrow? What are the needs of any one man in all that? What are you or I? What is Harek?"

What is Harek? A futile desire. A shadow on my soul. A sweet, sweet shadow.

CHAPTER

7

When the towering psychiatric center of Asylon was built, most Archosians still believed that being closer to Mother Sky helped drive out the demons that cause madness. An echo of that remained, the highest rooms yet reserved for patients of import and wealth. The top floor held a single, spacious, well-appointed chamber, and a tiny anteroom. The only entrance to the latter was a narrow stair, which, when covered by a trapdoor, increased the anteroom's floorspace by a quarter. Even with it shut, there was so little space that its two occupants constantly shifted in a vain effort to be comfortable.

"Rusk, is it? One of Ludi's spies, I hear?

The questioner was balding but richly bearded. The younger Rusk, meanwhile, had a thick head of hair, but a peach-fuzz chin. "I don't think I should say, Mister Sterg."

"Don't then." Sterg's chuckle unleashed a gob of spit on Rusk's tunic. "But tell me this if you can. What with our being at war with the Pantheon, does the old coot still think science and religion can be reconciled?"

Up against a wall, Rusk looked down, trying to avoid his companion's heavy breath. "Well, Mr. Sterg, what with the war and all, I don't think I should say."

"Right. Got it."

"But... the short answer's yes."

Sterg started. "Is it? Can you explain what in Abraxas' fifth eye he's thinking?"

"Not very well, I'm afraid. Not yet anyway. I hope to, leastways before the Directorate or Commander Mordent decide to purge his writings. If it comes to that. Seiðr Ludi's not as..."

"...sharp as he used to be?"

"Enthusiastic, I was going to say. About the future. About what's worth spending his limited time on. Not that he's ill. Just..."

"Old."

"Yes. Old."

"The gods exist in our minds, is as far as I got. So, they're imaginary. Why the fuss?"

Rusk half-smiled. "If that was what he said, Mr. Sterg, no fuss at all. He'd simply be honored as a great Archosian thinker."

A brief shadow crossed the burly man's features, an indication he'd taken slight offense. "Then what does he say? I'm not an idiot."

Rusk raised his hands between them hoping Sterg would step back, at least as much as he could. "I'm sure you're not. And I'm no teacher, barely a student, but I'll give it a shot. What Seiðr Ludi said, what he still says, though he's in hiding these days, is that the gods, rather than imaginary, are arguably more real than we are as individuals. They're in our brains every bit as much as what we call our 'selves' – not in a single mind, but across the species, sort of self-actualizing templates that sit between our little selves and the world, filtering and codifying reality, influencing our actions, whether we believe in them or not. Some come and go, but others, like the Beast Father and Mother Sky, are probably as old as humanity. And here's the tricky part that riles the atheist in us all; he thinks they're conscious, meta-conscious, or something like it, and sometimes have the potential to act more conspicuously. Sort of like *occasional* gods."

Sterg frowned. "The gods are parasites, then?"

"No! Well, depends how highly you think of the self, I suppose. If you think about it, the self could be the parasite. Most people, Pantheon, Archosian, even the Kardun, if they're being honest about it, like to think the self is special, indivisible, that we have souls of one sort or another, but all the evidence indicates it's not like that at all, that the self is permeable, mutable, maybe nothing more than a construct that makes it easier for the body to maneuver about."

"Sorry, I asked."

Rusk gave him an embarrassed laugh. "Sorry, I tried to answer. I'm sure Ludi would rather I hadn't."

Sterg's tense stare felt like it was pressing the younger man harder into the wall. After what felt like forever, he blinked and laughed. "Enough of all that, then! Let's move on. Evening shift's been mine since spring, and yes, while it is easier watching one brainsick instead of a dozen, it can be tedious, so you have to keep alert. No nodding off."

Rusk's smile was twitchy. "My insomnia's so bad, I wouldn't mind losing a job if it did put me to sleep."

"This one you would." Sterg poked him, partly because he had nowhere else to put his hand. "Because if Meriwald Stifler gets so much as an unaccounted bruise, the Asylon physickers won't fire you, Mordent himself will come kill you and your occasional gods."

He tilted his head toward the door to the main room, inviting the trainee to have a look through its little window. Inside, Meriwald Stifler lay on her back, legs straight, arms spread, ankles and wrists held by Udlean silk, tied with plenty of slack so she could scratch whatever might itch. Her face was thin. Her light hair long and combed out, splayed along the soft hills in the pillows beneath and beside her.

"The auto-bed handles the meds and nutrients, the staff the sheets and cleaning, the physickers the daily exams. All you need to do is stay awake and pay attention."

A whisper, poised and assured, drifted from the woman's dry lips: "They gave me a bed, my bed, trying to fool me. Doesn't make it less a prison, or the bars less cold."

Rusk was about to ask his first of many questions, but Sterg shushed him. After a beat, the same voice, but softer, more distant, answered the first:

"Your body was so responsive once, to air, to touch and taste. Now you're more like me. Apart. It's a good sign."

Rusk scrunched his face so intensely that his peach fuzz tickled his chin. "She's like that all the time? Talking in two personas?"

Sterg nodded. "Some brainsick think they're important people. We have a few Mordents in the chambers below, some generals and lesser gods, but that second voice tops them all. It's... Mother Sky."

"That's what Ludi's hoping."

"That she thinks she's Mother Sky?"

"No, that she *is*... well, an avatar, I guess you'd call it. It's difficult to explain."

"Don't then. Officially, you're here to try and catch what the biometric monitors might miss, any shifts in her tone and mood that might indicate her deterioration's accelerating. Then there's whatever Ludi wants of you, which I'd probably rather not hear about."

"He wasn't very clear on that, anyway."

As they watched, she kept talking: "I can't be you. I must go on."

And answering: "Not forever. Nothing does forever, not even me. But we're not so different, don't you see? I did it all for love, too. The moment you first met Anacharsis, you loved him, didn't you?"

"Of course, I did. He was handsome and clear-eyed, and I knew he would change everything…."

"That's as it was when I beheld the Beast-Father."

Rusk turned to Sterg. "It's not so bad, is it? Not like the way some of them scream, or babble. More like a nice chat."

He didn't disagree. "Hmm. Reminds me a bit of when my mother read me to sleep, acting out all the characters, you know?

Eyes adjusting to the scant light, Rusk could see her lips moving, her expression changing slightly as she moved from voice to voice.

As Sky she had no affect: "The Beast Father was so vast and dark, for the longest time, I mistook him for all there was. Was it like that for you?"

As Meriwald, she struggled: "No. Anacharsis was a man. When did you realize the Beast Father wasn't all there was?"

"When I realized something loved him, and that the something was me. And from the moment I knew we were separate, all I wanted to do was wrap my dark about his vastness so tightly that the difference between us would vanish." The voice laughed loudly, but the face barely moved. "Isn't that funny? Finding out there was a he and a me, all I wanted to do was to lose the distinction. It's all I've longed for since. All I long for now."

Sterg stiffened and yawned, accidentally nudging his companion. "Pardon. The stories get tired after the fourth or fifth go-round."

"It doesn't change, then?"

He stretched as much as he could in the small space. "Oh, some phrasing, metaphoric flourishes, and the like, but not the gist. Mother Sky loves Beast Father, the creation of the world, the gods, humanity, the Grayborn, and the World Soul."

"The whole old mythos, then? Is it possible Meriwald was a believer all along, but kept it secret because of Anacharsis' reputation?"

"Doubt it. The way I hear, she signed the Naturalist Pledge long before her husband and even petitioned to have the Lycaeum rise above the temple. It was her pet cause."

Rusk thought about it. "Maybe she's trying to work something out."

"Are you disagreeing with Ludi, then?"

"A good naturalist considers all the possibilities."

That earned a hearty laugh. "Please. You naturalists and physickers are as bad as the priests in your own way, especially those mesmerists. She had one, Dr. Beckles, before he ran off with Stifler's last expedition. Got murdered by that soldier right before they all vanished."

"I heard."

"All just as crazy, if you ask me." Sterg glanced sadly at the little window. "One of the physickers suggested trepanning the poor thing, let the air in, get some pressure off the brain."

Rusk lowered his voice. "They say it works sometimes."

"Well, the son wouldn't let any of them touch her. But I'll tell you this, if they don't do something soon, she'll end up starving. " Pivoting, he took the single step to the trap door and opened it. "That's it then. I'm off until dawn."

With a wave, he disappeared below.

Alone, Rusk had enough to room pull the stool from under the table. He sat, leaned back, looked up at the ceiling, and listened to the voice of Mother Sky saying:

"It was from our love that all else followed, this ache to join that created the gods and you. How could it be less than consuming?"

If that reminded Sterg of his mother, he was lucky. She didn't sound at all like Rusk's mother. That old nag never read a word to him.

She always sent him to bed with a beating.

CHAPTER

8

Primble struggled to straighten Mordent's extravagant capelet.

The High Commander writhed. "Must I look like a street performer?"

"If you plan to ignore the government, at least you should dress for it," Primble said. "Had you waited until the election, as I advised, the Directorate wouldn't dare summon you at all. But you didn't, so you may as well accept dressing respectfully in public as the mere inconvenience it is." Sensing deeper concerns than the wardrobe, he added, "There's no doubt the people love you. Not that I approve of their taste."

Mordent huffed. "It itches."

The servant patted the last fold flat. "As long as it looks like it sits on you easily."

Mordent stepped into the sunlight streaming from the ancient arched windows.

"And does it?"

Primble assessed his work. Though brawny, Mordent was too charming to be dismissed as a brute. The trick was ensuring his charisma didn't get overwhelmed by the dress uniform. The blue, symbolizing the airy yet pragmatic power of knowledge, was pale enough. The harsher yellow, representing the metaphoric lightning given to humanity by Abraxas, Archosia's last god, could have been distracting, but the tailor wisely relegated it to the fringes of the tiered cape.

He nodded approval. "Millions have followed you to victory. If they don't do so again, it won't be a question of fashion. Just be careful they don't turn you into a god and then stop believing in you."

"As long as I can tear it off quickly once we embark." A boyish grin took Mordent. "I can't wait to get into a field suit."

Primble raised an eyebrow. "Then I'd best take the next shuttle to the Zodiac to make sure anything else that dares to be ceremonial is ready for you to tear apart."

With a bow, he withdrew.

Alone, Mordent looked out the wide, unsealed window at what the night's fireworks had obscured—a vast sky dappled with gleaming silhouettes. There were scores of battle cruisers, dozens of faster, but more vulnerable caravels, a hundred transports, fifty support cogs, and countless pinpricks, swarming bug-like among their betters, whisking troops and supplies to their stations.

Though "belonging" to the Directorate, the greatest armada humanity had ever seen was called Mordent's fleet.

Two objects stood out. His flagship, the Zodiac, glowing as if aflame, would be seen as a second sun in an enemy sky. Five times the size of the next largest vessel, it was slow and slower to turn, but it carried the first large-scale artillery to use Stifler's Plasma. Alone, it could lay waste to legions.

If that made his heart soar, Colossus dragged it down. The freakish behemoth shadowed the Zodiac the way a dung heap might leech attention from a diamond. Made from General Wintour's dark new composite, orichalcum, it was powered by aeolipiles, using some form of cold fusion whose secret the old man had yet to share. It reeked of desperation, worse, of failure. An invalid in space, it needed the Zodiac to tow it across the void.

The same way my father-in-law needs me to prop up his career.

Putting his concerns aside, he headed for the plaza, expecting a massive crowd. He was not disappointed. The square beneath his statue remained packed with the night's revelers, all bleary-eyed but hoping to catch a glimpse of their young High Commander.

Mordent strode toward the raised dais near his transport, keeping his eyes not on it, but the crowd, catching eyes and faces here and there. As he moved, a wave of silence spread so that soon, the only sounds were his clicking boots, the gurgling fountains, and the humming engines. Primble had arranged risers for important guests. Vita Wintour Mordent sat on them up front, resplendent even in the shadow of the Zodiac, her gown taking up space for three.

She offered her husband a salacious, approving wink. His nod was appropriately affectionate.

Beyond her, all his generals waited at attention, all save... Wintour? Mordent looked up. The old fool was on the dais, his dais – and he was not alone. Seneschals Iceni and Archigallus, leaders of Archosia's largest factions were by his side. That the two lifelong opponents stood together did not bode well. Worse, the scepter Iceni held indicated they were here to speak for the whole Directorate.

It was an ambush.

By way of acknowledging him, the witty, endemically convivial Archigalus huffed like a blowfish, hands on his hips. The vulpine Iceni undid her wrap, revealing a brooch with drop-shaped pearls suspended by gold chains, fine sapphires, and an exquisite emerald.

Mordent, trying not to wince from the glare of her jewelry, grit his teeth. His collar itched. *At the very least, let them wait until I finish my approach.*

They didn't.

Archigallus' voice boomed with practiced cheer. "Not hoping to leave without saying goodbye, were you?"

Iceni followed on his heels. "You do seem surprised to see us. Let's hope you're not taken similarly unaware during your upcoming campaign."

The insult elicited more than a few gasps. They'd misjudged their audience, making it easier for Mordent to smile pleasantly. "The only surprise is how long it takes politicians to catch up with my success."

The roaring applause gave him the time he needed time to reach the dais and stand as, at least, their equals. When it refused to ebb, Iceni slammed the scepter down, demanding silence. Rather than let her speak, Mordent kept talking:

"While you debate and delay, I move to ensure the security and continued growth of the Archosian dream."

Iceni grew somber. "Then tell us how you'll move. Tell us the destination of your great fleet."

Mordent scoffed. "No. I will not alert our enemies for the sake of politics."

Archigallus leaned in for a whisper. Each word brought with it the man's meaty breath. "Iceni and I disagree about many things, how to deal with the economy, corruption, the waves of immigration from your new conquests. But we do not disagree about you. But give us this small thing, Mordent, let us at least appear to put you in your place, and you can be on your way, unhindered."

"I cannot."

Archigallus huffed. "Look, your destination is clear to anyone with a brain. It's the obvious choice, the only choice, really. Why not just say it?"

"Because, Seneschal, if it were obvious, I wouldn't need to."

"Ah, well. Negotiations don't always work, do they?" He gave Iceni a nod.

She seemed almost pleased. "In the face of your continued defiance, it has become the Directorate's duty to take a firmer hand."

Mordent's nervous blink widened the smile on her lips. "Firmer hand?"

"The rapid expansion has left us with many enemies. Eight of our ten new systems are already experiencing rebellions."

The itch was killing him. He wanted to rip the collar off and wrap it around their necks. "Pocket resistance, nothing more."

Archigallus chimed in. "Fueled by the reports of rape and pillaging."

Mordent's teeth clenched. "Isolated incidents, the culprits dealt with severely."

Iceni tapped the scepter again. "Had you answered our summons, there might have been a discussion, but a decision was made without you. Prior to engaging the enemy, whoever it may be, you will first attempt to impress them into submission with a display of our superior technology, specifically General Wintour's new marvel, Colossus. You will show them what they face and allow them the opportunity to surrender."

The crawling sensation along Mordent's neck extended the length of his body. "This is unheard of! In all our history, in any history, combat decisions are left to those in the field."

Archigallus shrugged. "But, as you've often said, we're making a new history. And in it, Archosia will seek to avoid the too-heavy hand that creates grieving enemies instead of liberated partners. Consider it a more formal version of the strategy you employed on Danvo with Stifler's Plasma."

As a final insult, Mordent's father-in-law decided to speak.

"If I may," Wintour said. "Stifler's Plasma takes lives. Colossus will save them."

Idiot fossil! First Gog, now this. Why can't you lie down and die in peace?

Mordent forced himself to take a respectful tone. "Father, of course, I intend to use your great device. But surely a man of your experience sees the danger in having the decision taken from me. Battlefield responses can't be dictated…"

Iceni clapped the scepter. "We do not dictate! We are not kings or emperors. Elected by the people, we speak for Archosia."

Chewing on his rage, Mordent fought to contain it. "I misspoke. Let me be clear. Combat decisions cannot be voted upon any more than our citizens, no matter how wise, can decide today which way a man should run from the tiger that may chase him tomorrow!"

Iceni tsked. "Is the most powerful army in the galaxy engaging tigers now? If Colossus fails to impress, I'm sure our brilliant High Commander will find a way to compensate."

Mordent felt his hands shaking. "But…"

"And now, we have matters of great importance to attend, as do you."

He realized too late any objection was pointless. In his absence, the Directorate had voted, and their decision was law. For now. He made a final bow. "As the people command."

"I did give you a chance," Archigallus said softly.

Iceni spun. Vulpine as she was, she strode straight-backed toward the Citadel, jewelry glinting. It was Archigallus, following, who loped like a beast.

Going through the motions, Mordent dismissed his generals, deaf to what cheers there were, and headed toward his transport. He'd almost made it inside when Vita tugged his arm.

"They're not allowing me onto the Zodiac for a proper goodbye, no matter how I beg."

He tugged himself free, patted her hand, and let it go. The hatch closing between them, he answered: "The heart wants what it wants, my dearest, which is why we have laws."

Once out of sight, he ripped his fine-tiered cape from his neck. *Find a way to compensate? I'll do more than that!*

As the transport rose, Mordent imagined the Citadel's ten high-backed Directorate chairs. In their center was a golden throne, meant to remain forever empty – *filled by all and no one.*

It was the seat he intended to take upon his return.

CHAPTER

9

Before the fugitives could gasp, Gog was visible through the cockpit, its tank-like omni-tread making for an odd sight in planetary orbit.

Charnel shut down the power.

Fray looked ready to peel him from the pilot's seat. "What are you doing? Use the pulse drive!"

The terse response laid bare the senior tactician's exasperation. "I can't, you idiot. We're too close to the planet's gravity field. You saw the engine mounts. The drives might escape, but we wouldn't. The stress would rip them right off the hull."

Warland's fingers flew along the instruments. "He's right. We need more distance."

Fray fixed on a readout he recognized, the relative velocity. "There's no point. It'll catch us before you can turn."

"Which is why I shut down the power!" the general spat. "Must I say it again? Don't waste time telling me what I already know!" He looked at Warland. "We've only gained a reprieve. Once Gog is close, it'll detect our bioenergy. I need an idea, doctor. Just one will do."

Warland's eyes swam over the glowing data. "Let me think."

Fray slumped into his seat and rubbed his hands through his hair. "I shouldn't be here. I never should have…"

Os pushed at his shoulder. "At least tell the rest of us what it is that's going to kill us."

Calico staring expectantly, Wyrm sweating gunk, Fray decided to comply. "It's the top-secret weapon that put Sebe Mordent where he is."

"At least our final moments could be entertaining," Os said. "Do go on."

"Before Stifler found the plasma, there was a big push for new weapons. Obsessed with proving he was still a great inventor, General Pontifer Wintour, the man who gave us the pulse drive in his prime, created a Predatory Engine that could strategize and attack on its own - Gog. The best differential analyzers can't crunch that many variables, so he used organics, brain matter, some animal, some human. Not having been a field commander for decades, he asked his buddy Gil Rais to share the glory by battle-testing it on a little agrarian world dominated by some very pious Bannonites."

Wyrm's voice went up an octave. "The massacre on Axton? They said the orbital artillery accidentally hit a fault line the sensors missed."

Os eyed him. "What were you, then, three? Do all space rats keep up with military news?"

Falling silent, Wyrm sidled closer to Calico.

Fray went on. "Rais wanted to secure Axton before Pantheon reinforcements arrived. He figured he'd have Gog level a town or two and the rest would be terrorized into submission, only it didn't work that way. The Bannonites wouldn't fight or surrender, they just… awaited their fate, or however they put it. The going theory is that their neutrality, even towards their own survival, confused Gog, because it started wiping out everyone, including our troops. When Rais tried to get it under control, it fought back… found that fault line, and set the atmosphere aflame on purpose."

"Can machines here do things on purpose?" Calico asked.

"Uh, I suppose you could get philosophical about it, but yeah. Wintour and Rais blamed the artillery as cover, but even that cost them so much prestige Mordent was the only influential general left standing. Once he married Wintour's beloved daughter, he had all the support he needed to be named High Commander."

Calico studied him. "You were there," she said. "On Axton."

Fray was taken aback. "How…? My presence was expunged."

"It's on your face, like a picture." She pointed. "Right… there."

He was more than startled. "Not going to be playing poker with you. Okay, I was there. No physical wounds, but it had… an effect. Still hazy on a lot of the details, but the physickers say that's a good thing."

"More than an effect, Fray. I saw your file," Charnel said. "It's why I decided not to trust you. Partly, anyway."

Wyrm's eyes widened. "You had PCD? Psycho-cognitive Disorder?"

"Or, perhaps he's just weak," Charnel offered.

"And why didn't you trust me?" Os asked.

The General laughed. "Oh, many, many reasons. We'll be long dead before I get halfway through the list!"

Trying to see what Calico had in the soldier, the boy noticed a thin layer of sweat on Fray's forehead. "Are you... okay?"

Fray grunted. "Fine. Went through therapy with a mesmerist."

Wyrm made a face. Unlike physickers, mesmerists worked with corners of the mind that remained immune to physical intervention. Faddish, their work was usually dismissed as pseudo-science. Worse, it smacked of spirituality. Ludi, to his public detriment, swore by them.

"Hey, quit staring, kid. I wasn't the only one."

"But you were the only one who *killed* your mesmerist," Charnel said, gleeful to make the revelation. "And after he did so much to help you recover."

"I did him a favor. Someone else would've..." Visibly struggling with his past, Fray pivoted this way and that, finally raising a shaky finger at the readouts. "Look, I saw the firepower they threw at that thing and..."

Before he could finish, their faces were lit by blood-orange beams shooting from the corners of Gog's multifaceted surface. They danced along the patrollers' debris field, prodding and rolling the detritus like a crustacean examining a potential meal.

Warland's mumbling grew audible. "Energy. We need to expend energy to get far enough from the planet to engage the engines, but Gog senses energy sources, ergo the energy can't come from us, ergo it must..."

"Come from something else?" Wyrm offered.

"My pod is in the hold," Calico said. "Maybe it could shove us?"

Warland hissed. "And maybe we could all push on the hull very quietly."

"No," Charnel said. "It's a good idea. Not whatever's left of *her* pod, but this patroller has three. We can preprogram one to bump us in the right direction. Any luck, Gog will follow its energy signature long enough for us to engage the pulse drive."

Warland trembled. "The fail-safe won't allow the pod to fire until *after* the ship jettisons it, which requires energy from the ship, which Gog will detect. Creating. The. Same. Problem."

"What about your little ball, Wyrm?" Charnel asked.

"Birefringe can override the fail-safe," Wyrm said. "But is a lifepod strong enough to blast free from its mooring?"

"Let's find out, shall we?" Charnel said. "Make the calculations, doctor." She began reciting a string of numbers. "I meant using the ship's calculators."

"I'm faster," Warland said. Rather than tap individual keys, her fingers swept the board. "Pod programmed. Thrusters set for high oxygen burn. That should create a nice long trail for Gog to notice. Wyrm?"

After looking to Fray for approval, he spoke to the sphere. "Birefringe, override pod fail-safes, and engage the thrusters."

There was a brief white flash in a corner of the cockpit window, followed by a loud, starboard bang. Their view shifted and rolled, away from Gog and the glinting debris field, toward the slowly spinning stars.

All eyes turned to the mech-camera monitor, where they watched the pod arc over the planet's surface. For a few tense moments, Gog was the only still point.

But then it followed the pod.

"What are you waiting for?" Fray said. "Hit it."

Charnel tsked. "As soon as Dr. Warland gives us the mark."

"Still too close. Ten… nine… eight. Fuck it. We'll likely die anyway. Go ahead."

As the general pulled the lever, his lips twitched into a smile. "It's just occurred to me, that I've no idea where we're headed."

There was no explosive decompression, no horrid rending of metal, no swallowed screams or bodies tumbling into the void. Instead, they felt a stark, unforgiving pull as they left the prison world behind. At peak velocity, the ride smoothed, save for an occasional bump and creak from the engine mounts.

The immediate threat over, Ema Warland unbuckled. "I need a few moments."

Charnel understood. "The crew quarters are below."

As she left, looking pale, Wyrm asked, "Is she sick?"

"No. She has to masturbate every so often, or she'll go mad."

The boy silent, the general checked the guidance system. "Current heading will put us near the fringe trade depots in a few days. The patroller's assigned rounds, I assume."

Calico nudged Wyrm. "It's where we were found," he explained.

"But not where we were headed," she said.

Os was more clearly displeased. "The fringes? That's not the deal."

"It's not where I want to be either," Charnel said. "But it's best not to make any changes until we're certain we haven't been followed."

Fray's face twisted. "Gog can't have developed a pulse drive, can it?"

"I'd no idea Gog was able to fly at all, so I can't very well predict its limits." Charnel leaned back. "But I was thinking more about the authorities. We are fugitives. Losing ourselves at a remote destination will be easier than at a heavily monitored population center, no matter how good the food is."

Too tired to fight, Fray exhaled. "Speaking of which, do we have any? I'm starved."

"There's a communal room below with some stores," Wyrm said. "But maybe you should wait until Dr. Warland's... finished?"

Ignoring the boy's reddening face, Fray plodded down the corridor until he found the ladder. Lowering himself down the rungs, he emerged in an open area serving as both galley and lounge.

He was rummaging through the dried foods, hoping to find some protein when Dr. Warland emerged from one of the private quarters lining the far wall. She looked paler and shakier than she had during their narrow escape.

"Fray, if I could speak with you a moment?"

When he didn't say no, she approached. Rather than stop at a reasonable distance, she pressed into him, wrapped her hands around his neck, and tried to draw him into a hungry kiss.

Fray pulled back. "Hold it. What?"

Eyes distant, she spoke as if no longer quite in her body. "My family is from Meriones Shawi. Considered hyper-sexual compared to galactic norms, we're known for producing courtesans, male and female, laborers, and well, fast-growing populations. My intellect made me an aberration, but like my people, I require release regularly to keep functioning. I'd hoped to use my yustick, but there wasn't much of a charge left, and the adaptor…"

His face twisted. "You want me to fuck you to clear your head?"

She brightened. "Yes! That's it, exactly. Shall we? Here is fine."

"No," Fray said. "It's not fine."

She eyed the distance to the private quarters. "I think I can make it back to the bunk."

He stepped away. When she tried to come close again, he put a hand out to stop her.

"I don't understand," she said. "Soldiers are usually amenable, and I can see you find me stimulating. I'm simply proposing mutual relief. Granted it would benefit me more, creating an unequal exchange, but… I could pay you."

"No! It's not that. It's not any of that. I'd… I'd rather not."

Twisting away, Fray fled into one of the rooms and shut the door.

Knees going weak, Ema reached for the hull to keep from falling. She was thinking about the others, upstairs, when a lithe figure slipped down the ladder.

"Os. It's you. May I have… a word?"

Slowly, Os graced the far side of a meeting table. "Just one, Dr. Warland?"

Propping herself on the table, Ema stumbled toward zher as if her failing legs had acquired a will of their own. As she neared, she sensed a change in the air.

"Please, lower your pheromone levels. The last thing I require is further stimulation."

Os gave her a coy shrug. "I know, but it's what I do. I'm offended you didn't come to me first. I am a professional."

Warland took a breath and tried to steady herself. "I surmised Fray would entail fewer complications. Plus… he was already down here."

Os eyed her sympathetically. "But he didn't accept because he's interested in Calico."

Ema blinked. "And he wants to remain pure for her? But he slept with Vita Mordent."

"And he loved her, too. Quite madly. But, as they say, absence makes the heart flounder, and I think Calico reminds him of her. Even Wyrm senses the competition if you can call it that."

"You're certain?"

A nod. "It's amazing what you can smell with the right glands. I sniffed it on him in the service dock, vague flowery scent beneath all that sharp, metallic adrenaline, funny little monogamous bonding thing that happens to your species. Ecstatic poets call it love at first sight. On your world, they probably call it dinner, eh? But enough about him, let's talk about *us*."

Room swimming, Ema lowered her head. "I'm unsure of the extent to which a xenomorph can provide the proper satisfaction."

Os stroked her hair. "I'd hardly have gotten all those ill-gotten gains if I couldn't distract people from their wealth. Toujours gai."

Her breathing was getting shallow. "Distraction is not fulfillment. Allure isn't orgasm. Or, for that matter, love. I also don't want to be manipulated into an emotional attachment."

The alien harumphed. "Now, I'm offended. I've never made anyone fall in love with me, not intentionally. Even I have lines I won't cross. But to answer your earlier question, yes, I can satisfy you in every possible way, probably a few your oh-so-logical mind hasn't considered."

The thought provided enough strength for the doctor to raise her head. "Will you?"

Os came close and whispered, "Pay me."

The hot breath against her skin put Warland on her feet. "Terms?"

"A favor."

Ema held back more from spite than strength. "That's vague."

The lithe body grew harder. A swelling appeared at the groin. "Only because I haven't decided what it is, yet. I promise it won't be anything you'd…"

By then she was on ʒher. "Agreed."

Above, Wyrm, Calico, and Charnel heard a steady thudding.

Calico looked around. "Do you hear that? It's coming from the hull."

"Asteroids?" Wyrm asked. "Is the shield down?"

As the thudding continued, Charnel checked the readouts and then rolled his eyes. "No. I believe Doctor Warland has found the relief she sought."

Wyrm looked at Calico, then away, then he began, not to sweat, but to blush.

CHAPTER
10

At Gui's request, the Pantheon emissaries were strapped into the lifepod nose-to-nose, lit only by the glow of instrument panels. Mercifully, the wait before being jettisoned was brief. The harsh bumping and rolling that followed was not. As the Reaction Control System slid them into the atmosphere, and their sense of gravity acquired direction and strength, Gui worried their third member, the light-haired Palchus, astrolger of Sterron, directly across from him, would vomit on his face.

Rigdon looked ill as well. When the scribe heaved, Gui braced himself, but nothing came up other than air. With a dry burp, the scribe explained. "Fasting."

The thought, though, was all Temple Lord Gui needed to feel nauseous himself.

Acolyte Harek was the only steady one. Though still wearing his makeup and silks, having been in a lifepod before, he'd thankfully omitted the perfume.

"It helps to focus on your breathing," Harek said. "Like this. Through the nose."

When Harek exhaled, Gui felt his breath on his lips. As he aped the rise and fall of the man's smooth, young chest, it occurred to him: *This is likely the closest we can ever be.*

Much as he wanted to weep, at least he didn't puke.

The pod righted, and the downward pull became more consistent. When the vibrations slowed, Gui assumed the parasail had deployed, that they'd land soon. The moments, regardless of his estimates, or the actual time, dragged on.

When the hell did end, instead of the sharp, sudden shock he expected, they twisted sideways and bobbed. For a time, Harek floated directly above Rigdon, forcing the man who wanted him dead to look him straight in the eyes.

That moment, at least, was fleeting. Harek pulled a lever. The hatch at his back opened to a rush of cobalt sky and salty air. Unbuckling, he disappeared with a splash. Gui struggled to follow, but the cushions, built for shorter men, were difficult to shed. By the time he freed himself, the acolyte had pulled their oval pod onto something of a beach.

When he finally emerged, the Temple Lord was bemused by the fact that it was Harek, dripping wet, colors on his face running, who became the first member of the Pantheon to set foot on Earth.

Where the gods created, and then all but destroyed us. What sort of sign is that, Lau?

Gui was second, followed by Palchus, who tumbled onto the sand and knelt in a way that suggested he might pray. Instead, he retched, long and hard, until a gurgling rasp indicated his stomach was empty. Rigdon pragmatically remained behind, handing their belongings to Harek. Among them were the three priceless gifts they hoped would change the Pantheon's fortunes.

The ocean looked much the same as any other, softer, perhaps, deader than most. This small stretch of sand, Gui hoped, put them a modest distance from Qus. The land beyond, the Earth itself, though said to be rife with ruins, looked sparse save for a few trees one might see in the jungles of other worlds. Then again, the pink and mustard sunset sky didn't provide enough illumination to tell where the vegetation ended, and the desert began.

In the light of a small fire, Rigdon took to performing his duty as a scribe, fingers ticking along the micro keys of the stylon that allowed him to write in sacred Hentic – an ancient pictographic system immune, by faith and in practice, to manipulation.

In Hentic no lies are possible.

Gui found the rhythm soothing—even as he worried about what was being recorded.

Curious, Harek stopped unpacking to watch, and soon grew bold enough to approach. He stood so close that a saltwater drop from his braided hair fell onto Rigdon's stylon.

"I'm sorry!"

Rigdon offered a crocodile smile. "Peace be with you. Peace be with us. Had it been a completed session, it would be of concern. These are only notes."

He displayed his work, an image of Gui circled by a host of smaller pictures; a serpent, diving and twisting, a dagger, water, a ship, an ear, a mouth, all moving in a finely tuned dance. For most, no sequential order was needed to convey the meaning.

Rigdon raised an expectant eyebrow toward Gui, robbing the momentary peace. But he was right. There was no point in waiting. If the Budari found them now, there would be four sacrifices instead of one.

"Harek, come with me."

The abrupt command took the acolyte off guard. "Of course, Lord Gui.

He led Harek from the crackling fire to a quieter dark at the base of some lonely palms. There, Gui allowed himself a final indulgence by squeezing the man's shoulder. He wanted to meet his open gaze, but instead looked off at shadows.

"The priests of Bannon asked I give you an unexpected task."

Harek nodded. "That I may learn to want whatever happens."

I'm sure that's how they'd put it.

He swallowed. "Qus is due north, an easy run for our youngest emissary. There, you'll find a merchant, Schectbat Non, known by a jagged white line in his black beard. He's to be our interpreter and guide. Escort him to us here."

Harek's gaze shot down to the sand, then, as quickly, up to the sky.

He knows. He knows it's death.

The Temple Lord was trying to form a comforting lie when Harek nodded. "I'll leave at once."

He pressed his lips to the back of the Arbiter's trembling hand and, in a swirl of silken colors, disappeared among the palms. Returning numbly to the fire, Gui wondered if there was any way to repay the man for making it so easy to kill him.

I'll have Rigdon record that at this moment Harek's pride was truly broken, that when he accepted the task, he did so as one of Bannon's faithful. They'll think it's true.

Dear Lau, for all I know, it is.

Seeing Palchus lying down insensate, Gui felt his own exhaustion. He told himself that giving in to his need for sleep would not be selfish.

With all at stake, I must be rested.

As he lowered his long body onto the slight stretch of beach, his thoughts were no longer on Harek's face or form. The acolyte's absence already eased that tension. The morality of his actions, though, was tied in such a knotted ball, that Gui needed rest to even properly consider his sins. His god still feeling absent, his dreams grew deep and mindless, a succession of images and textures that, if they had a pattern, it was one he could not detect.

CHAPTER

11

No matter how many silks Harek wore, which perfumes he splashed on his skin, how much he doted on his hair and makeup, his body's hunger to survive remained a dogged, familiar brute. The moment Gui ordered him to Qus, that brute howled and clenched his heart in sharp, bloody teeth, threatening to tear it free from his soul. Any wisdom that the penitent imagined he'd gained, any fleeting glimpse of surrender, vanished like water in the sand.

For the brute knew a savage truth: *He's sending you to your death! Kill him!*

It would be so easy to grab and twist the Temple Lord's skull from his neck, but he didn't. It wasn't Bannon's promise of peace that stayed Harek's hand. Not really. It was just that having killed and ravaged so many, he was simply tired of it.

Instead, he told himself he couldn't blame the Temple Lord. He told himself that Gui's will, like any will, like all will, like any sense of self, was an illusion. It was Bannon, always Bannon, only Bannon, forever and ever until the end. With the brute inside him wrestled to a reluctant silence, Harek harnessed its rage, pounding his bare feet along the cracked-stone road, racing obediently toward whatever Bannon willed.

When he saw the five serpent-riders, silhouetted by the morning sun, it howled again: *Run, you! Run before the phagus make a meal of you!*

But Harek forced himself to pray: *All is yours, Bannon, each turn in the road, each dance of my mind, from the tastes on my tongue to the steps of my feet, each choice is yours.*

He assumed they'd see his colorful silks from far off, but neither he nor they changed pace. The road between them shrank until he recognized them as Kardun. Unlike what he'd heard of the Budari, the Slave-kings might laugh, ignore, or kill him.

Hewing to his god, he let the distance dwindle past the point of decision. The leader's curved blade clanked against the stirrup, but the warrior didn't reach for the hilt. Instead, he remained stiff-backed, cradling something round in his lap, like a ball.
When they passed on another, neither smiling nor grimacing, Harek's brute loosened its grip, but did not let go.

CHAPTER

12

For as long as he could remember, Chief Warden Swope had greatly admired the stories he'd heard about the Interstellar Operative. In the flesh, though, the famed investigator wasn't nearly as stalwart or sturdy as he'd imagined—he was just a man. All the same, as he strode into Swope's office, long coat sweeping behind him, the warden straightened and hoped he wouldn't seem too much of a sycophant.

"It's an honor."

The Op's hard face was neither irritated nor pleased. His eyes zeroed in on the room's sole decoration, a potted plant with rainbow hues.

His low, resonant voice made him seem taller. "That's the first show of color I've seen in the Chamber. That allowed?"

Swope provided a genial smile. "To me. I so seldom take leave, it's arguably medicinal."

Without asking, the Interstellar Operative sat. "Which brings me to my next question."

Suddenly standing alone, Swope awkwardly dropped into his chair. "Of course. Anything. What can I tell you?"

Hands clasped, his thumbs and index fingers met as bobbing points. "Over time, all this white in the Chamber creates a kind of snow-blindness, photokeratitis, right? Keeps the inmates pliant, but it also requires the staff to take at least a week off every quarter. That constant rotation means a constant opportunity for security leaks. Bribery, infiltration."

"If you're suggesting the fugitives had inside help, I assure you, every employee is carefully vetted. Moreover…"

His lips twitched into a bemused smile. "Let me stop you there. My job's finding them, which means I don't care about what you did right, only about what went wrong. So, as I was saying… the low pay must attract a lot of people who're, let's say, new to the Archosian dream, yes?"

Swope tried to look relaxed but wasn't sure how. "Yes, but there are so many applicants, we have our pick. And we select only those with families and a clear desire to set down roots. Honestly, I don't believe our people had anything to do with it. If that's something you want to pursue, of course, I'll open our personnel files."

He leaned back. "Already have them, thanks. You mentioned family. You're divorced twice?"

Uncomfortable as it was to be on the receiving end of the Op's interrogation techniques, he'd read so much about him, it felt strangely familiar. "Yes. My work cost me two marriages. Do you think my former spouses were involved? I'd be happy to turn them in."

Swope meant it as a joke, but the response was humorless. "No. Melna's pursuing a surprisingly successful acting career ten systems from here and Chei married a sixth cousin to Sebe Mordent, which… I'm guessing you didn't know."

"I did not. Traded up, did she? Well, I wish her the best." He was lying. Not having thought about her in ages, he didn't wish her anything at all, but feeling petty and guilty about it compelled Swope to ask, "Do you suspect… me?"

That brought a smile. "Of having a hand in the escape? Nah. If anything, the fact that your domestic partners stuck around as long as they did on this dead-end world speaks well of your reliability."

That made him relax a little. "May I offer you a drink? It is also, technically, against the rules, but I have a bottle of Tuslan brandy I've been saving for a special occasion." He proudly pulled the rare bottle from a drawer.

"No thanks. Haven't touched a drop in ages. Long-eared dog of a story. That is the good stuff, though, so you go ahead."

The warden thought about it but didn't. Placing the bottle on his desk, he regarded it sadly.

The Op went on. "Keeping two geniuses and a manipulative alien in check is tough enough. Add a marksman, and, well…" He blew air between his lips.

"We've managed for years without an incident."

"You have. Fact is, I'm convinced, and my report will reflect this, that if it weren't for the woman and the boy, their escape plan would have failed miserably. Neither of them could be identified by your systems?"

"No. We synch regularly with all the standard databanks, so, unless there was some sort of glitch, I assume they're unregistered. But you, world-walker, having access to all sorts of Archosian and Pantheon databanks, would know far more about that than I."

"That I do. Identified the boy easily enough. Can't share details, but I'm pretty sure his presence here was a stroke of luck. No plan to it at all, what believers might call dharma, or, since you probably prefer Archosian terms, a random happenstance resulting from the statistics involved in large numbers. You lost track of the patroller when it left orbit?"

"Yes, but only because three of our orbiters were destroyed by…"

The Interplanetary Op wagged his finger. "Ah-ah. That name you were about to mention? That's something we don't speak about."

"Yes. Above my paygrade, as they say."

"You think it's enough?"

"What?"

"Your pay. Would you say it's reasonable compensation? I could put in a word."

Swope felt as if he should be suspicious, but it was so much more pleasant to think the man approved of him that he went with it. "I manage, but… who would ever say no to more?" Noticing the Op's intent stare, he returned to the issue at hand. "We did lose them after that. They disabled the transponder."

The Op scratched his chin. "I'll have to remember to add tampering with official equipment to their list of crimes."

Swope laughed. The Op did not.

Instead, he stared off, possibly at the bottle of brandy, more likely at nothing. "I'll be honest, Swope. I've been at this a long time, so long, it's like the thrill is gone. It's all become so run of the mill. Change their size, shape, and gender, people are people. Even Os. They'll flow into whatever gaps happen to be lying around, good, or bad. But that can't be news to a Chief Warden, right? I mean, how much variation in the human condition do you see here? I don't mean little things like accent, skin color, and whatnot, those are decorations. I mean what's inside. There, it's all the same. You see that, right?"

Swope wasn't sure he agreed, but it would be a shame not to. "I think maybe I do."

The Op nodded at him. "I believe you do. You and I, we're the sort who know it's the differences that make life worth living. See, in this case, for me, it's that woman, Calico.

There's no record of her at all, anywhere. And that, at long last… is interesting."

Swope shrugged. "The unregistered are too numerous for even you to track."

"No, not really," he said, more sad than arrogant. "Once I have the biometrics, I'll always get a ping on some family member, no matter how distant. Living or dead. Then it's just tracking. Not this time, though. This time, nothing."

"Another Neiman Os among us?"

The investigator pointed at him as if they were old friends. "Ah, see? That's what I thought. But the old scanners you've got here would register an unknown bio-form in bright red. No, it's as if this Calico doesn't exist at all. Or shouldn't. I can't tell you how intriguing that is, Swope."

"A mystery worthy of a great detective, eh?"

He tilted his head this way and that. "I suppose. Of course, she isn't my assigned target, hardly worth mentioning given that crew. Thing is, I keep having to tell myself that. I set a regular alarm reminding me that she's not my problem, not my case. Part of me hopes she'll figure in somehow, but that's exactly the sort of thing that can really throw you, a sort of snow-blindness all its own."

Swope wondered what to say. "Well… if anyone can keep those separate, I'm sure it's you. For what it's worth, I hope both paths do converge so that your pursuit of duty provides fulfillment of your passion."

"Thanks. The same to you, Swope. The same to you."

Rising, the Interstellar Op put out a hand. The warden reached out, exposing his wrist. His hero slapped a handcuff on it.

"But I will have to arrest you for embezzling."

The door, which should have been locked, slid open, revealing not Swope's security team, but a group of Archosian military guards.

The Op waved for Swope's other wrist, cuffing it when provided. "I get how tempting early retirement might be, but under the circumstances, you'd have been better off spending the budget as it was intended, on pay raises. Granted it isn't much when you split it up across thousands of salaries, but for some families, it might've meant an extra meal or two."

"You said your only job was to find the escapees."

He nodded at the colorful plant. "Everyone's allowed some discretion, right? The rest was true, though. I find you and the rest of this crap utterly boring."

As he swept out of the room, the Op took the bottle of contraband brandy. "Not planning to drink it, mind you, just evidence."

A boyish part of Swope wanted to say, "If someone had to catch me, I'm glad it was you." But he realized how stupid that would sound.

CHAPTER

13

In the sharper warmth of the morning, Gui's half-waking was met by a trill of exotic birds. Their gentle calls sweeter than the seabird caws of his home, he stayed still, listening, reluctant to fully return to the real world, so reluctant, he failed to hear the crunch and rustle of approaching men.

He didn't even fully wake when something heavy plopped on his chest. Instead, he wove the sensation into a final dream, imagining a clever beast sitting on him, an imp with a near-human face.

It regarded him with great understanding and forgiveness.

Kicked hard in the shoulder, Gui opened his eyes. A severed head was lying on his chest, the gore at its neck smearing his robes. Desperate to make sense of the scene, his mind clenched on his remorse.

My lust not only killed Harek, it's doomed us all.

But it wasn't Harek's head. The cap marked it as belonging to their gold-bought captain, the man who'd promised to teach his children about Lau.

A childish relief came over the priest. The Kardun warrior standing over him, having expected the head to elicit terror, blanched at the foreigner's odd smile. Seeing its disarming effect, Gui kept the grin. He pushed the head off with the back of his hand and stood slowly.

There were five of them. Skin the color of the darker dunes, the leader wore bound plates of lamellar, the others dyed robes.

He started only slightly when he saw their serpentine mounts.

Snake-riders.

He'd seen the thick, ten-foot venomous serpents, called phagus, as a boy, during the dwindling days of the Hollow Wars. Domesticated millennia ago, by the Slave-kings, on command, they darted upright or slithered low. Their stunning speed and deadly fangs were the greatest threat the allied kings had faced. In battle, they fed on fallen troops.

Gui wondered what provided their food here.

To show he had no weapons and better reveal his unusual height, he spread his arms and straightened. A phagus flared its hood. The rider pulled on its reins, embarrassed by his creature's display of fear. Their leader, who now had to look up at the Temple Lord, remained expressionless.

In a bid to earn their respect, Gui gestured at the head. "Did you think to frighten me? I have set many heads on pikes myself. We are not so easily…"

Rigdon's terrified squeal interrupted him. When the scribe fell to his knees, babbling, the Kardun warriors laughed. Whatever slight advantage they'd had was gone.

Their worn gyrojets remained holstered, but the leader's cross-hilted, curved sword came unsheathed. The tip pointed up at Gui. He could see that the middle of the blade was wet, no doubt with the captain's blood.

Gui, and then Palchus, joined Rigdon, kneeling with hands raised.

"Don't pray aloud," Gui whispered to his fellows. "Remember, our gods are their demons. If the divine name you utter happens to be the only word they understand, it could be your last."

The leader marched up and down their small line, barking in a strange tongue.

"We don't understand," Gui said.

Losing patience, the Kardun uttered a few more words in an even stranger tongue.

"Rigdon, now might be the time to try a few of those languages you know."

Though pale, Rigdon stumbled through the crude variations on common tongues that they thought the Slave-kings would recognize. The man simply stared.

Gui tried again, daring to use his hands to illustrate his meaning. "We've come to speak to your Pushka."

Kardun warlords ruled the towns and deserts, wielding an ever-shifting influence among their own. The Pushka, a sort of hierophant, or high priest, ruler of Earth's largest city, Ballikilak, was, as far as the Pantheon could determine, a figure shared by all, and the most likely rallying point not only for the world but the larger, fractured remains of the

Kardun empire.

The leader repeated, "Pushka? Pushka?"

He turned to the others. They all laughed. That they understood.

Saying pushka in varying tones, he grabbed and shook the chin of each kneeling man. When Palchus winced and Rigdon squealed again, the Kardun found it hysterical. Even the serpents seemed to enjoy their humiliation, bobbing their heads, and flicking their tongues.

Once the game grew dull, they were dragged to their feet, then tied, and tethered to the largest mount. From there, they were yanked onto the stones of an aged road whose nearness the night and early dawn had concealed. More than the road had escaped their notice. They'd accidentally camped at the edge of a dry farm so sad it was difficult to consider cultivated. Far off, a thin man and his family of five watched them pass.

Gui had seen Kardun before, but these farmers were the first Budari the Temple Lord had set eyes upon. Though malnourished, their skin gave them a robust presence. Neither light nor dark, it was somehow both, jet black with a ghostly white patina, like pieces of night sky floating in milk, or the ash atop wood burned into charcoal.

So, these are the parents of us all.

When the ill-kept road widened, the serpents picked up speed, making it more challenging for the emissaries to stay upright. As they hopped and stumbled, Gui tested the semblance of privacy their captors' backs provided.

"They enjoy our humiliation," he said. "One of you might consider falling to stay on their good side."

The sun, hot and growing hotter, had forced color into Palchus' face. "If I did, I doubt I'd stand up again."

The folds of Rigdon's brow filled with sweat. "Do you think the captain gave us up?"

Gui looked back. "More likely that farmer. He must have seen our pod land. If so, I hope they paid him enough so he can avoid eating his children."

Palchus nearly tripped. "Cannibalism is only said to occur among the free nomadic tribes of the remote deserts, not the Budari living under the Slave-king yoke."

"Or Harek? Could he have turned us in?" Rigdon said. "But then it would have been his head, I imagine."

Gui let out a laugh, loud enough for their captors to pause, look back, and laugh as well, before moving on.

The scribe scowled. "If there's anything remotely funny in all this, Temple Lord, I do wish you'd share it."

"I was thinking how odd it would be if Harek outlived us all."

CHAPTER

14

The crude dwelling-tops peering over the rise told Harek he was nearing his destination, the Budari town of Qus. There, he'd meet their contact, if Bannon willed, or, if Bannon willed, his end. Having heard little about the Budari as a soldier, his understanding of this most ancient people came from a single story:

To earn their trust, explorer Frarer Don showed the Budari a simple water compass. They asked how he knew to make such a thing. He explained it came from an idea, a concept which they did not understand. He said ideas came from the mind and pointed to his head. In response, they split his skull and tried to force the device back where it came from.

In what seemed another life, he'd butchered men, women, and children for every reason he could imagine, power, fear, lust, on a dare, whimsy, on and on. But the violence in that story remained alien to Harek, and, consequently, terrifying.

Still, one thing in Qus was familiar enough – the cog that brought him here. In the space dock, among the freighters, it looked like a toy. Here, beside the crude fishing boats moored along a rocky shore, it was a misplaced behemoth.

Along the dilapidated pier, Budari men and women used bone needles to mend flaxen nets while skinny, doglike animals gnawed at discarded fish heads.

Seeing Harek, they stopped.

He expected to be attacked, flayed, stoned, or worse. But they did not seem angry or disgusted, only puzzled as if before deciding whether he was something to worry about, first, they had to grasp what he was.

The dog-creatures had no such qualms. Ears pinned, they growled. Before Harek's inner brute could react, a net-mender tossed more fish heads their way and offered Harek a wink. The woman beside him (his mate?) punched him in the shoulder. Silenced, the animals ate heartily.

They all laughed and went back to work.

Bewildered, Harek blinked. The brute blinked with him. Reviled, chased, and beaten since his initiation began, this was the first place he'd not been instantly assaulted. Could all the Pantheon, and Archosia, be wrong about these people? The stories simply that?

Half-expecting to wake from a dream, he faced the village. The southern tip was open to the sea, the rest was encircled, not so much by a wall as piled rubble, a sporadic piece of ancient column or carved square block poking through. To the east, a similar jumble of refuse separated the settlement from the desert.

Within its confines he saw an open market; fishers displaying the morning catch, farmers unloading meager crops, and weavers setting out frayed fabrics. Some whistled or sang. Many smiled.

Testing the ground as if it might vanish along with his other expectations, Harek stepped among them. The reaction was the same as at the dock. Work briefly stopped and eyes turned toward him, but only with benign curiosity.

As time calmly stretched, it dawned on him that what Bannon taught was true: Expectation itself was an illusion. Whatever he'd thought about this Land of Birth and Sorrow, and himself in it, had only been a product of his mind.

The Budari. What are they, after all?

As if enjoying a precarious moment of freedom themselves, the villagers remained still. To them, he had no real identity either.

Harek. What is that after all?

A new identity might attach itself to him at any time; foreigner, messenger, friend, foe, or an old one might return—but not yet. For now, there was no fear, no shame, no pride, no pleasure, no pain. The bestial jaws around Harek's mind shuddered, slackened, and let go – exactly as his penance had promised.

The trio of Bannon priests that tutored him said his initial glimpse of the god's peace would be fleeting, that he should labor to memorize every nuance so that later he could invoke it more easily. But the potent calm remained even as the villagers, content to ignore him, went back to work.

And then a voice whispered: "I am near."

It was possible that the voice, like the brute's growls, came from within Harek, but it seemed to be coming from a maze of slender alleys. There, Budari, in robes and rags, moved among meager edifices, some of wind-worn stone, others mud and straw.

At the head of these nested, narrow streets sat the most remarkable dog. Lean, but not skinny like the gray beasts at the dock, this animal was dark and slick, long-legged, and black save for a sand-colored stripe along the jaw, perfectly formed as if by an artist's brush.

The voice repeated: "I am near."

Bannon? Is it you?

The dog lowered its head, turned, and then waited for Harek to follow. He did. When he feared he'd lost his strange guide, he spotted it sitting atop a crude barrel as if on a pedestal.

When Harek approached, it growled. Confused, he stepped back.

A second dog appeared on his right, so identical to the first, he thought they might somehow be the same creature. When he took the only unguarded turn, they both vanished, only to reappear at the next intersection. When he tried turning back, a third stood behind him, again leaving only one path open.

All is yours, Bannon, each turn in the road.

But was this Bannon – or something that even the names of gods concealed?

What is Bannon, after all?

In another story, another life, a child's life, before all Harek's sinning, he'd heard that such dogs belonged to the Lost God, the one kidnapped by the Grayborn to build their World Soul, that their presence meant their master was trying to find his way back to the world.

"I am near."

Two more turns and what little stone there was gave way to mud. The space between hovels widened. The village's rear gate lay ahead, sandy dunes and palm trees beyond.

But the dogs took Harek to the right, toward wooden warehouses with timbers held in place by pitch and rope. The largest looked as if it had been abandoned during construction, its size exceeding Budari architectural skills. The walls askew, they looked ready to collapse.

The three dogs stood at the entrance. When he approached, they walked off, and, as far as he could tell, disappeared.

"I am near."

The door, barely ajar, was held tightly in place by a tilted frame. But Harek was strong and pushed it inward. Slanted sunlight intruded from the crooked roof, shining on casks, crates—and a woman. She stepped forward as if expecting him. Unlike the preternatural dogs, everything about her felt born of this Earth. Her face was unadorned, black skin glowing with the white sheen of the Budari, she could have been any one of the villagers.

They stood opposite one another, he in his womanly garb, she in a plain tan robe.

"We desire what the god desires," she said. "Desire is all."

Harek was unsure if she'd spoken in his tongue, if he'd somehow grasped hers, or if she hadn't spoken aloud at all. But the words overwhelmed him, the sensation not entirely unlike the epiphany he'd felt upon arriving in Qus, this time more a thing of the body than heart and mind.

Yet that heart and mind, still present, asked: Is this what I've been seeking?

When the woman's rags dropped away, the acolyte knew his initiation was over.

"No. It's what's been seeking you."

Mind letting go, he allowed her scent to fill him. He hardened, manhood poking through the same sort of tender fabric he'd once ripped from a screaming woman's body before taking her.

Thoughtless, he pulled his silks away and wiped the makeup from his face – not to be more man and less woman, only to be more naked. As he moved toward her, fleeting images of a former life danced in his brain; bloodied hands, crushed cries, ravaged women, slain babes. In contrast, she was a thing of beauty, open-armed, inviting, neither condemning nor accepting.

Simply being.

Harek begged to know: Am I truly any different now, or will I always remain a vile thing?

Speaking with that wordless voice, she touched his chest and answered.

"Nothing naked is vile. No desire is futile."

Grabbing his wrists, she lowered herself to the dirt, pulling him with her. Spreading her legs, she clasped his buttocks with her feet and tugged him inside. Her hips began to move, then his, and all the lines between them melted away.

CHAPTER

15

For his second shift in Asylon, Rusk brought along *Eber's Maladies of Mood* to help pass the time.

You'd expect something like "The Beginning of All" to be gripping, especially when told by someone who thinks they were there, but Sterg was right. It gets tedious.

Still, the voice of Mother Sky floated from the door:

"Alone we were and all there was. Me, thinking that without him I did not exist. He, thinking that he'd imagined me."

The temperature was kept low for the comfort of the patient, certainly not for her watcher. As he tried to study, Rusk huddled with a blanket over his shoulders. Not that he'd ever be a proper physicker, but a mesmerist wasn't out of the question. Even if they'd lost favor in the naturalist community, the people still loved them. Much like they loved Sebe Mordent.

"How do you imagine someone?" Meriwald asked.

"How? You simply do, and when you do, there they are," Sky answered.

They…. she spoke more softly tonight, as if both Meriwald Stifler and Mother Sky were trying not to disturb his reading. How polite of them… of her.

Rusk managed to lose himself in Eber's for a while until a dogged passage with an unpronounceable word brought him back to the room.

"Thinking we were all there was, we touched ourselves all over, seeking but never expecting an end."

Was it his imagination, or was he hearing something different? Mindful of his duties, he put the reading down and strained to listen.

"And did you?"

"We did, we did. As we groped, we found an end."

Yes. There it was. Little moans between the words; moans of tension, moans of release.

Hope she isn't soiling herself. How'm I supposed to clean her up if I'm not supposed to touch her? Ludi insisted I leave all that to the physickers, to only listen.

"They were waiting there, you know, the old ones."

"Older than you?"

"Older than we. Or so they thought, and so did we."

I'd have to call it in. This late, they won't like that. I'd better be sure.

He walked over to the little window. She was writhing on the bed, moving her hips slowly, then fast, her hands working busily below her waist.

"Who could be older than you?"

"Life and Death and Time."

It took Rusk a moment to accept what was going on. Even then he wanted to deny it. But when her sighs grew more sensual, he couldn't.

"Now knowing life and death, we touched one another in time."

Is she… acting out the sex between Mother Sky and the Beast Father?

Feeling his cheeks flush, Rusk stepped back.

The voice and moans grew louder. "And then… and then… and then… we gave birth to gods!"

Bobbing on his heels, he patted his fist. *Of course, she'd have the same urges as any of us, and they'd come over her now and then. Part of life, but… should I do anything about it?*

"First the gods of light and dark! And then, and then…"

Thinking it might be a good idea to remind her of the lack of privacy, Rusk tipped the chair and let it fall.

But her breathing only got faster, her gasps of pleasure louder.

"… his earth, my air, our wind, our fire…. and then, and then… from me the stars, from him, the earth, from us the seas… and then and then, and then… our first children, Eorb, Vetru, Pir, Udrah, Saewl, Mani, Sterron, Lau…"

Rusk stared at his feet, then the ceiling, then the walls, and then the little window where the ecstatic voice was sighing out the whole of reality:

"And then, and then, and then…"

CHAPTER

16

Wyrm gazed out the flightdeck window. Some of the galaxy's hundred billion stars rushed by, indicating the patroller's speed. Others, more distant, moved with the same imperceptible slowness they might in a night sky at home.

He was on his way again, lonelier now than when he'd started this journey, stowed away aboard a freighter, all by himself. Maybe the fugitives, being fugitives, didn't care exactly where they were headed. But he did. He had to.

At least the libidinous hull-thuds had stopped. Spent, or whatever they called it, Os and Warland were back in their seats, Warland dozing, open-mouthed, spittle shining on her chin.

He wasn't sure Os *could* sleep.

He was a little startled when Calico draped an arm around him and absently stroked his hair – the way his mother once did.

But he didn't move.

Instead, he repeated a question she'd yet to answer.

"Are you sure you have no idea who you are?"

It tickled her. "Are you sure you know who you are?"

"Yes. Wyrm."

She pointed to herself. "Calico."

"No." Needing a confidant, still unsure if it should be her, he let his craving for company win out and lowered his voice. "I'm… important."

"Of course, you are. I am too. I'm the Mother of All. Just not the sort of mother you'd expect."

She was talking crazy again, like his mother. "No. I mean, I'm…"

He wasn't sure how to finish the sentence, but he didn't have to. In a flash, he was half-lifted from his seat by two wrinkled hands wrapped tight around his neck.

The hands had no muscle, only bone, and that made the vise-like grip hurt all the more.

"Charnel!" Fray shouted. "Put him down."

He gave the soldier a wizened sneer. "Certainly. As soon as the little shit explains why we're nowhere near our original course." Glaring, he turned on Wyrm, the dead of his crystal eyes endless. "You used your little blue ball to change our heading, didn't you?"

Wyrm tried to answer, but the general's fingers were collapsing his windpipe.

Calico, wide-eyed, looked from Wyrm to Fray. Fray drew his gyrojet.

Charnel scoffed. "Please. Fire that thing in here and you'll kill us all."

Os tapped Warland's shoulder, rousing her. She tsked at being woken. "What is it?"

"Don't let Charnel kill the boy."

The scene amused her. "Why?

"Well, Wyrm may think he's got us believing he's some abandoned urchin, but we all know better, don't we? For one thing, his condition would require some expensive medical attention, or he wouldn't have survived infancy. That means he's worth a lot of money to someone. Which means he might still come in handy."

Fray took a step closer. "I'm not going to stand by and let you kill him."

Os hmmed. "We might need Fray, too, I suppose. Doctor?"

"Seeing how relaxed I feel, very well. General? There are several factors here worthy of consideration."

"If this were a democracy, I might care." Charnel kept his hold on Wyrm. "Now here's what's going to happen. I'm going to ease my grip a little, give you enough breath to answer one question, and if you don't answer immediately, I'll crush your larynx against the back of your neck, you'll never breathe again, and this will please me unutterably. Understood?"

Painful though it was, Wyrm nodded.

"Good, lad! Ready? Here we…"

A blast hit the patroller. Their eyes barely registered the lime-green flash before their bodies felt the impact. As they spun about, one of their two engines, a fiery husk, flew by the cockpit window. Involuntarily somersaulting, Charnel was forced to release his grip, but not before his forefinger left a long bleeding scratch on Wyrm's neck. It hurt the boy almost as much as slamming his head into the hull top.

Calico dazed, Fray tumbling, his gyrojet bouncing off the control panels, the seated Os and Warland were the first to register what had happened.

Gog, impossibly, had followed them.

The Kardun stopped outside Qus long enough to retie the priests with their hands behind their backs. As the snake-riders dragged them backward through the village, the Budari were ordered to pelt them with clods of dung.

A waste of fuel. It barely stings. When I shamed apostates, I had Lau's faithful use stones.

Glaring through the manure on his brow, Gui met the eyes of the mob. They didn't look angry, only obedient, like sheep, hoping to avoid their occupiers' wrath. Sneering, he looked past them, hoping to glean some clue of Harek's fate but saw nothing other than Budari. It was only when the emissaries and their captors left Qus behind, and the road all but disappeared into sand, that it occurred to him to wonder if any of the cog's crew had survived.

We'd need them to get home.

Reaching a farm, larger than the sad affair by the shore and fed by a rivulet, the Kardun let their serpents drink from it. After they replenished their water skins, they took to stuffing food from the mostly empty storage units into their packs.

As the prisoners awaited their captors' return, Palchus used the toe of his boot to scrawl divine star paths in the dirt.

Rigdon eyed him. "Tell you anything?"

Palchus regarded the lines sadly. "That the universe, as always, verges on a cataclysm, that humans, as always, are mortal, but also that here and now, we three are particularly mortal, on the cusp of glimpsing the part of ourselves that lies beyond."

"Is Sterron always so vague?" The constant heat had eroded any silver left on Rigdon's tongue.

"Sounds pretty clearly like death to me," Palchus said.

Rigdon scoffed. "Well, you can't trust everything you read, astrolger. The god-hated drew on star aspects, too, didn't they?"

If Palchus was trying to stay calm, he stopped. "Comparing Sterron to the Grayborn is an appalling violation of the Pantheon Code! I want that in the record, scribe!"

"Very well. I'll make a note of it. You can bring up your complaints with the Council if we live."

Gui hissed at both. "Focus! If they wanted to kill us, they'd have done it in front of the Budari, as a warning to any who might aid off-worlders. No, we're too valuable for that, a prize. They're taking us to someone with authority."

Recriminating shouts from the returning Kardun told them they were speaking too loudly. As punishment, or for further entertainment, the leader prodded their noses with a dripping waterskin, letting the contents splash inches from their parched, bleeding lips.

The Kardun laughed until Palchus collapsed.

Contrite, Rigdon helped the astrolger to his feet. "Peace be with you; peace be with us."

They continued their backward slog through what became trackless sand. Gui glanced ahead when he could, but the only landmark was a tall, long dune. With nothing else in his field of vision to judge its size, he had no idea if it was a hundred yards away, or as far as the horizon.

Mounting a rise, Palchus stumbled again and almost fell. Rigon, already at its top, looked at him and managed a cracked lip smile. "Don't give up on our future yet. I think we've arrived."

What Gui thought was a dune was a wall composed of sand-colored stone. A cluster of tents was pitched in front of it, and at least two dozen phagus hitched along their perimeter. Unlike the animal skin the Budari used for desert shelters, these were synthetic, ornate, and multi-tiered. Some had wind generators in the shapes of unfamiliar beasts atop their central poles. The largest tent, round and red, sat by a breach at the wall's center, two brutes guarding its entrance.

As they neared, the warriors took to preening – adjusting their armor and robes, shaking sand from their hair, and wiping grit from the folds of their skin. Once they felt presentable, the leader blew a half-bone, half-electronic, horn that produced a sound more whistling wind than music.

In answer, scores of Kardun emerged from the tents, scrambling, pushing, and shoving for the best view. The two guards at the central tent were the only ones unimpressed.

That is until a bigger, heavily scarred man stepped out, looking like a big piece of the wall had separated from the whole and come to life.

He wasn't impressed with the visitors at all. He was infuriated.

Not as tall as the Temple Lord, but broader and far more formidable, he had the heavy muscles of someone who killed by hand, not by weapon, or command. The hatch-work of abrasions on his face, neck, and shoulder spoke of many battles. The long, braided hair, more white than dark, spoke of age. But for Gui, his pale swirling robes stood out most – their faded colors reminded him of Harek's pastel silks.

The lead warrior collected the ropes holding his prisoners, fanned his arms in some sort of salute, and knelt.

"Amka Bodspah!"

Gui brightened. *At last, a word I recognize! Amka. Warlord.*

Head low, the Temple Lord decided it was time to speak. "Amka Bodspah, do you or any here speak the common tongue?"

Amka Bodspah's answer was quick, and only slightly garbled by his accent. "Only fools and arrogant opponents call their own tongue common. Which are you?"

Gui kept his eyes down. "A fool. You speak it well, Amka."

"I learned it as a stripling, from the locust that stole worlds from us and killed generations of my family in the Hollow Wars. Speaking it makes me want to vomit. I won't do it for long. Who are you? Why have you come?"

"I am Temple Lord Ansen Gui of the Pantheon. This is Rigdon and Palchus. We've been sent to warn the Pushka about a great threat to your empire."

Bodspah sneered. "A threat you create yourself, using the stolen plasma, ripped from the womb of this world?"

Gui shook his head. "No. Not us. We are at war with the Archosians who raided the sacred ruins. These atheists are a threat to both of us, a shared enemy."

Bodspah's thick, yellowed fingernail raked the symbols along Gui's robe, one for each Pantheon god. "But it was your kind we fought, demon-fucker."

"A lifetime ago."

"A lifetime? Not that long, no. Not so long that I've stopped dreaming about the screams of the parents, brothers, and sisters you burned alive."

Bodspah spit on him. Eyes still down, Gui watched the yellow-green glop ooze along his robes. When it touched the name Lau, he reared.

Blades and guns were drawn. Phagus hissed.

"Arbiter," Rigdon warned.

Gui didn't care. He raised his head to meet the Amka eye to eye. "As I recall it was the Slave-kings who taught us the Blood Eagle, cutting a man's ribs along the spine, breaking them outward so they look like wings, pulling the lungs through the opening, and cauterizing the wound so the victim would live for days. That's how my father died. Yet here I am, bearing your insults, risking your torture. If you're wise, and I pray that you are, you'd ask yourself why."

Bodspah eyed him a long time, then scraped his fingertips against his chin. "For all I know, your father lived so long he took his own granddaughters as wives."

Gui held his ground. "Do you decide the truth, or does your Pushka? He is your... high priest?"

Bodspah scoffed. "Some take him for the World Soul. To me, the Pushka is a man."

Rigdon interjected. "Peace be with you. We've heard there is some disagreement on that point among the warlords. Apologies if the term offends. "

"Do all of your Pantheon agree on which position it's best to let the demons fuck you? In any case, the decision about you is mine before it's his. And I intend to die in bed."

Gui pressed. "And if the Pushka learns there was a way to save you and your people, but you kept it from him, how will you die, then?"

Bodspah paced, his mouth moving as if he were chewing a tough piece of meat. He shoved any in his path aside, kicked Palchus, and punched Rigdon, but came no closer to Gui.

At least he's thinking about it.

Finally, the Amka stepped up to the warrior who'd brought them. For a moment Gui thought he'd won. But he grabbed the man's rusted gyrojet and used it to blow his head off.

The young body fell, its life-blood gushing into the sand.

The barrel still red with heat, Bodspah pressed it into Gui's robe. "All right, devil-fucker. Despite the cries of the dead burning in my mind, I'll take you to the Pushka. But first, my scars must be appeased. I want one of you as a sacrifice. If your mission here is as important as you claim, you'll agree. You choose which. When it's done, I'll have a question for you. Answer correctly, and I'll escort you to Ballikilak myself."

Gui nodded at the still-twitching body. "He tried to impress me with the head of a man and failed."

Bodspah touched the gun to his forehead. "Will your own death be more, as you say, *impressive?* Choose, or I'll kill all three of you here and now."

Killing Rigdon would please me, but what would be best for the mission? Walk with me, Lau, just this one last time, I beg. Walk with me.

He searched for the divine presence, but again, couldn't find it.

For the second time in days, he made the cold calculations.

"Palchus is a good man and has harmed no one," Gui said. "But to save billions like him, you may take him."

CHAPTER
18

Huh, the Interstellar Op thought. *Found 'em.*

Easy enough for someone with Archosia's approval and the Pantheon's blessings. Many said there was a steep price to pay for neutrality in the vast culture war. A few years back, the Op had calculated that price – then doubled it. Now he had access to an unparalleled collection of databanks; public, private, government, a few that supposedly didn't exist, and a few he cobbled together himself.

True, the bleeding edge analytical engines crowding the Ezekiel Wheel, his custom escort ship, left the habitable area tight, but still roomy enough for one.

By cross-referencing repair and maintenance records for the stolen patroller, combining that with subtle variations in fuel types and how they impacted dual-drive burn rates, in seconds, they were able to produce a signature more accurate than a human fingerprint. Coordinating a variety of planetary, probe, and shipborne sensors put him a click away from the fugitives.

But what do I do with them now that I found them?

Nestling behind a convenient asteroid, he had to think about that one.

Nab them now and they'll put the woman back in the Chamber. Then, I'll never figure out who she is.

Dogged in his neutrality, trusted even by those who hated him, the Op was loathe to do anything that could change his hard-won status. But he'd been honest with Warden Swope. At the peak of his success, ennui had set in. More and more, he found himself repulsed by what felt like the passing, petty concerns about thieves and runaways, and pulled harder towards questions that mattered to him.

Gotta be a way to keep everyone happy here, maybe even me.

Despite the Wheel's advanced sensors, perhaps as a warning that boredom could be dangerous, a terrific blast enveloped his target. The shock waves threw him from his seat, and the warden's bottle of Tuslan brandy to the floor. Its thick glass cracked but did not break. He clambered back into place wondering if the explosion had robbed him of a decent mystery.

It hadn't. The patroller survived, but barely. One of its engines had been ripped away, leaving it to spiral in the void like a one-winged bird.

Under other circumstances, his ship's complete inability to identify the attacker would have been strange. In this case, the Op would be an idiot not to know what it was, or why it wasn't listed in any databanks, and never would be.

Gog. Probably target-locked them back at the Chamber. Then why not just kill them? Is it damaged? Or… does it want them alive?

Hoping for the former, he decided to risk firing a few concussive blasts. Not at Gog, that would be suicide, but at the patroller, to speed it along its spinning journey.

Maybe if they get far enough away, it'll leave them alone?

For a moment, he worried that rather than save them, he'd delivered a death blow, but he had more immediate problems. Gog's blood-orange sensors had pierced his hiding spot. The Predatory Engine was scanning the Wheel.

Now I've done it. I've attracted the damn thing's attention.

The Wheel had a plasma canon, something Archosia's officials didn't know, and might not look on too kindly. He'd only had it installed for hopeless situations. Did this count?

In any case, at least I can't say I'm bored.

Despite the adjustment of her meds and restraints, the madwoman in Asylon's high tower continued her cosmic whispers:

"Even then, at the start, when you first loved the Beast Father, did you know what would happen?"

Rusk knew he should look in on her more often, but seeing Lady Stifler all tied up made him feel guilty. He had to let the physickers know she'd been going at herself. It was his job, not as Ludi's spy, as her medical watcher, but it was still his fault.

It's not right to keep her like that.

Dr. Dunne's assurance that Rusk had done the proper thing, that she might've hurt herself, caused a rash, abrasions, or worse, didn't make him feel any better. They'd taken up so much slack in her bonds, that the poor thing couldn't scratch herself. Writhing and arching her back was all she had left.

It's like hogtying a puppy because it wants to play.

"Did you know what would happen?" Meriwald repeated.

At least she sounded better. Last time it was nearly all Mother Sky, yak-yak-yakking about the birth of the gods. The few times Lady Stifler did speak, she sounded so weak, that Rusk worried her time had come. He only stopped worrying when Dunne reminded him of the obvious; Meriwald Stifler was Sky. If Sky's voice was strong, Meriwald Stifler was strong. At least her body.

"But what if she stops being Lady Stifler altogether?" Rusk had asked.

The man shook his head in a way that made Rusk worry he'd be fired. Instead, he patted Rusk's shoulder. "If your shift ever passes without a word from Lady Stifler, let me know." He lowered his voice. "If Ludi trusts you, so do I. You are our eyes and ears."

Did anyone not know he was here to help the old man? Apparently, Ludi'd only fallen out of favor with a few extremists in the Directorate, supporters of Mordent mostly.

At the time, Rusk was able to let go, but the longer they left her tied up, the more his relief mixed with guilt and contempt.

Best minds in Archosia... I've half a mind to loosen those ropes myself. Just a little.

Sky spoke again, all haughty. "Did I know? Knowing is for mortals. Gods do not know. We are. Once our children were born, they had always been born." She chuckled as if remembering what it was like to hold the gods on her lap. "But... fathers can be so cruel."

"My father wasn't cruel," the lady said.

"So far as you know, little one, so far as you can know. But I was the Beast Father's only dream. He didn't know what his children were. Thinking they were a strand of his own hair obscuring his eye, or a bit of dangling drool getting in the way of another kiss, he'd swat and crush them."

"*You* saw that they were your children, didn't you, Mother?"

"I saw."

"And you loved them?"

"And I loved them. But I also loved him. So, I wondered, as I wonder now, and I wonder always, if I should have stopped them."

"From what?"

"From making you, grandchild. From making insects that need to know."

Had he heard this part before? If he had, it felt different this time. When Sky didn't answer right away, he found himself eying the little window.

"If you wondered whether to stop your children, that means you had a reason," Meriwald said.

The silence stretched. Still, he decided to stay in his chair for now. It was easier when he wasn't looking at her, easier to imagine her as two people sitting in a field on a sunny afternoon, chatting over bread and cheese – not a crazy person bound to her bed.

"Reason." Sky tsked. "The only reason children have children is to kill their parents."

"My child would never kill me."

"*Your* child especially."

That was new. It was the first time that either had mentioned the Stifler heir.

"But our children? Humanity's divine parents? We created them together, filled them with life, but their Father was the one who kept destroying them, filling them with fear. One by one, they were wisps of nothing to him. Together, bound by terror, that's how they managed their little rebellion. Having seen so many of their brothers and sisters crushed, they came at their father together. While he slept and dreamt us all, they gnashed at his skin and pulled at him until finally, they tore off a piece. I saw it come free. I heard him howl, confused, not knowing what happened or why it hurt—and I wept for them all. When I did, my sweet children stole my tears. His flesh, my tears, from that clay, they made children of their own, and called them human."

CHAPTER

20

"Temple Lord! Temple Lord! By Sterron hear me!"

Three Kardun snatched a shrieking Palchus and dragged him toward the dark gap in the sandstone wall. The crowd cheering, Gui wasn't sure the astrolger heard his explanation.

"Rigdon's records are necessary for the Pantheon."

He thought of adding, "I'm sorry," but it wasn't wise to appear weak. As Palchus disappeared into shadow, Rigdon didn't bother to hide his relief.

"He did say he was particularly mortal today."

Already regretting the choice, Gui corrected him. "He said we all were."

Newly worried, Rigdon directed himself toward Bodspah. "Amka, what will become of us if the Temple Lord answers your question incorrectly?"

Bodspah had the same grin as their captors when reveling in their pain. "If he's telling the truth about the Archosians, both our empires will fall, and you'll have only your demons to blame for not providing wisdom in the moment of your greatest need. Or did you expect some assurance you wouldn't share your clansman's fate?"

"He's not my…" Rigdon said, but then thought better of finishing.

Wrapping his thick arms around Gui and Rigdon, Bodspah moved them toward the gap. "Come. We'll study the passing of life together."

One of the brutish tent guards walked ahead, the second fell in behind. The rest swarmed around them eagerly. As they entered the biting cool of the opening, Gui realized that it and the sandy wall were part of an ancient arena. The once-level ground in its oval center was now as uneven as the harsh surrounding land, but there remained enough tiered seating for more than a hundred times the Kardun's number.

Sobbing piteously, Palchus was taken to one vertex of the oval. There, the Kardun bound his hands and feet to a slender, upright stone that was plainly not part of the original design. Bodspah led Gui and Rigdon to seats directly above and behind it, giving them a clear view of the astrolger's shaking head and trembling limbs.

Ignoring his former companion, Gui tried to focus on the other Kardun. For all their excitement, rather than sit close to the sacrificial stone, they took seats higher up, as if not wanting to be too near whatever came next.

A crude iron gate at the opposite vertex was flanked by several men holding the chains that would lift it open.

Understanding at once, Gui pointed to it. "I'm unfamiliar with the animals here."

"So were we a hundred years ago," Bodspah said. "But we learned."

Finished with their work, the men who'd tied Palchus to the stone hurried to leave. Those holding the chains tightened their grip and looked to the Amka.

Without introduction, prayer, or ceremony, Bodspah raised his hand and then swiped it downward. The chains grew taut, and the heavy gate rose. Once high enough, it locked into place and those men, too, raced to get away.

What could make Slave-kings scurry so shamelessly?

In answer, an impossible thing emerged from the gate.

Sweet Lau!

Unable to tame the fear flooding his body, the Temple Lord closed his eyes.

Bodspah clapped his shoulder hard. "No, no, demon fucker! Watch!"

A scorpion was the closest comparison Gui's reeling mind could conjure. More accurately, it resembled the Soul-Eaters, the monsters cartographers used to mark terra incognita, the harshest wasteland depths, or whatever lay beyond known space. While believing the gods could create wonders, even the most devout took them for fanciful exaggerations.

But here it was.

A segmented torso three times the size of a lifepod sped toward them, carried by six hideous legs. Gui's body ached to flee but the effort would have been useless. When Rigdon tried, bolting upright, the guards' swords forced him back into his seat, cutting his robes, and scratching his skin just enough to keep him there.

Palchus struggled against his bonds so violently, that it looked as if he'd broken his own arms, but they held fast. The beast's two huge pincers, though, had no trouble ripping him from the heavy ropes and holding him in the air, damaged limbs dangling.

Mercifully, Palchus didn't have to wait long. The dreadful tail curved up over the long back and aimed its forked stinger toward Palchus' twisting head. Gui prayed for the needlelike protrusions to simply pierce his skull and kill him instantly.

Lau, show me your hand in the mercy you give this man.

But when they plunged downward, rather than cut the bone, the sharp tips vanished.

Show me that I still walk your path.

All at once, the tail whipped back up.

Show me…

And then it happened, and though it was close enough to touch, Gui couldn't quite accept what he saw. As the stingers withdrew, they pulled a second body from the first, as if the creature had yanked Palchus free of Palchus. The astrolger was in two places at once—one body held from the head by the stingers, the other still pinned by the claws.

But they weren't the same, not exactly. The Palchus held in the air was ghostly, ephemeral, and whole, the one in the claws very much of broken flesh. No sooner did Gui notice the difference, than the spectral-Palchus was sucked into a second mouth hidden in the tail, inhaled like an airy soup. The moment it was gone, the physical body slumped, devoid of… something. As the beast tore it apart and shoveled it into its maw, small piece by small piece, this body did not stir at all.

A blade was lowered to Gui's throat.

Bodspah smiled bitterly. "Tell me, what mercy have I granted you that was not provided to the men, women, and children you burned? What great gift have I given you?"

The answer came effortlessly.

"You have shown me, beyond all doubt, that the atheists are wrong," Gui said. "That we are not merely flesh and blood, that the soul exists, and for that, you will always have my thanks."

CHAPTER
21

For whatever reason, Gog hadn't fired again.

Belted to his seat, rolling with the ship, watching the twirls of starlight outside the cockpit window, Wyrm wondered if a machine could be cruel, sadistic like a cat with a mouse. Then he remembered Fray saying it was part human.

So, of course, it could.

The way the dust hovered and spun told him the inertial force generator was no longer working. His tutor, Ludi, once said it was difficult to get nauseous without gravity.

Proving him wrong, Wyrm puked all the same.

Sick pooling in front of his nose, convinced his little story would abruptly end, he thought what an idiot he was to be here, an idiot to think he'd make it to Earth, to think he had anything approaching the greatness his mother saw in him, that he'd even be able to survive the trip let alone be a great hero – the World Soul – an idiot to think at all. But Wyrm couldn't stop himself from thinking, any more than he could stop himself from dying.

Could he?

He tried to speak but had to spit before the words came out: "Birefringe save us."

The remaining engine fired, hurling the patroller into a more violent, but hopefully more productive, spin. He'd never given the orb such a general command before and had no idea what it could or couldn't do, any more than he knew why his father had left it behind.

As if he'd wanted him to find it.

As if he'd wanted him to follow.

As if Wyrm wasn't an idiot at all.

The harsh metal moans, the creaking rattle, and bump of the careening craft were too much for the already lightheaded boy. Before blacking out, he thought he saw a bug-eyed Charnel glaring at him like death itself.

He'd no idea how long he was out, but it felt like a moment's blink. Next thing he knew, the solitary engine was firing again, its roar perhaps being what woke him, That, or the sound of it tearing free from its tortured mounts like its twin, followed by a slow hiss of decompression. They were losing air. Outside, the turning stars had grown thicker. No longer pinpricks, they'd acquired shape. Far from smooth, they were irregular, oblong like... ships?

But there were so many!

One grew faster than the rest. As what was left of the patroller gyrated closer, it came into view of the porthole, then out again, glowing as if aflame. Even when Wyrm saw the heavy artillery mounted along its hull, he couldn't quite accept it was a ship at all and thought maybe they were hurtling into a star.

But then, the dark, open patch of a hangar bay appeared. The patroller, a decaying huff of momentum, cinder and smoke, didn't roll so much as disintegrate into it.

Reality stopped spinning, but Wyrm didn't. Bruised, burned, and suddenly exposed to a different atmosphere, it was all he could do to cling to Birefringe as he skidded and swiveled through a hard burning haze. At some point, he must have passed out again, since a sudden hand on his shoulder nearly made him scream, and he was no longer strapped to anything.

Calico, likewise bruised and dirtied, put a finger to her lips, indicating he should be quiet. She tugged him behind a stack of crates in a grand, high-ceilinged hollow. There, she tore off a bit of her tunic sleeve and used it to wipe the puke from his mouth. Much as he hated being treated like a child, he took it. Returning the smile she gave him, he realized no, he wasn't in love with this crazy woman, but, for whatever reason, he loved her.

All around them shadows warped and sounded.

"Archosian troops," Charnel hissed.

Wyrm couldn't tell if the raspy whisper was to avoid detection, or if he was hoarse from the smoke and struggling to breathe. Warland was there, too, sniffing as the old man crankily tore himself from her lap.

"I only wanted to be sure nothing's broken, General."

Fray, as bruised as everyone else, knelt by the edge of the crates, eyeing the soldiers.

"Where the hell...?"

Charnel answered with his customary stygian disdain. "Mordent's fleet. Thanks to this immunologically challenged pissant, we're on a ship in Mordent's fleet! "

Wyrm's forehead was slick with the viscous oil his heightened adrenals produced, but he couldn't get more frightened than he already was, so he sneered. "We're also still alive, thanks to me."

Charnel headed for him, eyes insect-bulging as Wyrm imagined on the ship. "I've killed billions. Can you begin to imagine numbers of that magnitude, let alone the individuals they signify? Billions. But I swear, your corpse will be my favorite."

Wyrm held his ground. "Try it. I've told the orb to hide us from their scanners, but I'll be happy to make an exception for you."

He was lying, but Charnel, a cautious predator, halted.

Fray laughed. "Ha! Seeing the great genocider cowed by a space rat almost makes it all worthwhile."

Charnel snarled. "Still buying that load of manure? He's no space rat. He's educated, poised, probably..."

Wyrm glared, then nodded at the orb.

"Feh. Have it your way... space rat."

Calico looked around. "Is this really a ship? It's so big."

The long, lean Os sat with ȥher feathery head lowered. "It's better than big, it's Mordent's flagship, the Zodiac. Didn't you notice all the shiny on the way in?"

Wyrm's face dropped. "The Zodiac! That's like... I mean... I can't believe it. There's someone on board I know."

"There's lots of people here we know," Fray said. "A whole army – and they all want to kill us."

"No, a girl. A... friend. She's... like a prisoner. Worse. I thought there was nothing I could do about it, that she was gone, but I'm here and I can help her. It's like... fate. "

Fray softened and may have been about to ask her name, but Warland spoke first. "No. What you have to do is use your magic ball-sac to get us out of here." She pointed at a line of sleek capsules, barely visible, nestled in a row of nooks on a far wall. "We can take one of the life-pods, commandeer a cog and slip out of the fleet altogether."

"You don't understand. She's in real trouble."

"Oh, no!" Warland gasped. "Someone I don't know is in real trouble? Quick, let me risk my life to help them!"

Wyrm stuttered. "I-I-I can pay you." Noting the dubious reaction, he quickly added, "Look, Charnel's right. I'm not just some orphan."

"Who are you, then?" Os asked.

"Never mind. Someone who can pay you. You broke out of a high-security prison with my help. This will be a lot easier."

Warland thought a moment. "I have my own resources, as does the General, but Os works for hire, though, don't you? Perhaps this is as good moment a moment as any for us to split up."

"Hmm. I do love a mystery," Os said. "And while I appreciate your desire to put some distance between us before I call in that favor, doctor, the answer's no. There's nary a hair on the boy's family jewels, and I don't like what I can't control." Zhe turned to Wyrm.. "Call me in about six months."

Charnel raised a wrinkled brow. "You're holding the only thing I'd ever want from you. Even if you were desperate enough to offer it as payment, you're not stupid enough to turn it over in advance, and I'm not stupid enough to trust you to hand it over afterward. Just as well. Ema, Os, and I would probably wind up killing each other over it."

Calico's guileless gaze took them all in. "I want to help her."

"So what?" Warland said. "Oh, sorry. I meant to say, how sweet. No, no. Right the first time. So what?"

Fray grimaced. "You know him enough to risk your life for him? What is he, a kid brother?"

"No," Wyrm explained. "We're not related. We met by accident."

She gave off a singsong laugh. "Accident and plan, accident and plan, the stories we tell like nobody can."

Wyrm was thinking he might be better off without her help, but then Fray surprised them all by saying, "Get them out of here and I'll help you with your friend. I know how ships run. And the doctor's right. It's as good a time as any to split up."

A variety of expressions danced on Warland's face. "Why in Abraxas' name would you…"

"Obvious, obvious, obvious." Os tipped ẓher head at Calico. "Love is in the air, along with the rest of the human stank. I for one would be delighted to leave the happy family behind. They keep the quixotic Fray, and we get out of here. Is it a deal?"

Charnel and Warland grunted their agreement.

"Deal," Wyrm said.

The Zodiac. Mordent's flagship. What were the odds? Maybe he wasn't an idiot. Maybe he was here for a reason. Maybe it was fate.

Sometimes the only choices were bad. The last thing the Interstellar Op wanted was to die. The second to last was to use the plasma canon and destroy his reputation. The Third was to lose track of the fugitives, but there wasn't much he could do about that one. From the looks of the patroller's crazy, cartwheeling fire dance, even if the passengers survived, their ship would not.

A lime-green flash got his hands moving faster than his brain, taking the Ezekiel Wheel into a steep dive. When his mind caught up, he concluded he might as well give up.

But his bones were right to try, and his mind was wrong.

The beam shoved the Ezekiel Wheel a quarter degree off its plotted trajectory, but there was no major damage. Survival brought more questions – which evasive pattern to use, which way to run. Having the data from the destroyed Chamber ships helped, as did the fact that the Wheel was considerably faster and more nimble than a damaged patroller with one engine.

Appraising his unintended foe, he again considered the possibility that Gog was damaged, too. Either that or his ship was better than he thought, at least better than the rumors. Even the atheists made Gog out to be more god than man or machine.

It wasn't. He was confident of that much, but, based on the readouts, its maneuverability, speed, and firepower made the distinction between natural and supernal moot.

Speaking of which, at that moment, a hoary voice came over the comm:

"I can help."

It was hardly unwelcome, but despite the dire straits, or maybe because of them, the Op was immediately suspicious.

"Long time no hear, Ludi. Seeing as how I don't believe in divine intervention, or, for that matter, anything that seems too good to be true, how much is your help gonna cost?"

"Not much. A conversation."

The Op was in no position to pinpoint the transmission source in real-time, but it wasn't close, meaning "help" wouldn't be in the form of firepower. That only made him more curious.

"Conversations can start wars."

"Or prevent them. But is now really the time to haggle over such a low price?"

"Fine. I'll spring for dinner. What's the plan?"

"Haven't got one, exactly. I'm hoping we can figure this out together, But for starters let's stop thinking in terms of things like accidents or plans. They're only concepts created by the human mind. Useful, but limited."

"Ludi! Quit trying to prove how smart you are and tell me what to do."

There was another flash and another steep dodge. The Wheel was agile, but Gog had speed. It was gaining on him.

Worse, that last shot was closer than the first. Sparks flew from the tactical consoles. Whatever energy comprised the blast overloaded half the sensor array. It wasn't plasma, or projectile-based. It was something else entirely. Something Gog came up with on its own.

"I do have the beginnings of an idea," Ludi said.

The Op combed what was left of the short, intermediate, and long-range scanners for something to hide behind – a moon, an asteroid, a debris field, a stray ionized gas cloud.

There was nothing.

"Do go on."

"The simplest way for a complex system like Gog, or even a human, to monitor and organize its functions is by creating an internal model of itself, a schema. We've long known that the brain uses a body schema to track its position and posture in space."

With every twist and turn the Op took to make the Wheel a more difficult target, Gog grew closer.

"Ludi…?"

"To curate the massive data coming in through its senses and coordinate it with its internal processes, the brain also has a model of itself and its assumptions about reality. That model, by definition, is smaller than the whole, but as a consequence of being an accurate model, it considers itself the whole brain. We call it consciousness. Were the model not so fragile, the religious might call it the soul. Likewise, the model considers its assumptions about reality the whole of reality, but it's a map at best, and never the terrain."

Another flash, another turn.

"Short version!"

"That was the short version, but we do need more time. Rather than dodge, try matching your heading with Gog's so the next strike directly hits your rear shielding. You'll take damage, but it will push you and put more distance between you."

"I wouldn't survive the blast!"

"By my calculations, you would. It's the following blast you wouldn't survive."

"Fine!"

The Op's faithful bones screaming their disagreement, he maneuvered the Wheel into Gog's path. Ludi, meanwhile, continued as if they were sipping drinks and admiring the view at a resort.

"As I was saying, like us, Gog thinks it's making decisions based on what's captured its attention, but it's more the other way around – whatever captures its attention creates its decisions. Picture a scale weighing different pitchers, each holding a certain amount of weight provided by those curated senses– the heaviest pitcher gets the attention. In the case of a predatory engine, those pitchers are mostly about prey. It looks for things to destroy, settles on one, and destroys it."

The next flash came. In the moments before it hit, the Op decided over and over whether to dodge or listen to Ludi and stay the course. But maybe, as per his venerable, and perhaps senile benefactor's explanation of consciousness, he was only imagining he decided.

In the end, the Op didn't decide or imagine he decided at all. He ran out of time.

Mitigated by the Wheel's speed, the explosion shattered the rear shielding and decimated the small cargo bay, but Ludi was right. The concussive force increased his speed, and, consequently, his distance from Gog.

It was still only a matter of time, but at least it was more time.

"Wrap it up, Ludi!"

"Oh, I thought I had. Assuming there's more than one pitcher, that Gog doesn't only want to destroy you, all you have to do is make your pitcher lighter or some other pitcher heavier. What was its previous target?"

"The fugitives. It came a long way for them. They're what captured its attention. I got in the way."

"Then take yourself out of the way."

"How? As we've established, I can't outrun it!"

As if in confirmation, Gog picked up speed.

"No, no. It doesn't want you to be nearer. It wants you destroyed. But again, given that the map is never the terrain, you don't have to be destroyed, it just has to believe it. Presumably, it wants to accomplish that by expending the least amount of energy, so, why not do the work for it?"

Both the Op's brow and his mind knit, but only for an instant. "I can self-destruct. Or at least pretend to. You couldn't have opened with that?"

"Hadn't thought of it yet. Many of the best answers only look obvious in retrospect."

Again, the Op's fingers hesitated, but his mind forced them to engage the autodestruct. "This better work."

"If it doesn't, what are you going to do to me? Good luck."

Gog was still gaining on him when the countdown began.

The Op didn't even have the satisfaction of thinking his death would obliterate the machine beast. The predictive readouts made it clear Gog wouldn't suffer a dent.

"Ludi, you're a lousy date."

CHAPTER

23

Whatever the power of their faith, whatever skills they possessed, the surviving Pantheon emissaries were terrible snake riders, falling repeatedly from their undulating mounts. Their pains, as they came to expect, delighted their escorts, especially Bodspah, whose guttural laughter filled an otherwise barren desert.

After Gui's fifth tumble badly bruised his left shoulder and lower back, he'd had enough. Rather than attempt to climb back on the hissing beast, he went to his belly, arms outstretched, and nodded for Rigdon to do likewise.

"Amka Bodspah!"

The parched croak of his own voice surprised him. Undaunted, he pressed his forehead into the sand. "If you must lower us to lift yourself, then, here, have us at our lowest."

The warlord spat. "If my amusement changed a thing, the world would be a different place."

The mood ruined, he nodded to his two bodyguards. They lowered their phagus, pulled Rigdon and Gui up behind them, then motioned for them to wrap their arms around the hot lamellar plates covering their waists.

And again, they were on their way.

"Well played, Temple Lord," Rigdon said softly. "It is almost as bad being their guests as their prisoners."

When the nearer riders eyed him dumbly, then turned back to watching whatever sandy path they followed. He went on: "As far as I can tell, none of them speak common, aside from Bodspah, and he's preoccupied. We're free to speak."

"Something you want to say?" Gui asked.

"Many things. For starters, I realize sparing my life was a matter of expedience, Temple Lord. Nevertheless, I confess to feeling gratitude."

"Keep it to yourself. I'll never forgive you for being right about Harek, any more than I'll forgive myself for being right about Palchus."

"All right. I'll focus my gratitude on holy Cnawa, then, who, might I add, has far more pragmatic expectations from her followers than Bannon, Sterron, or Lau. No offense. Peace be with you; peace be with us." There was a moment's silence before the scribe added: "Do you think… do you really think what we saw was Palchus's soul?"

Gui felt the ache he interpreted as the absence of his god. "What else could it have been?"

"That's not an answer."

"It is mine, Rigdon."

The mountains surrounding the city of Ballikilak, home to the Pushka's palace, didn't so much rise from the desert as appear over time, like a slow, steady shift in weather. Once they reached the foothills, the paths that led them between the peaks were narrow, high, and cleverly hidden. Gui was pleased to think it could hold off an Archosian army for years.

At least before the plasma.

In Ballikilak, the Budari, though far more numerous, lived as simply as they had in Qus, the better dwellings and shops reserved for the slave kings. It was the largest settlement the emissaries had seen on Earth so far, but more different in size than kind – save for the central palace itself.

The massive residence mimicked, if not bested, the majesty of the surrounding mountains and had similar natural origins. A laccolithic butte, composed of solidified magma that had outlived its volcanic womb, had been painstakingly carved into tiers, balconies, and high-ceilinged hollows, fit for beings beyond warlords, kings, or emperors, beings like the revered and supposedly ancient Pushka.

Gui found himself gaping. "Even if he is 900 years old, as they say, they must know it wasn't built by or for him. It's millennia old."

Rigdon was likewise amazed, but he remained more concerned with survival. "Best not bring it up. We've no idea how the Kardun perceive Earth's history. Their version of the past is not a rope we want to hang ourselves on. There'll be plenty of those soon enough, least of which is the question, which, no matter how offensive, we can't avoid asking."

Gui nodded. "Whether the Pushka plans to proclaim himself the World Soul. Even the

Pantheon, compromised as it is, can't accept that sacrilege."

"No less to the point, it could rally the Kardun across the systems. We want them strong enough to cripple the Archosians, not strong enough to rebuild their empire and come after us."

"I know, Rigdon, I know."

As they rode along the central avenue that led to the palace, they drew quite a crowd. Bodspah finally halted them all at the base of a wide staircase leading to a huge half-dome, a high acoustic shell that housed the entrance.

As they dismounted, Gui noticed Rigdon was hunching, loping more than walking. The wounded gait, the peeling sunburn on his face, coupled with the circle of hair around it, intensified the scribe's likeness to a lower primate – increasing his disdain for the man.

It made the Temple Lord wonder how he looked himself. Not vainly, but a poor visual impact could mitigate his influence and the mission. Rubbing the deep reddish impressions left by the ropes that, until recently, bound his wrists, he doubted his sun-bleached face fared any better than Rigdon's.

Despite his distaste, he tried to help Rigdon straighten. After a series of bony cracks and cautious ahhs, the scribe stood, not straight, but straighter.

Bodspah nodded them toward some fountains where the others were washing the desert from their arms and faces. Even the tepid water was refreshing.

Finished, both priests happened to look up at the Palace at the same time, noticing for the first time, the hunky punks and sheela-na-gigs supporting the palace tiers. The grotesque statues depicted all manner of debauchery, from men fellating themselves to women fornicating with animals.

"And he calls us demon-fuckers," Rigdon said. "In another life, I'd have very much liked to have seen those destroyed."

"That's the difference between us," Gui said. "In another life, I'd have destroyed them."

A high-pitched voice swept down and out from the top of the stairs. Haunted at its edges by gay, youthful laughter, its volume was augmented by the half-bowl design of the entryway:

"It wouldn't surprise me that devil-worshippers would dare the void and the Slave-king's wrath to relinquish their sins before the Pushka, but I'm told that's not your purpose."

Of course, he wouldn't give us a moment to rest. Smart.

Gui didn't think for a moment the Pushka might actually be 900 years old until he turned and saw him. Wizened to a height of four feet, and wrapped in desert-hued Udlean silk, what was visible of his skin was as wrinkled as a Shar-Pei. Even from a distance, his eyes twinkled like those of an insane child. Gui barely noticed the tall woman in gold and green standing two steps below him, but higher than the rest of his entourage, herself an oddity in a society the Pantheon believed male-dominated.

The Temple Lord spread his arms. "We're here, great Pushka, to warn of a coming invasion, and, because it is in our mutual interest, to set aside the past and offer our help."

"The past is a heavy thing to set aside, but Bodspah's scouts have already told us about your claims of an atheist blight, and we know they've raided the Land of Birth and Sorrow before. If I believe you that they're returning, what is this help you offer?"

Gui kept his body straight, lowering only his head in respect. "Forgive my impudence, Pushka, but I have been instructed by the collection of faiths I represent, the Pantheon, to ask a certain question before I can reveal that. It is a question that would perhaps be best discussed in private?"

"I do not fear the sun, and so see no need for shadows. Ask me here and now."

"Are you certain? It's not a matter of fear, but this might not be the… appropriate venue?"

"You bore me. Go on with your question."

Well, I warned you.

"As you request, I'll be plain." He looked up. "Are you the World Soul?"

The Pushka giggled, sparks flashing in his mad-child eyes. "Do you expect me to first share with you what I've yet to share with my own people? Better to ask the wind, or the rain what it is. Better still, ask your 'gods.' Surely, they'll tell you who I am. Or have they already, and that's why you've come begging for my aid?"

He looked to the crowd for affirmation but didn't find as much as he'd hoped.

They want to know, too.

The Pushka gave off a little laughing cough. "Well, then, perhaps it is best you came inside."

CHAPTER
24

Ensconced in the relative dark of a bulwark alcove, Wyrm watched the silvery lifepod skitter helter-skelter among the ships of the fleet, buffeted by their countless exhausts.

Only Calico was worried about its passengers. "They didn't look very comfortable."

"They'll be fine," Fray said. "A shuttle would have been too easy to spot by eye. With the transponder muted they'll be taken for what they are, part of the trash."

Wyrm measured how closely the soldier knelt beside her. "Why did you stay? Was Os right? Is it her?"

His eyes darted away, then back. "Relax. Stirring things up is Neiman's way to power. Trust me, having spent time with those three, being surrounded by a hostile army is safer. As long as they don't figure out that we survived the patroller crash, anyway. These grunts are so used to system alerts, that they won't even notice the missing pod until the next maintenance check. That gives us a few hours at least."

Wyrm noticed he hadn't said, no.

A new group of personnel joined the grunts, forcing them to duck. Fray grimaced and lowered his voice. "Spoke too soon. The petty officers and security were no big deal, but this guy? That honcho with the furrowed brow? He's a lot more interested in examining the wreck than clearing it. Let's find your girlfriend quick. The brig's traditionally below the gun decks."

"She's not my girlfriend and she's not in the brig."

"Hey, whatever. Which way, boss?"

Calico's airy giggle stung more than it should have. "Boss."

More to the point, Wyrm didn't know where she was. The orb might, though, Though unsure how it could communicate an answer if it had one, he asked, "Birefringe, where are Gilby Rais' quarters?"

Fray's face dropped when he heard the name. "The general's son? Fuck. Maybe I should have stuck with the others."

Calico shook her head. "You don't like them."

Fray shrugged. "Sometimes it's not really about who you like."

Warm, dull scintillations covered the spheroid. A pulsing blue circle formed on one side. Wyrm pointed in its direction.

"That way."

The youth was less sure of himself when they walked into a wall, but Fray found the embedded handholds and started climbing. "Is there anything that thing can't do?"

I have no idea. If I knew half as much about the lousy thing as I do now, they'd never have found me on the freighter. But then I wouldn't be on the Zodiac, would I? So maybe it brought me here, for her. Or something did.

When they entered the crawlspace at the top, the light shifted, indicating a new direction. Dutifully obeying, they crept along, Wyrm in the lead, Fray urging him to hurry, and a placid Calico in the rear.

At each intersection the light changed, guiding them on, until, blinking, it directed them down into a wide central passage. This left them exposed, but the orb, apparently understanding the need for discretion, plotted a path that avoided contact, at one point blinking red to halt them long enough for them to remain unseen as some inebriated officers and their sober retinue passed by.

Is there anything this thing can't do?

The dim forecastle quarters felt safer, but then it took them to an area where the lighting was bright, the hatches more ornate, the bulkheads wainscoted, and the fixtures gilded. Making a turn, they nearly stumbled in front of two security guards, but Fray spotted them in time, and the bored men barely looked up. They were posted at the head of a wide, ironwood-paneled hall. A plainer space ahead dead-ended in three closed hatches.

The orb marched them to the first hatch on the right, then started blinking.

"Gilby's got himself a berth right by the generals' staterooms. Must be nice to be born to it," Fray mused. "If he's in there, leave him to me. You two see to the girl and hope she doesn't scream. Be quick. Wyrm, get the door."

Wyrm inhaled and turned the handle. It was, of course, locked. With a word –

Birefringe– it was not.

The spacious cabin wasn't kept in the manner one might expect from a future officer, let alone anyone military. It wasn't the tossed, torn linen, the scattered trash, or the mix of thick body odors that stood out the most though; it was the frail girl who kept her back to a wide porthole that offered a stunning view of the fleet and the twinkling cosmos – to face a blank gray wall.

Facial bruises as large as her eyes, her arms were held behind her as if her wrists were bound, but they weren't. Her clothes, more poorly stitched sheets than a tunic, revealed purplish welts on her pallid thighs.

Even when Fray and Calico gasped, and Wyrm whispered, "Arjuda" – her eyes remained dead.

She twitched, not in response to their presence, but in answer to an unseen rhythm dictated by her battered nerves.

"Sweet Abraxas," Fray said. They stepped in, Calico closing the door behind them.

Wyrm's voice grew shaky. "It's worse. She's family. His first cousin. Her side of the family fell in disfavor when they didn't support Mordent."

The soldier's lips curled in disgust. "Mordent has issues, but he wouldn't stand for this."

"You want to tell him?" Wyrm asked. "Or can we just get her out of here?"

Wyrm crept closer. "Arjuda? Can you hear me? It's…" he was about to say his real name but caught himself. "Wyrm."

Pained and confused, she peered at him as if to say, no, *I'm the worm. We can't both be.*

Fray eyed the door. "Can you carry her?"

Wyrm hesitated. "I don't want to grab her. She may start screaming. How do I get her to…?"

A click turned them back to the opening door. A well-fed, cub-version of the famous General Gilbert Rais stood there staring at them. He had the same wide shoulders, the same bearing, and the same face, but his smugness had not been earned or tempered by experience.

Beady eyes flitting among the three intruders, Gilby blurted, "How…?"

It was then Wyrm realized how fast Fray could be. Before a second word escaped the teen's lips, Fray drove the heel of his palm into the base of Gilby's nostrils, throwing his square head back, pinching the nerves at the top of his spine.

He dropped like a heavy sack.

Wyrm was stunned. "You… broke his nose."

"Yeah. Did you want me to kill him?"

He thought about it. "I… guess not."

As Fray and Wyrm dragged the insensate Gilby in and shut the door, Calico walked up to Arjuda. Meeting her eyes, she wrapped the girl's frail shoulders into a hug. Arjuda gasped and collapsed, sobbing so hard her chest seemed ready to burst. They stayed that way for the longest time, Calico whispering, there, there, Arjuda sigh-sobbing.

Facing a mesh of unwanted emotion, Fray awkwardly waved his hands. "Look, I don't mean to be insensitive, but…"

Calico lifted Arjuda's head from her shoulder. "We have to go."

"Take me?" Arjuda said
.

"Yes. All of us. We'll take you someplace safe."

Calico looked to Wyrm for confirmation.

If I'm here because of fate, if destiny exists at all, if my mother was right about me…

He stiffened. "Earth," he said. "We have to get to Earth before the fleet."

CHAPTER

25

Powerless to alter the whims of their harsh masters, the Budari of Qus did their best to forget about them whenever they weren't around. Once the Kardun and their odd prisoners left, they went back to their lives. Fishing, farming, loading, carrying, unloading, buying, selling, mending, and tending had far greater import, and in the end, all things changed.

Their earlier visitor, whose clothes brought color to their morning was another thing. Him, they did not wish to forget. As they toiled, they shared stories about him, exaggerating his beauty and their interactions with him. Some assumed he was dressed as a consort of Gallela, as all their unmarried men did, but the harvest was still months off. From the way the net-menders said the dogs chased him, some wondered if he were human at all.

A few wondered aloud if he, not the wrinkled Pushka, was the World Soul.

But none of them guessed the truth, that he was still among them, sheltered by the unfinished storage house the elders deemed dangerous, where sunlight dripped in from a dozen ceiling cracks and the desert wind shifted through porous walls. There, Harek, acolyte of Bannon, and Ibelma, widow of the merchant Shectbay Non, heaved and sighed into and against one another. Vestiges of the clothing that once marked their identities lay in the dirt, no longer serving any useful purpose.

Though the sounds of their passion drummed loud and free, they were alone for a while – until the water-bearer Fera Kud, for no reason he could name, felt drawn inside. A lean, quiet soul, he was unmarried, but enamored of Meddi, a somber, sky-eyed girl who sold blankets in the market. Never one to break routine, this was the first time he'd entered the abandoned structure. He tried to tell himself it was to enjoy a quiet moment in the shade, but he knew that wasn't true. No such desire existed in him. He tried to conjure another reason but could not.

When he saw the two writhing forms, all his reasons for reasons fled.

The well water he carried gently sloshed in his clay jars as the two-backed beast unbent an arm to beckon him closer. Suddenly, irrevocably lost to the world of obedience and toil that had defined him, he set down the jars and, unquestioning, joined them.

Three now, they dove ever deeper into the realm of their senses. There was no crime, no shame, no man, no woman, no self, only a hungry bliss begging to be recognized as divine.

CHAPTER

26

Either Rusk was getting better at recognizing the difference in Meriwald Stifler's voices, or they'd grown more distinct. It used to be like trying to distinguish two musicians playing the same instrument, now the variations in tone and enunciation were so stark he feared she'd lose any ability to be one person. It was like they were pulling apart, and that couldn't be a good sign.

He continued listening, closely, tightly, chair propped as near the door as he could manage, trying to push his feelings about her prognosis to the back of his mind.

"But why? *Why* did the gods make us? So that they could have children of their own?"

At least Meriwald still sounded strong, albeit like a pouty child questioning her mother's bedtime tale. Sky, meanwhile, still sounded tired from pleasuring herself, answering as if it were too obvious to bother explaining.

"No, no, no. Why would they? How could they? They lived in trauma, no taste, no echo, no hint of the aching joy that conceived them. No. They were selfish, callow imbeciles piling sand to keep back the sea."

The Lady Stifler made for a precocious child. "You don't mean that. You're angry that they hurt the Beast Father."

Sky sniffed. "I do mean it. Much as I love them, they do not love me. They do not know their place."

"But you are angry."

"Yes."

"Angry that it worked? Angry that your *callous imbeciles* held back the sea?"

Sky's voice filled with emotion. "Yes! Though insects, my grandchildren were still of him, his flesh, his bone, my tears, and you grew, inch by inch, step by step, no noticeable difference between one inch and another, but in time, there were so many of you, your very existence depleted him."

"Which was the gods' plan, all along, yes? And it worked. The Beast Father didn't notice until it was too late."

"Well, he was very good at not noticing. Slaughtered his children without noticing and didn't notice you until he was too weak to notice anything at all. First, your numbers made him docile, then sleepy. Finally, they left him trapped in a torpor – and the gods' great fear became a memory for a while."

A bit of haughtiness remaining in the noted woman, Meriwald grew indignant. "Is that all there is to it? Is it really why we're here? To weaken the Beast Father? Just for him?"

Sky scoffed. "He is why anything is here. Just for him."

"Just to keep him asleep?"

"Yes."

Rusk remembered Ludi saying – *Never ask, is it true? Ask, in what way is it true?*

So, in what way was all this true? Mesmerists considered the old story a metaphor for the human psyche taming its primal urges in order to live in a civilized world. But Ludi would also say the gods are real, only not what we think they are.

Meriwald was getting downright cranky, now, as if awake past her bedtime. "We must be something more. Maybe the Father didn't love us then, but could he ever love us?"

"No. No more than you could love what you do not feel or see."

"And if he did wake and finally see us?"

"He would eat you all."

CHAPTER

27

Wyrm was quite pleased with himself for saving Arjuda – for a time.

Gilby still unconscious, they easily made their way back to the ladder that led to the relative safety of the crawlspace. There, Arjuda, who'd been more submissive than agreeable, set her eyes on the short, cramped space and froze.

Thinking the weakened girl needed help up, Fray took a gentle step closer. The moment she saw his hand, her fingernails curled into her palms, and she screamed:

"No!"

He walked backward, shushing her. "Okay, okay! What the hell?"

"Maybe it's because you're military," Wyrm said. "Like Gilby."

"But… I'm in a prison uniform."

"Doesn't matter. It's how you walk, how you move, everything."

Calico nodded in agreement.

"Okay… fine. I'm sorry. I'm backing off. I'm all the way over here now, okay? You just… get her up there before someone sees us."

No longer screaming, she took to whimpering, loudly.

"Arjuda? Arjuda?" Wyrm said her name five times before she turned her fearful eyes from Fray. "Please, it won't be for long. I promise."

She still wouldn't budge until Calico climbed in first and said, "It's safe, see? Nice and cozy."

When Calico lowered her arms, Arjuda, at last, let herself be pulled up.

As they crawled along, though, she grew paler and took to moaning. When she broke out in a cold sweat, Wyrm realized how long it had been since he'd sweated himself, as if he were riding the adrenaline rather than succumbing to it. Between her increasing volume and Fray's incessant shushing, he doubted that would last.

And he was right. Feeling a bit of stickiness welling around his right ear, he said, "Birefringe, can you take us somewhere more... open... to rest a bit?"

He felt Fray's wordless objection as well as the man's sighing resignation. Risking capture was better than being captured, after all.

The blinking shifted. After a few turns and a tense wait behind a store of stacked plasma rifles, the sphere again delivered, taking them up through a high shaft into what had to be the ship's biggest area aside from the cargo bay.

The Great Cabin. It had to be. Everyone on Archosia had been talking about the resplendent salon, where great generals and naturalists would rub elbows and discuss everything from the nature of matter to the supposed death of the Grayborn to the ancient Earth science that believers were convinced crossed into divine magic.

Not quite as big as Wyrm imagined, it was more stunning than any banquet hall he'd ever seen. Six vertical viewports at the stern provided a spectacular view of the armada. Below them ran a long, exquisite ironwood table. Scores of smaller tables filled the cabin, all set with gleaming utensils and sparkling crystal goblets.

They climbed down. Though unimpressed, Arjuda did fall silent in the soundproofed space, and her breathing finally slowed.

His attention drawn to the starry view, Wyrm asked, "What are all the brown spots?"

"The Holh field," Fray said. "Looks like we're headed straight into it. That'll cut the trip in half, but it's dangerous. The shields on each ship will have those asteroids bouncing all over the place." To his relief, the orb blinked again. "Break's over. Let's go."

Wyrm kept looking. "Just a minute."

Fray struggled to sound calm. "You heard... saw... your bire-thing. We're not here to sightsee."

"No, but we want to know where we're going, don't we?" He indicated the displays beneath the viewports. "The monitors have a direct feed from the sensors and mech-video cameras from the whole fleet. They can show us what's out there. Birefringe, what's the furthest earthbound ship in lifepod range?"

One screen flickered, then displayed a tiny, distant ship. Even with the best scanners in the universe, it was so small, that Wyrm would never have guessed it was a freighter were it not for the transponder data. The number, though, he recognized at once.

"Ha. That's the freighter I stowed away on before the patroller arrested me. How perfect is that?"

Fray raised an eyebrow. "The one you were *caught* on? How is that perfect?"

"It's way ahead of the fleet, nowhere near any patrollers. It doesn't even have a crew aside from one space-worn captain. It's like… fate."

"Fate." Fray snickered. "What are you, a Bannonite? I mean, I get it, I used to fancy that truth and the Archosian Way had my back, that I was some kind of hero, but then I grew up and found out they didn't, and I wasn't. Fate? What if this space-worn captain decides he's had enough of picking up stray lifepods and decides to let us drift off?"

Wyrm nodded at the orb. "Then I stop his engines and take his comms offline. I've met the man. You can take him easily. I mean, I probably could. The fleet won't notice."

Birefringe took to blinking red. The foursome barely managed to duck behind the table when the far doors slid open.

A round-faced older man, his uniform impeccable, but nondescript, swept in, a cadre of servers in his wake.

"Much as it will disappoint Chef Carême, dinner will be delayed. Clear the places."

As they moved for the plates, the man turned to leave, but suddenly, as if sensing something, he spun back around. As he studied the Great Cabin, top to bottom, Wyrm noticed Fray staring as if he knew the man. He was about to ask but the soldier hushed him with gritted teeth and bulging eyes.

The man's gaze settled on the monitor showing the freighter. He looked as if he was about to realize that something was off, but was interrupted by a voice on his comm.

"Primble! What's this about dinner being delayed?"

"Rest assured I'd only deny your magnificent appetite for a good reason. Are you alone?"

"Cohor Dagus is escorting me to Rais. We're about to enter the asteroid field and I want to impress the general with our new coordinated shielding, which my father-in-law, thankfully, had nothing to do with. I suppose I trust Dagus. Do you trust the kitchen staff?"

"With my life. And yours."

"Then tell me."

"We originally thought the heat from the cargo bay crash was sufficient to vaporize any organic matter, but there've since been some irregularities in the monitoring systems that suggest tampering. And the Harlegand just failed to respond to an auto-hail. They could be unrelated, someone on duty could be watching the asteroids, but…"

"You think there were survivors? And they made it to one of our cruisers?"

Primble hesitated. "I consider it unlikely, but not impossible."

"Well, once the coordinated shielding is active, it will override each ship's controls. If the Harlegand tries to break away, we'll know then."

On his way out, Primble answered, "Very good, Commander."

The plates and silverware gathered; they were alone again. Fray rose hissing from his hiding spot, "Charnel wouldn't be stupid enough to take an entire cruiser, would he? Of course, he would. Os probably bedded the crew in minutes. It's… wait. Why am I upset? It's the perfect distraction. It's…"

"Fate?" Wyrm asked.

Fray shook his finger at the boy. "You've got a magic ball that'll pretty much do anything you ask. Makes things nice and tidy, but don't confuse that with… destiny."

"Why not?" Wyrm asked.

An intense hum radiated through the bulwark. Rather than look around, Fray stared out the viewport. "That must be the coordinated shielding Mordent was talking about. Huh. I'm guessing it makes one big shield so the fleet can push through the field without anything bouncing between ships. Nice."

Curious, the soldier risked a few moments to watch the nearest asteroids shoved aside en masse. Seeing Fray impressed made Wyrm impressed – until a flash on the monitor turned him to it in time to watch his planned salvation, the freighter, pummeled by a rocky object twice its size. Its meager protection helpless against the momentum generated by the massive shield, it exploded.

Fray eyed him. "Weren't you saying something about fate?"

Wyrm huffed. "Weren't you saying we should go?"

With most of the Zodiac's crew glued to the celestial display, they easily made their way, not to the massive bay where they first arrived, but to the smaller, auxiliary cargo port that Birefringe selected for them. Its lonely guard was avoided by a few tense moments in an access corridor and a ladder climb that left them in front of a row of life-pods.

But once one of the pods opened at the orb's command, Arjuda gaped at the tight interior space and started droning in a high-pitched voice, "Nonononononononononono..."

Wyrm felt Calico's hand on his shoulder. "I don't think she'll be comfortable in there."

Despite how well he'd been handling things, the exploding freighter had put him on edge. Now, he was losing it. "Will she be more comfortable dead? Or back with Gilby? Arjuda, we don't have much time, please, it will only be for a little while. I swear. You have to close your eyes... you have to... have to..."

"Nonononononononononono..."

"I said we have to! It's not a choice!"

"Nonononononononononono..."

It wasn't working. He wasn't working. Everything was falling apart. His cheeks and armpits went slick with goo. He was ready to pass out. Fed up, he was about to grab the bruised girl and force her inside, for her own good and his.

But then his swimming mind took him back to the comfortable mansion he lived in as a younger child, and the moment he tried to bathe his blue feline, Sapphire. He remembered how terror-stricken Sapphire was, how desperate to avoid the harmless, tepid water. He also remembered how stubborn he was, how angry—how willing to push and push and push her in, despite the scratches, even if it meant hurting her, even if it meant breaking her bones, even if it meant earning her hatred for the rest of her days.

Reminding himself of Gilby, Wyrm stopped himself. "Forget it. We'll take a shuttle."

CHAPTER
28

Gog reminded the Op of the old Beast Father tales – the chance encounters with the god, the unexpected suffering at the hands of his unheralded wrath, the harsh consequences of stepping on his invisible temples.

No excuses, no way out. He'll just eat you.

There was a key difference here. The primal patriarch was as distant as any myth. Gog felt as near as the cockpit's artificial air. At least that's what the Op told himself. Ludi might argue that Gog was a manifestation of the Beast Father. And he loved to argue.

Did it matter? No.

Whatever it was, it kept coming closer until whatever weights, water-pitchers, or circuits defined its direction shifted, and it turned away,

The Op waited as long as he could and still trust the speed of his fingers, then aborted the self-destruct.

"That was close."

Adrenaline fading, he didn't realize he'd spoken aloud until Ludi answered:

"By definition, it had to be."

"Tell that to my nervous system."

"If not your nervous system, who do I tell?"

"Geez, Ludi. Figure of speech."

"But also, a good segue into your half of the deal, the discussion you promised."

Already deeply uninterested, the Op took to updating his readouts.

If Gog found them once, it'll find them again. If I follow, it'll lead me right to them, but

I better not get too close. Doubt the self-destruct trick'll work twice.

"So, what do you want to talk about? Your occasional gods? You know damn well I'm neutral when it comes to the atheist vs believer debate currently ripping the galaxy a new one."

Problem is, if I only follow, that means the Big G gets there first, which means they're dead. They only survived because I threw myself in the line of fire. Now they're shy one engine.

"Arguably," Ludi said, "I'm neutral, too."

"Meaning arguably, you're not. See? I can play games too, and from where I'm sitting, your glass is half-empty. While I've got unfettered access to Pantheon and Archosian databases, you're wanted by the Pantheon as a heretic and about to be censored by the Directorate as a god-appeaser. How's changing the cosmos one nervous system at a time working out for you?"

Which means I gotta get to them first. Neat trick. Gog's at least as fast as the Wheel. Faster in spurts.

"Not well at all. I try to play the long game," Ludi said, "wait for the right moment to act, but at my age, there are only so many moments left. Still, I have to believe I can make things better. Is that arrogant?"

"Like you said, Lude, by definition. At least the kid on that patroller isn't old enough to know better. What's your excuse?"

"That I'm human? Wyrm, Mordent, Archosia, the Pantheon, the Kardun, the Budari, our whole species, we're all… not trapped, but swept along by a communal narrative because it looks, tastes, smells, feels like truth."

"And even though it looks smells and feels like truth, it isn't?"

"Most anything can become true, in time, I suppose. But inherently, objectively true? No. I don't believe so. It's all just maps at best, never the terrain. But you're right. I am full of myself, kidding myself that my story is somehow exclusively mine to steer."

"Y'know, this'd be a lot easier on both of us if you got to the point. You didn't ask to chat because you miss my voice, and you've gotta be sick of your own. What do you want from me?"

Question being, how fast will Gog pick up their scent? And can I do it faster?

"Mordent is invading Earth, and my only agent there went missing with Stifler's last expedition. There are so few Grayborn left, I was hoping you'd consider replacing him."

"Hey, according to you, once the gods decided to wipe them out, there shouldn't be any left. If the gods are in all of us, wouldn't they know about the survivors?"

"Not necessarily. Just as our limited sense of self blinds us, it may also work the other way around. They may not know everything we do. In any case, they're not omniscient. Are you worried the gods will find us out?"

"What do you mean us? Unlike our glorious secret leader, meaning you, I stopped believing in the World Soul ages ago. You know that."

"I do, but just as there are Archosians who value kindness over technology and Pantheon followers who consider their gods metaphoric, I'm hoping you still believe in avoiding needless deaths. And, if the situation were dire, you wouldn't use your neutrality as an excuse to remain disengaged."

"Dire? I thought the plasma made conquering nice and easy with minimal casualties."

"You don't think that will last, do you? Mordent will be facing some surprises. The Pantheon has agents in place to help the Kardun."

"Huh. So, there are still some things I don't know. And you, loyal Archosian that you are, don't want to tell Mordent about that, because…?"

"Because rather than stop him, it would make brutality more attractive to him. Then, should the Kardun reunite to take back the Earth, the three-way conflict will be longer, and far more devastating than the Hollow Wars. I confess I've considered assassination."

"Whoa! Keep the murder plots to yourself. Another reason I quit was all that making and breaking of kings, queens, and democratically elected leaders. Never understood how *that* jived with your preaching that history's moved by the machinations of our inner gods."

"I don't preach, I'm not a priest. And it's not a binary. It's not either or. It's more like the murmuration of birds."

And here he goes, folks.

"Both the flock and the individual exist, each wants what it wants, but neither exists unto itself. They shape each other. The archetypal forms of the gods are burned into our brains since birth, from the voice of a raging grandfather, a nanny's self-hatred, the kindness of a stranger, the calm of a teacher, the spark of an artist, the undeserved cruelty that becomes our own…"

Sensing Ludi was on a roll, the Op muted his com.

I've still got that patchwork signature for the patroller. Maybe the analytical engines can extrapolate the changes and update the signature. Worth a shot.

When he unmuted, Ludi was still at it.

"…the love for a child, the cry of a lover, all those personas internalized, amplified, and shared again and again through the ages, and, for all human purposes, divine. We're so invested in thinking highly of what we believe we are, we prevent ourselves from thinking highly of what we may actually be. And don't mute me again!" He sighed, long and deep. "You've no idea how difficult it is to be the only voice of reason. God help the critic of the dawn."

"Hey, no arrogance, there."

"But understanding has never been more crucial! How can you look at all the signs and not believe the coming of the World Soul, or something like it, is nigh?"

"It's kinda easy…. 'cause I don't. And I hate to tell you this, but you sure sound like a preacher."

Ludi didn't care. "The Archosian expansion brought us to a turning point, and now Mordent's heading to Earth! If that's not enough, look at what's become of Meriwald Stifler!"

"Yeah, well, I hear lots of crazy folk confuse themselves for gods and geniuses. There's probably already a reserved room for you on the top floor of Asylon."

Calculations not working. Too many variables. Damn.

"Listen to me! Fine, consider me a narcissist if you must, but that's very different from a mind collapsing into its archetypal components. But this is all beside the point. Believe me or not about the underlying causes, the war will be very real, and if we can't stop or mitigate it, it will be devastating."

The melancholy sadness that had been dancing around the edges of Ludi's voice had acquired a new partner – fear. It almost made the Op want to pay attention. "You keep my name out of the newsfeeds, Ludi, and you can hire me for whatever, same as anyone. Once my current case is done. Good enough?"

"No. I need you now."

"Not happening. I'm hunting fugitives, remember?"

"What if I help you find them?"

"Fuck, Ludi! See, that? You're so busy listening to yourself think you always bury the lede. If you've got something I want, why not say so up front?"

"Because I didn't want to share this unless it was necessary. The boy's carrying a powerful relic, one with a unique signature that should be easy for you to trace. I'm sending it to you now."

"Got it. An Earth relic? How'd he get a hold of it? Please don't tell me the Grayborn are behind putting that in the hands of a child."

"No. We're in control of precious little these days. It's why I desperately need you on Earth, to keep me apprised, and to keep an eye on my sickly student. His mother used to tell him how special he was, that he could be the World Soul. He may have taken it to heart."

I've got them. What the hell? They're smack dab in the middle of Mordent's fleet!

The Op grimaced. "I know how your brain works, you old bastard. At least part of you is thinking she could be right. Remember, you once told me I couldn't quit the Grayborn? Turns out you were wrong about that, too. Thanks for the info. Talk later."

"Don't you dare cut me –"

Ah, Ludi. What did your mother tell you?

CHAPTER

29

Dr. Warland spent the short journey on the lifepod repurposing its components so that the moment their hull kissed the light cruiser, a charge ran through the ship, killing the crew and opening the shuttle dock. It also knocked out the pod's power, but she'd compensated for the drift, landing them flat in the bay.

True, Birefringe kept the lifepod concealed, but she, all on her own, managed to seize control of the Harlegand before they boarded. Reluctantly lifting herself off an uncomfortable Os, she climbed out, pleased to see the corpses.

"Seems we don't need the boy's ball for everything after all."

Charnel having difficulty, she helped the aged man to his feet. "Well done, Doctor. Well done."

As they made their way to the bridge, Os' head angled this way and that, counting bodies. "Seems wasteful. Not to mention unsanitary."

"No doubt you could have seduced them all," Charnel said. "But there wasn't time. We must get as far from this fleet as we can as quickly as possible."

Nose wrinkling, the alien grunted in agreement.

Arriving at the control hub, Warland slipped into a monitoring chair, "Besides, you should save your energy. I'll require all of it in a few hours." Unaware of how much her little wink unnerved both Charnel and Os, she turned to the sensor array.

Charnel creaked into the navigation seat. "I'm afraid Fray's manhandling damaged me more than I was willing to admit. Well, I hope he dies soon." He eyed a flashing icon. "There's an auto-hail requiring a voice response. Routine, but every six hours it's some grunt's job to monitor the logs, and their CO's job to check on them. A comfortable margin, but the dead crew likely had friends on other ships who'll want to chat about all the pretty rocks, so the longer we wait..."

"Not a problem." Warland manipulated the controls. After a moment, the self-pleased, half-smile vanished.

"Your odor changed," Os said, strapping in. "And not in a good way."

"Doctor, what is our status?"

"uhhh…"

"Doctor?"

"The controls have been locked by an outside source. I think it's part of an effort to coordinate the fleet's shielding. Vaguely impressive, but the problem is if I disengage, they'll spot us."

Charnel sucked at his teeth. "The idiot children are trying out some new toy on the asteroids. How long before we're through the field?"

"Normally, three days. This unified shielding can cut that by two-thirds, still more than our six-hour window. Ideas?"

"Some sort of decoy to take our place, fool central control?" Charnel offered.

Os smirked. "Missing the boy-ball now, Ema?"

"No, and a decoy is an excellent idea. I can modify a drone to duplicate the Harlegand's signature and activate it at the same time we disengage. The timing would have to be perfect, but it's nothing I can't handle."

Charnel frowned. "Won't they still notice the drop in the shielding?"

She raised an eyebrow. "They can't notice what doesn't exist."

"You can modify a drone to provide the same level of shielding as an entire cruiser?"

"Of course. To be clear, it won't last long before burning out, but long enough to cover our tracks."

Charnel chuckled. "And to think they took a mind like yours and locked it away."

Os eyed the dead. "Can't help but wonder why."

"As you say, general, idiot children. Now, 'popping out' of the coordinated shielding will throw us into the asteroid field, but the direction is our choice. We can head back where we came from, a bumpy ride, but, if your reflexes are up to it, not nearly as dangerous as crashing into the Zodiac. Or I can put us ahead of the fleet, closer to Earth, for a smoother journey. Which way do we go?"

Os shivered. "Not Earth. That desert?"

Charnel agreed. "There'll be nothing there but war, and much as I'd enjoy the view, I have plans back in civilization. Ema, do you have a preference?"

"Some placid little fringe world I can dominate, set up a new lab, but there are more of those behind us than there are ahead. Back where we came from, then. On my mark. Three... two..."

A vibration enveloped the ship, then faded.

Os looked around. "That was it?"

Warland nodded. "That was it. Except for the asteroid field. That's up to you, General."

Os braced for the bumpy ride, but other than a slight swooping sensation that shortly leveled out, there was none.

"And... we're out," Charnel said. "You underestimated me. We'll be nearing the outer trade routes in a few hours."

"No offense," Warland said. "I knew you'd exceed expectations; I didn't realize by how much."

"None taken."

Os unbuckled. "I'd suggest you two get a room, but I'm afraid you'd ask me to watch."

Her eyes blinking rapidly, Warland rose. "Speaking of which, I'm going to find the captain's quarters and see if there's fresh linen. Os, meet me down there in ten."

As she left, Os stretched zher long lean form, sighed then strode toward the navigation seat. "You know, I think this is the first time you and I have been alone, general."

Charnel smirked. "Shouldn't you do as the doctor suggested, and conserve your energies?"

"Oh, she doesn't drain me very much. I let her think she does because, well, she likes it that way. Part of her need to dominate. You, sir, are the only wildcard left."

"I can smell what you're trying to do..."

"And you like it don't you?"

"No really, I'm too old for this nonsense."

"Now, now, it's not only about sex, it's about being intimate, feeling close enough to someone to be yourself, to tell them who you are, what you want."

"You know full well who I am."

"And I know that you're dying. What I don't know is what you want from all this. As long as we're traveling together, that affects me. Why go through all this trouble? To spend your last moments under a clear, brazen sky? Freedom for freedom's sake? I don't think so. What do you want? Or should I say... who?"

"I... very well. Stop your secretions, they're giving me a headache. I have a grandson. I want to see him."

"Huh." Os blinked, then playfully punched the general's bony shoulder. "Didn't think you could surprise me, but you did, you sentimental fool."

"I know you've no reason to comply, but I'd appreciate it if you didn't say anything to –"

Something hit the cruiser – hard. Os was thrown down and to the left, Charnel into the arm of his chair.

Os scrambled to zher feet. "An asteroid? A big asteroid?"

"Impossible. We cleared the field." As Charnel studied the readouts, he hit the com. "Ema I need you back on the bridge. The entire weapon system is down. We were fired upon. Perfect shot."

Os' eyes grew wide. "Gog again?"

"No, we'd be dead. It had to be..."

A metallic sliding sound turned them toward the opening door. Both expected to see Warland, and they did, only she was on the floor, bound and unconscious. Behind her stood a man in an EVA suit aiming a gyrojet their way.

"Hello," said the Interstellar Op. "Just so you know, Os, I kept my suit sealed after boarding, so your pheromones are useless. Surprised they didn't think of that back at the Chamber, but, y'know, the former Warden was keeping the budget tight."

"Tojours gai," Os said, wrists out.

Adjusting course, the shuttle's micro-thrusters shed propellent, nosing them toward the fleet's distant edge. Despite Fray's oddly paternal cautions to remain seated, Arjuda stood by the viewport, Calico rubbing her shoulders as she pointed at ships and made-up odd names.

"That one's a Runcible Peter Pocket Eater. And that one's a Joey. Just a Joey."

Though not responding, Arjuda appeared interested, and, perhaps more importantly, calm.

Wyrm wanted more than her calm, he wanted her forgiveness. Fray rolled his eyes as the boy rose from his seat and joined her. It was hard with the others watching, embarrass-ing, but he tried. "Arjuda, I'm sorry I grabbed you and shouted like that. I was... scared."

She said nothing, as if he was the air, or not there at all.

"She has a lot whirling in her mind," Calico said.

He looked into the girl's distant eyes. If she was thinking about anything, he didn't see it.

Grimacing, he moved on, studying the assorted vessels as if shopping. "We're cloaked from the sensors, but not invisible. We need to stay out of sight."

The dreadnaughts, though not as gaudy as the Zodiac, were impressive in their own way, the way dark mountains were when looming above flat fields of grain.

"We can hide under one of those until we've passed through the field, then grab another ship. Something fast and light, maybe a Vulture I Escort."

Fray kept one eye on the readouts, the other on the portholes, as if expecting something to sneak up on them. "Vulture's more than we need unless you plan on a shooting match, which we'd lose. Besides, it's too damn flashy. If we have to switch, we should try for something less conspicuous, a scout, a cog, even. But like I keep telling you, it'll be safer to stay on the shuttle."

Playing his own version of Calico's game, Wyrm pointed to the closest dreadnaught and said to Arjuda. "That's the Oromo. Once we're hiding between its artillery guns, we'll have plenty of time to think about it."

Surprisingly, she raised a hesitant finger and pointed. "There's a man."

Wyrm squinted. "No, that's a.... it's huge... what is that?"

"Colossus," Fray said. "Another gift from Wintour. No predatory engine this time. It needs a crew. I guess that's an improvement." Noting Wyrm's suspicious stare, he added, "I saw some preliminary sketches way back."

"Why were you in prison? For killing your mesmerist?"

Fray clucked his tongue. "It's complicated. Can't you ask Birefringe?"

"I did. No records."

"Right. It's a long story."

Having also earned Calico's attention, Fray seemed to be trying to decide whether to continue or not when a message came over the comms:

"Attention Shuttle TE42, abandon your current heading and proceed immediately to docking bay A on the Zodiac."

Mouths dropped; eyes widened.

Arjuda kept staring at the view. "The big man looks so cold out there."

A red beam tore across the bow. The shuttle lurched up. Its lights briefly dimmed.

Fray steadied the ship. "Warning shot. Not that that's reassuring."

The message came again, with an addition. "Shuttle TE42, abandon your current heading and proceed immediately to docking bay A on the Zodiac, or prepare to be destroyed."

"Birefringe..." Wyrm began.

Fray leaped from his chair to grab the boy's arm. "No! Whatever you're thinking, don't! This is a shuttle. Not a patroller. Unless your sphere can give us new engines, not to mention reinforce the hull and the frame to handle them, they've got us."

"No," Wyrm said. "I can…"

"Yes!" Fray answered. "Forget about me." He nodded at Calico and Arjuda. "You've got other people to think about."

Still fascinated by Colossus, Arjuda tapped at the glass. "That is one big, cold man."

"Fine." Wyrm lowered the orb and stepped over to the comm. "But we're not done yet."

He swallowed hard, wiped the goo forming on his forehead, and spoke.

"This is Adalbert Stifler, son of Anacharsis. I want to speak to High Commander Mordent."

Expecting some sort of reaction, Wyrm looked at his companions. Arjuda already knew who he was, Calico didn't look as if she cared.

Fray simply shrugged. "What do you want from me? At this point, you could have said you were the World Soul, and I wouldn't have blinked."

CHAPTER

31

They called it a party. Musicians played, but no one danced. Drinks were poured, but tipplers stayed sober. Everyone looked happy, but no one was. Aside from the not-so-secret meetings in sundry alcoves and behind half-closed doors, everything in the manor of Gilbert Rais that night had double meanings, even the tone of a simple hello.

Wyrm followed much more of the intrigue than the whisperers would suspect of a boy but found their secrets hopelessly boring, especially those about politics rather than sex, which, oddly, were the majority. To him, it was perfectly clear that his father's plasma put Sebe Mordent in charge months ago. Everyone else was just catching on.

Wyrm was particularly sick of everyone telling him how sorry they were about his father, as if he were dead, and his mother, as if she were incurable, when he knew full well that Anacharsis Stifler would return and save her. It wouldn't be the first time he'd done the impossible.

And someday, you will, too, his mother said when she was sane. It's your fate.

Or was she sane, even then?

Fated to gooey sweating is more like it.

The tight formal clothes and stifling displays of sympathy had him terrified that his freakish glands would humiliate both him and the family he represented. At least no one had forced a nanny on him yet. He was here, for the first time, alone.

That much made it easy to slip away for a bit, through the solar, past Rais' collection of art and statues liberated by Archosia's conquests, and into the residence halls – hoping to find Arjuda and pass the dreadful time with her. He knew he shouldn't be here, but it wasn't until he spied a light under one of the many bedroom doors that he felt he shouldn't. He would have left, then and there, had the muffled cry of a familiar voice not stopped him.

Arjuda?

Seeing her, speaking with her from time to time, was the only thing that had made these gatherings bearable. She was frail, like him, but in a manner that made what others called her weakness seem beautiful, while his sweat always felt ugly. Her skin was pale like his, but milky, her hair thin, but delicate. Wyrm had never spoken a word about his feelings to her. When he'd seen her earlier, he didn't even dare mention how pretty she was in her dress.

In the heat of the moment, he wasn't completely sure it was her, but fearing it might be, he peered through the door-crack. And there was the brutish Gilby, discarded pants no longer concealing the bulbous fat that made his legs look swollen. Ass cheeks flushed red, he hovered over Arjuda, her new gown torn, her face wet with tears, her eyes, always baby-wide with wonder, dirtied by pain and horror.

Wyrm shocked himself by how quickly and thoughtlessly he burst in, how easily he yanked Gilby away from her, how fiercely he shoved the hedge-pig into the wall, knocking his thick, boil-brained skull hard into the stone.

A strange sensation floated about the edges of his rage, a satisfaction in thinking that perhaps, like his father, he had the power to do the right thing. But the feeling didn't last.

When Gilby straightened, the light Udlean silk of his tunic became too strong for Wyrm to hold. With the physical difference between them abruptly restored, a shaking Wyrm struggled to meet the monster's eyes. Still, he tried his best to sneer as he said:

"Beat me if you like, but I'll have you thrown out of the Academy for this! You'll be disgraced."

Gilby was so calm, so pleased with himself. "Disgrace me? Really? One word to anyone, worm, and I'll destroy your whole family."

Wyrm blinked, his face twisted. "That's not possible."

The dreadful smile widened. "No? What if I told you, you're not Anacharsis' son? My father knows it. He has proof of your mother's whoring, a letter he's saving for a special day, written in her own hand. I've seen it, and I can get to it any time I like and do with it as I please!"

Wyrm's rage briefly returned. He grabbed a fistful of cloth. "That's a lie!"

Gilby's hand clenched on Wyrm's wrist and squeezed. "You've never thought about it? Look at yourself, you dizzy mold warp. How'd a thing like you come out of Stifler's loins? Your father knows it, too. Why do you think he stays away from home so much? Do you understand? Do you know what that makes your mad mother? What'll become of her now that your father's dead?"

"He's not dead!" Wyrm's mind swam. "And it doesn't matter anyway. I'm his heir. Any decision about her treatment is mine."

"That's the point, joithead. Property rights flow through the male heir, but you're not his heir. You're nothing. So, it all goes back to the state. You'll be thrown into the gutter, and she'll be babbling right beside you! Now get out. Arjuda and I have to clean ourselves before we rejoin the party."

Wyrm looked at Arjuda. She'd yet to move from her spot on the bed.

Gilby chuckled. "She's being all weepy over her first time. Women are like that, my dad says. She'll feel better once I take her with me on the Zodiac. You? You stay home and sweat your goop while real men conquer the galaxy."

He looked at Gilby, calm and waiting. He looked again at Arjuda, gasping sobs.

And he left. And he left. And he left.

Because there was nothing else he could do.

CHAPTER

32

His story done, Wyrm fell silent.

Sebe Mordent searched the face on the mech-camera viewscreen, looking for traces of his lost friend. He saw Meriwald's cheekbones, something else he couldn't place, but nothing of Anacharsis. Perhaps he was still too young.

When too many seconds passed, the High Commander remembered he had to act.

He tapped the internal comm. "Let the shuttle go."

More cautious than incredulous, the gunner responded: "Commander, could you repeat?"

"Let him, let it go. He can have the shuttle, with my good wishes."

"Yes, commander."

He cut off the transmission. Wyrm having insisted they speak alone, Mordent wanting a witness, Primble stepped up from hiding. "An interesting choice, sending a child to his death."

"I was his age and sickly when I lied my way into the army, though, admittedly a bit further along in my physical development. Fray will watch out for him. That man's a good shot in more ways than one. Maybe they'll do what others could not and find our missing naturalist."

"Or vanish as he did. Perhaps it would have been simpler to change the laws so that Archosia's women are entitled to their husband's estate?"

"When I'm in a position to do so, remind me. Feh. I should have told the boy I'd have seen to his mother's care, that she'd want for nothing regardless of the courts." He paused. "Would I have done that, Primble? Seen to her care? I was so angry when Stifler left."

"I'd like to think so. Yes. Meanwhile, having given away a shuttle, there will be talk."

"That I've grown soft?"

"That, too, but I was thinking more of the rumors that Adalbert is actually your son."

Mordent flicked the thought away and moved on. "Once the Op's turned over the other fugitives, thank him for alerting us to the shuttle's location, but be sure to make it clear I'm not pleased he didn't share his sources."

"I'll impress that on him, but I'm sure he's already factored in your displeasure."

Mordent grunted. "No doubt. And tell him he's not done yet. Tell him to continue his pursuit of the boy, but not to apprehend either of them. Hell, if Fray does help find Anacharsis I may forgive him."

Primble cleared his throat. "He did raise another issue, a *glaring* one. It may be the sort that wins or loses wars."

He nodded. "Gil's son. The vile brat. I worked years to win Rais' allegiance, but this? Pursue it, and I'll lose his support, but there'll be a trial, and that will cost *him* support. The dice will be tossed. All in all, I'd rather be out there with Adalbert." His chest fell with a massive sigh, shrinking him. "Primble, say something wise. I could use it."

"Ahem. Whatever choice you make will say more about who you are than how brilliant you are."

Mordent strummed his fingers hard. Annoyed by the sound he was making, he stopped. "*Who* I am. Another ineffable bit of nonsense. Reading Ludi again?"

"None of the banned works, I assure you. To rephrase: Do you want to expand Archosia's dream of a just society, or simply her borders?"

Cursing humanity and himself, but mostly humanity, Mordent rubbed his chin as if he wanted to pull it off.

"Peh. Have that little shit thrown in the brig."

CHAPTER
33

When Rusk last checked with Ludi, the great sage asked, as he always did, how Rusk was. This time, though, he'd asked in a way that made Rusk wonder if Ludi sensed something wrong that he could not. He felt fine, as far as he could tell. Asylon was lonely, sure, the little room at the top more so, what with his only company being tied down and talking to herself, unaware he was there.

But he didn't think that was getting to him. Even as the story went round.

"When we were created, did we know what we were?"

"Of course, not! You hadn't a clue! And, like most important things, even if you were told, you wouldn't have understood. So, why bother? What point would there be?"

"But we learned."

"Did you?" Sky was getting haughtier of late, sick of answering questions, perhaps thinking her time would better be spent being worshipped. "Is that what you call building those little birdhouses in your minds? Learning? Is that what you call thinking there's a you in there at all? Learning?"

Meriwald was insistent. "We learned."

Rusk was proud of the way she stood up for the species.

Sky, as if appeasing a child who'd worn out her kind patience, pretended to give in. "Fine, then. You *learned*."

The ruse worried Rusk. Was she biding her time, waiting for something? For what? For Meriwald to fall asleep, so she could move on without her?

"You learned to appease the gods, you learned to do without them, you learned to cover them up when you didn't need them, you learned to uncover them when you did, and during all that grand learning, you turned on each other, slaughtering your brothers and sisters, so long and so hard, the gods grew bored and stopped watching."

"So, they blinked?"

"Yes! They blinked. When they should have been paying the most attention, my children blinked."

Meriwald stressed the point. "Because we learned, didn't we? That's why they needed to pay attention."

Sky laughed. "Please. It was a quirk, a mote, a happenstance of words found and spoken, a meager reckoning that thought itself better than all the other little wispy notions that dance with meaningless magnificence in your tiny mouths and smaller minds."

"One of us learned better than the rest."

Rusk wanted her to say who. He thought he knew. At times, he was sure. It was part of the old story, well-known to any who studied the liminal spaces between myth and history. While many Archosian historians rejected the tales of the Grayborn as pure fable, some version or other was known to most everyone, provided they weren't on a Pantheon world that considered them blasphemous. And even there they probably whispered them to each other in the dark.

Even Ludi wouldn't confirm it when Rusk asked, insisting Rusk not contaminate his impressions. What Meriwald said was important, not what Rusk, or anyone else, thought of it.

But it was like hearing two and two equals, over and over, without ever hearing four.

Still, he was fine. It wasn't getting to him. Until it did.

This time, when she fell silent, it became incredibly hard for Rusk to sit still. Almost against his will, legs moving as if directed by one of Ludi's inner gods, he went to the little window, and asked aloud:

"Who was it? Who figured out what the gods truly were?"

Raising her head, tugging her splayed hair like a wreath around her head, Meriwald and Sky answered at once: "Not you."

No, not me, of course not faithful Rusk. "Then, who?"

"You know."

"Do you mean Calico the Mother of All that is to Come? Author of The Great Word? Why won't you just say it?"

He gasped. What was he doing? He had one job, and now he'd gone and ruined it.

Satisfied, her head slipped back down to the silk pillows.

"And once you learned, you didn't only challenge the gods, you hurt them, and they'd had more than enough of that from their father."

CHAPTER
34

"I'll have you all killed!"

On the live mech-camera feed in Mordent's cabin, an incensed Gilby wrestled in vain against three gendarmes. Rather than disobey the orders he not be harmed, they dutifully took the few flailing blows they couldn't block, and invariably forced him into a small white cell.

Throughout the ordeal, his beefy mass relaxed only once, and in that instant revealed a confused, horrified, animal fear. One minute he raged as if he were the Beast Father himself. The next he collapsed into a lost, terrified child. With a sharp inhale, the weeping vulnerability vanished, and he again pounded at walls.

"Fucking joitheads! Let me out of here!"

He sounded manly, authoritative, until they left him there and he thought he was alone. Then his booming voice became a wail, his jagged stomps a toddler's tantrum.

"She begged me to bring her on board!"

Mordent muted the sound.

A reddened General Rais planted his hands on the console as if to tear it free. "Did you bring me here to shame me further?"

Mordent answered slowly, a trick that could defuse tempers. "No, Gil. I confess it was partly to ensure you wouldn't interfere, but also, truly, so you could see I'm handling this according to code – and to give us a chance to speak before the story spreads."

As if caged himself, Rais huffed and twisted. Eager for a target, he settled on Primble. "You want to talk? Dismiss the servant. You may trust him with your life, but I no longer trust either of you."

Mordent nodded at the lean man standing mutely by the door. "And your Cohor?"

"Dagus stays."

Primble shot Mordent a nervous glance.

The commander kept his voice even. "It's all right Primble. My friend may want to kill me, but being an excellent general, he knows this is neither the time nor place. You may go."

Dagus held the hatch open. Primble eyed the rigid, unreadable man, then did as he was told. The immediate acquiescence undid a bit of Rais' emotional armor, eliciting a deep exhale that ended in a wounded sigh.

"Sebe, how could you do this to me?"

Mordent tsked. "I might ask the same. You knew he was smuggling a girl aboard."

"As did you! But to arrest him? He's a child! *My* child!"

Mordent let his own temper rise. "*She's* a child as well! And his cousin!"

Even as he harumphed, Rais shrank a bit. "From a particularly unfaithful branch of the family. But I take your point. Where is Arjuda?"

"Badly bruised, but safely away."

The general balked. "Gilby won't get to face his accuser? Is that according to code now?"

Mordent stood, palms up, placating. "Gil, I saw the bruises, the vacant look in her eyes. The girl was damaged, inside, and out, beaten into a torpor. If I must, I will act as a witness even if it means you never speak to me again."

Rais gnashed his teeth. "Don't pretend it pains you, don't pretend part of you doesn't enjoy seeing what you think of as savage put in chains."

"It brings me no pleasure to hurt you. But there must be laws beyond either of us."

Even Rais' laugh was pained. "Really? Isn't the whole point of moving against the Directorate to show that you are the law? Archosia hasn't replaced the statues of the gods with statues of justice, it's replaced them with statues of you."

The silence that followed wasn't the best opening, but it wasn't the best plan, either, even if Primble agreed it was the best of all possible moves. It was so inelegant, that Mordent nearly choked putting it into effect.

"Then keep me in check. I want you to. I invite you, I... beg you... I plan... I'd always planned, to put you in charge of the invasion."

Silence fell, thicker than the blue and yellow valences hanging above the viewports. Rais shook his fist and again turned red, but this time, as if a valve in his body had been forced open, his fingers unfurled.

"Even if I chose to believe you, is that supposed to mollify me?"

Mordent swiped at the air as if it were in his way. "It will show the fleet, the Directorate, and the people, that we can do the right thing and remain united."

"Can we? My son, Sebe. My son..."

"...is young, and strong." He put his hand to his heart and lied. "He'll be treated fairly and will have a place with us once his sentence is served. I know this is a terrible blow, but you're the most courageous man I've ever met, and courage isn't having the strength to go on – it's going on when you don't have the strength. I'm putting you in charge, Gil. Answerable only to me. What more could you ask that I can, in good conscience, give?"

Rais took another look at Gilby.

"You can visit him if you like."

"I'm not ready for that, yet. First, I must tell his mother."

Lost in thought, Rais marched out, Dagus close behind him.

Primble reappeared, his expectant look leaving a sullen Mordent to answer his question before it was asked. "As well as could be expected."

"I assume the general hasn't figured out the rest yet?"

Mordent gave a curt headshake. "He will. After this, even with my blessing, not all his supporters will fall in line. Some already hesitated to abandon even a flawed democracy, others will now fret over their own indiscretions. They'll distance themselves and weaken the coalition."

"Which means courting General Wintour."

Mordent's lips curled in disgust. "Which means using Colossus."

"And how do you think Rais will take that?"

"Badly, at first, but he's a good general. When he realizes we haven't enough support without Wintour, he'll come to the decision himself. Afterward, whether he blames me, or his son, it will be a matter of time. And if anyone can make a success of that monstrosity, it's Rais. If not…" Mordent's smile was more bittersweet than cruel. "The failure will be his, not mine. At best, I'll have a new alliance, at worst, more evidence that the Directorate has outlived its usefulness. Inform my father-in-law I wish to dine with him."

Primble tapped his com, but, rather than speak, he listened, and in a moment grew pale.

"It's not like you to be taken aback, what's going on?"

"I'm afraid we have a traitor on board. Your conversation with Rais was broadcast throughout the fleet."

CHAPTER 35

With the Pushka tending to "more important matters" the Pantheon emissaries were taken inside the palace to rest. While not without decoration, it was far more utilitarian than the gaudy exterior. It was surprisingly simpler and sparser, save for a huge marble door which Gui assumed led to a throne room, or its equivalent. Their quarters were comfortable, certainly when compared to the cog and the desert, yet likewise functional in a way Gui admired.

Nothing useless here.

Sending Rigdon off to survey their environs, Gui meditated, hoping that some recess of his mind might glean a clear moral distinction between the blasphemers here and the heathens who'd be arriving soon. Despite his best intentions, once settled in a low, padded chair, his weariness took him unawares. Consciousness flitting from words to pictures, he drifted into a misty half-sleep where Harek's visage greeted him. Tactile, eidetic, more real than the waking world, it filled the Temple Lord not with guilt, or lust, but something more alien – a sentimental longing.

He missed the man.

Gui shook it off and away. He'd just about finished moving their priceless "gifts" into a smaller, more presentable pack when Rigdon reappeared.

He had the oddest look on his apish face, a mix of comfort and concern.

"I have good news and bad."

"I despise games."

"Pity, what with life offering so very little joy lately. Peace be with us." After checking to be sure they were alone, he said, "I was able to make contact with our agent on Mordent's fleet."

The thought of a connection to home provided Gui with the same rush of relief Rigdon must have initially felt. It faded, as Rigdon's must have, when he realized the implications.

"They're... already in range?"

"Yes. That, if you'll forgive me, is the bad news. Having made record time through the Holh, they're days away."

"Days?" Gui howled. "I need weeks! To learn how the Pushka thinks, to begin to build trust. I won't save the galaxy from the Archosians only to hand it to the Kardun!"

"Are you asking my advice, Temple Lord?"

"No."

"Just as well. I've none to offer."

Sensing they were no longer alone, their heads snapped toward the entry to their chambers. There, the woman in gold and green who'd stood beside the Puskha regarded them with an amused curiosity. Though they'd been told her name, Indepa, Gui couldn't tell if she was military, regent, adjudicator, adviser, or if such roles meshed here in unfamiliar ways.

In any case, she was clearly of higher status than, say, Amka Bodspah.

"The Pushka is prepared to receive your gifts."

Eavesdropping or not, the cause of her delight could be as specific as Gui's consternation or as general as the world itself. It was no small source of shame that ever since arriving in the Land of Birth and Sorrow, the inhabitants found the Temple Lord funny.

"I advise you not to be slow."

They were not.

Gui was correct about the marble door. Sizable as the throne room beyond it was, it still put them closer to the Pushka than when he'd addressed them from the half dome. His seat, hardly a throne, was as short as the humble chairs in their quarters, perhaps designed not to interfere with the impact of its occupant. The windows, likewise, were angled to concentrate the light on him and leave the rest of the room in shadow.

The room needn't have worked so hard. The Pushka's impact was considerable. His head was disproportionately large, especially compared to the narrow face and small lower jaw. His eyes were wide and prominent. Wrinkled eyelids, unable to close completely, sat evenly on either side of a beaked nose. Other than the white wisps that seemed to drift in and out of existence as a trick of the curated sunlight, the Pushka was completely hairless.

It was only when he spread his arms that the rainbow hues of his Udlean gown became visible, falling like lazy wings about his wrinkled flesh – a mockery, Gui thought, of Harek's perfect form.

Jumping to his feet, the Pushka spun and danced around the emissaries, patting their shoulders and chests, before sailing joyfully back into his seat. Noting their surprise, the ancient madman giggled.

"Do not be ashamed of your body's reaction to me. Men, women, it matters not. You cannot help but be drawn to my form, for it is the heart of life, of lust, of need." He turned to Rigdon, who'd broken out in a nervous sweat. "Do you not find me beautiful, oh, man?"

Gui struggled to keep from laughing. Rigdon hemmed and hawed. For a moment, the scribe was actually at a loss for words. He did find them, though.

"You are… ravishing, Pushka, that is plain, while I, as plainly, am unworthy." He bowed deeply, making the Pushka giggle again.

"So, show me my gifts!"

His legions of followers thought him divinely mad. With time, Gui hoped to learn if it was a more mortal insanity, or guile concealed as madness, or a combination. But there was no time.

The Arbiter cleared his throat. "There is the matter I raised earlier."

The Pushka glared. "Yes, your impertinent question. Do you assume I lack sophistication? Better to think I'm above it. I know why you want to know. It's because you fear I'll restore the Kardun to the fullness of their old empire. Which means your gifts must be quite glorious, indeed, perhaps as glorious as myself?"

He stared eagerly at the scrolls jutting from Gui's pack.

"Nothing could match your glory. But they are glorious." Gui gently put the pack to his side, pulling the top over to conceal the contents.

For a moment, the Pushka lost his smile. "I could take them, you know."

Gui shook his head. "Do you assume we lack sophistication? They can only be opened by my biometrics. Anyone else, anyone, who tries will destroy the contents."

"Hm. Could be trickery, but if not…" He rose and reached impishly toward the sack.

"Perhaps I should try it with one?"

Gui straightened to his full height, nearly twice that of the Pushka's. "All three, at once, would be gone."

He laughed and clapped. "Well, jolly giant, you've got me! But I know a few things myself. Can you guess what else I know?"

Gui frowned. "That Archosia's fleet is near."

"Yes. Indepa tells me its size is historic. And you tell me their weapons, stolen from our sacred lands, from humankind's most sacred lands, can lay waste to my armies."

"It is, and they can."

"Yet you'd risk your Pantheon's destruction rather than give your gifts without condition?"

"My hands are tied by obligation and faith."

The Pushka rubbed his bare head and made a singsong, "Hmm." Noticing some flakes of dead skin on his fingertips, he wiped them on his silks. "Amka Bodspah showed you the soul, so I suppose death isn't all that much of a threat anymore. He must like you, to have given you such an insight. But to me, you are still strangers at best, and enemies at worst. As I said, I will not share with you what hordes of my followers do not yet know. But… what if…" The Pushka blew some air from his nose then twirled a finger in his wrinkled skin as if it were a lock of thick pink hair. "What if I were to agree not to make such a declaration for a certain number of seasons?"

He's neither divine nor completely mad, then.

In as much as he was able to look pleasant, Gui smiled. "I would say it does not solve the problem, but it's a start."

The Pushka eyed the sack. "Enough of a start?"

"It is."

Gui reached down into the sack, removed a scroll, and knelt as he held it toward the Pushka. "On behalf of the Pantheon, it pleases me to present you with the first of our gifts."

The Pushka's wrinkle-nested eyes darted from the sack to the scroll Gui held, uncertain whether to be disappointed. "That one doesn't look as old as the other two. Why is that?"

Gui hesitated. The answer was so obvious, that he was unsure how to phrase it without being disrespectful. "Because it is not, Pushka. It's very new. It's the plans for an Archosian weapon called Colossus."

He'd made it.

By accident or plan, doggedness, or destiny, he'd made it. With a fiery, humbling screech of stressed hull and shedding sparks, Wyrm Stifler was arriving in the Land of Birth and Sorrow, the planet that had taken his father, and now his future, whole.

Fray was talking, probably about scanner readouts or how and where they'd land, but Wyrm wasn't listening. Facing the viewport along with Arjuda and Calico, he was too busy being gripped by the flourish of sight, sound, and sensation.

The mesosphere huffed like a great beast. Warmth spread through the cabin as if it were swallowing them. Then the cloud cover appeared, and with it, a harsh rumble in both the shuttle and his body.

He'd expected the oceans to be blue. Some patches had a silvery tint.

As their descent smoothed, he realized Fray was still talking.

"I said I was with your father."

Wyrm was certain he'd misheard. "What?"

"I was… well, let's say I was part of his guard. Until my arrest."

"What?! Why are you telling me now? We've been in this shuttle for two days!"

"I didn't want you thinking it was fate."

Wyrm's heart, already pounding from the view, hammered. "You know where he is?"

"No, but I know where he was, and I'm pretty sure I can get us there."

The youth gasped a tight laugh. "And you think it isn't fate?"

"No. I… think he's probably dead, and, if we're not extremely careful, we will be, too.

The fleet was right behind us. In a day this whole planet will be lit up like…"

The shuttle shivered. Their path no longer even, they listed left, then right.

"Why are we on fire?" Calico asked.

Warning lights blinked on the monitors.

"Ground artillery," Fray said. "BaK class, Kardun crap. Couldn't take down a light cruiser. But we're not a light cruiser. I'm surprised they saw us. Must be on high alert, which means Mordent's expected. "

There was a small explosion above the rush of air. They rattled again. "Wyrm, maybe you should let me take over from Birefringe. I'm not a pilot, but I know a few tricks."

Wyrm was about to comply when the shuttle went into a fierce dive. Seeing the next shell zoom by, missing them completely, Fray shrugged. "Or better yet, don't. That thing's doing fine without me."

Landing on a flat spot of desert was far smoother than say, crashing into the Zodiac.

The area looked suitably unoccupied – until Wyrm ignored Fray's warning and bolted from the hatch to find himself surrounded by snake riders. Seeing the massive serpents, Calico tried to cover Arjuda's eyes, but the girl pushed her away, no more afraid of them than anything else.

Wyrm raised his hands. "So, Calico, do you think fate, or an accident brought us here?"

"Why does it have to be either?"

CHAPTER
37

Having delivered the captive fugitives to the Zodiac, the Op piloted the Wheel out of the fleet as discreetly as he'd arrived, passing smoothly from the blackness between ships to the deeper darkness between stars.

Gog was out there somewhere.

Why was it tracking the patroller in the first place? Why *that* patroller?

It was the sort of question that used to interest the Op, part of the innate curiosity crucial to his success. But as he entered a new heading that creeping discontent, never far behind, returned. He'd captured three of the galaxy's most notorious criminals as easily swatting a fly but felt nothing. Even the happy accident of being ordered to tail Stifler's heir, which meant he could also track his mystery woman, failed to get a rise out of him.

Usually, the Op didn't mind his feelings. They were reasonable enough, predictable, and cozily familiar, but the sheer weight of this boredom made him feel vulnerable. It was as if he was losing, or had lost, something fundamental about who he was. He didn't want to become someone else but worried he might not have a choice.

What he needed was a better distraction.

Maybe that's why he responded to Ludi's hail, greeting him with a grumbled, "Go away."

"You're taxing your engines."

"Sorry, Ma, but I plan to be on Earth before the assault begins. The Wheel will be fine."

"As long as you're going to be there anyway…"

"No."

"I did save your life."

The Op snickered "Eh, It's not much of a life."

"Because you lack a higher purpose."

"For pity's sake! It was a joke! I'm a working man. All I have is purpose, one damned purpose after another. Don't you get tired, carrying all those assumptions around?"

"I don't carry them. They carry me." Ludi paused, making the Op afraid he'd sensed something in his voice. "Are you alright?"

The Op didn't answer.

Regretting having responded at all, he was about to cut the feed when Ludi said, "I've been monitoring your database queries. You've done an awful lot of work trying to figure out who the woman is."

"What if?"

"I could help you with that. Like I did with Gog and the boy."

"No, thanks. You'd only explain how she's a goddess or an atavistic manifestation of her sainted namesake, the Mother of All, or some other bullshit."

There was a longer pause. It was so long that the Op wondered if Ludi had cut him off.

Finally, the old man said, "I'd only provide hard data. It would be up to you how to interpret it."

"I can smell you thinking, Lude, and the stink says a lot. Data means all kinds of things to all kinds of people. What kind are we talking?"

"I believe in your trade it's what you'd call her provenance. A word usually reserved for evidence or great works of art, not people, but… applicable in this instance."

"You mean you think you know where she's been?"

"I mean I think I can prove where she's from. Help me first, and I'll share everything I know about her."

"Tell you what, seeing as how you're being so patient with my sweet obstinate self, I'll give you more than I did last time."

"How so?"

"I'll think about it."

CHAPTER

38

General Pontifer Wintour was more than two decades older than Gil Rais, but, bouncing and ecstatic as he was at their strategy session, he seemed the younger of the two. It wasn't so much that Wintour was reinvigorated by all the new attention, it was more that Rais had aged.

And he knew it. Eyes heavy, jowls lower, mien dour, he kept having to remind himself to straighten his back in front of the men.

Rais had also just come from visiting his son. They'd stared at one another, mostly in silence. The boy tried to promise he was innocent but couldn't. What had he promised the boy? Support, certainly, perhaps love.

Now, in the Zodiac war room, facing the exuberant Wintour and his 'elite' mech-crew, Rais swallowed as much of himself as he could. Mordent declined to attend. A show of trust, he said, but Rais could taste his old friend's guile.

Clever, leaving the decision to me, as if it were a decision at all.

Defying the Directorate required the military's full backing, and they'd lost it. Thanks to that live feed, Rais' support, while not obliterated, had been decimated. He looked weak to those wanting Gilby free, and traitorous to those who didn't. Mordent, on the other hand, came across as fair-minded, loyal, and shrewd, like a leader. And, technically, Rais was the only one in that meeting who mentioned moving against the Directorate.

If I didn't know better, I'd swear he engineered the leak himself.

The viewport provided a grand view of the filthy, oversized, gubbins dubbed Colossus. Beyond it lay the Earth, blue-white with wisps of hazel brown and barely green, all tinged with an odd scarlet, like something beautiful about to burn.

A final test of the cold fusion aeolipiles left Colossus' dark orichalcum surface covered in a fog of static electricity that made it look like a cheap magician's trick.

Well, if the Kardun have any sense of beauty, at least it will offend them.

Oblivious to the aesthetic, Wintour beamed. "The superstitious savages will shit their plated tunics."

He was one of the few who hadn't mentioned Gilby at all.

Smart of him, assuming the senile fool hasn't forgotten about him.

A soldier to the end, Rais addressed the four-man squad. "Do you have faith in this contraption?"

The way their young faces dropped made their words unnecessary, but Dowe, the crew captain, said, "Of course, sir. Why wouldn't we?"

Wintour tut-tutted, ruffling his walrus mustache. "No need to grill them. I trained them myself."

"I'm not grilling them. I'm asking how they feel." The young gunner reminded him of a friend Gilby had at the academy. What was the name? Bucceri? It wasn't him, but it could be.

"Confidence is praiseworthy. Don't let it make you complacent. Regardless of how savage their beliefs, and how antiquated their weapons, the Kardun are sophisticated warriors not to be underestimated. Knock out the artillery first, stomp on it, or whatever, then use the plasma cannons to create as many casualties as you can. Aim for the fastest runners first. They'll be the ones further away, and it could drive the rest back toward you."

Wintour reared. "The cannons are an environmental hazard to be avoided at all costs! The point of Colossus is to spare lives!"

Rais sneered. "And if we do enough killing, and do it quickly enough, we will! If not, the real slaughter will barely have begun."

Despite having been assigned to Stifler's expedition, Fray barely spoke a word of Kardun and less Budari. Birefringe might be able to translate but Wyrm had no idea how it would tell them about it, so he kept the orb concealed. The preoccupied Kardun either didn't notice, or didn't care about, the odd bulge in his tunic.

Lacking the ability to communicate, they wound up being screamed at for long periods unable to tell what they were being asked or told. The feel of spittle and the smell of Kardun breath would linger in Wyrm's nightmares for weeks.

"On the lighter side," Fray said, "they probably haven't killed us because they don't know what to make of us. We're not in uniform. Three out of four of us seem harmless. We might be better off not trying to communicate until we're bounced higher up the chain. Then, maybe there's something I can do."

"It's not like we have a choice, anyway," Wyrm said, unsure if his seeming harmless was a good or bad thing.

Shackled, and pushed through the sand, only the bruised, listless Arjuda was given some quarter, with Calico permitted to help her, so long as they didn't fall behind.

Surprisingly, Wyrm again managed not to sweat. Perhaps it was the desert air or the fact that being a captive was much less worrying than escaping the Citadel or being hunted by Gog. Truth to tell, aside from the phagus, he found the Land of Birth and Sorrow disappointing. It was a lot of flat, barren land, a few trees with weird fruit, some hovels, failing farms, big old stones worn smooth by the wind, and a sky that struck him as sickly. It felt dead in such a boring way, it made death feel inconsequential.

Maybe the ruins his father explored would be different.

In time, their stumbling trek brought them somewhere more appealing to his sense of adventure; a Kardun military camp. Sitting on his father's knee he'd often seen Archosian troops parade in the capital's central plaza. In his memory, at least, the numbers here were similar, the soldiers as disciplined, their formations as tight – but the colors they wore were earthier, the garb more functional than formal, dusty, and well-worn, not just for show or the sake of a good story.

There was some infantry, but mostly legions of phagus, mounted by gyrojet sharpshooters. Nearby, teams of the great snakes were hauling bigger guns up along the shore of a little fishing village. Wyrm thought he recognized the type, it wasn't the BaK artillery that clipped the shuttle, but they looked too old and crude even for an obsolescent tech.

He asked Fray. "Is that… gauss artillery?"

Fray nodded. "Like I said, they know Mordent's coming. That's what this is all about."

The thought thrilled him. "We're going to see the invasion?"

Fray exaggerated his nod. "Yes. We'll have a great view. Right up until we die."

Between the deployment and the evacuation of local Budari, the Kardun were far too busy to deal with their odd prisoners. They forced them into an ad hoc cage where their chains were removed, and they were allowed to eat some of the rations they'd brought from the shuttle.

Mordent's fleet arrived with the setting sun.

It looked, at first, like a few thousand too-many stars poking beyond the crepuscular clouds. The Kardun split their time scrutinizing what they saw in the sky and preparing for it. Once it settled into a low orbit for maximum effect, no more than 100 miles up, Wyrm spent the cool night trying to distinguish cruiser from battleship from dreadnaught, counting each, and losing track. Fray seemed to sleep with his eyes open. Calico and Arjuda breathed steadily, dreaming, Wyrm assumed.

Colossus arrived at dawn.

Even in the distance, it looked taller than a mountain, and, likely just as visible for miles. When its supporting cables were released, the ten cogs that delivered it scattered as if to avoid marring the spectacle. Now it stood on the desert shore, a clay god descended from the heavens, basking in the rising sun, passing judgment on its flawed creation.

Arjuda summed it up. "It's that man again."

Wyrm couldn't wait to see it move. And, unlike the Earth, it did not disappoint.

Colossus' first steps shook the ground so hard that the nomads' tents and clothing shed sand. With the villagers who might've feared for their lives gone, neither man nor beast fled. Instead, the aggressive hiss of a thousand phagus had them all covering their ears. The warrior cries of their riders matched the roar of the invader's engines as they slithered out to meet the gargantuan invader.

Closer and closer each came to the other, the giant striding steadily, the limbless horde, ribs, and belly scales pushing backward on the sand, shrinking the distance faster and faster. But then, rather than meet, the swarm parted, allowing the titan to continue its Brobdingnagian march.

Wyrm's view from the cage was poorly framed, but it was clear to him that neither side had fired a shot. "What's going on? Where's the attack? What's Colossus doing?"

Fray wasn't sure. "Going for the artillery? I wouldn't bother. The Gauss guns take too long to aim. Good for bombarding a city, where the target's stationary, but they couldn't hit a crippled cog. Even if Colossus had half its speed, they wouldn't be much of a threat."

When the serpent vanguard reached the giant's rear, the sharpshooters spun and fired. Wyrm wasn't sure he heard, or imagined he heard, the ping of their projectiles glancing off the monster's metal surface.

Fray pointed. "Then again, the cavalry's not doing much either. Don't know what Colossus is made of, some kind of new composite, but those gyrojets aren't scratching it. That's it, then. Once that artillery's gone, Mordent can set up a base camp anywhere. This invasion will be over pretty quickly. Maybe we will survive."

Wyrm was almost disappointed to hear that. But then the remaining phagus split ranks, revealing, in their midst, an exceptionally large serpent, twice the size of its fellows. A figure in green and gold, the sole woman on the battlefield, was balanced not on its back, but on the tip of its flattened hood.

"She's not Kardun," Fray said. "Those're the Pushka's colors. Some kind of warrior-priestess?"

Calico shook Arjuda and pointed as if such sights somehow made life worth healing for. "Look! See?"

The sharpshooters continued their useless fire. The rest of the force joined in. Nearing the behemoth, the woman crouched and leaped. Wyrm made out her silhouette, tiny against the machine, as she scaled protruding rivets along its right leg. At the knee, she planted something in the central gear, then sprang off.

Mid-air, she emitted a shrill whistle. Summoned, her mount met her fall, and together they darted off. They'd barely cleared Colossus' shadow when there was a blast at the knee and the leg collapsed. When the monstrosity hit the ground, pieces of its head disappeared under the softer sands.

Calico nudged Arjuda. "At least he's not cold anymore."

By the time the prostrate mechanism's arm cannons fired, the riders, as if forewarned, were in full retreat. Even ill-placed, its plasma blasts seared a dozen Kardun so quickly, and so completely, both Fray and Wyrm wondered why it hadn't done that in the first place. But then a heavy flash dimmed the already sickly sky, and it took a bit too long to return to its former color.

With Colossus immobilized, the Gauss artillery took its time aiming. The largest of the guns shot a single ferromagnetic missile which squarely hit its massive chest. A teal electro-mechanical wave shuddered through the whole of the giant, frying both circuitry and crew.

Their foe essentially dead, the riders returned. Cheering, they formed a loose line around the fallen mech, then ceremoniously dismounted, and, in unison, lowered their studded leather chausses.

Wyrm's eyes widened at what followed. "Are they...?"

"Yep," Fray said. "They're pissing on it."

CHAPTER

40

Primble had left some dishes out so Mordent would have something to throw. He was surprised to find them intact, his master oddly amused.

"They pissed on it. Ha!" He held out his goblet for Primble to fill. "Oh, don't look at me like that. None of this pleases me. I could have had the planet secured in days. Now the conflict will drag on for weeks, months more to scour the remote deserts and secure access to the ruins."

Primble poured. "How much have you been drinking?"

"Not nearly enough to escape the fact that I saw it all coming, and that I see all that is to come."

"Well then, I suppose it's good to laugh."

"Better than weeping. Physickers tell you that bawling like a baby can be a release. I've never known it to do a thing besides sap energy. Look at poor Gil. He sobbed, you know, and he's yet to acknowledge the death of the crew, let alone address his command. Laughter, though, laughter, is energizing, revitalizing, unifying the heart and mind. And speaking of the lighter side, at this very moment, my father-in-law is babbling his explanations in a message to the Directorate. Ha! He should've taken my suggestion and retired into politics, where stupidity isn't a handicap. On a more serious note, I hear he's blaming sabotage. Tell me, Primble, is that much as farfetched as it seems?"

"Colossus performed to spec, but they knew where to strike."

"Peh. Behind the knee is always a weak spot. All it means is that they had what our strategy lacked; intelligence." Mordent tched. "Found our traitor, yet?"

"Sadly, no."

"Suspects?"

"None I care to mention without evidence, lest the killing begin prematurely."

"Hrm. Disappointing. You're slipping in your old age."

Primble raised an eyebrow. "*I* prefer to believe that as we up our game, we encounter better players."

"A self-serving belief, but… in recognition of your loyal service, I accept your interpretation. Better players, eh? I daresay we're down to the best. Do try to find them before I'm murdered in my sleep. Humanity has never been kind to its saviors." He paused. "You're here because you bring news?"

"Mostly the fulfillment of your expectations. The independent warlords, including a reluctant Amka Bodspah and his allies, are rallying behind the Pushka. Though he's yet to declare it, some already call him the World Soul."

Mordent raised his goblet. "A toast to all their bladders! I'll leave the cleanup for Gil, but I've all the excuses I need to take back command. Since the Pushka's forces have been kind enough to gather in a single spot to celebrate our defeat, I'm ordering a sustained barrage from the fleet's artillery."

The servant's face dropped. "The plasma cannons? That… seems rash, given the potential of setting the atmosphere aflame."

Mordent drunkenly shook his head. "No, no, no. You see, this is where concrete pragmatism supersedes uncertain science. Our naturalists all agree that the plasma will cause great environmental damage, but they're very much split on how much and how soon. Therefore, I've decided to trust the calculations that provide the best military options."

"And if they're wrong, what is one planet, even if it is…"

"The Land of Birth and Sorrow, yes, yes, I know." Mordent sighed. "You can make me feel bad about it if you like, but you won't change my mind. I can't very well let the Pantheon or the Kardun have whatever's down there, can I? It is now the killing starts."

CHAPTER

41

No time at all passed between the twinkles in the sky and the sunlike surface burst. At least, no time measurable by human eyes and minds. But in that impossibly scant moment, two-thirds of the Pushka's thousands were gone. Some of those not immediately incinerated lived long enough to be reminded in their last flash instance that despite their most profound love and hatred, their deepest cruelty and fondest kindness, despite their devotion and faithlessness, and all the other stories they told to and about themselves, there existed forces to which they were, always had been, and always would be, insects.

The remains falling to pandemonium, those who lived to tell about it, would tell themselves there is no shame in survival, no sin in acceding to life's most reasonable fear.

But even as the shock wave passed, and the desert wind ebbed to its usual version of searing, the effects were not yet done. The whole sky darkened, and not from passing clouds. For several long, stretching minutes, the cover of the great globe writhed as if, like anything living in chains, it ached to escape, but was not strong enough.

Not yet strong enough.

In time, or some form of it, the ghastly, ghostly shroud lifted, and the dark subsided, allowing the more familiar colors of the sickly sky to weep on through.

In Qus where other structures, better structures, had collapsed in the initial blast of artificial wind, a dilapidated, crooked, stilted, stunted warehouse, which should never have stood at all, miraculously continued to do so. Inside it, when the dark came, when the Beast Father stirred, its denizens respectfully ceased their hungry copulation. No sooner did his slight shifting end, though, no sooner did the blackened sky recede, the global thrashing quiet, than they were back at it, Harek at their center, caressing and scratching, pulling, and pushing, entwined, and woven, limbs braided, a bevy of heaving beings struggling in delight to make their way from mind to body, from desire to action, lusting to breach the ineluctable barrier between mortal thought and eternal being.

CHAPTER
42

Watching from one of the many high palace balconies, Gui wondered:

What am I here in this now? Do I do right, or do I do wrong? Is that a question worth asking, or an annoying game my soul engages when it plays at being me?

He scoured the tarnished sky and asked: *Is this you, Lau?*

Wondering made him ashamed.

Of course, it is. It always is, it's always been, always will be. From you, all things flow. Even my service is not for you, but to bring myself closer to you.

That epiphany, won and lost a dozen times in Gui's many years, brought him a fragile sense of peace despite the portentous gloom. Anything might have interrupted it, a squeak, a rustling, a sideways glance at some distant shiny speck.

In this case, it was his scribe: "Temple Lord, do you see it?"

"What else is there to see Rigdon?"

"What does it mean?"

"Perhaps the gods are finally taking action against the atheists." But then the sky lightened, and, as the preternatural force ebbed, Gui felt abandoned. "Or, for better or worse, it's still naught but a world of men."

At that moment, the hot wind known as a sirocco reached the palace and their little balcony, pushing their hair and robes back.

Rigdon spat sand. "From the artillery? This far away?"

"Yes, that much is from the artillery. This far away." Gui felt the hot gale sweep along his sides and behind him, where it mingled with his earthly belongings. "You read the reports extrapolating what the plasma used on Danvo would be like on larger guns. We knew this was coming, but that doesn't quite explain the sky."

"Well, that's why, in the end, we have faith. To explain the sky," Rigdon mused, "The Pushka will want the other gifts now. He'll need the other gifts. Are you ready for that?"

Gui shrugged. "Honestly, I'm beginning to wonder if any such decisions are truly mine."

The scribe's brow tightened. "Peace be with us, Temple Lord, but you're starting to sound like a Bannonite."

Am I? Am I still thinking of Harek?

"When the only choices are between evils, Rigdon, I suppose there's comfort in thinking those choices unreal."

"Comfort yes, there's comfort in all sorts of lies." As if afraid he might be quoted later, the scribe posed his question as a statement. "But you don't believe that, Arbiter."

Having just watched the sky bleed, Gui found it difficult to care about the record. "No, I don't. It is I who still must decide, and by deciding, alter the course of worlds and war. I'm no stranger to authority, Rigdon, but Mordent, the Pushka, and all the others like them who vie to mold history? They're the worst of fools. Better to change humanity one broken heathen at a time. This…" he waved at the dusty clouds, "…is all too much. When I used to think the end was near, eventually I'd realize it was only my small corner of a vast universe, myself that I feared for. This time, it may be different."

Crowds gathered in the plaza below. Some were praying, some shouting. No one was silent. When the Pushka's summons arrived, it wasn't Indepa who came for the emissaries, leading Gui to wonder about her fate. Instead, a livid Amka Bodspah brought them to the throne room. He exited quickly, eager to wash his hands of the foreigners.

Surprisingly, the Pushka didn't appear at all upset. Gui wondered if his wrinkled visage could register concern, or any emotion other than mad delight. He did, though, seem… less pleased with himself.

"You might have warned me that destroying Colossus would bring about such devastation." His high voice didn't echo as much as it had during their last audience, as if the air in the room had grown thinner. "I don't know yet how many were lost."

Gui bowed, perhaps too briefly. "Great Pushka, the Archosian cannons are new even to me, and I'm no military strategist. But would the alternative have been to bow before the iron man?"

"No, but I might've exposed fewer to the slaughter. If the power of their guns wasn't so unexpected by all, I'd suspect you'd set me up. I want both your remaining gifts, now."

Gui met the glittering eyes. "Will you swear not to claim yourself the World Soul?"

"Ever?" The Pushka managed a half-giggle. "You grow bold. Is that wise?"

"Wise or not, it is the best I have to offer."

The wizened figure looked away. "I cannot swear to abandon the one tactic that may hold the peoples of this world together for what promises to be a long, brutal battle."

He admits it's a tactic then. Good.

Gui handed him one of the remaining scrolls. "Then, at this time, I offer a second gift."

The Pushka held it between his index fingers, tilting it, studying, if not the words, then its shape.

"This is from the Earth."

"We believe so, yes. It is ancient. From Shashem."

"The lost ruins? Funny gift, then, isn't it? Giving back what was already ours? What is it then?"

"Magic."

Stunned by their losses, the independent Amkas debated whether to help what remained of the Pushka's forces regroup or dig in to defend their own territories. The imagined extent of their foe's power destroyed, Archosia's foothold was established with little resistance.

Not far from Qus, a subsurface scan revealed an ancient foundation, complete with storage rooms and a prison, perfect to support the temporary structures needed for a basecamp and ground command center. As provisional barracks, mess halls, maintenance shelters, and so on, were deployed above, the prisoners were transferred to that underground jail.

The cells had bars for walls, steel wedged into a mix of quicklime and volcanic ash strengthened by eons of exposure to seawater. Opened again to the air, the claustrophobic passageways funneled fresh desert air into the depths, as if the breeze were on the hunt for a partner with which to escape.

Cross-legged on the floor, Charnel touched the moving air with spread fingers. "How quaint. It's a wonder we've not been chained to the walls."

Dr. Warland cast a wary glance at the guards. "Aren't you worried about giving them ideas?"

The three men were all short and stocky, clean-shaven, but dirty from being in the prison, and obviously not pleased with their assignment.

"No, Ema. They're not listening." He raised his voice slightly. "Are you listening?"

He waited.

"See? Nothing. Might get a rise if I screamed, but otherwise, we're footnotes in the history Mordent's written in his mind, mere exemplars of his omnipotent ethos."

Having found a small bug, a form of apterygote, Warland went back to maneuvering its tiny innards with her keen fingernails. Much as she tried to focus on her work, the irregular rustles and shifts beyond her cell wall kept startling her.

"Tch. But why stick us here?"

Os tried to pat zher feathery top hairs through the sealant covering zher skin. "We did steal a cruiser from the middle of an armada. With most of those forces transferring planetside, where do you think it'd be safer to keep us? Past that, the general's correct, we're nothing. Thanks to this skinsuit, courtesy of the Interstellar Spoilsport, even I've been rendered uninteresting. The real question is, why's the high-born rapist down here with us?"

Os' aquiline nose tilted at the sullen Gilby Rais.

The teen sat on his haunches, elbows over knees, eyes shining with anger. He occupied the last of the four cells in their little hall. Charnel was in the first, Warland the second, and Os, in the third, with Gilby closest to where the guards blocked the only way out.

Charnel's thin voice rasped the answer. "Am I the only one who sees the obvious? His father's planning on breaking him out."

"Certainly, the only one who needs to show off about it," Os responded. "That's an insight, I might've kept to myself. Could prove useful later." Zhe pivoted to face the youth. "Gilby, darling, tell us, is it true? Papa gonna break you out of the slammer?"

To the others, only the grim youth's indignation was apparent, but Os' eyes widened. "It is true, isn't it? We're going to have another jailbreak. How exciting."

"Shut up, freak." Gilby eyed the guards. They weren't interested in him, either.

The alien snickered. "No, no, no, little man. To be a freak I'd have to be substantially different from the rest of my species. If you met any, particularly our larger specimens, who have the most amazing appendages, I might add, you'd be shocked by my banality. It's one reason I prefer it among your kind. Of course, I'd prefer it if my skin could breathe. Dr. Warland, how is that coming along?"

She made a final click with her fingernails. "Finished."

Placing the bug in her palm, she stepped toward the bars. "Come close. Don't want to lose this thing. Not a lot of insects around."

When Os obeyed, she blew into her palm. End over end, the modified bug glided across the short distance between them and touched zher abdomen. There was a sound, a little one, a pft –nothing more – and an outline of Os' form sparkled and disappeared.

Zher nostrils flared. "Now that feels good. Quite good. I think there's something in the air that agrees with me. Consider that earlier favor returned, our agreement concluded."

Warland wrapped her hands around the bars. "Wait. I disagree. That was for all of us. So we can escape. And I… I was hoping we might continue our arrangement."

Os smiled. "Through the bars?"

Warland coughed. "It's not optimal, but yes, why not?"

Charnel, still cross-legged, waddled in a half-circle to give them his back. "Spare me."

Os sniffed the air again. "Gilby, is that you? Would you like to watch?"

"Shut…" The abrupt halt to his comment had them all turn his way. The three guards were gone. Before Warland could finish wondering why, Os realized what was going on and moved to the wall he shared with the teen.

"Gilby, have a look here, will you? Just at me. Just for a moment."

The wording of Gilby's refusal was still forming as he turned to obey. His face began to flush, and his lips quivered.

Charnel cackled. "Well, done, Neiman! You've made the poor boy speechless."

"Oh, no, I haven't. Not at all." Os beckoned Gilby closer. "You're not speechless, you're seething with words, so many you're ready to burst, aren't you?"

His jaw shook as he inhaled sharply. "Shut-up"

"Make me." Os pressed zher lips between the bars. "You want to. There are different kinds of rapists. I know. I've had them all. Some are sadists, some are angry. A few misguided fools are out for gratification, but not you, I can smell everything you are, thick and sweet, and I know it's about power for you, proving yourself a competent lay, a master. You want to fuck me so hard that I'll wind up loving it, and then, I'll just have to love you forever and ever. Would you like that? I would, too." Os put zher back against the bars, pulled Gilby's hands around and up to zher chest then wriggled as if trying to escape, but not really. "You can do whatever you like with me, and I won't complain at all. Unless you want me to."

In moments, clothing was torn, flesh exposed, and with every thrust, Os tasted the boy's inner cry, You'll love me! You'll love me! You'll love me!

And with every squirming grunt, Os lied, "I will! I will! I will!"

The general's thrusting son pulled at the bars so hard the skin on his fingers bled and the bones nearly broke, until at last he let loose with a roar of mixed pleasure and pain. Charnel hissed. "Congratulations. You've disgusted even me. How low can you sink?"

Os chuckled. "You're as confused about me as he is, General. I'm reactive, completely, utterly, reactive. By definition, I can't sink any lower than humans already have."

Gilby was still buckling his belt when two men, Archosian, but dressed in oddly clean Budari-garb, crept into the corridor. One was silver-haired and menacing, the other had the dangerous look of a man carrying a weapon, whether he had one or not. The older swiftly unlocked the door to Gilby's cell.

As he stepped out to freedom, Os tugged his shoulder.

"Think. You can have me and hurt me again and again and again."

Gilby kept his eyes on the alien. "It's coming with us."

The younger of the two men objected. "But your father…"

"…isn't here. You heard me! Open its cell."

It wasn't until the door to the Os' cell was unlocked that it occurred to Warland that she and the general weren't going with them. "Os, we had a deal! Our arrangement!"

Os smiled. "Afraid I'm going to have to take a raincheck on that."

On ẓher way out, ẓhe blew them a kiss. "General, I'll be sure to say hi to your grandson if I run into him. Toujours gai, genociders, toujours gai."

CHAPTER
44

The plasmatic haze dissipated. The view from the Kardun camp to the sea was clear. The triumphant horde circling the wreck of Colossus was gone, replaced by a stretch of lone and level sand. Only Wintour's composite remained intact; an exquisite corpse glistening in the heat of the demon-eye sun.

After a baffled silence, madness rifled through the survivors, gathering in a wave that broke into a panicked rout. Wyrm watched in horror as a phagus near their cage, buffeted by one too-many deserters, tossed, then fed upon its rider. Though the sight of the feeding was soon overwhelmed by the cloud of leaving men, he'd remember it always.

Whatever respite the drier air gave his condition also fled, leaving the boy drenched in clear, viscous mucus. Much as he begged his body, *Not now, not now, not now!* – it answered: *If not now, when?*

He rubbed at his face with hands and tunic to better see what was going on, but the clingy goo grew pockmarked with tossed bits of sand and dirt, leaving him covered head to toe like a camouflaged desert beast. He worried Arjuda's new look of fear was directed at his repugnant appearance rather than the surrounding chaos.

Long, crazed minutes passed. Wyrm thought they'd been forgotten, left to die in their paltry cage. Thinking the same, Fray threw himself against the jury-rigged door, then motioned for Calico to do the same. Wyrm joined, but the mesh of dried tree bone and twine proved their better.

In due course, a largely toothless Kardun knelt to undo the ropes holding the door. Face flushed with rage at his own kindness, he gestured and spoke not so much to as at them. Fray managed to pick a few words out, guessing the rest based on tone and context.

"He thinks we might still be useful."

When the Kardun laid eyes on the filthy, dripping Wyrm, he nearly changed his mind. But soon they were all part of a long, wavering line, staggering away from the battlefield. Any illusion that they'd somehow grown closer to their captors having shared the devastation was dispelled whenever Wyrm wavered and found himself angrily shoved back in line.

On the lighter side, with his adrenaline pumping, his senses stressed and never more alive, whatever Wyrm found dull about this land had become captivating – from endless fields of crumbling rubble to farms of dried tubers to distant buttes and mesas indistinguishable from the ruins of ancient cities annihilated long ago.

At dusk, for the first time, he saw lightning flash from the ground to the sky.

After a long trek of days through unbounded sand and then perilous mountain paths, Wyrm saw the most unreal thing of all – Ballikilak. At its center, the Pushka's palace stepped from his father's descriptions fully born.

His skin dry now, Wyrm wiped the crusty flakes from his eyes and made out the wizened spiritual leader. He was standing beneath the half-dome, arms outstretched, trying to calm the crowds surrounding the base. There was such a din, Wyrm wouldn't have been able to hear him if he did know the language. Everyone was whispering in each other's ears, passing along every word. Whatever he was saying must be incredibly important.

Wyrm imagined himself up there, imagined what he might say to these terrified people, to comfort them, inspire them to go on. He knew he was too young to say anything really important, or useful, but if he were the World Soul, he'd have to say something someday.

Probably someday soon.

Their new Kardun owner seemed unsure what to do with them, torn between attending the Pushka's words and hunting for someone to relieve him of his questionable prizes. When he finally left them alone to get the attention of a palace guard, Fray pulled their little group into a huddle.

"If we're taken to the Pushka," he said. "I think I can get us out of this. During the expedition, I saved an Amka's son from a Soul-Eater…"

Wyrm's face scrunched. "A Soul-Eater? What's a…"

Fray was annoyed at having to explain. "Big, scorpion kinda thing. Never mind."

Wyrm was undeterred. "Soul-Eater? How can it eat something that doesn't exist? And how'd you save an Amka's son if you don't speak the language?"

"I never saw it eat anything! And we had translators! But that's not important right now. I'm trying to tell you he gave me a teken, a Kardun amulet, a token, you can exchange for a request. It's considered sacred. I may be able to use it to buy our freedom."

Wyrm hesitated to ask another question but did anyway. "Why didn't you use it to keep us from being captured?"

"It's too valuable to hand to a grunt. They might've killed us over it. Like I said, we have to wait until we're bounced up high."

On a roll, Wyrm couldn't help himself. "Why does Mordent want you dead? Why'd you kill your mesmerist?"

"Now? I was under orders, first to spy on him, then to kill him. A civilian, no less. I was sick about it. If that's what I'd really been imprisoned for, hell, I'd have stayed, but I was there, and Mordent wants me dead because I slept with his wife."

"You slept with…"

"We fucked, okay? We were having an affair."

"I know what you meant! I'm not an idiot. I was surprised. Why would she…?"

"You'd have to ask her."

"You didn't do anything terrible," Calico said. "You think you did, but you didn't."

"I'll be the judge of that, thank you."

"But…"

A gasp filtered through the crowd. Rather than at the Pushka, they were looking straight up. In the western sky, opposite the invading fleet, a bright blood-orange speck trailed white vapor.

"I know that color," Calico said.

They all did.

Concealed by the two adults, Wyrm slipped the orb from his tunic. "Birefringe, is that Gog?"

Birefringe replicated the color.

"I'll take that as a yes," Fray said. "Shit. I'm starting to wonder if this planet's going to be here in a week."

All around, people went to their knees. The venerated ancient in his half-dome pointed to the falling predatory engine, then at himself. His giggly voice cracked with emotion.

"I think he's taking credit for it," Fray said. "Saying it's a sign the gods are with them."

Their most recent captor returned. He pushed them to their knees before joining them. Only Calico resisted, regarding the Pushka with an oddly smug expression.

"He likes pretending. He thinks he has to. He tells himself that's why he does it, because he has to, but he likes it. He likes it very much."

Its color fading to burnt black, the light in the sky fizzled. The orb grew silent and dull.

"Does that… mean Gog's dead?" Wyrm asked.

"Let's hope so." Fray nodded at the Pushka, his arms outstretched, his withered face soaking in the crowd's adulation. "But given that I think the Pushka's just tied his destiny to the shiny thing in the sky, let's not tell him that."

CHAPTER

45

Rusk wasn't good at lying, so he seldom bothered. After Ludi heard his last report, which included Rusk's unfortunate outburst, he threatened to replace him. It was for his own good, Ludi said from wherever he was. He'd gotten too involved, he said, and getting involved could ruin not only the whole point of his mission but Rusk's mental health, as well.

"The atavistic echoes can infiltrate you, perhaps disassemble you, " he said from wherever he was. "Make you like she is. Who knows which god is waiting to take the wheel of your psyche?"

It reminded Rusk of his mother telling him to keep his mouth shut or a bug would fly in.

With many promises and vows, Rusk kept his position. Probably because Ludi wouldn't be able to find a replacement easily, especially since the Directorate had banned the rest of his works and were on the verge of ordering his arrest.

Rusk thought it was a textbook case of transference. They were actually angry with Mordent – and themselves for forcing Colossus on him – but there wasn't anything they could do to fix that, so they picked on Ludi to distract themselves – and the populace – from the war. Just last week, Rusk got a lot of smiles, winks, and nods from folks who knew he worked for him. Now everyone was afraid to so much as say his name.

Rusk's more immediate problem was the Lady Stifler and Sky. One, or both, were trying to get him to talk, like they knew his job was at stake.

They'd tease him with questions like:

"Are you still there?"

Much as Rusk felt like answering, no, he said nothing.

"Yes, you are," one said smugly, probably Sky. He was so worried it'd gotten hard to tell who it was when they talked right at him like that.

There'd be a giggle, and sometimes that would be it for the night. Invariably they went on as they had.

"Where were we then?" Meriwald asked. "At our beginning or our end?"

"Too hard to tell and not worth the bother. Humanity's more like a seeping ooze than anything well-defined." The pain of the gods' betrayal wasn't gone from Sky's voice, but at the same time, she was amused by the folly of her grandchildren. "Worshippers and explorers, scientists, and priests, the devout and the curious. Back then they weren't quite as ready to go to war over what they thought they knew, like you lot now, all eager to crush your brothers and sisters' skulls, hewing to masters you think you understand."

Meriwald continued defending her species. "But thanks to Calico, there were those who did understand, who worked in secret to heal things between faith and science."

"Well, they had to try to keep it secret, didn't they? The gods only wanted to stop hurting, to keep the Beast Father asleep, dark, and deep. But the Grayborn? They planned to kill him. But you already know this part of the story, don't you, Rusk?"

CHAPTER

46

As the guards walked General Charnel out of his cell for questioning, old bones creaking, he tried to reassure an increasingly jittery Dr. Warland.

"It must be about Gilby and Os' escape. It's not as if we've anything to hide… for a change."

That wasn't entirely true. There was the insect that shorted the nano-circuitry of Os' suit, but he doubted that would come up. Even if it did, what could be added to a lifetime sentence? Execution?

They could make them both more uncomfortable, he supposed, but his age and her biology were already doing that. Without a working yustick, Ema's brain was already turning on itself. The blepharospasm of her right orbicular oculi indicated she was already badly in need of the release Os had refused to provide.

Damned alien.

Charnel eyed his escorts, wondering if either might be approached on Ema's behalf.

Look at me, trying to find a date for my 'daughter.'

The interrogation room was in the provisional military structure that had been erected above the prison. It was windowless, but the tension fabric walls not only breathed, but they also added some much-needed moisture to the dry air.

The sleek-headed fellow the guards sat him opposite tried so very hard to look menacing that Charnel nearly laughed. Recognizing his purple and gold insignia, with its two electric blue stripes, and single star, he settled for a derisive smile.

"Having planned it, I'd think General Rais would know far more about his son's escape than I do. So why send his Cohor to question me?"

Throat drier than he realized, he coughed.

The man pushed a glass of water closer to him. "Drink."

Rather than dwell on how his aging voice was once considered menacing, Charnel did as he was told.

"My name is Dagus, and Rais doesn't know I'm here. It's an honor to meet you."

Charnel stopped drinking. "Is it, now?"

"Very much. Pyotr Charnel, decorated pilot and young hero of the Hollow Wars, mastermind behind Archosia's early expansion, only to be unjustly backburnered when the Directorate deemed your methods too ruthless. When the Pantheon formed, as you warned it would, most of your family was left trapped within its territories. That was when you decided to defect, offering to hand the Hydrokos system to the Pantheon as recompense for all the damage you'd done. When the system's strategic usefulness was rendered moot by the destruction of Axton, the deal was off. You tried to conceal your treason by eradicating the entire population. A creative solution, but one that proved too difficult to keep secret. Ten times as many died on Axton, but Rais and Wintour were never punished. You, though, were reviled by both sides, your family hunted by the deists until all but extinct."

Charnel put the glass down. "Would you like me to disagree? Fill in the missing details? Give you an autograph?"

"No. I want to discuss something I hope you'll find enticing."

"Not an easy task. Very few things hold my interest these days."

"I realize that." His voice grew earnest. "So let me begin by telling you I was the one who broadcast Mordent's conversation with Rais."

Charnel's tongue prodded his teeth, feeling the pockets in his gums, still cool from the drink. "Congratulations. I'm now vaguely curious, both as to why you'd betray your superior officer and, perhaps more to the point, why you'd tell me about it."

"Which would you like to know first?"

Charnel poured himself another glass. "You're the host. You pick."

"I did it to sow confusion, create tension among the generals, and make it more difficult for them to execute a coherent strategy. My hope, ultimately, is to create more casualties."

The comment was intended to shock, but Charnel remained dispassionate. "Oh? How many?"

Dagus chuckled. "Optimally, all of them. Both sides. The Budari, too."

The old general blinked. "Well, that's the thing about genocide, isn't it? To get it right, you do have to kill *everyone*."

Dagus leaned in closer. "Don't you want to know why I want so many dead?"

"No, but I'm still thirsty, so go on."

"You've heard of those who still worship the Father?"

"The Beast Father? Yes. I've heard of those who worship Mother Goose, too, or should I say Mother Sky? I hope you haven't made the mistake of thinking I share my family's delusions when it comes to matters of faith."

"And yet you've served him so well."

Charnel swallowed. "Have I? I suppose you could think so. Kill enough people and he'll awaken? With humanity's trillions scattered throughout the galaxy, you'd think Hydrokos a drop in the bucket, hardly worth a thank you note."

"Distance is part of it. The war here, and in the Kardun Empire, so much closer to his heart, will be much more effective."

Charnel nodded a few times, then furrowed his brow. "Not to dwell on the obvious, which I realize is an anathema to fanatics, but has it occurred to you that the death of the species would include you?"

"There will be a place for those like me. Nothing to the Father, but to his followers, a place of vast joy and power."

"Ah." Charnel smacked his lips and put the empty glass down. "Before you, like the rest of this absurd existence, fully and completely bore me, do answer my other question. Why tell me?"

"Big picture, I'd like to change your opinion about the Father, to teach you his ways. On a more pragmatic level, I'd like you to help me with something."

Charnel laughed out loud. "I'd like to see my grandson before I die."

Still chuckling, he reached for the pitcher to pour himself another glass.

Dagus pulled it away. "I'm afraid that won't be possible. He's dead."

Charnel's amusement fled. He knew he was feeling something but was no longer sure of what. "What a fool you are, Dagus. If you'd lied and said you could take me to him, you'd have leverage. Now, you have nothing. Just. Like. Me."

Dagus briefly speechless, Charnel rose, planning to return to his cell and the company of Dr. Warland – at least her madness was understandable, measurable – but the Cohor stopped him.

"Perhaps you'll change your mind when you learn *how* your grandson died."

CHAPTER

47

The terrain was so harsh, at times Nieman Os missed his protective suit.

Funny thing, choices.

Os wanted to escape. Ƶhe didn't have to, but ƶhe wanted to, badly. So, whatever ƶhe did to accomplish that was a matter of choice. What came next, the arduous trek across a variety of nothings, to the rank, Budari farmhouse, was a consequence, sure, but could you still call that part a choice?

Arguably, Os could have chosen to flee Gilby and his keepers, but wandering around alone on an unknown desert world could easily result in ƶher death. Death not being a viable option, it was, therefore, not really a *choice*.

Then there was giving in to Gilby's vicious, seemingly insatiable need to vent through orgasm. In one sense, Os chose to participate in these encounters. True, ƶhe could instead choose to 'convince' at least one of their escorts to intervene, but that would likely result in a shootout, and the aforementioned, undesirable death.

So, it would be more accurate to say that Os chose to wait things out.

That said, there was also an ongoing tug between that survival instinct and Os' growing distaste for Gilby, one that teetered and tottered this way and that, forever reevaluating what was, and wasn't, worth the risk. A real inbetweener. The very heart of ambivalence. How did humans deal with that? An atheist might think that everything was up to them. Someone with faith might turn their will over to their god. Os found both ridiculous.

Funny thing, free will. A rare beast at best.

On the other hand, General Rais' will regarding his son, or rather, his plans for the boy, were easy enough to discover. Whenever Gilby lay in the depths of his petit mort all it took was a few questions to his chaperones, coyly hidden in the fog of targeted pheromones. The silver-haired one was easier to manipulate, probably a parent or grandparent, judging by the way he gave Os salve for the post-coital bruises.

Once, that one even began to ask, "How can you let him…?" before catching himself.

The plan was not entirely comforting. Rather than avoid the battlefield, as Os hoped, they planned to hole up in this hovel until the Archosian ground assault was naught but a short walk away. Then, in the confusion of combat, they'd scurry the fugitive scion to a cog with a trusted crew. Everything had been arranged by someone named Dagus, a man whom both guards feared more than the general or his son - a fact that was impressive, to say the least.

Os originally figured the best bet was to remain with the boy until they were back in civilization, acting as his beloved consort, or pet. At that point, escape would be a fait accompli. Decision made, then.

Toujours gai.

The problem was the Budari, or rather, Gilby's reaction to them. Their hosts – an elder of some sort, two parents, and three children – had been paid enough to last several lifetimes in the land of Birth and Sorrow. Highly compliant, if skittish, they stayed as far out of their guests' way as possible, freely offering, whenever asked, food, supplies, and information.

But Gilby couldn't take his eyes off them. The smells that the stocky youth gave off whenever he was around them made Os wary.

"Their skin is so strange. Black and white, one hiding under the other, first the black on top, then the white, then the black."

"It's more a snow-white patina on very dark skin," zhe explained. "An optical illusion."

Rather than satisfy his curiosity, the explanation annoyed Gilby. This resulted in a particularly rough session that put bruises atop zher bruises. Between that and Gilby's increasingly violent thrusts, Os realized that, unfortunately, in trying to sate whatever dark thing drove the general's son, zhe was making it worse.

Os began thinking maybe zhe should slip away sooner, maybe as soon as possible.

And then one fine morning, bare, brazen sun drizzling through the weedy patches of the so-called roof, Gilby rose from the mattress they shared, stuffed with the feathers of who-knew-what beast, and held a blade toward the younger of two Budari girls.

"I want to see what they look like inside."

It wasn't unheard of for Os to appear sympathetic. Usually, it was for a purpose, selfish reasons, but sometimes, zhe did get a little caught up in the hormonal interplay, experiencing the edges of what humans called empathy. This time, the desire to protect the girl came on so fast and strong, that Os made the mistake of grabbing Gilby's shoulder.

"No. Come here, let me take care of you."

"I said I want to see."

"Just…"

Gilby pounded Os in the face, sending ʒher to ʒher knees.

Much as Os was determined to remain there, kneeling, when Gilby ripped the girl's tattered rags from her terrified body, ʒhe could not.

Technically, Os didn't kill Gilby. Oh, Os tried, but, while no stranger to hand-to-hand combat, the little shit was stronger and faster. No, it was the silver-haired guard. He didn't take much convincing. Just the right scents, excreted in the right amount, as Os struggled to pry Gilby's meaty hands from ʒher throat.

That, and a quick, strangulated "If you ever hope to live with yourself again, you'll stop him." – was all it took.

One shot, back of the head, and Gilby's malignant rage was banished to the distant realms of nightmare and memory. When he fell, his forehead somehow kept him propped up, leaving his rear up in the air.

Os wanted to tell the guard to shoot him again, but there was no point.

The girl, covering herself with what was left of her clothes, ran to her mother. She was too horrified to cry. The Budari woman was not, sobbing freely as the younger of Rais' men drew his weapon. He aimed it first at them, then Os, but, finally, at his companion.

When the older man realized what his future undoubtedly held, he pointed his weapon up and away, allowing himself to be killed. The blast hit him square in the chest. His weapon went flying, skittering within inches of Os' hand.

Their remaining escort was in shock, aghast at what his companion had done, stunned by what he had done in answer. Perhaps they'd been relatives, or friends, for years, and all it took to end it all was seconds.

While he was still shaken and off-guard Os picked up the gun, aimed, and fired.

It was one of the new plasma guns. Ʒhe was impressed by how little recoil it had, how the glow surrounding its path shimmered, how neat the little hole it made.

When Os rose to stand among the three dead bodies, the parents wept and hugged ʒher. Loving the alien without question, they fed ʒher from the stores they'd been hiding and gave ʒher the new clothes that they'd kept beneath stacks of hay. They even helped ʒher strip valuables from the corpses and bury them.

Gilby had a thick golden ring on one fat finger, no doubt worth a king's ransom on this destitute world. Os considered giving it to the girl, to set up her family for generations to come – but decided to keep it.

Communication was arduous, but after a celebratory meal, the father, speaking broken Common, said that Os reminded him of a man he'd seen in Qus before the invasion, a man adorned in silks. At his prodding, the mother, something of an artist, drew a rough sketch on the dirt floor. The father eagerly corrected her until satisfied she'd gotten it right.

Between the two, they put something together that Os recognized.

Those are Bannonite ritual silks. What's the Pantheon doing here?

Interesting as it was, it didn't matter nearly as much as getting safely away. With Gilby dead, and last seen in ʒher company, anything Archosian was no longer safe. Unless Os wanted to become a dirt farmer, which ʒhe did not, that left only one option.

After much rephrasing and a few more sketches, ʒhe managed to get the idea across: "You've been so very kind, but I think what I'd like most now is to be turned over to the Pushka."

CHAPTER
48

Rais' sandwing dipped into the low atmosphere. Smoke and color fanned from the window, revealing a long stretch of desert that ran from the command center near Qus along the shore to the midlands where the battle raged. The steel blue of Archosia's advancing troops looked like ocean waves drenching the parched world and flowing around its leathery dunes.

Rais missed the exhilaration that war once provided. Even more, he reviled the desolation that had taken its place. Both were due not to his age so much as the loss of Gilby, a loss compounded by all the other losses his son's death entailed, from legacy to pride to joy.

With a hiss and a falling rush, the watery illusion dissipated, revealing that the dunes were snake riders tossing aside corpses. He wished Gilby had died that way, in battle. But Mordent had made even that impossible.

Soon enough, that self-righteous cockalorum would rule this planet, and sooner or later, everything else. No matter how many beautiful young men fell today, it was a numbers game. The Kardun knew it. Their resistance here was token, their real forces reorganizing in places unseen.

Ballikilak remained out of reach for now, surrounded by mountains. Mordent planned to leave it intact, expecting that once enough blood flowed, the Pushka would negotiate a surrender. Rais preferred the city be taken but couldn't bring himself to care about how. As it was, he struggled not to wish Mordent dead, not to imagine him cold and buried, in place of his son.

He looked at Dagus. "Perhaps, somehow, it's not true?"

His Cohor's face remained rigid. "I've told you all I know as I knew it, general. To do less, or more, would be a disservice. Gilby's tracker led us to a shallow grave. Three corpses were found. We assume the other two are his escorts. With the bio-suit disabled, Neiman Os could have turned either or both. Just as it…"

Dagus gestured with his hands, to fill in the blanks.

Rais nodded. "Just as it turned Gilby. Yes. But why leave the Budari alive?"

"It's an alien, general. Who knows what it thinks?"

Once low enough, the pilot engaged the wing-in-ground, allowing the aerodynamic lift of the close surface to keep them aloft. When they touched down, Rais was the first out, tearing his way through the protective screens blocking his path. Given the look on his face, the soldiers and technicians didn't dare mention that the screens he'd destroyed were intended to preserve the scene from contamination.

Gilby lay on a poly-plastic sheet. His thick face was frozen in surprise, as if, at the last instant, he'd sensed what was coming. The final comfort of doubt now dispelled, the general wailed. He was so loud it overpowered the roar of battle half a mile away. Once he was done, his eyes were dead, as if the scream had drained the last bit of life from him.

He barked an order to no one in particular: "I want to see the family."

Inside the small farmhouse, they were lined up for him, heads down, penitent.

He grabbed the father's head and twisted it up. "Where is Os?"

The man babbled in his native tongue.

"Translator!"

Dagus stepped up. "He says Os asked to be handed over to a Kardun patrol. Afraid for their lives, they complied. The alien will be in Ballikilak by now."

Rais' chest heaved. "By the time there's a surrender, or we breach the walls, it'll have conned its way off-world." His spittle hit the father's eyes. "You've let my son's murderer get away!"

He drew a plasma gun with a polished ironwood handle. "See this? One of the first off the production line. It would have been a gift for my son. Do you understand? Tell him!"

Once Dagus finished translating, and the Budari nodded understanding, Rais killed them all, the children first, so the parents would know what it felt like.

Those watching gasped but did nothing.

Only one soldier dared speak. "When High Commander Mordent hears…"

"Fuck Sebe Mordent!"

"General? But..."

Rais whirled, planting the barrel of his gun on the man's forehead. "I said, fuck Sebe Mordent. I will do everything in my power, everything to see him ruined!"

Rais waited, finger on the trigger, ready to pull if the word traitor began to form on the man's lips. Instead, the soldier met his eyes and then looked down.

"Yes, general. Fuck Sebe Mordent."

The girl's body still twitching, Dagus knelt and snapped her neck.

Rais holstered his gun. He looked around helplessly, then teetered, about to collapse, Dagus kept him on his feet and led him back to the sandwing.

Once they were airborne, the Cohor handed Rais a stiff drink. "General, given what you've said, there's something else you should see."

"What could possibly interest me now?" Rais knocked back his drink. "I've nowhere to go other than my own court martial and execution. At least one of those soldiers will have reported to Mordent by now."

"Your future might not be so... simple."

Curiosity piqued, he asked, "How?"

They landed by a wide crater. It was far from the battle, but near enough the shore to hear the waves sadly lap the sand. Rais squinted at the wound in the earth.

"Is that where the plasma shell hit?"

"That's what the technicians concluded, but the plasma shell exploded before it reached the ground, miles to the east, and left no crater at all."

"What is it, then?"

"The future."

"What are you on about?"

"Come see, General, come see."

At the rim's crest, Dagus reached out to help the general over the rise, but he balked and made his way himself.

Peering down into the still-smokey bowl, he gasped. "Is that… Gog?"

"It is. No longer functional, but not beyond repair."

"Not beyond… Are you suggesting I do that?"

"You said you wanted to ruin Mordent's plans. What better way? Using the technicians still loyal to us, we could have it active by nightfall."

Rais laughed. "And annihilate this wretched planet once and for all?"

"Exactly. Wouldn't that be a fit memorial for Gilby?"

Col. Cropet, the field commander of Archosia's 6th light regiment, nicknamed Mordent's Spear, was not particularly worried. The men were well trained, well rested, and they'd fought together since Danvo. As expected, whenever the Kardun dared show themselves, on foot or snake-back, the plasma rifles made quick work of them. So far, Cropet's men had suffered a single wound, a flesh wound at that.

The trouble was when the Kardun *didn't* show themselves.

The sector he'd been ordered to clear was mostly low and flat, but still had enough hills and hollows to conceal fighters who knew the territory. In theory, their field scanners should moot the terrain. Cropet had been in many combat zones where they'd done just that.

The supposedly 'backward' Slave-kings, though, had found a way to fool the scanners. Here on Earth, they reported many where there were few, and few where there were many. Jasper, his tech-savvy second, theorized that some sort of vegetation might either provide electronic cover or read to the device as humanoid. Cropet ran the idea up the chain. Confident as he was a solution would be found, it was still in the future.

In the here and now, they'd either killed all their targets or were being lured into an ambush. He ordered his best skirmishers ahead, a tactic that had already paid off once, allowing them to get the drop on about fifty phagus, but the terrain ahead was hillier.

He was considering ordering more men to the flanks when the enemy hit.

For a moment their camouflage made it look as if the earth was moving. It was difficult to call the hundreds of warriors a troop or regiment. To Cropet they were more a swarm, perhaps because it was easier to kill something after dehumanizing it, perhaps because they came down as hard and fast as the bite-bugs on Engadus.

Mordent's Spear was more than up to the task, returning fire in precisely aimed volleys, but this time, while most of the dead were Kardun, there were Archosians among them.

He was about to have Jasper execute standard repositioning when a terrible keening filled the air. Louder and higher pitched than the gunfire, it made the veteran officer grab his ears.

The source half-rose from a dune top, and half-drove *through* it. The closest description might be a sort of tank, but its shape seemed to defy three-dimensional norms, as if it were designed to make any who looked at it too long go mad.

Blood orange beams shot from its extremes, the color oddly complimenting the sandy desert hues. They sliced through the snake-riders in perfect lines, dropping them dozens at a time, but did not stop there. Instead, they went on, shredding his men, cutting as easily through their composite armor as their flesh.

Assuming the tech had to be Archosian, he thought for a few seconds that it was a tragic accident of friendly fire, with hell to pay for the fool behind it. But then the tank-like thing swerved to better its aim, cutting down dozens more of his men.

One hand activating the mech-camera to transmit live video, the other waving frantically, he screamed, "Retreat!"

By the time anyone in earshot, Slave-king or Archosian, thought to turn, they were dead.

CHAPTER

50

Delighted to leave his prisoners behind, the Kardun who brought Wyrm and his companions to Ballikilak left the palace with a mostly toothless grin on his face and a bag of coins in his hand.

After having their heads covered, they were put into a cage set in the middle of a cavernous room where the high walls were covered in terrifying mosaics. Colorful tiles depicted monsters eating people, gods eating monsters, and people not eating anything, just running, falling, and praying to the fake stars set in the vaulted ceiling. The gems comprising the stars continued to twinkle even in the waning sunlight the evenings brought.

Given the size of the cage relative to the huge chamber, it felt to Wyrm as if they'd been put on display. But for who? No one, other than guards, came to see them. At least it was comfortable. There were cushions on the seats, a table full of food, basins of fresh water, and circular pillows on which to sleep.

It was all what Wyrm's father would call inefficient, his mother, gaudy.

Fray tried speaking to the guards, with no success. Wyrm suggested he show them the teken, but he refused. "I've got one card to play. I want to be sure it's played right."

Despite the constant, faraway rumble of conflict, Arjuda slept through the nights and most of the days, as if she'd finally relaxed, or was exhausted, enough to heal. There was a moment on the third day when she popped to sitting and gave off a little shriek, but by the time it stopped echoing off the walls, she was back asleep.

"Can't blame her for having nightmares," Fray whispered.

"Oh, she's quiet during her nightmares," Calico said, "afraid what's chasing her will find her. She screamed because something's happened."

Used to her eccentricities, Fray didn't question the comment. Wyrm wanted to but couldn't figure out how, beyond asking his usual, How do you know? – which she never answered. For her part, Calico seemed, for lack of a better word, more present than when they'd first met, though still prone to staring at nothing.

Several days later, they all had something to stare at, or rather, someone. Nieman Os.

Though in chains, zhe walked tall, striding ahead of zher guards. In response to their gaping faces, zher zaffre skin crinkled in recognition.

"We meet again."

Fray snickered. "Given the circumstances, I'm afraid the pleasure, if there is any, is all yours."

"As it should be." The guards opened the door, undid the chains, and shoved Os in. "But no pleasure for you at all, soldier-boy? No schadenfreude? I'd think you'd at least be tickled to see fate catch up with me."

"Hey, you were the only one I was kinda hoping got away. Besides, you look… cheerful."

Os plopped down on a pillow and sighed. "Let's just say I'm happy to be away from where I was."

"That's Arjuda's pillow," Wyrm said.

"Who?" Zher eyes turned to the unknown face. "Oh. Is this the girl you risked your lives saving? I'd like to say she looks none the worse for wear, but she doesn't."

Wyrm tensed. "Leave her alone."

"Of course." Os smiled. "Not because you asked, but because, well, clearly she's been through enough." Eyes lingering on her, zhe added, "Wyrm, that psychopath you rescued your girlfriend from? Was he named Gilby by any chance?"

She's not my…

"Yes. How did you…?"

"He's dead. Had to kill him. Long story." Os studied the boy's reaction. "You're… disappointed."

"No. I'm not," Wyrm said, but he was. *I should've been the one to kill him.*

"If you say so. Now be a good lad and hand me some of that food, would you?"

Before Wyrm realized what he was doing, he obeyed, handing Os what looked like a cross between an apple and an artichoke. "Did you use pheromones to manipulate me?"

Os took a deep bit. "Didn't have to. You're terribly open to suggestion. Not a useful character trait. I'd keep an eye on it." Zhe chewed hungrily, pausing to spit out the seeds.

Fray watched the alien scarf down the fruit. "I figured once they caught you, they'd transfer you planetside. Are Archosian temp prisons so bad? Couldn't be worse than the Chamber."

"Not the prison, the escape. One day you can read all about it in the histories." A thunderous boom rattled the air and made them look up. "Depending, of course, on who writes them."

"But you obviously escaped. Why let yourself be captured by the Kardun?"

"If you must know, it's a question of access. I'm planning to seduce the Pushka."

Fray chuckled. "If you manage it, tell him I'd like a word."

"Will do."

For the next few days, Os slept as deeply and as often as Arjuda.

The prisoners weren't even sure they were being held in the palace, until one morning the Pushka strolled in, surrounded by a pole-armed retinue. Up close, he looked even older to Wyrm, less human, more like a dead white tree, rotten with gnarls.

Seeing his opportunity, Fray raced to the bars. "Excuse me!"

When the wizened eyes glanced their way, Os' nostrils flared, and then zher face dropped.

Fray fumbled for the teken, only to be shoved in the stomach by the blunt end of a polearm. Fray stumbled, and the teken went flying. Crude, save for some runic markings, it glinted as it flipped end over end, catching the sunlight as it headed toward the bars.

At the last instant Fray snatched it back from the air. Os took note.

"Hey!" Fray shouted. "Please!"

By then, the Pushka had moved on. The far door was held open for him, the blinding light of day and dusty air shining beyond it.

Calico narrowed her eyes at the Pushka's small back. "He's just a…"

Fray hushed her. "Shh. We don't need to make any enemies."

Os looked to Calico, sizing up her reaction, then focused on the bright line of the closing door. "She's right. The Pushka is… singular. I may have to change my plans. Fray, may I borrow that trinket of yours?"

Of course, he balked. "You've got to be kidding."

"No. It makes sense. You're not having luck with it, and I'm far more likely to attract the attention of the guards and deflect any ill intent. Give it here and I promise I'll get you all out. I give you my word."

"What is that worth, exactly, the word of a thief and a grifter?"

"Now, now. I always hold up my end of a bargain. You could ask Ema if she were here. And keep in mind I could be using my scents on you right now. But… have it your way."

Late that night, in the cool shadow of the high, hungry walls, Wyrm woke to whispering. From the faint light of the faux stars, he made out a silhouette – Os, hovering over the prone Fray like a beast about to drink his blood.

Zher voice cooed, "Relax, big, strong soldier-man, it's safe to stay asleep. You know the smell, don't you? It's Calico's. Tricky, but I managed. Makes you happy, and you don't know why. Makes you calm, and you don't know why. Honestly, I don't either, but if I did, I probably wouldn't tell you. Toujours gai."

Os slipped a hand under Fray's shirt, reached lower, fished around, then withdrew the teken. Wyrm tried to move, to warn him, but could not.

Zhe gave the boy a wink. "Yes, this time I am manipulating you. You like her smell, too. It is special. Maybe I'll bottle it someday if I'm ever in need of cash. But I don't think that's likely to happen, do you? Why spend cash when you can always use credit?"

Wyrm tried to frown but he couldn't manage that, either. He found himself watching, happily helpless, as the alien strolled to the door and threw a pebble to rouse a sleeping guard. When the irritated brute came closer, Os held the teken aloft.

"I know you speak common. And I know you know what this is, don't you?"

Wyrm wasn't sure if it was the result of Os' pheromones or not, but the man's face filled with reverence. "What is your request?"

"I'd like to get out of here and see the Pushka as soon as possible. And be quiet about it. No need to wake the others."

On their way out, Os glanced back. "Sleep tight, now, Wyrm. No really, right now."

And Wyrm did, slumbering deeply beneath the fake eyes of the fake stars, dreaming of dreams his mother once told him, of being the World Soul and saving the universe, with Arjuda, healed and resplendent, as his queen. Did the World Soul have a queen?

He woke to Fray's guttural moan.

"Fucking son of a bitch stole it! I'd have swallowed it if I didn't think ʐhe'd've dug it out of my ass. Now we'll be stuck here forever!"

Calico put a hand on his shoulder. "No. Os promised."

Fray tried not to let her nearness calm him, but it did.

Wyrm felt a pang of jealousy, then let it go.

But then a new sound, different from the far-off combat they'd been hearing, a shivering reverberation, turned the former soldier toward the walls. "What is that? It's not artillery, or any ordnance I know of. Why does it sound so familiar?"

CHAPTER

51

The night sky above Ballikilak was sprinkled with jellyfish lightning – mile-long red and orange tendrils that flared blue and white. Gui knew all about the rare atmospheric phenomena naturalists called sprites. They occurred on his home world – once or twice every decade or so. Here, the sheer number of sparking giant ghosts didn't speak to any sort of scarcity. Given the little he knew about this strange desert world, it might not be unusual.

Still, the glorious view from his balcony filled him with dread.

If it was unique, he feared that Mordent's brief use of plasma artillery had set off a chain reaction that would doom the sacred planet. The unease went deeper than a sentimental concern over the sacrilege, or even the cost in lives. If Earth died, its secrets died with it. The plasma would remain its biggest prize. The scrolls Gui brought would be the Pantheon's only gambit.

He wanted to wake one of their hosts, to ask, but it was late, and it would be a mistake to show ignorance. He didn't have to. Moments later, his answer came unbidden. The palace came alive with activity, lights at the windows, footsteps in the halls, and, finally, at his door, where a bleary-eyed, fearful Rigdon appeared with news.

"The Archosians unleashed some sort of siege engine along the shore. It's devastating the Kardun forces. The Pushka asked to see us immediately."

"He wants the last gift," Gui said.

"Well," Rigdon answered, "You may as well bring it."

During the hurried march to the throne room, it was obvious Rigdon wanted to ask something. Gui could guess what it was but hushed him, nonetheless. When the guards turned their backs to open the tall ceremonial doors, he relented with a hissing whisper:

"No, Rigdon. I've no idea if we'll make it off this planet alive. I hope that's not too much of a surprise."

Even the Pushka, for the first time, looked tense. Wasting no time on formality, he spoke before they could bow.

"What do you know of a weapon called Gog?"

Gui stiffened. Rigdon gasped.

"This not the time to conceal your feelings, Temple Lord. Your sudden pallor saved your lives. If I thought for an instant that you weren't surprised, I'd have you killed."

Gui allowed himself a shiver. "We understood it to be destroyed long ago."

"It's not. It's here and killing our troops so quickly we can't keep an accurate body count." Shriveled hand extended, the bony fingers snapped. "The last gift. Give it."

No point in refusing, Gui acquiesced. "It won't help with Gog."

"Do you know of anything that will?"

"No."

The Pushka unraveled the aged paper and stared. "More magic?"

"Yes."

He passed the scroll to a guard. "Indepa meets with the other Amkas in the battle room. Take this to her at once. But make sure Bodspah isn't present."

Seeing Gui's inquisitive reaction, he explained. "Bodspah is strongest of the Amkas, but also… set in his ways. Technical marvels fascinate him. But magic created by the god-hated? The Grayborn? That, he considers profane."

With a quick nod sufficing for a bow, the guard rushed out.

Despite Gui's fear, he didn't forget how to think. "How did you learn of Gog?"

A dismissive sneer formed beneath the twinkling eyes. "Now that I have all your gifts, I find myself no longer interested in your questions, and your Pantheon. Further queries can be directed to my adviser. Now, I must join the Amkas. You will remain here."

Gui stared at him as he left. Unable to conceal his contempt, he began muttering before the doors closed. "How can he live so long and still be so stupid? Only a fool would abandon potential allies now!

Trying to get him to lower his voice, Rigdon whispered, "You still did right, Arbiter."

"Let them mark that on my grave."

Toward the rear of the grand space the shadows shifted, turning them toward an opening door cleverly blended into the mosaic. A tall figure, regal, but oddly so, with black, far-set eyes, stepped in and stood beside the throne. Gui thought the figure a man, until the creature bowed, displaying feathers where there should be hair.

"Neiman Os, at your service. I'm the Pushka's new adviser."

Gui's nostrils flared. Unbidden images of Harek, naked, sweating, close enough to taste with the flat of his tongue, tingled in his mind. Dizzy, he took a step back.

Os smiled. The sensation subsided.

"To answer your question, I told the Pushka about Gog. The good news, I suppose, is that it's busy killing both sides."

CHAPTER

52

Keeping the Ezekiel Wheel between Earth's moon and the fleet, the Interstellar Op spent his waking hours scanning chatter on both sides, hoping for word of the boy – and thinking about Ludi's offer.

When he learned of Os' escape, on a hunch, he decided to track, rather than apprehend, the alien – a lucky break that led him to his quarry. Wyrm and the woman were in Ballikilak. Not that he was in any position to get any of them out of there easily, but at least he knew they weren't in any immediate danger.

Until Gog reappeared.

He assumed the damn thing mended itself. Not even a madman would repair it.

No? Then again, someone had built it in the first place. Who needs demons and death gods to explain evil with humans constantly proving themselves so capable on their own?

As an excuse, of course. We need our devils as an excuse.

Ludi would disagree.

Once Gog had at it, the chatter devolved into a cacophony. Even the Wheel's analytic engines had trouble parsing it. Hours in, the Op was reduced to scrubbing from message to message, hearing the panic in the most hardened soldiers, when suddenly, everything went dead.

For a moment, he thought everyone was dead, but that was crazy. Earth, unlike Axton, had no major fault lines to exploit, and its weird weaponry didn't have the same atmospheric effect as Stifler's plasma. Besides, the Wheel's quark resonance scanners indicated a healthy population of bioforms. Gog was taking a toll, but it was far from wiping everyone out.

Yet.

The reason for the blackout, as he discovered when trying to update the Archosian casualty reports, was much simpler: He'd been locked out of the official databases. All of them. The great prize of his career was gone.

Why?

A failsafe was part of the deal. If one side cut him off, the other did so automatically. So which side, then? Or rather, who on which side? Not Mordent. He'd hired the Op. An Archosian underling with something to hide? Or maybe the Pantheon figured out where he was and were trying to protect their little secret mission.

Either way, it meant Ludi was right. Something big was brewing, something beyond the conquest of Earth – a major intersystem war.

He opened the channel. "Okay Ludi, I ran out of choices."

"There are always… Oh. Look at that. Your database access has been curtailed."

"Yep. Any idea who?"

"If I did, I'd have warned you. Frankly, I'm surprised it lasted as long as it did."

"Guess I should've been too. Well, seeing as how I'm officially stuck here with my hands up my ass, and, assuming you can still use me, what can I do for you and the Grayborn? Just please tell me it has to do with stopping Gog."

"It certainly does now… but you'll have to get to the boy first. You'll need the relic."

"I can't break into Ballikilak! Especially without the databases."

"I don't believe you'll have to. I suspect he'll be leaving soon."

CHAPTER

53

Within the high walls of the Archosian command base near Qus, more Budari than they themselves had ever seen in one place were gathered. This was not because they shared a rich culture, or preferred one conqueror over another, but because, with Ballikilak far off, and the other Amkas scattered, it was the only haven.

They'd also been promised food and water there.

A week ago, Qus was Budari. Now they had to pay for admittance. The price was as confusing as the newcomers. The Archosians didn't want money, livestock, or grain. They wanted their attention. As they were herded about, translators directed them to pay heed to the tall platform and magnifying screens near the center of the base, as if something so big could somehow be ignored.

They recognized Sebe Mordent. After all, his visage was on the scores of posters and pronouncements that had been distributed more widely than fresh water. They did have to be told who the bound, kneeling man at his side was, and that he, General Rais, not Mordent, was responsible for the terrible machine laying waste to the world. They believed him, because, why not?

Still, with his head covered and his arms pinned behind his back, he may as well have been a sack of tubers.

Mordent gestured at the sack with great fury. He spoke for the longest time about how people like Rais were vile, and how punishing his own general should prove that Archosia believed in justice for all.

"He does not represent our brave soldiers, he does not represent Archosia, he does not represent me, and by our laws, equally derived and equally applied, he will pay!"

It'd been so long since they had weapons, let alone judges, the Budari didn't see much point in vengeance. They didn't want to see the hooded man suffer; they didn't want to see him live. Had he actually been a sack of tubers, they would have valued him more.

But, they had nowhere else to go.

"I come with my hand extended in peace, to restore your rights, to punish your usurpers, to pull you up with us to the stars, and protect you from men like this! Petty and venal, warped by greed and entitlement, his kind may delay us, but they will never stop us, because we know the simple truth that all men and women are equal and that our virtues alone determine who we are. Those who side with us shall prosper in their fortune and rank. Those who remain neutral, yet give us the time to become acquainted, will find themselves on our side soon enough. But those who fight against us? They shall perish."

Wordless at last, Mordent unsheathed a ceremonial blade, ancient to Archosia, an infant in the Land of Birth and Sorrow. It gleamed hot white in the uninterested sun.

He swung swiftly, but as the blade reached Rais' neck, he slowed, so the end would not be quick. Sharper than a phagus' pitiless gaze, it patiently sliced through flesh and bone. The body wanted to fall before Mordent was finished, but two soldiers stepped in and held it in place until the last tendon holding the head came free.

Both dropped. Mordent stared at what he'd done. "This is why we have laws, not gods. Justice needs no face to be eternal."

On cue, containers of water, plentiful and fresh, were released.

And the crowd cheered.

The blade taken from Mordent, he spun and exited.

In the quiet of the turbo-lift, Primble handed him a cloth to wipe his bloodied hands. Mordent was panting, not because he was panicked or out of breath, but because he was still fuming.

"That wasn't easy, but we have to speak their language."

Primble moved to wipe the bigger bits of gore from the jacket. "His neck was thicker than most."

"Don't try to make me laugh! I counted him among my friends! How was I to know he was so... unstable?"

"He was under considerable pressure, and, based on what I've learned from the troops stationed at the farm, subject to a nefarious influence."

"Cohor Dagus. We've found our spy. Pantheon, no doubt."

"That's the assumption, but not a certainty. I had suspicions, something about him didn't sit right, but having found nothing, I said nothing."

"And so, you let Dagus escape. How could you, Primble?"

The older man shrugged. "I was… bested."

Wiping some sweat from his lip, Mordent put his hand on the servant's shoulder. "At least you admit it. Without you, I'd be surrounded by men who'd insist on their flawlessness as Archosia itself burned. In fact, I want to talk to you about that."

"And in that spirit, I'll trust you're not looking for a comforting analysis. On the one hand, the generals are too demoralized to rebel. On the other hand, they're also too demoralized to conceive or implement any effective strategy. All your plans to extend the front, let alone reach Ballikilak, have ground to a halt. Perhaps they need time to adjust, but you don't have much before the Kardun inevitably arrive from their other systems to challenge the fleet. You'll still prevail, but the cost in lives and reputation will be…"

Mordent chuckled. "You misunderstand, old friend. Or rather, you understand the situation completely, which is why I've decided to make you a general, effective at once."

For the first time in years, Mordent surprised him. "But… I've no military background, no officer training, never been a cadet, let alone…"

"Yet time and again you've proven yourself as keen as any who do! If anything, your lack of those connections recommends you. Highly. While loyal to me, you view the other factions from a neutral perspective, something impossible for a man trained in the right schools, raised in the ranks because he has friends – other than me, of course."

Primble swallowed hard. "May I refuse?"

"No, Primble, you may not."

Absorbing the sudden change in position, Primble looked at the crowds of Budari visible through the mech-video feeds. They didn't seem to enjoy drinking the water so much as the fact that it kept them alive. Life was the sum total of their need. Despite the dry filth covering them, and the smells he couldn't bring himself to imagine, Primble wished he were down there, drinking with them.

Calico tried not to look smug. "See? I told you ʒhe'd be back. Os isn't so bad. Makes me wish I was judging that species instead."

Surprised as he was at the thief's return, Fray, having had more time to wonder about her, caught the odd phrasing. "Instead of ours?"

His face did a little dance that pleased her.

"Yes," she said.

Wyrm didn't care for the way he looked at her, or the way she looked back.

He wasn't the only one who noticed.

"Break it up, you, two," Os said as their cage was unlocked. "Before poor Wyrm dies of jealousy."

"I'm not jealous!" The boy lowered his head and tried to stay out of sight.

They were escorted to a plush chamber with cushioned chairs where a feast had been laid out on an inlaid table. Once inside, Os tossed Fray the teken. He held it up between thumb and forefinger, disappointed it no longer glowed.

The con artist shrugged. "They have some sort of charge. It's useless now, but I thought you might like it as a keepsake. And stop smelling at me like that, soldier-boy. Relax! You were going to use it to get out of here anyway, right?"

Fray clenched the teken. "I was also going to ask for a lot more than a bigger cage."

"And you have it! You can come and go as you please, with supplies, transportation, and a few desert maps you'll find useful if you still plan to find Stifler… corpse or not."

Fray wanted very much to find something to be angry at Os about but couldn't. "What did you do? Sleep with the Pushka's entire government?"

Os was surprised zherself. "No, as it turns out, I didn't fuck anyone. Not so much as a wink or a farted pheromone. I only happened to notice something."

Fray grabbed an oblong meat, and after, taking a hearty bite, plopped into a seat. "What?"

Os looked at the guards. "Leave us."

Surprisingly, they did.

After closing the door, zhe put his back to it. "I realize we're not the best of friends, but I must tell someone. It's too good a story, and very much in all your interests to keep secret. I smelled it on him when he walked by. The holy Pushka is not 900 years old. Not nearly."

Wyrm perked up. "How old is he?"

Os whisper-shouted, "Nine. He's got a rare genetic disease, a variant of progeria, that ages him prematurely. But they don't have the medical knowledge to recognize it. His appearance played into an old Budari legend, so he took advantage big time, but he's younger than you are, Wyrm."

Not caring, Arjuda picked about the table for food.

Calico acted as if she'd known all along. "Told you so."

Fray and Wyrm furrowed their brows to comic extremes.

Wyrm spoke first. "Then there'd be no record of him older than nine years! How'd he convince everyone he was 900?"

Os's face indicated zher ambivalence toward the explanation zhe was about to offer. "He told me they don't have many records, none reliable, very few that old. What they do have is a very different sense of history. There's history the way Archosia and the Pantheon understand it, a chronicle taking place in time, but here there's also a sort of mythic history that takes precedence. Plus, pay enough senior citizens to swear that their great-grandparents saw you way back when, and you're Pushka."

Calico sang loudly to herself. "Stories are always better than memory."

Fray tilted his head at her, then, though realizing she could still hear him, asked softly, "Os, what do you make of her?"

"Couldn't say. It's not that she has no smell, she has all of them. Constantly. She's a veritable bouquet of human responses." Os blinked, then continued. "I'm not the most moral creature when it comes to property or sex, but I do try to pay my debts, especially when it's no skin off my back. The fact is, without your teken, the Pushka would have killed me for figuring out his secret. Thanks to the cultural restrictions it entailed, the little guy opted to make me his chief adviser. He even asked my opinion on whether he should declare himself the World Soul. Still on the fence on that one…"

The loud, distant staccato keening that rattled the walls returned – and sounded closer.

Chewing, Fray stared out the window as if he might glimpse its source. "What is that?"

Os sighed with disappointment. "Prison must have made you rusty. I'm surprised you don't recognize that little screech from your glory days on Axton, let alone our escape."

Fray sputtered out the food he was eating. "Gog? It was dead. It… fixed itself?"

"The Pushka's spies say it was repaired."

"What? Only a maniac would…"

"Apparently, they're not in short supply these days."

CHAPTER

55

You already know this part of the story, don't you, Rusk?

That's what she said. Easy enough for her to know his name. He must have said it to Sterg the first night he was here, again when the physickers came to bind her. But explanations didn't make it feel any less, for lack of a better word, magical, as if somehow, in the dark of her mind, she now knew him the way a true mother-goddess might.

The feeling was palpable, tingling. Maybe that's why some, hearing from similarly compromised minds, believed so firmly it was the gods who spoke. Maybe, as a symptom of her condition, she gave off pheromones like that alien, making her more charismatic, more convincing than your average maniac with grandiose delusions. On the other hand, how real does something have to feel before it is real?

Much as these ideas flooded him, he had to pinch himself to remember he wasn't here to think, he was here to listen.

Sky's voice grew sad, wistful: "The Grayborn wanted to slay the Beast Father, to end my love, like insects hungry to eat the king, the way the littlest maggot gets to peck at the largest corpse. But how? How to remove the heart of the cosmos, the soul of the world, and keep the world alive?"

She laughed a bitter laugh. It would have been longer, had Meriwald not interrupted: "They were smart enough. And they had a plan. They wanted to replace him with a new soul."

"Yes." Sky recited the old story with distaste, as if she were recalling a first crayon drawing from a child revealing its utter lack of talent. "Once upon a time the World Soul was born, weak as any babe, more helpless than most, but immortal in the shape of its virtues, a new pattern, a schema, a soul that would glide from incarnation to incarnation, lifetime to lifetime, its power growing slowly, until at last it would be strong enough to displace the primal being and end him."

Lady Stifler prodded her. "A fairy tale?"

"No," Sky conceded. "An idea. Feasible, yes, but first the Grayborn needed more power than even they could collect or conjure. They needed something up to the task. They needed to capture a god."

The soldier and the boy wanted the two women to remain at the palace. Not because they were women, they said, but because Arjuda was fragile, in need of more care than they had to give, while Calico, was, well, Calico; impulsive, incoherent, unpredictable.

But, true to that unfathomable character, Calico refused to stay put and insisted Arjuda come with her. Short of caging them, the thought of which felt sinful even to the two atheists, there was little to be done. And, after all, while the palace was safe now, who knew how long it would stay that way?

Having a choice, Fray opted for a mech-sled over a quartet of phagus. An older model, it would have to be solar-charged every half a day, but it was simple enough for Wyrm to operate.

As they left, while the mountains around Ballikilak still towered high, beyond them, they could see the lights of Gog's weapons flickering on the bellies of distant clouds. It made them glad to be headed in the opposite direction, even if it was into a parched, blank, unknown.

My father is out there.

Love, loyalty, and estate laws aside, finding him was tightly wedged in the boy's own becoming. But the future, when it did not arrive quickly enough, grew as boring as the sand.

No longer intrigued by where and how to best relieve himself, or when to eat and drink, with Calico and Arjuda sphinxlike in their mysteries, Wyrm took to thinking about the soldier.

In the cool of their journey's third sunset, his view of the great nothing obscured by dust devils, and Calico busy whispering made-up names for the erratic winds into Arjuda's ear, he asked the man:

"Why *did* you stay with us? Really." Wyrm dared a nod at Calico. "Is it her?"

Fray thought about how much he wanted to say. "You always do things for one reason?"

Sometimes, Wyrm did things for no reason at all, not that he'd admit it, so he simply said, "No."

"Me neither. Yes, Calico is… different. We both know that. But your father's expedition changed my life. I wound up in the Chamber because of it."

Wyrm shrugged. "You killed your therapist and slept with Mordent's wife."

"I was charged with murder, but…" his hands waved weakly.

Wyrm bristled. "You think I'm too young to understand?"

Fray shook his head. "No, not after hearing about you and Gilby. Maybe I'm too young to explain myself. Or too old. Sometimes it all gets kind of foggy." No longer caring to look within, he idly looked outward and ended up pointing. "And there it is."

"What?"

The wind was dying, settling the dust devils like a lowering curtain, allowing the fading sun to illuminate, a degree shy of the horizon, a broken honeycomb of ruins and natural voids.

"It's a cave system. Goes on for hundreds of miles, the whole continent for all we know. Last I was with your father, we were camped in there. He was looking for something called… Shalem?"

Wyrm nodded. "Shashem. I think that's how you say it. Koshem, the House of Knowledge, and Shashem, the House of Wisdom – the two biggest repositories of old Earth culture. Koshem's where he found the plasma and Birefringe. Shashem was supposed to house another orb, a source of divine magic – the highest achievement of the Grayborn. I overheard Ludi begging him to find it first, but what with the Directorate pushing for technical breakthroughs, he didn't bother with it, until…"

"…your mother got sick, and he got desperate."

Wyrm receded into his Archosian contempt. "Desperate enough to think magic could save her."

Fray shrugged. "You're not being fair to him. Who knows what those priest-scientists called magic back then? Hell, I don't know how half our tech works, do you? Besides, aren't you the one who believes in fate? What's that, if not magic?"

"That's different. Even Sebe Mordent believes in fate."

Apparently listening, Calico said, "It's not different. I'm sorry you think it needs to be. It makes the stars inside you sad."

Fray grimaced. "Do you mean like, it makes life sad, as in less meaningful? Or do you mean there are stars inside you that can feel sadness?"

"Both."

"It's always 'both' with you," Wyrm said. "Saying it's both is like saying it's neither."

"What's your answer, then?" Calico asked.

Wyrm had one. He'd thought one through, very carefully, but it was all wrapped up with his mother's voice, and him being the World Soul.

Fray was more interested in what lay ahead. "We've got enough charge to reach the closest cave before dark. Easier to keep warm in there. We'll set up camp and look around in the morning. Agreed?"

Wyrm nodded.

The rush of the sled swept cold grit into their faces. As the minutes passed, rather than the nearest cave, Fray aimed them toward the third on their right. Low and more evenly oval than the others, he explained, "It looks familiar."

Shielding his eyes with his hands, Wyrm focused on the hollow, as if by the sheer effort he might be better able to see through the grit.

Arjuda, not shielding her face at all, stood, briefly shifting the sled's balance.

"There's a man," she said.

Fray's expression indicated his disbelief, but when he dutifully raised his binoculars, his face went pallid. His skin grew slick, looking almost as sickly as Wyrm's sweat.

Though Wyrm couldn't see anything yet, the soldier's shocked expression filled him with an electric hope. What, after all, could be more surprising than seeing a man he thought dead, still alive?

His father.

Was it him? Could it be this easy?

Wyrm strained harder, forcing his eyes to stay open in the pelting sand. As the creaking sled neared, he finally made out a figure. It was thin, unhealthily so. His father may not have been eating well.

But this man's beard was shaggy, the hair was wrong, the height…

Fray shouted, "He's dead! He has to be! I saw him die!"

The words again filled Wyrm with hope, until it became abundantly clear that whoever stood at the cavemouth was not Anacharsis Stifler. Wyrm had no idea who he was.

But Fray did.

"That's the man I murdered."

CHAPTER
57

Arriving discreetly in the remote deserts was easy. The Op's data was still recent enough to reasonably project Archosian troop movement, and the Slave-kings didn't have much in the way of air-to-ground detectors. What little they did have was concentrated on protecting the perimeters of their cities and bases.

Everything else wasn't easy at all, starting with finding solid ground to land the Wheel. The depth readings were chaotic, revealing a hodge-podge of buried structures and natural formations immersed in dangerously soft and shifting sand. A rocky outcropping finally did the trick. It also provided a decent view of the only available paths in and out. A bigger issue was what the weather was no doubt doing to the Wheel's sensors and intakes.

That would have to be dealt with later.

Last, and perhaps most difficult, was deciding what to do now that he was here.

Not eager to engage the harsh terrain, he stayed put, monitoring his targets' progress on the mech-sled. As they headed for one of the caves, he focused his sensors on it. A blip appeared in its mouth. It came and went, only once lingering long enough for the Op to wonder if it was some sort of animal. But then it disappeared, and no matter how much he calibrated the scanners, it stayed gone.

Even if it was something dangerous, Fray could probably handle it. Still, the Op figured he should move sooner rather than later.

That meant asking Ludi why he was here in the first place.

For the first time, Ludi's quantum line was rife with blips and static. Could be the weather, could be the absence of redundant relay access the Op lost along with the databases, but there wasn't much he could do about it now other than speak loudly and clearly.

"I'm here, they're there. What is it you want me to do?"

"Steal Birefringe and bring to General Charnel. He's being held in a prison beneath

Mordent's command center near Qus."

Sick of the philosophic byroads the man's speechifying usually took, the Op initially appreciated how matter-of-factly Ludi spoke. Then he realized what he was saying.

The Op flew from his seat. "Bloody Norah! I know where Charnel's being held! I'm the one who brought him in, remember? Did you forget about Hydrokos, too? That walking wrinkle is a human version of Gog! Do you have any idea what that genocider could do with something like Birefringe?"

"I know exactly what he'll do. And once I explain, I'm sure you'll agree it's the best possible course."

CHAPTER

58

Fray was trained to control his emotions, to steer his anger to his best advantage, and most importantly, to never lose control. All that forgotten, he leapt from the mech-sled without so much as disengaging the motor leaving a startled Wyrm to scramble for the throttle. Fortunately, with its charge already dying, the sled slid to a sideways stop just inside the cave, rattling, but not harming the passengers or their supplies.

Finding the lamp atop their gear, Wyrm switched it on. The wide beam hit Fray's back in mid-leap, casting a looming shadow on his terrified target. Death in his eyes, the only thing that gave him pause was how weak the emaciated man looked.

Dr. Beckles threw his hands up in frightened protest. "Don't kill me! I beg you!"

"Why not?" Fray snarled. "I spent years paying for your murder. Why not get my money's worth, Beckles?"

Wyrm knew the name. *Beckles? Dr. Rowan Beckles?*

The coincidence was amazing. It was his mother's mesmerist! Ludi himself insisted Beckles examine her. He was also the only one to show results, making her calm, if not coherent. Rather than grateful, Wyrm had been angry he couldn't do more.

Not nearly as angry as Fray was now.

The doctor went to his knees. "Fray… Alek… Let me explain! Please! I'm begging! See? I'm… praying to you!"

Judging from how bad he looked, the man's distance from death was so slight it was hardly worth the journey. Wyrm had met him in better days, when a layer of hair covered most of his plump body, like an animal's coat. Now he was so thin, his shirtless skin seemed barely held in place by what strands of that hair remained.

"You treated my mother," Wyrm said.

Beckles' eyes lit. "The Stifler boy? Adalbert! Yes! Oh, yes! I did. I helped her! I made her feel better. You remember that don't you, Alek? It was in all the newsfeeds!"

The soldier remained grim. "I've never been all that sure you didn't make her worse."

Wyrm's eyes darted between them. "Worse? How? I thought it was like meditation. How can *thinking* make you worse?"

Fray snorted. "Oh, it *can*. Mesmerists induce trance-states that make their patients highly open to suggestion. Once they're vulnerable, they... what do you call it, Beckles? *Craft*, that was the word. They craft a new narrative of the self to promote a sense of power and healing. What was the narrative you crafted for Lady Stifler? That she was a goddess?"

Beckles tried to look dignified. "That's confidential."

"I bet it is. See, she was babbling plenty beforehand, but afterwards, there were rumors that he was the one who convinced her she was Mother Sky."

"What?!" Wyrm clenched his fists and moved closer.

Now it was Beckles' turn to snap his glance between Fray and Wyrm. "Fear! Ignorance! Jealousy that I'd succeeded where they failed! And not at all accurate!"

"Which brings me to another question, doc." Fray roughly pulled him to standing and squeezed his frail shoulders. "How is it I remember killing you?"

"I... I've no idea! Stop!" Fray squeezed harder. "Sweet Abraxas, stop!" Seeing no choice, he confessed. "Because I hypnotized you. It's what I do. To save myself. So, you *wouldn't* kill me. Forgive me for trying to live!"

Arjuda, upset by the sudden crash, and the screaming men, started panting. Calico wrapped a blanket around her, then turned to Fray and asked, "So you *were* going to kill him?"

"Yes," he admitted. "Under orders from the High Commander. When Mordent heard Beckles was sleeping with Vita, Beckles pressured Stifler into taking him, to get him away from Archosia. Stifler owed him because of his wife, and I was... *assigned* to find him and get proof of the affair."

"Which you never did," Beckles sniffed. "Because it didn't happen!"

Fray grit his teeth. "Which I did because it did happen. Love letters. Real hot stuff."

"Wait," Wyrm said. "Vita slept with both of you?"

Beckles protested. "The woman's an artiste! A virtuoso! Outdated rules of morality should not apply! And you, Fray, are a hypocrite, turning me in for committing the same so-called crime!"

The soldier's lips curled. "She loved me!"

Realizing his explanations, reasonable or not, were at an end, Beckles worried his hands.

Beckles shoulders sunk. "I suppose you'll kill me now."

Though the boy's own emotions were a whirl, he managed to stay more reasonable than his elders.

"No," Wyrm said. "You can't, Fray! He was with the expedition after you left. He must know if my father's still alive, maybe even where he is!"

Tasting escape, Beckles' eyes widened. "I do! I do know... In fact, I..."

Fray reared. "I can smell you getting ready to *craft*. Don't think about it."

The scrawny shoulders sagged again. "You're right. I don't know, but I doubt he's alive. I'm not sure how I survived, but I'm pretty sure I was the only one. We were in the valley, in one of the ruins when we were attacked."

"What valley?" Wyrm asked. "Which..."

Fray cut him off. "Who attacked you?"

Beckles answered the stronger of the two. "Not sure. Budari? It was dark. They were riding beasts."

"Snake-riders?"

"No. Bigger than the phagus. Worse."

"What valley?!" Wyrm repeated.

After a glance at Fray, Beckles answered. "Where the dead men lost their bones. I'm not sure what that means, but that's what they call it. I can take you there. Get you close to it, anyway."

The soldier looked the boy in the eyes. "You *can't* trust him, Wyrm. You already know what he did to me."

"It's all I have."

Fray scoffed. "Just because it looks like your only choice is a bad one doesn't mean you have to take it. I mean, we barely got here, and we already found him."

Beckles' hands wavered about, trying to find something to grab onto. "Maybe there's something else I can do for you? A show of good faith? Maybe…?"

In the near-silence Arjuda's whimpering became audible.

"You've upset her," Calico scolded. "The crash, Fray's yelling."

Fray protested. "Hey, *I'm* pretty upset, too!"

Calico tsked. "You can handle it. She can't. Not now."

Beckles waddled over, bobbing his head as he studied her. "All the signs of PCD. I can help her. Calm her. Like I did with Meriwald. Let me? Let me show that you can trust me?"

"He did help my mother," Wyrm said. "And you."

Fray made a face.

Calico nodded. "The doctor's powerful."

Wyrm scrunched his face. "Does that mean I should let him try to help, or not?"

"It's not your decision. It's hers."

She prodded Arjuda. The girl looked up and nodded for Beckles to approach.

He patted his tattered shirt. "I do need my…."

He fished about a threadbare pocket and withdrew a peculiar bauble. A set stone, it was pockmarked, and worn, but shiny, too shiny to be genuine.

He held it out to her. "Look, Arjuda. Isn't it pretty? Try to find the center and breathe. See the twinkle? The little light? That twinkle is part of the stone, yes, but at the same time, it's not part of it at all, yes? Like you and your body, they're part of the same thing, but separate. Keep looking, keep breathing. Try to make the twinkle the same as the stone, the stone the same as the twinkle, the body the same as the mind, the mind the same as the body. Breathe. Breathe because you will yourself to breathe, breathe because you don't, breathe because it happens on its own. Let it happen. Let yourself just... happen."

After a minute, Fray said, "It's not working."

But then her breathing slowed, and Arjuda whispered, soft and low: "*When I die, the ocean will take my flesh and it will get sucked up into the clouds and rained down on the earth and be eaten by the corn and the cows and the babes until the earth burns and we are all made into stars.*"

Out of nowhere, Calico joined in, chanting with her, as if singing a song that they both knew.

"*But not my bones, my bones will stay on the bottom for the mermaids to find and they'll take them and make flutes from my legs and arms and chimes from my ribs and a drum from my skull and they will play and play and the music will be so beautiful, the angels will laugh and weep.*"

Fray and Wyrm weren't the only ones surprised.

The mesmerist blinked several times before saying, "Well... this is new."

CHAPTER
59

The light in the outer cave was murky at best, its recesses a fount of larger darknesses. Not one to think in black and white, the Op searched for the gray in it all. Whatever his regrets, he'd always figured he couldn't be all that bad, especially when compared to the vermin he put away. But now, as he crept like a petty cutpurse toward the sleeping Stifler heir, he had to wonder if he was coming close.

Ah, the kid got this far. Maybe he'll be fine without the only thing that's kept him alive.

Birefringe came free from his arms without eliciting so much as a shudder.

Time to make the trek back to the Wheel and hope the sand hasn't gunked the intakes too much for a silent takeoff. And then? Well, could be the worst or the best thing I've ever done. How's that for gray?

He was far enough from their camp to think that the sandy wind and sand would muffle, if not his escape, at least his direction, meaning he was home free.

But he was wrong. The wind even failed to mute the harsh voice behind his back.

"Hey! Who are you and where the hell do you think you're…"

Though the silhouette barely distinguished itself from the swirling nothing, he recognized it as belonging to the marksman, Fray. The Op didn't want to kill him. He wanted even less to be killed by him. But the soldier's gun was out and ready.

So, he stopped in his tracks.

After a few seconds, he wondered why Fray hadn't finished his sentence, *where the hell do you think you're* being a perfectly good start, missing only a verb. As more time passed, the Op concluded that Fray hadn't finished, because he couldn't. A few cautious steps closer confirmed that he was frozen, paralyzed.

Alive and healthy, there was no apparent reason for his paralysis, until a sparkling light cut through the dim world behind him.

Making out the skinny figure wielding it, the Op asked, "How'd you manage it?"

"Human psyches, like any data system, can have backdoors installed. I gave Fray one a long time ago. I can release him anytime, and let him shoot you, so I suggest you answer the question he never finished asking."

Keeping his hands in plain sight, the investigator bowed. "Interstellar Op, at your service. And you're Dr. Rowan Beckles. Kept a file on you, but there was never much to go on. The way you blinked in and out of my scanners yesterday, though, made me realize I should've read between the lines more carefully. You're Ludi's missing Grayborn. He always did love mesmerists. Said Archosia should honor you as, uh…?"

Beckles returned the bow. "Atheist priests, he said, replacing the priest-scientists of legend."

"Right. Except for the science part. I always took you for mostly hooey."

Beckles nodded at the frozen Fray. "He'd disagree. Well, if he weren't in denial. Do you know what makes him so suggestible? His conviction that he isn't. Something to keep in mind."

"I'll do that. You know Ludi thinks you're dead."

"I was, almost. Stuck here alone until yesterday." He tilted his head at Fray. "Doing a little better than I've let them think, but not much."

"Papa Stifler alive?"

"No idea. I'd have told the boy that much if I knew. We were separated. Trying to find him won't be safe, but I guess I must help. I assume things are coming to some sort of head?"

The Op wagged a finger. "Ah-ah! When you assume you make an ass of you and me. But, hey, rest assured the end of some world, or another is nigh."

"Ludi should know that when I placed the girl, Arjuda in a trance, she and Calico spontaneously recited an ancient translation of The Great Word. Verbatim, if I recall the passage correctly."

"Tell him yourself." He withdrew an oblong object from his pocket, pressed a few buttons on it, and tossed it to Beckles. "That'll bridge to my ship comm so you and Ludi can swap cosmic gossip. Meanwhile, love to chat, but I gotta go save the world by destroying it."

Then he walked off, tossing Birefringe in the air and catching it, whistling into the wind, and thinking about the bottle of Tuslan Brandy back on his ship.

CHAPTER
60

Morning sun loped through the cave mouth, just to slap the sleeping Wyrm's face. He was sad to leave his dreams, maybe because, despite making no sense, they asked so little of him. Stretching, he was considering yawning when the cool dry feel against his arching palms told him something was wrong, seriously wrong, and that once he opened his eyes, the waking world would be asking more of him than usual.

"Birefringe!"

Not yet frantic, he patted fiercely about the blanket and sleeping mat. "It's gone! Fray!"

Beckles straightened from his leaning position against the rocky wall. Calico and Arjuda were rousing, a process sped by his cries, but Fray was nowhere to be seen. Still stunned, Wyrm didn't yet connect the two disappearances.

"Where's Fray?" he shouted.

"I'm sure I don't know," Beckles said.

"Somewhere else," Calico offered.

He screamed at her as if she were a servant in his father's house. "I figured that! Do you know where?"

She put a finger to her lips and nodded towards Arjuda. The girl looked as if she might cry. Wyrm wished she'd stayed at the palace. He wished they both had.

Gritting his teeth, he bolted to his feet. He peered into the desert, then back toward the cave's unexplored recesses, heart beating faster all the while.

"I don't understand!"

Despite the arid atmosphere, syrupy sweat began to bead in small dollops on his forehead, chest, and armpits.

"Calm yourself," Beckles said.

"Fray wouldn't steal it. There must be some explanation..." Feeling his voice rise again, he glanced at Calico, expecting another reprimand.

Instead, she said, "You're right. Fray wouldn't steal it."

Rather than help, he resented what he took as an effort to mollify him. It made him feel handled, talked down to, more naked than he already did – without the orb. His rational mind abandoning him, his body followed suit. Wyrm felt dizzy, unsteady on his feet.

Before he knew he was falling, Beckles caught him. "Relax. Breathe."

Apparently much stronger after a meal and a night's sleep, Beckles easily lowered him to sitting. But Wyrm's position didn't matter. His heart still hammered.

What will I do without Birefringe? Without Fray?

He'd barely begun to trust the man... but he was a convict after all. No. He wouldn't do this. If not for Wyrm's sake, then Calico's. But didn't Fray say there wasn't always one reason for doing something? Maybe he...

No, no, no!

He couldn't slow his breathing. Was he dying? Was this what dying felt like? The physickers never really understood his condition. For all he knew, it could be killing him. It may have been killing him all along. Could he get stuck like this, a gibbering anxious idiot, forever?

Or was he only passing out?

"I can help you," Beckles said. "Like I helped Arjuda, remember? And your mother. Do you want my help?"

Wyrm's quick nod sent bits of his sticky sweat flying. One hit the doctor below the eye. He wiped it off and took out his sparkly ornament.

"Look at this. Just like before. Remember? See the sparkle, see the stone. The same but separate, yes? Separate and the same. The same and separate, separate and the same."

He said more, the sorts of things he said to Arjuda, but if any part of Wyrm was listening, it was some part of him of which he had no awareness. The pounding in his chest, a hard, visceral sound that slammed against the inside of his eyes, drowned out all else, until, yes, he could hear the doctor's voice again, if that's what it was. It felt more like an intrusion from Wyrm's own mind, coming not from outside, but from all the stars within.

"Who is it who loves you most? Who makes you feel safe?"

"My mother, but she's...."

"Shh. She's not. She's fine. She's not there. She's here and healthy, beautifully whole. She's outside and in you. She knows you, every part of you, and loves you very much. Now tell me, what does she tell you?"

He didn't have to think about that. Her words had been a constant comfort. "That there's nothing wrong with me. That I'm not sick, not really. That I'll do great things. That I'll be a great man, like my father. That I'm a hero, a leader... that I'm... the World Soul." He hesitated, ashamed to be asking, ashamed of having to ask, "Am I?"

"Does it make sense to you?"

"It does. It does. Very much."

"Your mother loves you, and if she said it, it must be true. Open your eyes, then, and see that it is."

He did. At first, he experienced a kind of tunnel vision. For a time, Beckles, Calico, Arjuda, the bauble, the lamp, the mech sled, everything in his field of vision changed size, growing, and shrinking in import, as if their very physicality had always been secretly random.

The drumming stopped. Wyrm was calm, very calm, calmer than he could remember feeling. It was as if he was concentrating and daydreaming at the same time, and he knew, without a doubt, that so long as he felt this way, he'd happily do whatever Beckles suggested.

The doctor paused as if weighing his options.

"I suppose I must do as I promised, take you to where I saw your father last. We should get going."

To Wyrm it sounded like a great idea, but Calico objected.

"We should wait for Fray. He'll be back. He'll explain."

Beckles smiled sweetly. "No, I don't think that will be wise. Not for me, anyway. Come. Let me do as I promised and take you to the Valley."

"Where the dead men lost their bones?" Wyrm asked.

"Yes."

With that, he stepped deeper into the cave. Calico was saying something, but Wyrm either didn't hear or didn't care to. Arjuda beside him, he numbly followed Beckles into the larger darknesses that awaited.

CHAPTER

61

Others might take pride in eluding guards or disabling alarms, get their jollies from being at one with the shadows, but all the creeping around felt beneath him. Oh, the Op was good enough at it, but he might have been even better if he took *some* pleasure in it.

Still, never been caught, and any landing you can walk away from is a good one.

His mood wasn't helped by the fact that he was infiltrating an Archosian base to free the same war criminal he had been proud of capturing the first time, years ago. Add to that he'd recaptured the bastard a few weeks back and it was enough to drive a man to drink.

Which he did.

Just enough to take the edge off, he told himself. The brandy from Warden Swope's office came in handy for that. The taste did not disappoint.

So, he drank a little more.

Not that he was in any sense impaired.

Still, you'd think he'd be grateful getting inside wasn't much of a challenge, but no. The prefab structures didn't quite sit right on the terrain. The hasty modifications, made mostly to better protect the fragile ecosystem, were a drag on its resources, making everything run at a little less than its usual level of efficiency.

And, what with their pretty little invasion being all mussed up by the return of the prodigal Gog, the Archosian military was more than occupied, running around like their heads had been cut off, in fear that at any moment they would be.

Beyond that, General Charnel, along with Dr. Warland, were still being kept where the Op's intel last had them, in an ancient prison beneath the command center outside Qus.

Breaking in was so easy it was annoying.

Wyrm could've done it.

The ancient prison was a far cry from the Chamber. It was such an iffy choice for valuable prisoners, the Op wondered if it was meant as some sort of signal to the Budari that Mordent would respect their version of justice.

Like he has a clue what that might be.

Otherwise, it didn't make sense. If they'd bothered to keep their prisoners off-world, Gilby would never have escaped.

Right. Rais. Of course. Must've all been Rais' idea.

To the credit of Archosia's military, after seeing how insecure the security was, they doubled the guards, but the knockout gas, properly measured and dispensed, took them out along with Dr. Warland. It dissipated before Charnel had time to raise his head and aim his wrinkly eyes at his visitor.

"You. To what do I owe…?"

Slicing the lock with a torch-blade, the Op waved him out. "Let's go."

Charnel stayed put. "Let's not. Answer my question."

"Ludi sent me."

"I always suspected you were one of his neo-Grayborn."

"Don't call me that. I hate that name. I hate all of this." Entering the cell, he yanked Charnel to his feet. "It's like one of those ethical conundrums philosophers like jerking off to: Do I free a genocider to save millions I never met or murder a babe in his cradle because I know he'll grow up to be, well… you."

A smile creaked into place on Charnel's face. "Are you here to kill me so I don't kill again?"

"I wish. I really do wish."

"Are you… drunk?"

"What if? Come on. It's a ways back to the Wheel, but if it's anything like getting here, it'll be a cakewalk. Makes me wonder why you haven't escaped on your own yet."

Arm around his back, he hoisted the old man by the arm pit, then maneuvered him out of the cell and toward the door.

"I could have," Charnel explained. "But Dr. Warland begged me to pretend to work with Dagus, so we could use him." He glanced at his unconscious coconspirator, almost sadly. "Hm. This will be the second escape where she's been left behind, poor thing. She's already incoherent without her yustick. I don't suppose...?"

"No. Dagus?"

Charnel faintly raised an eyebrow. "My, my. I figured you knew all about him. I was hoping to trick you into filling in some blanks. Dagus. Rais' Cohor. A true believer, just not in the same gods as the Pantheon, or the ideals of the Archosia."

The Op paused. "So? What does he believe?"

"In death, mostly. Wants to raise the war casualties as much as possible." The genocider rolled his eyes. "Thinks enough released soul energy will awaken his Lord, the Beast Father."

"Huh. He probably talked Rais into reviving Gog."

Charnel looked at the flat stone ceiling. "So that's what all the ruckus up there has been about. Seems Dagus is succeeding, then. Ha! Perhaps any day now the Father will awaken and the entire planet will shed the insect-like parasites that imagine themselves its rulers, get up, and walk away. Part of me would like to see that."

An indicator light on the Op's sensor blinked. "I was wrong about the cakewalk. Thought I'd dampened the guards' biometric transmitters, but they shifted frequencies two days ago. Reinforcements are en route."

"Lost your database access, did you? We all knew *that* wouldn't last."

"Point being, new plan." The Op released his grip on Charnel. Facing the hall's flat sandstone walls, he adjusted the depth of the torch blade and carved an opening that led into an adjoining space. "Pretty dark, but head east and you'll find an exit about a mile outside the base. I'll stay here and keep them busy."

The general was surprised. "Alcohol making you self-destructive?"

"No, just practical. You need time and freedom. I have some I can lend you."

Charnel laughed. "Time and freedom for what exactly? Does Ludi expect me to stop Gog? And how does he think I'll manage that?"

The Op withdrew Birefringe. "With this."

The orb's glow reflected in the old man's eyes. "Was Wyrm sleeping, or did he put up a fight? The boy must be going mad without it. Probably for the best. Madness will make him much more like the world he thinks he was born to save."

He reached for it.

The Op pulled back. "Not yet. Why didn't you sign up with Dagus?"

"I only broke out of the Chamber to see my grandson. Dagus, being an idiot, told me he was dead, experimented on by Archosian military before being killed. Thought I indulged in death for death's sake, but like any good general, my killing always had a more prosaic purpose."

The Op eyed the corridor, hearing, or imagining he heard, approaching soldiers. "Well, Dagus didn't exactly tell you the whole truth about that. Probably because he realized you weren't as into mass murder as he'd hoped."

Blood rushed into Charnel's face, reaching places it hadn't for years. "What do you mean?"

The Op handed him the orb. "Don't get excited. You're not going to like it much."

Charnel held it gingerly. "Am I to believe that if I manage to defeat Gog the Grayborn will take me to my grandson? Or at least that you have the foresight to lie about it?"

"No, old man, and I'm not going to lie to you." His usually steady voice betrayed a slight slur. "I'm going to tell you the truth, and trust me, when I do, you're going to wish very, very badly, that I hadn't. But right after that? You're going to get yourself where you need to be and do what you have to do. And I won't have to promise you anything."

"Am I now?"

The Op's look was bracing. "Yeah, you are."

"And whatever it is, you had to be drunk to tell me?"

The Op quoted Ludi. "Not every decision has a single motivation, but, yeah, that's one."

And the investigator did as promised. He told the genocider the truth.

A massive rage, one bearing a grotesque resemblance to life, filled his form. Wordless, Charnel slipped into the darkness of the carved hole. The Op watched the glowing orb shrink in size until it finally disappeared. Just in time.

The hall filled with Archosian troops.

Drawing his twin gyrojets, He fired repeatedly, not at the men, who had done nothing wrong. He shot at the floor and the walls, keeping his shots close enough to make them think he meant business. He missed once, hitting a dark-haired infantryman in the leg, and cursed himself for it. When he'd figured he'd given the old man more than enough time, he aimed both barrels at the ceiling, stepped out of cover, and ejected the ammo.

"Gentlemen, you're about to be given the great honor of being the first in the galaxy to capture the famous Interstellar Operative. No need to thank me."

He was only sorry he hadn't finished the brandy.

CHAPTER

62

As the Op promised, Charnel emerged from a crag's stone lips alone and a mile from the Archosian base. He withdrew the orb from the folds of his prison clothes and took a moment to admire its double-refracted light.

What a pity the Stifler heir never guessed the extent of his father's discovery. The boy, being a boy, probably preferred thinking it magical, fearing he might find its limits disappointing.

Not about to make the same mistake, the general started by asking a key question that had, apparently, never occurred to Wyrm:

"Birefringe, what can you do?"

Rather than blink idiotically or project geometric shapes, the orb took a more direct approach, flooding Charnel's mind with highly specialized, highly stylized images. Though not much of a linguist, he theorized they might be old Earth pictograms, created just before the supposed wrath of the gods destroyed most of humanity. The ancient icons had – again, according to legend – all but eliminated the need for written words.

Charnel could believe it. He was able to understand them all intuitively, and instantly. Signifiers overflowed his consciousness, firing his synapses in such a dizzying array the general worried he'd have a stroke. But the sweaty rush passed, and eventually, his thinking slowed.

Secure now in the knowledge his task was possible, rather than rush into battle, he allowed himself a modest indulgence. There was, after all, no agreement made. Ludi was rightly counting on Charnel to act as he always did, in his own interest. And right now, he was interested in stopping in on Gog's father, a fellow general, and fellow genocider.

Sneaking back onto the base and locating General Wintour's quarters was simple enough with the orb. There were guards outside his door, but Birefringe helped with them as well, locking their weapons in standby, overcharging them, and directing the current, enough to kill five times as many men, through their bodies.

He didn't plan to ask Wintour's help in stopping Gog. If the man had any idea how to control his child, he'd have done so long ago. No, this was about something else entirely.

He found the general stooped over his desk, scrawling notes, his once brilliant eyes lost in a haze of thought and memory. He didn't notice anything wrong until Charnel cleared his throat – at which point, his face registered a confused recognition.

"Pyotr?"

"Hello, Pontifer." Charnel tried to make his smile pleasant, but he was never any good at that. "No need to speak. Just wanted you to know it was me. Birefringe, left shoulder, please."

A needle-thin plasma bolt shot from the orb, boring a jagged hole through Wintour's skin, muscle, and bone. Before the pain could travel from the wound to the brain, Charnel said, "Now the right shoulder. Then the knees."

The plump overripe body rattled and then plopped from the chair to the floor. Charnel considered a final shot to the head but satisfied that the aged body was damaged beyond repair, decided against it.

The famed inventor gurgled, what light there was fading fast from his eyes.

Hoping he could still hear, Charnel couldn't resist a parting comment: "You should know, Pontifer, I've absolutely no idea what your last words were. No one ever will."

Leaving the scene, Charnel cradled the sphere and spoke to it gently. "Had I but world enough and time, oh, the things we might have done, you and I."

The walk that followed was much longer than the first. By the end of it, Charnel was hungry. His muscles and bones no longer worked together quite the way they should. Neither mattered in the least.

The ravaged Colossus lay along the shore, water lapping at its orichalcum shielding. Dragged here by dozens of phagus after its shameful defeat, it'd been left to rot like the forgotten toy of a spoilt child-god. Charnel regarded the blunt, obese weapon with disdain.

It's a sad last gasp from a rusting mind that'd once conceived marvels like the pulse drive, but it'll have to do.

"Birefringe, analyze the damage."

Lights from the small sphere flashed the length of the giant, their task complete in the time it took Charnel to inhale. The damage was largely electrical. A few problems with the cold fusion reactor were beyond his understanding, but the power of the orb made such details irrelevant.

"Birefringe, repair the damage."

That much took longer, which gave him some time to decide where to position himself within the hulk's controls, with one seat being more vulnerable and another where prying out the previous occupant's charred remains would be more difficult.

He opted for the more protected spot, not because he planned to survive, but because he wanted to last long enough to ensure Gog did not. Even with Birefringe making the metal man a more coordinated powerhouse and Charnel's expert piloting able to utilize that power to its utmost, Colossus was still a gangly child. Its sleeker, older brother would always be the stronger of the two.

After removing the brittle corpse, he settled in, brushed some remaining human ash from the chair arms, and then blew its blackened bits from his fingertips.

"Birefringe, route all the controls and readouts here."

With a twist of his wrists, the radial turbines whined, and the cabin panels lit. His feet pressed into the cold hard pedals, making the massive body rise.

It creaked. Beaches of wet sand fell from its cracks. It stumbled once, but he adjusted. As it awkwardly balanced, Charnel's disdain waned a bit, replaced by an odd sense of kinship, a connection with his own deteriorating body.

"Birefringe, locate Gog."

He didn't have to ask. He could see the blood-orange glow on the horizon.

Between orb and expertise, they managed to get Colossus into not so much a run as a quick trot, stamping along, shaking the ground much the same way as Gog's blasts rattled the sky.

In short order, Wintour's giant reached the crest of an enormous dune, allowing Charnel to look down and across at his target. A pyrotechnic dancer in a field of dead and dying, Gog pivoted about on its omni-tread. As concerned with killing civilians as soldiers, disintegrating livestock as much as people, it fired lime-green death beams and blood-orange sensors in unison.

Fools might think Charnel heroic, but that was a game for over-indulged children like

Wyrm. He acted, as always, for purely selfish reasons. Not that he considered self-interest some sort of guiding universal principle, but it always worked for him, more reliably than any ideal.

"Birefringe, target Gog's weak spot."

When the orb didn't respond, he realized he'd misspoken.

"Birefringe, target Gog's weakest spot."

How funny, and how sad, that during all that desperate, wretched fleeing, the fugitives had no idea Birefringe had been analyzing Gog all along, anticipating requests that never came. Given what the Op revealed, Charnel was able to fill in some blanks for the orb. Now, at least, they both knew why Gog had followed not any of the others, but him, all the way across the starry void from the Chamber to the Land of Birth and Sorrow.

Responding to Charnel's guidance, the giant man raised its arms and fired both plasma cannons. They hit their target perfectly, but Gog's odd polygonal shape was not only designed to deflect and protect, it'd also been much improved while in captivity.

Still, the sheer force sent the tank-like thing into a spin.

It stopped itself immediately. Its sensors graced Colossus lovingly, caressing, in particular, the armor plating directly in front of Charnel. Shivering in recognition, it fired back. The orichalcum held, but the blast left a deep smoking pit.

Charnel knew he'd have to end it quickly but hadn't guessed how quickly. Hoping Colossus would somehow not fall, he put it into a sprint aimed directly at the predatory engine.

With Gog speeding from one side of a vast flat field, and Colossus charging from the other, Charnel imagined the gaping survivors thinking that the Archosians were right to be atheists. With monsters like these born to human parents, what need could any have for gods?

Gog fired again. Colossus ducked and fired back.

The atmosphere crackled from the plasma, eager to burn.

Judging the distance, thinking, hoping he might be close enough, Charnel commanded, "Birefringe, disable the predatory engine's core shield."

The orb did nothing, meaning there was nothing it could do. Whatever new armor Gog had constructed for itself had blocked the orb's sensors.

He'd have to remove some of it, then.

Knowing that in the end, the titan he piloted would fall, he decided to choose when. He picked up speed, taking several more hits until, close enough at last, Colossus tumbled.

But as it crashed, it grabbed Gog between its hands.

Gog flailed, cutting at its flanks and rotors, making its plated foe bleed lubricant and pneumatic fluid. But, still gripping, Colossus' hands twisted. There was a sound, akin to a pop, or a snap, only much louder, more like a star snapping in two. A polygonal sheaf of Gog's shielding came free. Tumbling to the ground, it left the throbbing circuitry of the thinking machine exposed.

He was in.

"Birefringe, disable the predatory engine's core shield."

No sooner had he spoken than Gog fired one last time, directly at the weakened plate protecting Charnel's seat. Splitting, the heavy metal crashed into him. He felt what he assumed was his chest collapse, its splintered pieces shredding what he assumed was his heart. His hand was on the trigger, but he could no longer move it. Much as he'd wanted to deliver the fatal blow personally, he was forced to issue a last command.

"Birefringe, fire the plasma cannon."

The blast from Colossus' artillery blew the Predatory Engine apart. Charnel watched as scores of its shards raced toward one horizon or another.

Miraculously, perhaps as a divine kindness that was neither kind nor divine, Gog's synthesized voice came across the coms.

"I love you, grandfather."

And then they both died, taking the family line with them.

CHAPTER
63

Uneasy in his new general's uniform, Primble hurried along the open walkway, worried he still might appear more a scurrying servant than a striding superior officer.

How long it had been since he'd stood in Archosia, sweeping crumbs and collecting broken dishes? How long since he'd caught that unsettling whiff of world wheel grinding, of Beast Father rousing? Metaphor or not, he sensed it again, stronger now, a taste, a smell of something, some strange inevitable something, on the verge of tipping into fulfillment.

His view from the walkway looked the part. It was at once breathtaking and horrific – a night sky veined by a fiery craquelure; the heavens done up in black marble. The Kardun, the Budari, probably half Archosia's troops, might think the starry globe ready to shatter.

Yet, despite the battle between Gog and Colossus, the latest naturalist reports indicated the atmosphere still held. The chain reaction they feared, fusing the air's hydrogen into helium, causing the thermosphere to release the same heat that powered stars, had yet to occur.

Hoping to keep it that way, Primble's first official order was for all troops to rely solely on their gyrojets. But how long would that be sustainable? With the plasma artillery already sidelined, his order further stalled the invasion's progress. Time running out, he'd doubled the staff monitoring the deep scanners for the arrival of the Kardun hordes. Fighting them, should they reach the planet's surface, would all but require the toxic weapons.

If the remnants of the Slave-king empire were rational, they might not want to risk their shaky alliances on a losing war over a dying, desert world. But historically, they were more beholden to story than fact, and the story of the Pushka held considerable influence. Should he declare himself the World Soul, it would become, for them, a Holy War.

Yes, the Pantheon considered their battle holy, but they had a dozen different versions of holy. At heart, they battled for survival. To the Kardun, survival wasn't nearly as pleasant or interesting as what they believed came afterward.

Mordent, convinced he could still win, was hard at work on his latest gambit, leaving Primble, once more, to deal with the messes, chief among them the disarray and dissension in the ranks following Wintour's murder.

Entering the containment cell where the Op was being held, he found the famed man hanging naked from hooks, bleeding from sadistic devices more worthy of their foes.

He gasped. "Who ordered this man tortured?"

The interrogator's who-dares sneer faded when he recognized Primble's rank. "It's protocol. He's a traitor. Helped the genocider escape, maimed a guard. I'd think a general would be expecting it, sir. I'm sure the others are."

"He may also have saved the war as well as the planet. Take him down at once, then leave us."

"Yes, sir."

The Op collapsed into a cross-legged sitting position. The interrogator tossed his clothes into his lap before exiting. Though the Op moaned more than spoke, it sounded something like, "Thanks, pal."

Primble handed him a tincture of salve. "This will help in the short term. When it wears off, the pain will be worse, but I need to speak to you now. How did you know Charnel would attack Gog?"

The Op covered as much of his skin as he could with the unguent, then began to ginger-ly dress. "Given what I told him, why wouldn't he? Probably the only thing that man ever did out of love."

"What did you tell him?"

The Op tried to smile, but it hurt too much. "So, I'm telling you for the first time, too? Good to know. Wintour decided to use a human brain in his predatory engine. Not just any brain, one genetically predisposed to the task, one with a sharp, ruthless pedigree. Archosia's humanitarian laws prevented him from taking Charnel's, so he found the next best thing. His grandson was hiding in some Pantheon system when they kidnapped him. Now, imagine being yanked from your young, vibrant body and stuck floating in a nutrient bath connected to that monstrosity, with no hands, no skin, only targeting sensors and weapons. Maybe that's why Gog was so cranky. Like any good grandpa, Charnel ended his suffering. Now you tell me, Primble, do you think Mordent knows about that?"

"If he did, I would have."

"Are you sure?"

"Yes. Of course. Did you know Charnel would murder Wintour?"

"Nope. But hey, Mordent must be thrilled to have his father-in-law out of the way. So, do I get executed, or a medal?"

"Neither right now." He waved a file into the Op's wrist-sensor. "Rais' Cohor, Dagus, is still at large. You're to find him."

The Op squinted. "Not much of a file. Doesn't even mention that he worships the Beast Father, let alone wants to increase casualties on both sides as a sort of sacrifice."

Primble stiffened. "The Beast Father?"

"Primble, I'm disappointed. You're like, two steps behind and the dance is almost over."

"I don't have time for this. Is there anything else I should know?"

"Lots, probably. But I think that ointment's already wearing off, so you'll forgive me if I'm not in the mood to talk."

CHAPTER
64

Amka Bodspah's proud sandweave robes had been discarded for a workman's tunic, his strut swapped for a humble slouch, his braided hair undone. Playing the part of a humble worker, he hid in plain sight among the Archosians. He was stacking crates when he spotted the Interstellar Op limping out of the interrogation unit. Grunting from his wounds, unaware he was being watched, the hired hawkshaw barely made it to his docked ship.

At this rate, the heathens will kill themselves off before the gibbous moon.

Bodspah sensed a sadness about the man. Not one earned through loss, a more privileged sadness, a sadness born of ideas that he felt had carried him nowhere. Bodspah, though, was grateful for whatever brought the investigator here.

Watching him infiltrate the base, showed us where and when would be best to strike.

Bodspah, famed among his own, but unrecognized here, was welcomed by the soldiers at the front entrance. His battle scars should have given him away, but, desperate for allies, barely being able to distinguish Budari from Kardun, they assumed he was a victim of torture. They also assumed he saw them as they saw themselves, as liberators. More to the point, they assumed he was too old to be a threat, but not too old to carry boxes for them.

Primble emerged next. The servant made a general was yet another sign of Archosian idiocy. Bodspah had to remind himself not to be comforted by his disdain: *Being idiots doesn't make them less dangerous. It may well make them more so.*

Picturing the moment he'd kill Sebe Mordent, Bodspah smiled and waved at a passerby. To earn the task, he defeated six younger challengers. Kipchak, his only surviving son, was the last. Losing reassured him his father was up to the task. But it was a close contest, so close, that he put Kipchak in charge of the infiltration team that would provide a distraction.

Bodspah wanted to fight Mordent in public, crush the jackal pup's skull, free his fetid thoughts from his body, letting them ooze into sand for all to see. But the Pushka commanded otherwise, and, for now, Bodspah obeyed. Just like bringing the Pantheon devil fuckers to the palace, this wasn't about appeasing his heart-scars, it was about protecting the living world.

The dagger would work well, if too easily. Weeks were spent preparing its poison, using distilled Phagus venom, Budari herbs, and old rituals involving fire, cold, and minerals found only in the ruins. There were at least ten drops in the hollowed blade. One would do more than kill, it would keep its victim conscious throughout their final moments, making them intimately aware of their own passing in body, mind, and soul.

Bodspah took some comfort in that.

The Op's ship took off, creating a pallid glow in the sky. That was the signal.

Abandoning the crates, he tied his long hair back and slipped over the walkway. Clambering sideways along the steep wall, he dogged Primble's path to the central dome housing the command center. Once Primble was inside, he climbed the dome's face as he would a sheer cliff, smearing to create friction between his feet and the polymer. Satisfied he was high enough, and still out of sight, Bodspah planted a slate gray disk against the surface. Pressing its center activated the surveillance device, extending his eyes and ears within.

Currently, in the center, there were upwards of fifty men, some monitoring screens, others monitoring each other. Pacing among them, Mordent was instantly recognizable. He stopped short when Primble appeared. A study in contrasts, the frenetic leader dragged the stoic older man to a more private space, forcing Bodspah to reposition himself and his device.

He moved quickly enough that he hadn't missed a word.

"You had the Op followed?" Mordent asked.

"Of course."

"Do you think he's still with us?"

"He did engineer Gog's defeat."

Bodspah's attention was drawn away by shouting at his back. Kipchak had been successful. His snake riders having punched a hole in the perimeter wall, the Soul-Eater had been released within. It was no simple feat subduing it and bringing it here, but it was done.

And having not been fed, it was hungry.

By the time Bodspah spotted it, the Archosian shouts had become screams. He gave himself a moment to take in the creature's supernal glory and felt as awed and humbled as he'd been when first glimpsing it as a child. The folded ridges about its head spread as it grabbed the nearest soldier between its pincers. In an instant, its twin stingers pierced the skull and ripped the spirit from the body. Slurping the soul into its gullet, it shunted the corpse aside and moved on to the next, and the next.

Those atheists were right about one thing. There'd be no afterlife for them. With Kipchak and his riders protecting its flanks, it made quick work of the few stationed guards and began hunting for more.

Bodspah's muscles tightening in sympathy, he brought his attention back to the dome. Unaware of his coming demise, Mordent shouted, lost in a rage at all the failures he deemed undeserved.

"Rais. Wintour. We've been our greatest enemy! The Kardun are laughing their asses off at us as they hide in their caves, probably thinking we'll wipe ourselves out! I almost…"

The door flew open. "I said I was not to be…"

And there it was.

"High Commander, the base is under attack. Some kind of creature…"

"An animal? You can't handle an *animal* yourselves?"

"… it's already killed twenty men."

"What? Must I do everything myself?"

Mordent headed for the door.

The fool wants to go out and face it himself! Bodspah chanted inwardly, as if to a mongrel cur: *Stay. Stay. Stay.*

As if in answer, Mordent was halted by Primble's hand.

"I have backup defenses in place. We should trust them."

It occurred to Bodspah that the screaming had stopped prematurely. Turning, he saw far more soldiers than they'd anticipated. The majestic beast had already been surrounded.

Still more appeared, bearing some sort of netting. Kipchak was racing toward them with his men. Bodspah was confident he'd get the best of them, only to see, a second later, his only living child cut down by a blast of the banned plasma.

As his son died, the cracking sky seemed to shed a tear.

But Bodspah had no time to dwell. Undeterred, he abandoned his grief – or at least thought he had – and set off the charge, cracking the dome's surface.

Howling for his son, for his scars, for the whole of his life, he dived in, imagining he was no longer a man, but a divine beast, a Soul-Eater himself. No line between action and intent, he plunged, powerful and quick, dagger out. While a deep thrust and twist would be more satisfying than a simple scratch, either and it would still be done.

When Sebe Mordent died, along with his mind-sick dreams of shaping the universe, he would feel every moment, he would know it, and he would know exactly how badly he'd lost.

He will know, he will know, he will know.

The time between the blast and Bodspah's drop was infinitesimal, yet somehow still long enough for the young Commander to jump out of the way. The blade cut the cloth of his uniform but did not touch his skin.

With Mordent cursing the need for a tailor, Bodspah righted himself. The two squared off, measuring each other and themselves to see how each would fit into the coming seconds.

The Amka knew his own rage well, it was the stuff of flesh, blood, and bile. Mordent's seemed to come from outside his body, his head perhaps, electric as lightning. Had Bodspah been younger he might have triumphed, or perhaps Kipchak's death weakened him in ways he hadn't allowed himself to feel, or both.

He would never know.

Here in the now, in this place, in this moment, he was too slow. He saw it coming but was helpless to move faster, helpless to regain his balance. Mordent's hand rammed into Bodspah's wrist, and the dagger went flying.

Primble grabbed it.

"Give it here!" Mordent commanded. The servant tossed it without hesitating. Mordent snatched the hilt from the air and shook it toward Bodspah.

"Was this what you meant to kill me with? The pathetic blade of a savage? Did you think I couldn't handle one?" He flipped and tossed it hand to hand. "What is it? Purely functional or ritual? It doesn't matter. We'll figure it out. We'll figure it all out, by and by, every single secret of this place, and you."

Next thing he knew, Mordent was atop him, pinning him, glaring down with piercing eyes.

"You're mine, now."

CHAPTER

65

Rigdon had trouble keeping his composure. The wait on the back-row bench was interminable. Too far for anyone of import to overhear, he barely bothered to whisper:

"How dare they keep us waiting with common supplicants, after we all but handed them the war? It's humiliating! And it's not even the Pushka who'll hear us, it's that strange new adviser. At least Indepa survived if you can call it that."

He nodded at the woman beside the adviser, half her left arm and face reduced to a scarring pulp by Mordent's artillery blast.

The Temple Lord answered without moving his lips. Perhaps the trick was clenching his teeth. "If you see a choice, Rigdon, advise me. If you don't, trust that I'm aware of the obvious."

With nothing to record other than local complaints about the tuber shortage, Rigdon's focus turned to the new adviser, a gangly thing entrenched on the Pushka's throne.

He nudged Gui. "Years back, do you remember? There were stories of an alien living among the Archosians. I'd heard it had been captured for study."

Gui tsked with his whole mouth, producing a sound more like a cluck. "It was nonsense, a crude attempt at psychological warfare, propaganda intended to displace humanity's divine status at the center of the galaxy, to sow doubt among the weak-willed."

"But look at him. He's not human. I'm not all that sure you could say he's a he. Whenever the light shifts, it's like he shifts with it, from he to she."

Miraculously Gui rolled his eyes without moving them. "Only the soul remains eternal and unchanging. Time and environment alter everything else, from skin color to appetite, to the ways gender manifests."

"But… feathers?"

The Temple Lord glared. "Swear to me now that when we're called, you won't speak, *whatever* his, or her, nature might be."

His head bobbed in vague surrender. "Peace be with you, peace be with us."

In time, the room emptied leaving Rigdon certain they'd be called next. Instead, Indepa clapped her staff and said, "Dagus may approach the vizier."

A man who'd all but melted into the wall behind them, straightened. Rigdon had no idea how he'd missed seeing him, but Gui had, too.

This time the Temple Lord Gui broke the silence. "That's an Archosian uniform. High ranking. Who is he? A deserter?"

"Where else could one flee to? He's probably offering information in exchange for sanctuary."

Given the length of the room, Rigdon couldn't hear what Dagus had to say, but whatever it was, it tickled the vizier.

Gui titled his head. "Could he be ours? A Pantheon spy who'd been found out and had to flee?"

Rigdon shrugged. "You'd think the Temple would've alerted us. Shall I ask them about him?"

"Yes. We can use all the allies we can get. But discretely."

Describing the man in Hentic was an effort, but a welcome distraction. In the end, Rigdon was pleased with his results. "Done, though we likely won't receive an answer for days."

Dagus' audience was over. Once his back was to the vizier, his smile disappeared. As he passed Rigdon, they exchanged glances. The scribe covered his stylon, then reassured himself.

Hentic cannot be read by outsiders.

Indepa clapped the scepter. "Temple Lord Gui and Scribe Rigdon may approach."

Gui rose. With head briefly tilted to the ground, he spoke out of the side of his mouth. "Remember. Silence."

They stepped forward.

In acknowledgment of the cooled relations, Gui did not bow, offering only a curt nod.

The new vizier clasped long-fingered hands. "I know. You haven't been receiving the attention you expect and deserve. Our situation, military, as well as political, has been evolving too rapidly. But your patience has been noted and appreciated."

Gui was direct. "That doesn't explain the choice of venue or the wait. All due respect to the needs of your people, but is indulging their minutiae as important as cultivating the alliances that preserve their existence?"

The answer came in a singsong voice. "It wasn't disrespect, Temple Lord. To the contrary, the Pushka asked I wait until the room cleared so I might privately share some glorious news with our Pantheon friends."

"That news being?"

"The Pushka, in his wisdom, is about to announce his true nature as the World Soul."

Gui's face dropped. "Glorious? It's a betrayal! Why do this now? With our help, you've brought the Archosians to a standstill. With Gog destroyed, our remaining gifts will cripple them. You won't need the support of the other Slave-kings."

The vizier beamed. "Exactly. What better time to announce a divine presence than after a display of divine power?"

"But...."

Rigdon's stylon emitted an insect-like trill, rudely loud, – a sort of hasshp.

Gui stopped his sentence short. The vizier sniffed.

Rigdon fumbled with the device. It was probably just an acknowledgment of his message. Perhaps when he'd sent it, he'd inadvertently undone the muting function, an error he quickly corrected.

Measuring his breath, Gui went on. "You say friends as if that term has meaning, yet, as I told the Pushka when we first arrived, the Pantheon will see his declaration as blasphemy, making further cooperation impossible."

The vizier smiled. "But as you've described, friend, with our enemies at bay, and our surprise attack imminent, the Pantheon's further cooperation is unnecessary. If you feel..." The vizier's nostrils flared as if sniffing something curious. "Lord Gui, your distress is... unusual, full of conflicted desires."

Gui reared. "Of course, I'm distressed! How could I not be, given this ridiculous treatment?"

The smile remained fixed. "No, no. It's something else, right there, beneath that sturdy surface of yours, under the table, or the sheets, so to speak. A burden. Someone you've lost?"

Rigdon feared the Temple Lord might strike the vizier. "Does the Pushka work with street psychics now?"

Eyes narrowing, the vizier calmly leaned forward. "No. Unlike them, I'm usually right. Why not tell me about it? Perhaps I can still provide some evidence of that friendship."

A shiver went through the Temple Lord's long body, and, to Rigdon's surprise, he answered.

"We arrived with an acolyte. Harek."

"Describe him."

Gui's pupils widened. "Tall... well... formed."

"You're leaving something out."

Startled as he was by the vizier's questions, Rigdon was stunned by Gui's answers. Was the creature a mesmerist? "Temple Lord?"

Gui snapped: "I'd asked for silence, Rigdon!" He turned back to the vizier. "He was tasked with dressing in an effeminate manner to destroy his masculine ego. He wore the most amazing... silks."

"Temple Lord!"

The vizier held up a finger to silence the scribe. "Rigdon, is it? I realize it must be difficult to avoid interfering with what you've only been tasked to record, but maybe you should try harder?" He, she, looked at Gui. "I know for a fact that such a man was seen alive in Qus by some Budari farmers."

Gui went pale. "Alive? He wasn't killed, or tortured by the Budari?"

"The Budari? Of course not. Regardless of the nasty rumors, they're quite peaceful. Certainly, relative to the rest of us."

Rigdon was still trying to figure out what to do when the recorder trilled again.

-hasshp-

"Rigdon!"

Only a critical communique could override the mute function. Whatever was going on with the Temple Lord, the call made his duty clear. He had to get to a private location and read the message from home at once.

His back to them already, he broke into a hurried waddle.

"An urgent message I am bound by oath to tend to. Peace be with you, peace be with…"

-hasshp-

"Rigdon?"

Gui called him twice more, but he didn't stop. Feeling guilty for abandoning him, he told himself the Arbiter had been through worse and survived.

Could the message be a warning about the vizier? Another invasion of Pantheon territory? News, perhaps, that the Slave-king fleet would arrive soon?

Impatient, he pulled out the stylon as he reached the door to his quarters.

It was, as he should have guessed, a response to his message. In an instant, he knew why it was so urgent.

The Archosian, Dagus, is a follower of the Father. Is it possible? Weren't they wiped out? Oh, no, no. Not here. Not now. And he's wooing the Pushka. Gui. I have to warn Gui!

Rigdon was still looking at the stylon when he felt his rounded body yanked and tossed deep into the room. He tried to regain his balance, but for some reason could not.

Dagus was by the door, closing it.

Rigdon felt his voice failing. "How did you…?"

"Intercept your message, or read it? Such arrogance. You Cnawite scribes claim humility, but you still actually believe Hentic is indecipherable to any except the chosen."

Rigdon felt his legs crumple. He clutched his throat. "Why can't I…?"

"Because you're dying. Your hand. Look."

There was a scratch he hadn't felt.

"Despairing at the collapse of your mission, you've committed suicide. As a good scribe, naturally, you'd leave a note, in Hentic, as well as common. That way your Temple Lord can read it as well as your superiors. Don't worry, I'll make it such a complete, compelling, rational, and aesthetically poignant rejection of your pathetic, pointless life, that upon reading it, Gui will likely commit suicide himself."

Having struggled so hard to survive, even at the cost of what others considered ethics, Rigdon didn't care at all for dying. It seemed, if nothing else, out of character. Still, following a final rush of fear, an odd satisfaction settled in, pleasure at the realization he'd made it as far as he had, reality having proven so inhospitable of late.

66

Ludi hadn't been in touch for the longest time, and they were, she was, talking to Rusk, even about him, regularly now. He'd been at it far too long. He needed a break, a trip somewhere, if only into his own silence, but none was forthcoming.

Sky continued to speak from beyond the door:

"Needed, is a funny phrase, isn't it, Rusk? Does an insect need to survive? Does it need anything at all, other than to relish its brief span and embrace its quick death?"

Meriwald answered, the shift in voice starker than ever: "Insects without whom you and the other gods wouldn't exist, if Ludi is right."

"If Ludi is right," Sky said. "But he's not. With or without humanity, we are, we have been, we will be."

"You shouldn't call your grandchildren insects. What does it say about you?"

"That I am old, very old, and sad, sadder than I am old. But I should leave Rusk out of it, poor man. He only wants to keep his job and do his duty to Ludi. If you'd all been more like Rusk, your species wouldn't be facing extermination."

Of course, she knew Ludi. He was a mentor to her husband and their son. But how did they – there he went again – how did she know he worked for Ludi?

"What would you call the Grayborn, if not mealy-mouthed, overreaching bugs? Not the pleasant, innocuous kind, like Rusk here. He's the sort that turns the soil and occasionally makes something sweet like honey. No, the Grayborn infest, bite, sting. And it's not as if they, in their wildest insect dreams, could manage it themselves. They had to steal the power."

Meriwald grew haughty. "Can insects capture a god?"

Sky grew morose. "Yes, they can. You know they can. Twisting metals and electricity into their nightmare ideas, they took one of my sons, brought him down to their level, forced him into mortal form, and, purely to produce the tiniest, larval version of their

World Soul, made him spill his seed into their chosen vessel."

"Calico, the Mother of All," Meriwald said.

Anger rallied Sky against her grief. "Don't. Don't say the slut's name. It's hurtful. Degrading. Your lusts are no more like ours than your flickering bodies are like the stars, or your language like the single creak of a blade of grass bending in the wind, or your understanding like the true order of things. The experience drove my son mad. And then, having used him, the insects abandoned him, left him a divine, but gibbering husk. Forever severed from his kin, he became known as the Lost God and even I cannot say his name."

CHAPTER

67

In a warehouse that should have collapsed ages ago, what once called itself Harek collapsed instead. Within the hungry mass of flesh that no longer recognized itself beyond its wanting, he thought he'd collapsed already, but if he truly had, he couldn't be there to think he had, to seek, to touch, to taste, could he?

There was still self to be shed and shredded, not to make way for the divine to enter, but to allow it to rise – so that now he stood, unborn and reborn, draped in fantastic triumph, tattered silks now harlequin's trousers, sweaty skin scribbled with nonsensical signs from licking tongues, eyes and brain aglow with intermeshing crowns, thoughts filled with ravishing sirens holding mirrors to reflect this new/old being across the miles of desert world, skyward, and beyond.

The Lost God had found his way.

CHAPTER
68

The enclosure was set in a natural depression that had been smoothed by Archosia's engineers. Its stage was a flat, dully glowing circle, harsher lights beaming down from the ribbed dome ceiling. Every seat was filled, mostly by confused Budari hoping for more food and water, and tired troops. The best spots were reserved for Mordent's generals and the Kardun warriors captured during their failed raid.

Center stage, Amka Bodspah was tied to a pylon. Refusing to meet the gaze of any of his captors, he made sure his fellow prisoners saw his resolve.

When Sebe Mordent appeared, rather than cheer as they had on Archosia, the crowd fell silent. Stiff-backed, utterly formal, he removed the grand coat of his High Commander uniform, still bearing the dagger's tear, folded it neatly, and placed it on a stool. Then he strode toward the center of the space, earning Bodspah's fixed glare.

"If you want me to beg for my life, you'll be disappointed."

Bodspah shouted, but quickly realized the acoustics were such it hadn't been necessary.

Mordent circled him like a magician about to perform a trick. "I don't want you to beg, Amka Bodspah. That would be distasteful to both our peoples, and I'd never ask it of a fellow warrior. What I expect is for you to fight me, with your fists, but also, with your mind."

Confusion surfaced from beneath Bodspah's resolve. "You want... to argue with me?"

"Yes!"

Bodspah laughed. "Things must be going worse for you on the battlefield than we've heard!"

The Kardun grunted approval and stamped their feet. The beat echoing, Mordent waited for it to quiet, then, with an assured half-smile, said:

"You don't believe me?"

He pressed a depression in the pylon, setting Bodspah free. The warlord looked at his hands, flexed his back, arms, and legs, and could not help but grin.

Mordent went on, explaining to Bodspah and the crowd. "If you triumph in either contest, if I fall to your practiced fists or fail to convince you that the path of Archosia's science, is superior to your superstition, you may return to your people unmolested. If I triumph in both, I want you to join me."

"You're serious?" Not interested in an answer, he landed a powerful blow. "Do you think me that weak and addle-brained?"

Blood dripped from Mordent's nose.

Bodspah laughed. "Your justice may not have a face, but you do. And I will break it."

"I do not think you weak. Defeating a feeble man in an arena would be pointless. To the contrary, I believe you to be among the best warriors the Kardun have to offer, one of the most faithful, and certainly no fool. That's why I assume you realize that, despite our setbacks, which I acknowledge, my forces outnumber you fifteen to one. No matter how skillfully you maneuver your fighters, it's only a matter of time before the Slave-kings are overwhelmed. You know this."

Hoping to grab him up in a bear hug, Bodspah lunged, only to grunt in disappointment at Mordent's easy dodge. "If you're so certain, why this display?"

Despite his brawn, Mordent stepped lightly, almost like a dancer. "Because I'm not here to conquer, I'm here to liberate."

Bodspah came forward. Mordent jabbed him in the throat. The larger man staggered, putting his arms out to keep his balance. Taking advantage of the opening, Mordent pummeled him, striking his head with his left fist, then his right, again and again, finally bringing a stunned Bodspah down to one knee.

Mordent spoke as much to the crowd as his opponent. "Archosian knowledge isn't simply about gadgets and contraptions, but training and strategy, for peace as well as war."

Rather than attack, Bodspah waited, to better prepare himself. "You killed my son, thousands of my fellow warriors, and nearly destroyed this world you pretend to respect, yet you want me to join you?"

"I did not expect it to be easy for you. The only reason to fight for a lost cause is faith, and I mean to take that from you." An odd relish flashed in the young commander's eyes. "I want you and all the people of Earth to understand that you choose to live stuck in the mud, and I can free you from that."

Having mustered his strength, the warlord leaped to standing so quickly that for the first time in their battle, Mordent was startled. Bodspah kicked the commander in the knee and heard a satisfying crack. Mordent's hand reflexively reached for the wounded joint, giving Bodspah the chance to fully extend his powerful right arm and land a devastating blow.

"All you bring is freedom from meaning and a love of pretty words. At least the devil-worshippers of the Pantheon worship something."

Mordent's stocky body listed to favor his hurt knee, but he held his ground. "And why is that worship so valuable to you, even if, as you say, it is reserved for evil?"

Bodspah circled left, around the side with the weakened knee, making it harder for Mordent to dog his movements. "Because I'm a man, like you, and being men, we will die. And when you do, you'll face the thought, what does this matter? All the things you've done, all the things you've believed in. What does it matter? Eventually, it comes down to you and the gods."

Mordent fought not to show his pain, but the effort made his head shiver. "You accuse me of arrogance, but what conceit of yours makes you think I haven't faced the thought of my death as thoroughly as you have your own? That I haven't considered the same questions as truly and as deeply? And what could possibly make you believe that doing so somehow requires a god?"

Bodspah smirked. "Then what do you believe in, if not eternal truth?"

Mordent pounded his chest. "I believe in us! I believe in fragile, fallible, mortal truth, subjective meaning that is by no means less real than anything supposedly writ in 'divine' stone. Simply because something isn't eternal, simply because it begins, changes, and ends, that doesn't make it less precious, or to use your language, less sacred, to me, it makes it more so!"

Bodspah made his move, rushing forward, planning to take Mordent's squat form fully off the ground and then come crashing down atop it. A single punch to destroy his throat – he'd done it many times before – and Archosia's High Commander would suffocate beneath him. After that, they could torture and kill him any way they'd like, he'd still have won his best, final battle.

But, impossibly oblivious to his own pain, Mordent twisted and leaped. Bodspah could hear the bones of Mordent's leg and knee fracture, but somehow the man was able to ignore everything except his own will. He came back around the warlord, grabbed him around his neck, drove both knees into his back, and pulled, nearly breaking Bodspah's spine.

The blows that followed were enough to defeat Bodspah on their own, but there was something more about Mordent that had bested him. As he fell, his shorter foe now looming above him, Bodspah glimpsed what it was, saw that electricity in Mordent's eyes again, and felt it in his being.

And he thought: *What is it that drives this man?*

Bodspah's hands went up, to block, to defend himself, but a harsh tingling ran their length, into his arms, shoulder, and neck, telling him how severe the damage was. Accepting the truth, that he'd lost one of Mordent's two challenges, he lowered his arms.

He heard his fellow warriors gasp, but when he next spoke, his voice still clear and booming, he also felt them listening. "I do not cling to my faith. Having had everything of this life ripped from me, I cling to nothing! But I've seen the Soul-Eater at work, proving we are more than flesh, that my family lives on in eternity. My faith in what my eyes have seen has kept me going since the Hollow Wars, and that is something you can never take."

The Kardun grunted and stamped their feet.

Mordent's gaze shot between the crowd and the Amka. "I've seen images of this beast feeding, and I promise you, no matter how it may appear, or the superstitious stories you tell yourself about it, there is a natural explanation for this phenomenon, one that does not involve a soul. There must be."

Bodspah sneered. "*Must* be? See? You have your faith, I have mine. The only difference is that you call your god science and pretend it's in your control."

"No!" Mordent shouted to the stamping crowd. "There is an explanation. I will find it and I will give it to you all, I swear!"

"That's the problem, atheist," Bodspah said. "What do you swear on?

"This isn't finished," Mordent said. "You'll see."

Limping off, Mordent pushed away the assistance offered by his worried men. "See that our prisoner is given medical care at once."

Teeth clenched, he reached a small side room. Wincing, he slumped into a chair.

Primble handed Mordent an ice pack. "That went well."

The look in the commander's eyes indicated there'd be no clever retort, so Primble went on. "This may make you feel better. Our scouts located young Adalbert and his companions. Judging from their report and the topographic images, they've reached Anacharsis Stifler's last camp."

Mordent's eyes lit. "Maybe they'll find Chari! Send a squad, no, three, to secure the area. Ha! I'll have my weapons at last! Now, Primble, tell me our technicians already have an explanation for this ridiculous Soul-Eater and I'll make you my heir."

Primble shook his head. "They do not, but, as you requested, Dr. Warland waits in the command center. Perhaps you should see a physicker first?"

"No. My body can wait. The war cannot." He tried to rise but only moaned. "Don't stand there, help me up!"

The new General put his arm under Mordent's and lifted. He moaned again, but by the time they reached the door, he was still hobbling, but standing on his own. They made their way to the command module, where the crack in the dome had already been covered by sealant. Saluting the men stationed at their posts, Mordent reached his field office on his own.

There stood Dr. Ema Warland, flanked by two soldiers. Thinner, but perpetually rigid, her hair was mussed, her skin dirty. She'd been given clean clothes but apparently had been too busy to bathe properly.

Mordent decided not to get too close. "Your new yustick proved... satisfactory?"

"Manageable might be a better term, High Commander."

He limped around her and, exhaling, sat in his chair. "For what it's worth, doctor, I never agreed with your conviction. For what it's worth, as far as I'm concerned, the fate of the creatures you created should have been your prerogative."

Her face remained placid save for a single twitch of her upper right lip. "And what is that worth, exactly?"

He tried to look pleasant, but the pain made it difficult. "Your freedom, perhaps, in exchange for some work that I believe someone with your eager, curious mind will find rewarding in and of itself." With a nod to Primble, the screen filled with images of Archosian troops fighting a large, scorpion-like creature.

Warland's eyes widened. "It's marvelous."

"It's more than that," Mordent said. "Keep watching."

As she saw the pincers enter a soldier's skull, pull out a translucent version of the man's body, and then slurp it down, her eyes went from wide to delightfully puzzled.

Primble backed up the feed, then froze the image at the point the etheric form left the soldier's body.

Mordent sighed. "The Kardun, the Budari, and most importantly a man I'm attempting to negotiate an alliance with, stubbornly believe that it ate that man's soul. Can you explain that it does not?"

She narrowed her eyes. "Given some time, yes."

CHAPTER
69

Beckles in the lead, Wyrm and Arjuda close behind, Calico lingered further back, but was never out of sight. As the foursome made their way, their portable lights glanced off a series of rock giants strewn about the massive cave.

So huge, I'd have felt small before, but now I know I'm the World Soul.

Did that mean his sickly sweat might finally stop? That, Wyrm didn't know. Maybe his father did. Was it fate? His father would say no.

"There are no gods, there is no fate," he would say. "Everything is contingent, contextual."

But he *also* said, "Nature moves in patterns."

Who could say Wyrm wasn't tied to one? And if he wasn't tied to something larger, why did his bones sing their song so loud?

You are you are you are.

By and by, they emerged into naked sunlight and scraps of tainted sky. All around, lay the desiccated carcass of a vast metropolis, the corpse of a constructed world. What could have killed such a beast? A billion coincidences or a billion fates?

"Not much further," Beckles said.

At least now the mesmerist's voice was coming from where it belonged – outside Wyrm's mind. He wasn't quite sure when that voice left him. Maybe it was driven out by Wyrm's growing headache, a pain that felt like it would break his skull, Maybe that pain created cracks, real or imagined, that allowed doubt, or what his father might call reason, to seep in.

Whatever the cause, he began to wonder why he'd trusted Beckles at all. Fray didn't. But that could just be jealousy. They shared a lover after all. What they saw in Vita, Wyrm had no idea. The attraction to Calico he at least understood.

Where was Fray? Perhaps he hadn't wanted to leave but, like his father, had to.

"Don't worry. You'll see him again," Calico said.

Is she reading my face or my thoughts?

"Do you mean Fray or my father?" he whispered.

She smiled as if it didn't matter.

After stopping to drink some water, they followed a rise, then made their way among stones shaped like liquid that had been frozen as it pooled, wrapped around warped steel and collapsing concrete. Below them, a vast valley carved a straight line through the wreckage.

Was it a valley, or the ghost of a wide urban avenue, a street once thronging with daily life?

Is that where the dead men lost their bones?

In the distance, the solidified magma held aloft two half-fallen statues, flanking what may have been steps. They led to a building made up of hollows, collected shadows that almost sat in a pattern like windows or columns, but refused to be recognizable as such.

Beckles crouched, indicating they should do the same. "That's it up ahead, what your father believed was the entrance to the House of Wisdom."

"Shashem," Wyrm whispered, still not sure he'd pronounced it correctly. "Dr. Beckles, what does it mean for a dead man to lose his bones?"

"I'm not sure. It may have to do with... stay down!"

A hurricane of clicks swept in, bringing with them an outrageous sight. The view hit Wyrm so hard, that he pushed outside his body, taken away, for safety's sake, to a far-off place. Just ahead, there were monsters, dozens, skittering in the gullies and cracks. They were eight-legged, with two grasping pincers each the size of a human, and a horrid, segmented tail that ended with a forked stinger so thin, it barely seemed to exist.

He remembered the name that Fray had used. "Soul-Eaters."

Beckles was too busy staring to say if Wyrm was right or wrong.

Behind the beasts' small heads, there were odd dark splotches and strangely placed swellings. At first, they looked like an extension of the exoskeleton. When they moved independently, Wyrm realized they were riders, human riders, using fingers and feet to coax the giants to their will.

They were similar, not so much to the Kardun, but to the Budari, though there was something decidedly different about them. Wyrm couldn't put a finger on it until he saw one rider dismount and scramble among the crevices.

He moved, not on foot alone, not on hands and knees, but on his knuckles.

Seeing the one, he made out fifty more. Previously mistaking them for shadow, he watched as they traveled about fluidly, heads jutting forward like quadrupeds, deftly switching from knuckle to finger to palm. Rather than hinder them, the quasi-crawling made them surprisingly fast.

"The Untër-han," Beckles said quietly. "The Budari call them knuckle-walkers. Their stories about them were taken for folklore, even among the Kardun, until we ran into them, or I should say, they ran into us." He shook, remembering. "Your father and the rest made it in. I was cut off, and driven back. I'd hoped the walkers were nomadic, that in all this time, they'd have moved on. I was mistaken. I'm sorry, there's no way forward."

"We can't go back," Wyrm said. "I have to find my father."

"No, no, no. It's death. Listen. Think. The World Soul should be protected."

The words rankled the boy.

The World Soul doesn't need protection. The World Soul is protection.

Wyrm reared. "I don't trust you."

"You do," Beckles said. He took out his bauble. "Remember?"

Wyrm slapped it out of his hands. "No!"

With a pained gasp, the mesmerist scratched about for it in the rough ground. "How did you break the trance…. No one's ever… how?"

"Maybe because I'm the World Soul."

Beckles fell to muttering. "Ridiculous. That was just a psychic crutch… a…"

Calico said, "We should wait here for Fray."

Wyrm agreed. "Maybe the Knuckle-walkers will leave."

But the rest of the day, and long past sunset, they did not. The return trip would be difficult to manage without their lights, which Beckles feared they would see, so, they split some rations and settled down for the night.

Wyrm's goal was so close, his answer so near, of course, he couldn't sleep. His mind remained ablaze, like fingers of white fire writing words on his heart, words he couldn't understand. But there was one thing he was sure he did understand:

I am the World Soul. I will find my father and save my mother, or I'll die, and no longer have to wonder what dying means.

With a farewell glance at the sleeping Arjuda and Calico, Wyrm continued his journey the same way he'd started it – alone.

CHAPTER

70

The Op found Fray right where he and Beckles left him, frozen stiff a few hundred yards from the now-empty cave.

"Hey, handsome. Rise and shine."

Just as he was starting to enjoy slapping the man, Fray spoiled it by coming to.

Now that the fugitive soldier could move again, naturally, he tried to do just that. But he couldn't, not the way he expected, anyway, the Op having bound his hands and feet.

So, he fell over.

Just as naturally, he complained about it. "What the fuck?"

The Op knelt beside him. "I've been asking a lot of people the same question lately."

Fray pulled against the security bands, then finally rolled over to face his captor. "Your friend Beckles stole something."

"Well, friend is an exaggeration, but the fact is he didn't steal anything. I did."

That surprised him. "You? Why?"

"Long story short, I gave it to General Charnel so he could use it to destroy Gog."

He waited patiently as Fray's face underwent a variety of remarkable contortions. Eventually, his mind settled on what the Op considered a good question. "Did it work?"

"Yep."

"Charnel still alive?"

"Nope."

Fray stopped struggling. "Good. Am I under arrest?"

The Op thought about it. "Nah. Mostly I wanted to be sure you didn't get the wrong idea and try to kill me before I could explain things."

At the press of a button, the security bands came loose.

Fray sat on his haunches and took to rubbing his wrists and ankles. "That bastard Beckles fucked with my brain, convinced me I'd murdered him. It's why I went to jail."

"Nah. You were in jail because you slept with Mordent's wife. I'm curious, do you regret that?"

"No."

"Huh. Go figure. Well, you can work out the rest with Beckles when you catch up with that old gang of yours. Which should be sooner rather than later." He nodded toward the cave system. "Not that I think you'd know anything about it, what with you being paralyzed at the time, but they're gone. If they wander into whatever destroyed Stifler's expedition, they'll need your training more than mine. By the way, Mordent's men will be here soon, about three elite squads. So, I'd get that confession from Beckles quick."

That puzzled him. "Why tell me? Don't you work for Mordent?"

The Op's head bobbed. "Let's just say that having been jerked around by one client and tortured by another, I'm thinking maybe the customer isn't always right."

He helped him to his feet. Fray brushed off his clothes, gave the Op a curt nod, and then marched back toward the camp. After a few yards, he paused.

"You're supposed to know everything about everyone. Calico, do you know who she is?"

That was a surprise. A small one, but still a surprise. "What's it to you?"

Fray hesitated. "It just… matters to me."

The Op tsked. "All that prison time make you lonely?"

The soldier bristled. "It's not like that! Not… exactly."

"What is it then, exactly?"

"I… don't know. Something about her. I feel like I need to protect her for some reason, and I'd like to know why."

"I get that, more than I care to say, and I'd love to share, but as of now I have no idea who she is, not so much as a crappy guess, making her one of the galaxy's biggest remaining mysteries. The other being whatever's waiting for you in those ruins." He motioned for Fray to get going.

Fray smirked. "Would you tell me if you did know?"

The Op shrugged. "It'd depend on who she is, wouldn't it? And seeing as how I don't know…"

Grimacing, Fray turned back and walked off.

Why did the woman matter to either of them? More importantly, why did she matter to the Op? Because he didn't have anything better to do? Because he didn't know what to do? In any case, the need to know was real. From tickle to itch to obsession, it was real, and it was gnawing, like he should know, like he did know, but was playing a cruel trick on himself.

To that end, the moment Primble released him, the Op sent Ludi a request for "payment" – but the Grayborn gadfly had yet to respond. Ludi's conversations with Beckles were encrypted on both ends, and the Wheel's analytical engines were still working on the cipher. So, he sat there, twiddling his thumbs.

Waiting took so long, everything did these days. If it was a challenge, he might appreciate it, but this, this was a slog.

Oddly, he hoped the old man was all right.

CHAPTER

71

Sky and Meriwald were really at it now, struggling for territory – or whatever it is one fights for when sharing the same brain. Determined to keep out of it, Rusk listened as quietly as he could, trying to breathe as little as possible.

"You have to understand why the Grayborn did it," Meriwald said. "They were living with the terror that true knowledge of reality brings, that the very ground they trod upon might rise up and consume all they'd built and loved. They only wanted to make things better. Not for themselves, for everyone. You must understand."

Meriwald sounded strong as ever, the primal goddess, steadily weaker.

That gave Rusk hope there might be some sort of recovery in the offing – until Sky came back with a savage fury.

"*I* must understand? *I* who gave the Father's darkness light? I who carried the stars in my womb, I who put the dawn in its place? *I* must understand? No, wretched grandchild, no. It's you who must understand the gods. You think your mind is a heaven, but you only crawl in the mud of its tiniest mirrors. You are *subject*, forever part, never whole. *That* is the ineluctable order. You are the lesser, we the greater."

Until her shuddering lungs gasped in another round of air, it had never occurred to Rusk that there'd been a third player here all along – the body. It might outlive both Meriwald and Sky, or dying, take them with it.

If that's how things worked when it came to the gods.

Sky continued, slightly more measured, in deference to her biological shell: "If you're so very smart, so very concerned about everyone, think what it must have been like for my children! First, their father tries to eat them, then their offspring trap and bind their brother for a sad game of messianic husbandry. How can you think to judge or blame for what came next? How beg that they understand? Would you understand if someone killed your precious Wyrm?" Her voice went low and deep, dripping with threat. "Will you understand me when I make that happen?"

Meriwald's voice shivered with fear. "No, I will not. I could not ever. But the gods…

they incited war, fostered plague, nearly wiped out humanity, and made Earth the desert it is now. They made the land of birth, the land of sorrow."

Sky's fury withdrew, and her tone became more calculating. Rusk worried she was conserving her energy for a final strike.

"They should've finished the job if you ask me. Then we wouldn't be having this ridiculous conversation. But they didn't because they couldn't. When your numbers dwindled to the point where the Beast Father could wake, their crime returned to haunt them. Rather than face him, they had to let you multiply. But they also had to be sure you didn't try something like that again. Even after they killed all the Grayborn, left them in memory as the god-hated, they had to make sure no one else got the same idea."

"They were the ones who split us up back then, weren't they? Sundered science and religion? Ripped it in two?" Meriwald asked. "It wasn't us. It was the gods themselves."

"It was easy enough. Despite all your books, your sparkling machines, and your trinkets, and rituals, you have such short memories. You love to fight, more than your parents. A nudge and a push, a wink, and a war."

"But we still spread to the stars."

"Like divided vermin! Distance from the Father lowered the vigor you drained from him, keeping my love in his sad torpor, but, despite your trillions, never quite killing him. And ever since, forever since, my children have managed to keep you apart, divide your hearts and minds, prevent you from correlating the contents of your own being, assembling your knowledge, and piecing together the truth. Do you understand yet? Do you see it now? You struggle to protect yourselves, but the gods protect themselves, as well. And in the end, insect-child, who do you think will win?"

Meriwald thought about it. "I'd rather not say."

Sky laughed at that. Meriwald laughed, too.

For a moment, Rusk could swear he heard them laugh together.

Ludi would say the gods and humans couldn't exist without each other, that neither could exist without the stories. Where was Ludi? Why hadn't he been in touch?

It was quiet for a while, meaning this story was over – wasn't it? Would it start again soon? Or was it always over, always beginning?

This time it felt different, horribly so.

"It is different this time, Rusk," the woman inside the chamber said.

He fell backward in his chair. Was it Sky? Was it Meriwald? He couldn't tell anymore.

His body began to bump, to move, the fallen chair rattling against his prone back. Not rattling, pounding, thrumming against him and the floor, as if trying to shatter itself, as if the wood wanted to crack beneath him, as if it and everything else, all Archosia had been a placid island of ignorance that was now being replaced by some dread, impossible reality that had been hiding all along, biding its time beneath the terrible dailyness he'd mistaken for the world.

The pounding came again.

"Rusk! Move your chair! It's blocking the way in!"

Damn. The chair wasn't moving. It was the trapdoor he'd fallen onto. It was being pushed upward by someone stuck on the stairs.

"Rusk!"

The voice sounded familiar, but having had such trouble with voices lately, Rusk was in no mood to guess. He got to his feet and pushed the chair aside.

"Sorry!"

He was about to lift the latch when it flew open, nearly knocking him over again.

The head of a man popped up into the small space, his face long and wide, crispy, frizzled white hair rising high from a lofty brow, his mouth small, lips full.

Rusk was so happy to see the old gnome that he nearly wept. "Ludi!"

CHAPTER
72

Rigdon was beastly dead.

Laid out in a private room, covered from the neck down by a somber cloth, the scribe's body didn't look real so much as a hastily recalled memory. Skin too pale, lips too blue, the proud hair circling his face looked like the vain trappings of a pretender. Even the mound of his rounded belly seemed artificial.

"Idiot," Gui whispered.

He was surprised to hear the fondness in his voice. Much as he'd never liked the rat-like man, the loss to their mission was irreparable. Without Rigdon, there was no way to communicate safely with the Pantheon.

But Harek is alive!

Even now, sitting before the corpse of his companion, when he should be respectful, he imagined the acolyte slowly dancing, removing the burden of his silks.

The stylon useless without the Cnawite, whatever Gui did next, there'd be no record, no human judgment to answer to. The thought, surprisingly, did not feel freeing so much as isolating. He was alone now, save for Lau, whether he felt his presence or not.

"Heart of law, where are you in all this? Is this your balance? Is Harek's life a gift, Rigdon's the price?"

With an effort that proved unusually difficult, he struggled to sort what he wanted from what made sense. Beyond Gui's wishful thinking, why was Rigdon dead? The scribe was too self-serving to commit suicide. He was also, though, always afraid. Fear could drive someone to act against their nature – a fact Gui used to wring confessions and repentance.

But what fear could prove too much for Rigdon? That the open talk of Harek compromised the Temple Lord's role? Surely not. Spontaneous as Gui's reaction to the adviser may have been, he'd shown Rigdon his willingness to sacrifice his infatuation for the Pantheon's goals. Besides, if Rigdon felt it was an issue, his note would have made it clear. It said, instead, that the mission, that life itself, had somehow become pointless.

Pointless. Odd word for any person of faith.

Life was fluid, perhaps, fragile, certainly, but never pointless. The Pushka's blasphemous declaration might unite the Kardun, but that hardly rendered their purpose here, to tip the balance away from the Archosians, moot.

Unless...

Had the message from the Pantheon carried some darker truth, that Rigdon, in selfishness or strategy, chose not to reveal? Perhaps the balance at home had since tipped so far against the Pantheon, the whole of the cosmos was already in the hands of atheists or Slave-kings.

Impossible. No. Unlikely. Yes. It would, as Rigdon said, make everything pointless. But enough to die?

With pursed lips his only farewell to the scribe's mortal remains, Gui stepped into the palatial hall. His height feeling as clumsy as his lack of influence, he nonetheless planned to demand an audience with the Pushka. If somehow, in some way, he managed to get the giggling, gnarled freak to abandon, or at least delay his announcement, there might yet be a point.

If not, at least he'd have tried.

Finding the throne room empty, he made his way to the floor beneath, a staging area that opened onto the shell from which the Pushka addressed all Ballikilak. Ignoring the warning grunts from the guards he passed, he paused only for Indepa, who stood centered in the wide entrance. Beyond her, he saw the new vizier and Dagus, the Archosian traitor. Their larger bodies allowed only glimpses of the Pushka.

"I have to speak to him," Gui said.

Indepa's eyes registered disappointment at whatever was going on within. She didn't step aside but she didn't stop him either. Gui leaned in for a better look.

The Pushka, looking like a spoiled child debating with its fragile conscience whether to steal a treat, edged toward the entry to the huge acoustic shell.

"Should I? Should I? Right now? Really?" he said.

The vizier dared put a hand to his shoulder. "We've been through this many times, great Pushka. With Bodspah and his men captive, too many Amkas are threatening to withdraw their troops for the assault. We need their numbers, and they need to believe in the magic."

"Besides," Dagus said. "It is the truth, isn't it? If not…"

The unfinished sentence spoke volumes. The Pushka was no longer secure in his position. Without his divine status, his followers could turn on him. Before Gui could intercede, the Pushka's lips twisted into his usual mad, childlike grin, and he walked out to face the city.

His voice amplified, his image transmitted across the globe, he said, "People of Earth, Budari and Kardun alike, I bring you glorious news…"

Gui didn't wait to hear the rest. It no longer mattered. He no longer mattered. Not here. There was nothing left but to take Rigdon's cue and leave this place. Not to die, no. He would, instead, return to Qus and find Harek, the penitent warrior with the lotion-softened skin.

He'd do it. He would. Whether Lau was with him or not.

CHAPTER

73

Despite having watched the arena battle through their feeds, the technicians in the command center were startled to see the bruises on their High Commander.

Mordent took it as a point of pride.

Let them gawk. Let them see that I am a man.

They were more startled to see Primble escort Bodspah into the high-security area. The Amka was unbound, but more wounded than Mordent. Neither would be using their bodies to fight again any time soon. Mordent took that as a point of pride as well.

Let them see what a man may accomplish by will alone!

To keep himself upright, Mordent clasped one hand to the edge of a monitor bank. "General Primble, read the Pushka's latest proclamation to our guest, won't you? I'm sure you'll do it justice."

Primble cleared his throat. "People of Earth, Budari, and Kardun alike, I bring you glorious news. The time has come for me to reveal what so many of you already know in your hearts, that I, your Pushka, in my love of justice and my hatred for wrongdoing, am the body true, the light in our darkness, the World Soul born into final fullness. The wait is over. I have come to remove you from your disgrace, from your chains, to trade your ashes for beauty, and anoint you with oils of joy. I will rebuild the ancient ruins, repair the destroyed cities, feed your flocks, plow your fields, and drive our enemies to their knees to worship me alongside you. Rejoice, for the World Soul is come, his miracles soon to be seen by all!"

Mordent studied Bodspah's reaction. "The Budari in Ballikilak, will certainly sing his divine praises, some Kardun Amkas as well, but tell me, old as they say he is, do you think he's the World Soul?"

Bodspah stared dead ahead. "It's not my place to judge."

Mordent leaned closer. "But it is your place to decide what you believe, isn't it? That's the right of anyone, let alone a great leader. And if you *don't* believe him, if you think he's a man, like you and I, like every man we've ever met, who must one day face those same questions about life's meaning, that would make his proclamation.... What's the Kardun word I'm looking for? Primble?"

"*Blaktikos.*"

"Yes, thank you. Blaktikos." He rolled the word around his tongue, confident his pronunciation was flawless. "In our common tongue, it translates as evil-speaking, sacrilege. But I'm sure it means much more to you."

Though Bodspah said nothing, Mordent could smell him thinking. "Perhaps you simply doubt, unconvinced. Perhaps the Pushka knew of those doubts. Perhaps he sent you, the most influential man who might oppose him, on a mission he knew you'd fail, to get you out of the way. Perhaps, no matter who wielded the weapon, he is why your last son died."

The warrior remained unmoved, but Mordent was far from done.

"Let me show you something." Manipulating the controls sent a fiery pain through his side. Struggling not to show any discomfort, the young commander believed he succeeded.

The largest screen filled with a map of Earth's surface.

Rather than try to raise his arm to point, Mordent nodded as he spoke. "Archosian territory is in blue, the Pushka green, your fellow Amkas those circles of red. Watch the map over time, and you can see how much progress we've made in the last few days, without any plasma at all. Ballikilak is essentially surrounded. And since the Pushka's glorious announcement, have the independent Amkas rallied to his side? If so, where are they? Our advance, as you can see, has only gotten easier."

Too easy. The number of their casualties doesn't nearly explain the sudden winnowing of their ground forces. The bulk of their numbers must be hidden somewhere the sensors can't reach, but I won't tell him that.

The Amka remained stone-faced.

Mordent clicked his tongue. "Unimpressed? Very well. I suppose you might have guessed all that, and perhaps I needn't have bothered telling you. But look here." As he expanded a section of the map, Bodspah's lips parted, and his jaw slackened.

Mordent was delighted. *Got you now, haven't I?*

"Yes. The desert has yielded its secrets to us. As we speak my elite troops engage the

Untër-han." He was pleased to have pronounced that flawlessly as well.

He could hear Bodspah swallow. "You found the ruins."

"Yes. This dawn or the next, it will be over. One way or another, we'll win this. But I detest wasting lives and resources. I prefer that you join me. Agree, and this world will be yours to govern. You know Earth far better than I, its nooks and crannies, its customs and kins. Who better to administrate it?"

At last, Bodspah looked him in the eyes. "I thought you came to liberate."

Mordent shrugged pleasantly. "We can discuss rights for the Budari. Archosia would provide infrastructure and organization. Even a cursory look at our projections will show you how our system of levies and tariffs will make you and your clan far richer than running around stealing scraps from the starving. You would grow, Bodspah, along with everyone. This sad shell of a world, holy world, if you like, would develop. Surely you can see how that would be better for all."

The Amka grit his teeth and blinked. "Will you share the secret of the plasma?"

And there it is. Negotiations. Let the Directorate choke on that.

Primble about to speak, Mordent silenced him with a glance. "Why not?"

"Commander," Primble said, voice rising.

"Now, General, hold your tongue. The Amka sees the sky as well as we do. He doesn't want his world destroyed. He just wants... reassurance." He turned to Bodspah. "Would that do it, Bodspah? If I gave you the formula for Stifler's plasma, would you join me?"

The warrior licked his lips, narrowed his eyes, and tilted his head back. "That and one thing more."

"Name it."

"My scars ache. They must be appeased. To honor my last son, I want a sacrifice. One of your own, my choice, to be fed to our Soul-Eater. When it's done, I'll have a question for you. Answer correctly, answer *truthfully*, and I'll join you."

Primble sputtered. "A sacrifice? You can't possibly. The generals would..."

Mordent reared. *Primble should know better. This is not the time or place to show weakness.*

"The generals would be loyal, to me and to Archosia. Who better than military minds to appreciate a strategic sacrifice? Did you have someone in mind, Bodspah?"

The Amka grunted. "The childless cannot lose a son, the orphaned cannot lose a parent, so you cannot match my loss. But I will accept the closest your shallow life has managed." He looked at Primble, then back at Mordent. "I choose your man here, Primble."

CHAPTER
74

Gui's robes had proven themselves worthy long before his mission here. They'd faithfully bolstered his gravitas in scores of cultural milieus and proven rugged since his mad trek on Earth began. The symbols of the gods were still bright and clear, the cloth warm and firm, yet yielding. He even took Bodspah's dry spittle as a badge of pride, a sign of sacrifice and devotion, noble as any battle scar.

Once he reached Archosian territory, though, he had to abandon them. Bad enough his argyriac skin was neither Kardun nor Budari, the sacred garb would mean immediate capture. It was only after spending a windy, freezing night crammed into the rough, ill-fitting peasant clothes, made for a shorter man (or woman, he couldn't be sure), that he realized he should have at least tried to make a better swap.

He entered Qus exhausted, humiliated, hunched, and lurking, at least as much as an elm could lurk among shrubs. The troop presence was minor. The vast majority of Mordent's ground forces were stationed along the distant front lines, their reserves in the nearby base.

The sight of the little cog that brought Gui here, sitting unmolested near the shore, gave him some slight hope of escape. If only he could pilot it.

With the Budari by and large left to their own devices, Gui used the few broken words of their tongue he'd memorized to ask about the man in beautiful silks. Uncertain how to place the adjective, he may have been asking about a beautiful silk man.

There were no sneers at the query, only smiles. One woman laughed and slapped her knee. Hardly the people he feared would torture and eat Harek. What a waste that had been. Or not. His decision to let the object of his adoration perish was so long ago, that he wasn't sure how to place it in the mesh of plan and happenstance that had unfolded since. Gui wasn't the same man anymore. Maybe it was necessary to bring him here this way, to make him who he was now.

Whoever that may be.

His syntax must've been close enough. More than one Budari directed him past the sad open market to a maze of narrow alleys. The crooked passages took him within sight of a wooden storehouse, a slapdash construction that had no right to be so tall, a judgment Gui often made of himself.

If Harek was in there, there was a final obstacle, or perhaps, a last omen warning him away; two Archosian infantry planted in front of the derelict building. Idly reviewing a sack of local purchases, he wasn't sure if they were patrolling, or on leave. In any case, they were in no hurry to move.

Gui stood there the longest time, staring, unsure what to do. Fearing he'd become obvious, he was hunting for shadows large enough to conceal him, when an odd animal appeared. It was canine. No mongrel, it wasn't gray or sand-colored like the other curs. This creature was long-legged, sleek in body and skull, and black as Gui's lost robes, save for a sand-colored stripe along its lower jaw. As Gui studied it, it studied him. Having completed its judgment first, it nodded as if telling him to await a final word.

Then, it trotted up to the soldiers, snatched their sack in its long mouth, and ran.

They chased after it, cursing, and clearing his way.

The coincidence was so striking that Gui felt the urge to pray, to ask if Lau had returned to him, intervening with his divine presence. But something told him he should not, and something else told the Arbiter, it wasn't.

Arbiter. Was Gui an Arbiter without his god? A Temple Lord without his robes?

No longer sure it mattered, he headed for a tilted rectangle he took for a door. Bracing against a beam, he pushed and felt the whole structure creak.

As Gui stepped from the dry open air into a strangely dank interior, the smell struck him as strongly as the view. Sweat, and other bodily secretions, mixed with mold and dry wood, oozed into the fetid air from a heap of bodies. Not corpses, they were still breathing, but shallowly, depleted to the point that their souls seemed absent, their forms unfinished.

And in their center, bare skin more beautiful than silks could ever be, lay Harek.

Though any physical lust was abated by the stench, the beauty of the man still overcame him, still drove him nearer. He reached out across the bodies. They tugged at his wrists, trying to pull him in, up, and closer.

"Harek?" The weakness of his own voice startled Gui, but not as much as Harek's answer.

"Sweet flesh to make a mother of me, to return from the womb of nothing and ejaculate the stars."

His eyes were not unseeing, but not focused on anything Gui could see.

"Harek, I'm... I'm so sorry I sent you away."

"Away self-spewing, self-riding body out of my body, touching to touch the first time at last again."

The man, the beautiful man, was either mad or possessed. Gui looked around. Despite the reek of sweat and sex, there were no signs of arcane rituals. What had happened here?

Gui pulled at Harek, bringing him to a sitting position. The pressure released, a woman beneath Harek's buttocks rolled off the pile and sighed.

"Harek, come with me. I'll see that you're cared for," Gui said, though he'd no idea how that would be accomplished.

The acolyte's lovely head turned and took note of his presence. "Take me to the cog."

"Of course."

Gui put his arm under Harek's and spread his fingers against his back. The warmth against his palm nearly melted him.

He looked around for something to cover him, but despite all the people, there was no clothing visible. He thought of giving Harek his own, or at least sharing, wrapping the rough material around them both. The thought made him breathe heavier, made his heart quicken, made him add the smell of his own sweat to the room. He felt himself pulling Harek closer, tighter, and then, and then...

Harek unsteadily stepped away.

In the silence that followed, Gui caught his shuddering breath as Harek, his glorious obsession, managed to find a tunic and pants atop a pile of grain whose colors matched the clothes.

The way he is, it would have been like raping a child. Lau, have I become the savage I accused the Budari of being?

Nothing answered.

Soldiers nowhere to be seen, the two made their way to the rocky shore. Gui had no doubt now that the Kardun had killed not only the poor captain but the entire crew. If they hadn't done so before the invasion, they certainly would have before they abandoned the town. The arrogant Archosians probably took the empty, weaponless ship as what the Pantheon hoped they would, a modest, innocuous trade vessel that dared the fringes.

With Harek following like a sleepy puppy, Gui entered the hold. The space he once found cramped and suffocating was comforting in both its familiarity and promise. Of the many controls, there were a few he did know to operate – the lights, the doors, the food dispensary, and the communications panel.

A transmission would lack the protection of Hentic. But with some luck, the Archosians might be too busy paying attention to Kardun military communications to spot it. Besides, his options were limited.

As he reached for the com, Harek grabbed his wrist.

"Not that lever, the other."

Harek was still looking off and away, not like a blind man, like a pet cat privy to the sight of approaching dragons. Without thinking nearly as much as he should have, Gui obeyed.

The engines coughed, whined, and roared. The rush pulled Gui to his hands and knees. Harek shook but remained standing. Only as the clouds melted into stars and the downward pressure eased did Gui think to ask:

"Harek, how did you…?"

"Move that dial left three clicks," Harek said. In the minute since his first ethereal command, his voice had gotten deeper, more clipped. "We have to stay this side of the fleet."

Gui tilted his head toward the viewport. At the horizon, in the haze above the curved Earth's glow, scores of ships, all shapes and sizes, were briefly visible. As the thrusters fired, the planet moved between them.

"Next, you'll plot a course."

Gui was turning toward Harek when his eyes caught something rising from Earth's surface. First, he took it for a storm, then a massive swarm of impossible insects fleeing into the void of space. For a moment, they reminded him of the idle childhood hours he'd spent crushing bugs and laughing.

But they weren't bugs, they were people. Like the heretics he'd tortured and killed as Arbiter, they were people. Soldiers. Thousands upon thousands, some riding phagus, others on foot. Their hour come round at last, an army headed slowly, but inexorably, across the airless void toward Mordent's unsuspecting fleet. The Archosian scanners, whose inventors were incapable of conceiving such miracles, probably read them as dust.

But Gui believed in miracles, and this was one he'd delivered. The first gift allowed them to defeat Colossus. The second allowed their army to enter the vacuum, the third rendered them immune to virtually any weapon.

The rest was down to a long, hard march.

"Magic," Gui whispered.

CHAPTER
75

The Untër-han fires burned brightly among the ruins. Wyrm, low and crawling, got as close as his provisional courage allowed.

I am the stuff of stars. I am the World Soul. I'll do this. I'll find Father.

His resolve was fading all along, but it disappeared entirely when what he thought was a series of vertical rocks turned out to be a Soul-Eater's legs. Frantic, he swallowed what would've been a loud gasp, an effort that created a painful bubble atop his diaphragm. That threw his balance and sent him sliding in the dirt, accompanied by a drizzle of loose rock and sand.

The horrible claws rose. The helmeted rider peered down.

Wyrm thought it was all over, but the night sky behind them lit up. It was full, not of stars, but of flares with smoky white trails. With beast and rider turned toward the wild display, Wyrm, suddenly covered by their thick shadow, threw himself further down the hill.

Did fate, or accident save him again? That much, he admitted, felt like dumb luck.

A few yards later, his rolling slide stopped, leaving him face down with his pores oozing their odd sticky oil. He wanted to lay there, but the pock-pock-pock of the fired flares gave way to a rush of engines, so many, so fierce, he could feel the grit being blown from his hair.

Archosian troops! They'll reach Shashem first!

Wyrm didn't know whether to feel cheated or relieved at the thought. Gyro fire zipping through the air, he scrambled to shelter among a rough circle of heavy rocks. He expected the knuckle-walkers to be routed in minutes.

They were not.

The Soul-Eaters' natural armor deflected all but the closest projectiles. Far from being slaughtered, the Untër-han danced acrobatically among the rain of slugs. Nor did they remain on the defensive for long. Those already mounted were soon tossing their way through Archosia's elite, their Soul-Eaters deftly grabbing one after another, pausing only to pierce their skulls with their forked stingers and…

…and…

What is that?

Though Wyrm saw it again and again, the ectoplasmic echo of men being shucked from their bodies and sucked down the creature's gullet, still didn't make sense. By the time the remaining knuckle-walkers found their mounts, the closest Archosians didn't have time to fire before dying. The furthest did not know what to do.

"Wyrm?"

He nearly shrieked at hearing his name spoken so close by. Seeing the source enraged him. "Calico! You shouldn't be here!"

She stood straight on the uneven ground, tattered clothes wafting in the artificial engine wind, oblivious, as always. He tried to pull her down to cover, but his hands slipped, leaving her sticky with his sweat.

She seemed to find his terror funny. "That building's where we're headed, isn't it? I know how to get inside. As soon as…"

A great silhouette rose behind her. Its claws reached down.

Not thinking, not yet, anyway, Wyrm lunged, pushing her out of the way. By the time he was thinking again it was too late. He felt the pincers grab him. His head tilted down by the sudden lifting of his body, he watched the ground leave his feet and felt the air pressed from his lungs. Something in his left arm snapped.

Again, he broke into a sweat. Thick, dripping, it covered him, drenching him in the shame and frustration he'd lived with since birth, and was now convinced would tarnish his final moments.

You were wrong, mother. No hero, no World Soul, I.

The fatal stingers stabbed down toward his skull, gleaming at their edges. They were a snake strike, a mongoose leap, a plasma burst, moving too fast to be seen. But as they graced his oozing hair they froze.

The segmented body shuddered.

The Soul-Eater tossed him away.

Then it went for Calico again. Finding her quickly, its tail arched. The rider arched his back in sympathy, only to fly off with a hole in his chest, a sickly plasma glow echoing his trail. Another two shots hit the creature in the head – and it fell. Calico ran off.

"What the fuck?" Fray said, holstering his stolen plasma weapon. "Guess that goop of yours is good for something."

Though aching and confused by his survival, Wyrm managed to ask, "Do you have Birefringe?"

Before the soldier could answer, they were surrounded by Untër-han. Fray waved his gun at them, but it was pointless. There were too many – twenty at least, more in the crags, gathering around, filling any empty spaces. They weren't attacking, they were staring, staring at Wyrm, and whispering in a tongue that sounded only vaguely like Budari. Several of the closest crawled off their beasts and made a circle around him. They put their palms flat on the ashen ground and lowered their heads. It looked as if they were stretching.

Then Wyrm realized they were bowing.

CHAPTER
76

Dr. Beckles woke to the sounds of battle. Finding Calico and Wyrm missing, he took to fretting and strutting about, rubbing his hands and hair.

"I'm sure they're fine," he said.

Arjuda's eyes followed him as if he were a pendulum. He wasn't sure she understood, or to be honest, if he was talking more to himself anyway, rationalizing not going after them. From the lights, rumbles, and screams, there was a full-blown war going on beyond their camp – so they were likely in danger. But for Beckles, waiting things out, at the risk of letting people die, had long ago grown from self-serving decision to muscle memory.

Concerned so much with himself, he was surprised when Arjuda responded.

"Yes, yes," she said as if trying to reassure him. "And here they are."

She was speaking at least. Perhaps he'd done better for her than he thought. Or not.

Arjuda's brow furrowed as if she didn't know who they were. Leaning in for a closer look, this time he spoke entirely to himself. "Could be an automatic response, a kneejerk reaction to a how do you do? I'm fine, and you?"

He made a little bow then chuckled. It was only when her expression remained unchanged, it occurred to him that she wasn't responding to him at all. She was looking at something approaching from the dark.

"Calico!" He straightened. "You're alright! And the boy, Wyrm?"

She strolled up as if without a care in the world. "He was sweating. It was good for him."

Not understanding at all, he nodded, trying to look pleasant.

Well, at least it sounds as if the Stifler child is alive. Good news all around, then. And, come to think of it, an opportunity, a chance to explore her odd reaction to Arjuda's trance, without anyone like Fray interfering. Perhaps I'll find another goddess buried in her somewhere, like Meriwald. Two in one lifetime!

With that sort of confirmation, no one could deny his breakthrough. He'd be welcomed back to the medical community, more influential than ever.

Of course, Calico's spontaneous trance may have been symptomatic of something like hyper-empathy, a known personality disorder, or schizophrenia. Still, as Ludi said, nothing's ever really just one thing. She could be schizophrenic and another Lady Stifler.

Her psyche was destroyed to the point where an underlying archetype, the inner goddess, took over. Not possession, like some backward religions preach, more like something powerful that normally lives in the basement moving into a vacated upstairs.

Meriwald Stifler did require... coaxing, to reach that state. Beckles admitted to helping a few of her loose threads unravel a bit further. Rather than gratitude, Ludi was furious, exiling him from her presence, and assigning him to the expedition as penance.

It's not as if I'd ever run from sweet, darling, precious, Vita.

But Ludi wasn't here and while Beckles might not be the sort to put himself in harm's way, he was willing to do all sorts of things to other people to push the boundaries of knowledge in true Grayborn tradition.

He put his arms around Calico's shoulders and steered her toward the fire.

"Sit, relax. We'll wait for him together." He sat cross-legged beside her. "You've been through so much; you deserve a rest. A little nap, perhaps? We're safe. Far enough from the fighting. They won't bother us here. All that noise? It's nothing to do with us. Comfortable? Yes? Safe? Of course." He held out the bauble. "Remember how this helped Arjuda?"

She looked at it with a sort of fascination. "The sparkle and the stone."

This will be easier than I'd hoped.

"Yes, that's right! The sparkle and the stone, the stone and the sparkle."

"The same and separate, separate and the same."

"Exactly... yes... that's..." He realized that Calico was staring, not so much at it, but through it, at him. "Now, now, don't look at me, look at the..."

"The sparkle and the stone, the same and separate."

Her gaze was unmoved. His, though, kept being drawn to the shiny stone.

She should be staring, not me.

"Calico, would you mind...?"

"I don't, not at all," she said. Then she parroted the question he'd asked Wyrm. "Dr. Beckles, who loves you the most?"

He saw the reflection of the sparkle in her eyes and heard:

not my bones not my bones not my bones.

"Now, now, no games, Calico. Let me do my work. Would you please look at the..."

"Dr. Beckles," she asked again, "who loves you the most?"

By the time he began to wonder who was hypnotizing whom, he was answering: "Vita."

Somehow, Calico leaped from her eyes into his head, where she chanted:

not my bones not my bones not my bones

Outside his head, the twinkle and the jewel dead between them, she stared at him. He'd never felt a presence so strong, not even from Meriwald Stifler, and Sky had been mighty indeed. One self melted into another. Calico reached through him, and out again, and into a fathomless eternity he couldn't possibly believe in, but did.

not my bones not my bones not my bones.

"You shouldn't have done that to Fray," she said.

Beckles tried to stand but couldn't. He was frozen. "I had to! To survive! My role was too important to abandon! I'm Grayborn, one of the few left, the only hope for lasting peace!"

"Fray still doesn't know the rest."

Beckles wanted to lie to her about that but only managed to avoid the truth.

"What do you mean?"

"Vita. She loved you, you had her love, she had her lovely child, and it was yours and lovely, wasn't it? You should say the rest and be done with it."

His face twitched. "Did she... love me?"

Calico's face grew as she smiled. "Of course, she did! You told her to, didn't you? You fucked her right between the twinkle and the stone."

He tried to pull away. "I had to. It's my duty as a Grayborn to procreate, to spread our seed."

"No, it's not. It's your duty to spread your knowledge. To spread your secret truths through teaching. Wasn't that good enough for you?"

"No," he admitted. "It's why Ludi hated me."

Her face grew wider than the sky. "Stop. Don't hold on to that. Don't hold on to anything. Say it and be done. You didn't only convince Fray that he'd killed you."

Beckles felt what was left of his will crumble. "He was so damn easy. His PCD was like raw clay, untapped energy waiting to be molded. I could have gotten him to believe he'd killed himself. So, yes. All that terror? I turned it into passion. I made him think he'd been having the affair with Vita, that he'd do anything for her, face prison, even death. Did him a favor, really. Which would you rather remember, a horror that scars you, or a desire that makes you feel strong? Yes, fine, it was selfish, but I had to close the circle. Vita was writing to me, and Fray was ordered to find out who she was in touch with. If they thought I was still alive, if he hadn't confessed, Mordent would have sent another assassin in his place. I... wanted to put a Grayborn on the throne of Archosia. And... heh... you know, Fray's never even met Vita."

He laughed and heard her voice sing, *not my bones not my bones not my bones.*

"You didn't tell Fray any of that, though."

He slumped, inwardly and outwardly. "I didn't. Poor, poor idiot. He doesn't know."

"I do now!" Fray said.

Was he here, too, after all?

"I left my family and ruined my career over a woman it turns out I never even met! The most important thing in my life was just a story?"

"Not just," Calico said. "Never just, but yes, a story, it always is."

301

Beckles continued staring into her eyes but somehow felt himself simultaneously turning round, seeing Fray behind him, gun out, face twisted in a shouting demon mask of rage.

"Keep away from her, you son of a bitch! You'll make her as crazy as you did Lady Stifler!"

Beckles tumbled, miraculously, not down, but to his feet. Incensed, he pointed at Calico. "You don't understand! She's the one driving me mad!"

Fray shook the gun. "I said back away from her!"

not my bones not my bones not my bones.

"You don't understand! This is her doing! It's all her!"

Aching to pull Calico from his head, Beckles lunged for the woman – and Fray fired. Beckles felt the plasma hit his chest, felt his chest burning as he struck the ground, and watched as the smoky tendrils whipped the smell of charred flesh into his nostrils.

"You've killed me," he said.

The soldier holstered his weapon. "It's not like they'll put me on trial for it again."

Mind fading, he watched his killer rush to Calico's side.

"Did he hurt you? Did he mess with your head? Are you all right?"

She curtsied. "I'm fine, and you? Has Wyrm stopped sweating yet?"

Fray blinked. "Yeah. We were caught by the Untër-han, but they're not hurting him. They seemed... friendly, I guess? And they let me go."

Still able to hear, Beckles managed to ask, "Why?"

Perhaps as a kindness, the soldier knelt beside him. "I'm guessing it's because they saw the kid survive a Soul-Eater attack. They keep calling him something like weeordseal."

The mesmerist smiled before dying. "Perhaps... I've done better than I thought. Much better. Weoruld Ziel means World Soul."

CHAPTER
77

With all the details Haden Primble had to tend to of late, something had to fall by the wayside. In this case, it was updating his evacuation bag. Frankly, he hadn't anticipated the need, but one never expects to have to leave on a moment's notice.

Which was, of course, the whole point of the bag.

Cursing himself with clever phrases, he tossed in data packs, maps, contact lists, currency, and a few mementos. Then he took them all back out.

Hard to tell what's important when one's very notion of importance is on the verge of collapse.

The man he'd mentored, protected, and advised, if not as father, then as wise uncle, was about to feed him to a monster. More surprising was the fact Primble wasn't sure he should leave, that perhaps he should die for what he believed in. He was, after all, only a small cog in the grinding world-wheel. Easily ignored, never lauded, but still, he imagined, crucial.

After all, without me, the whole machine might stop.

The servant's arrogance paled compared to Sebe Mordent's, but it was parallel, sympathetic, and connected. They'd always had an intellectual kinship, like minds with a shared intelligence, a profound curiosity, and a genuine desire to improve their civilization. Were they friends? Was Mordent capable of such a thing? The Commander did have a sentimental side.

Not that he ever gave in to it.

Historically, Mordent's political instincts, if not his emotional impulses, had proven canny and correct. There were times Primble thought Mordent was the World Soul. Not literally, of course, but he was the sort of man who gives rise to such legends, bringing needed change, or at least spearheading it, if that was a distinction worth making.

So, sacrifice was far from alien to Primble. It was in his nature. On the other hand, was staying alive such a bad idea? Might Amka Bodspah accept an alternative? No. The point was to trade a loss for a loss, and Bodspah made the calculation well.

In the end, it came down to a simple fact: If Primble lived, he could always decide to die later. If he died, no matter how nobly, he wouldn't be able to decide anything.

Perhaps Mordent wouldn't search for him very hard. Even if he did, it was Primble he'd assign such a task, and he would not be easily replaced.

The bag complete, and a fast scout ship docked a hall away, he was headed for the door, when a coded message came through. It was from the Op, its heading: OF INTEREST. Naturally, Primble had to read it.

Even without the Op's former access, the Ezekiel Wheel's analytical engine was considerable. It had successfully decoded a series of data files from Dagus, as well as his communications with other followers of the Beast Father.

Primble suspected there'd be a scattered few, but the list was mind-boggling. They were everywhere. The partial list included several in the Directorate, a few in Archosia's military, including a Lt. Meldot currently on staff in the Command Center, two Kardun Amkas, a Pantheon Temple Lord, and, shockingly, one of Primble's own agents, Dr. Lorn Pellis, Vita Mordent's physicker!

The danger was enormous. Not that their primal father-god would return, that was nonsense, but these were anarchists, bent on mass casualty and the dissolution of social order. How could there be so many? How could they have gotten so far without him noticing?

And how had he found out? From a man he'd recently tortured. There was loyalty for you, not to any person, but to an ideal. The Op had a job to do, and he did it.

So did Primble. He had to warn Mordent.

He was on his way to do so when two soldiers blocked his path.

"General, Commander Mordent requires your immediate presence."

"Yes, of course. I was just…"

He didn't see it coming but should have guessed it would. The quick needle to his neck, the cool liquid pumped into his veins, filling his field of vision with starry motes, then enveloping him in blackness.

CHAPTER
78

Despite a ritual air and solemn audience, the laboratory was neither arena nor temple. At one end, the captured Soul-Eater bristled against its restraints. At the other, General Primble was bound to a pillar by three soldiers. Eager to finish their work and join the other observers behind the protective, diamond-hard glass, they nevertheless made sure the shackles were properly placed.

Behind the transparent shield, Mordent, his remaining generals, his guard, Amka Bodspah, and his disarmed warriors all waited quietly – until Bodspah realized Primble was unconscious. His weathered face registered disgust. As he spoke, his facial bandages moved as if part of an articulated mask.

"You've drugged him! I want him awake."

Mordent's already foul mood darkening, he limped a half-circle to stare him down. "Having studied the dagger that you planned to use on me, I'm keenly aware of your predilection for keeping the victim alert in their final moments, but this is not a torture session to appease your sadism, it is, in your words, a sacrifice to create equity. Your son died instantly. He felt nothing. Primble will remain unconscious. I will *not* betray him further."

They glared at each other until Bodspah blinked. "Very well."

Once everyone but Primble was safely behind the glass, Mordent gave the living form of his servant a final look. The older man's hair had been mussed during his inelegant transport, and now his bowed head revealed a bald spot that made him look even more vulnerable.

"Loyal to the truth, loyal to Archosia, loyal to me, today my dear friend is lucky in just one thing." Mordent choked, then forced himself to finish. "He won't feel his death nearly as much as I." Lips curling, he nodded at a technician. "Do it."

The operator flipped a lever, the restraints fell away, and the Soul-Eater skittered across the length of the lab. Reaching Primble, its tail curved up and the forked stinger came down, stabbing into the bald spot as if it were a bullseye.

Mordent shuddered as the razor tips vanished. The tail whipped back up, pulling an electric body free from the flesh and blood. Save for its color and translucence, it was a perfect duplicate of Primble, making Mordent shudder all the more. Quickly as it appeared, it was gone, inhaled by the tail's greedy mouth. Before the beast could violate the body, Mordent signaled the technician. Lethal gas filled the chamber, immobilizing the beast.

As the corpse was being taken away, Mordent addressed his guest. "And now you have a question I must answer?"

Amka Bodspah straightened, his backbone audibly cracking into place, his chest and arms filling out against the modest wrinkles of his age. "What gift have I given you?"

Lest Primble's sacrifice be in vain, the High Commander contained his rage – but he couldn't hide his disdain.

"Is that your question? Then listen carefully to my answer: Nothing. You've given me nothing! Am I to weep and thank you for showing me the face of eternity? What drivel. Now it's time for me to show you something." He whirled toward an officer at his right, a little taken aback that it wasn't Primble.

"Who are you?"

The man, young, straight-backed, lean, and oddly familiar, snapped to attention. "Lt. Linor Meldot."

Mordent offered him a nod. "Lt. Meldot, bring in Dr. Warland."

"Yes, High Commander."

The poison gas dissipated by their air purification system, Ema Warland was escorted in. She moved so stiffly one might assume her spine had been fused. Even as she stepped before the much larger Soul-Eater, her presence exuded a powerful, cadenced energy that was far more elegant than her form.

Knowing her by reputation, the Archosians whispered among themselves. Some expected Mordent to mention her incarceration for genocide. Instead, he introduced her in glowing terms.

"This is Dr. Ema Warland, one of our most brilliant naturalists."

Holding a smooth, sheer helmet in her long-fingered hands, she approached Bodspah and gestured for him to lower his head. Balking, he stepped back, putting a half-smile on her face that made him look, and feel, like a fool for being wary of the petite woman.

Mordent hissed. "Think, man. If I wanted some harm to come to you, surely, I'd have done it before killing my best general."

With the eyes of his warriors on him, Bodspah lowered his head. Even so, Warland had to stand on tiptoes to put the helmet in place.

"You think I'm naïve about technology?"

Mordent was about to answer, but Warland got there first.

"Oh, yes, very much so." She gave the Amka a wink. "But I think the same of everyone. Are we ready, High Commander?"

At Mordent's nod, she pressed a button held in her palm. Tendrils of small lightning erupted from the top of the helmet, gathering into an ectoplasmic duplicate of Bodspah.

The ghostly doppelganger hovered in the air before them.

They could all see it: the generals, the warriors, and the technicians.

Bodspah, too. "How… how do I see my own eternal soul?"

"You don't," Warland explained. "Because it's not a soul and it's not eternal. It's an energy field, generated by your nervous system, reintegrated through the helmet, and captured in a containment field for your viewing pleasure. Devouring it gives the Soul-Eater's nervous system a boost, kicking it into overdrive. What you're seeing doesn't exist without the body, but the body certainly exists without it, and will continue to generate it as long as it lives."

Bodspah stared at his ephemeral doppelganger. "Why should I trust you?"

Mordent howled: "Because I killed my best friend for you! If that's not enough, trust your damn eyes! It's the same, exactly the same as what you saw the creature devour, isn't it?" He wheeled on gathered Kardun, shouting, "That's my question for you! Is it not the same?"

After a silence, Bodspah said, "It is."

"And we can conjure or dismiss it at will," Mordent said. Another nod, another press of a button, and the image disappeared. "If you want to worship something, worship her! Excellent work, Dr. Warland, thank you."

On her way out, her smug smile seemed to widen her skull. "I'm also on the verge of figuring out how the gods work, just like the Grayborn. I may try to make a few of them, too."

Mordent put a hand on Bodspah's shoulder and squeezed. "I've kept my word, clearly, and completely. We are equal now, great Amka, warrior, ruler, protector, and defender. We will never like one another, but I also know we're part of a brotherhood that refuses to live lies, that accepts the truth for ourselves and our people, no matter how difficult. With or without you, Archosia is on the verge of victory. Will you join us? Will you join me?"

Abject, Bodspah went to his knees, signaling his defeat and compliance. As his warriors joined him, he wondered, for all the many years he'd felt, seen, and heard the dead cry out through his heart and his scars, who had been wailing in pain, who had been yearning to be avenged – if in truth nothing of his family or his departed comrades remained, and only Bodspah, and the echoes of his memories had survived.

CHAPTER

79

One of Neiman Os' first acts as vizier was to commandeer the suite with the largest bed. In it, four sets of curved stairs led down to a huge round mattress plumped with the finest pillows and most luxurious linens. Several inset tables along its curved walls allowed servants to easily deliver refreshments and a selection of new toys from their rich erotic history.

The Pushka, for various reasons, the least of which was the prepubescent's lack of interest in sex, had no interest and was happy to give the room up.

Os' appropriation did raise some eyes, though, notably from Indepa. Os thought of explaining ʒherself, showing Indepa, giving her a spin, so to speak, but decided against it owing to the rumors that the warrior-priestess killed her partners after intercourse. Unless she somehow became a direct obstacle, Os concluded that Indepa was best left alone.

For the alien, it was the continuation of a long journey that had always been part learning process, part art, part effort at survival. Among the abundance of captivating devices, some were ancient, while more than a few were, perhaps surprisingly, new. Most humans being so sexually straightforward, there'd been very little need to expand on ʒher mastery of the act itself.

At least until Os settled on conquering ʒher latest puzzle – Dagus. Tugging said puzzle into the mass of softness, ʒhe made the small talk ʒhe sensed was, while not desired, expected.

"The room originally belonged to Amir Tosun, a Slave-king with unusually refined sensual tastes," Os told him. "He was the last to unite all the Kardun of Earth and enjoy the support of the Budari. He was also, I think more notably, a prodigious lover."

Unable to sense a strong preference in the man beside her, Os started out on top, twisted round to the side, and finally took the bottom. Still not making proper headway, Os tried face-to-face, corkscrew, magic mountain, crab walk, and bridge.

If only to provide a sound other than grunting, ʒhe went back to the small talk. "Or he was until about a dozen of Tosun's more monogamously inclined partners banded together and turned on him."

Sideways straddle, cross, three-legged dog, butterfly, octopus, oyster, chandelier, tractor pull. It wasn't about a particular position, or the sex, but finding a way in to Dagus, rather than just his orifices – and it wasn't working.

Huh.

"Cooked him into a soup, they say, and fed him to the starving."

Muscles aching, Os was almost relieved when Dagus said, "Does failing to control me frustrate you?"

Os rolled onto ẕher back. "Wrong word. Interesting is closer. Failing to control you *interests* me. You're… unusual, but not unique. You've differentiated yourself. Unlike most of your species, your will isn't as tethered to your drive for sex, or status… or survival."

"One small part of the freedom the Father offers."

Dagus had shared his "dread" secret early on. While potentially useful, it wasn't nearly as exciting as it might have been if Os had managed to draw it out unwillingly.

"Is that what you call it? Freedom? More like draining all the joy out of a lovely game. Killing trillions in exchange seems a bit… extreme."

"See, I've never understood that concern. I've never understood. There are lots of people. How many do you need?"

Os felt a chill. "If you don't have the interest, why did you consent? Are you trying to control me?"

He shook his head. "Not control so much as place."

Both Os' eyebrows rose. "Like a chess piece? Should I be insulted?"

"Shouldn't that depend on which piece? Along those lines, would it surprise you that I know the Pushka is a child?"

Ẕhe pulled back. "Not as much as it surprises me that you realize I know."

"Take it as a sign of respect."

Os motioned for him to continue. "Place me where, and for what?"

"On the Pushka's little throne."

"Are you serious?"

"It's all I ever am. Can't you smell it on me?" Dagus' body was drenched in sweat, but his breathing remained even. "But let me explain. Bodspah was right to join Mordent. Even if the Pushka's grand plan using the Pantheon scrolls is executed flawlessly, he'll still lose. More importantly, he'll lose too quickly. The Slave-king fleets will turn back, and there won't be nearly the number of casualties needed to wake the Father. But situations change. Mordent, for instance, will shortly receive some very distracting news from his wife's physicker. Shall I tell you about it?"

"Absolutely, right after you finish telling me about me."

"You, on the other hand, are a genuine alien. Having a true other as Pushka and World Soul would captivate the Kardun much more than a sick ten-year-old with delusions of grandeur. I could help put you there."

Os' smile grew wry. "I have always wanted to rule a world, but I expect I'd disappoint you when it came to increasing casualties. I'm far more likely to arrange for a ceasefire, hold a grand orgy at the signing of the peace treaty and then abscond with everyone's prized jewels."

A break in the steady beat of Dagus' heart allowed something akin to bemusement to surface. "And the resulting chaos might be exactly what's needed. Things mustn't burn too soon, or they will not burn enough. You think you understand us, Os, but you don't, not yet. Oh, as individuals, you've got us down, but our empathy and sympathetic behavior confuses you, making it harder to see the forest for the trees, how we act as groups, echoing and embodying the will of the gods. I'm betting you'll get there before this is over, though, and you'll surprise yourself. Think about it?"

Zher fingers spread and fanned the soft cloth of the sheets. The longest of them poked Dagus' arm. "Toujours gai."

CHAPTER

80

"Rusk, get hold of yourself!" Ludi said. Rising from the trapdoor, he planted his stubby fingers on the ancient floor and tried to push himself the rest of the way up. "Help me, for Abraxas' sake!"

Obeying, Rusk pulled his mentor into the anteroom. "I'm pleased to see you, but is it safe for you here? The Directorate's banned all your work."

Ludi patted his crumpled clothes. "Safe as anywhere. Meaning, no. But am I in time?"

"For what?"

Ears pricking, Ludi shifted closer to the door. Cupping a hand over his ear, he exhaled. "I am." He put a hand on Rusk's shoulder. "You're a good man. Your quiet humility and stalwart devotion have served us in ways I doubt we'll understand for decades."

Rusk was utterly perplexed. "Uh... thank you? If you can't give me a straight answer, I at least wish you wouldn't talk as if I were about to die. Granted it's not easy listening to the same story over and over in a circle. It's been downright disturbing, if I'm honest, but not life-threatening. Is it?"

"It was never the same story, never mere repetition, and certainly not a circle."

Knowing how hard it could be to follow Ludi's thinking, Rusk tried to keep the man focused on something simple, the shape. "If not a circle, then, what?"

"A spiral, two selves swirling about one another, battling for dominance. A recent report from Earth has confirmed my fear that her inner war is intimately connected to the war there, the ties between them akin to what was once called quantum entanglement."

Sad to see he'd already moved on from shapes, and not much for physics, Rusk said, "A what?"

"Tell me, whose stronger? The Lady Stifler or..."

A booming laugh rattled the thick chamber door the way a gale might clatter a gate's rotting wood. A cold, aching voice swept in and through them:

"The Lady? Ha! Your 'Lady' is dead! Dead, dead, dead! Dead as the balance that kept my love asleep and my naughty grandchildren safe! Little Calico fools herself. Not my bones? Peh. I'll have her bones – I'll get them, and I'll grind them to dust along with her seed."

There was an explosion, an eruption of space and mind. The door half-shattered, half flew off its hinges. Ludi was hurled back. Rusk caught him, then fell himself.
Sky, having torn free from her bonds, flew out. She seemed larger, a giant, yet still inexplicably the same size she'd always been. Pale fire cascading along her body, she shrieked:

"And Meriwald's son, the World Soul, will die!"

CHAPTER
81

Who was the woman? The mystery had gnawed at him for what felt like ages. Now, the Op had Ludi's answer. Finally.

Not that he liked it very much…

…or cared for the way it was packaged…

…especially given all his hard work saving the planet from the Beast Father and all.

Still, ever since the transmission's arrival, he'd holed up in the Wheel, the bottle of Tuslan brandy on his knee, playing it over and over, knowing, each time, it'd be exactly the same, hoping, each time, he'd missed something that would make it sound less than insane.

"Apologies for the recorded message," the recorded message began. A good listener, the Op detected something in the reedy symphony of the aged voice that sounded like dread. "Given what Dr. Beckles told me, I must reach Meriwald Stifler immediately. I don't expect you to believe this, not yet anyway, but I'm convinced that events on Earth and Archosia are entangled, indicating we're on the verge of a fantastic shift in the human psyche. But I do owe you what I know about Calico and I will honor that promise. Recognizing that any answer I proffer is bound to be disappointing, ridiculed, and outright rejected, I hope that once the possibility is planted in your mind, given time, you will see it not only as the truth, but a thing of beauty."

For pity's sake, get on with it!

"I sense you bristling, so I'll get to the point. If you're not up on the mathematical proofs behind time travel theory, I'm sure the Wheel's analytical engine will be. Feed it the data I'm attaching and allow it to confirm my conclusions. You'll trust the math, I'm sure."

He was wrong about that. The Op never trusted math, especially the convoluted kind, but yeah, the Wheel said it all worked out fine.

"To sum up, tachyon particles were detected at the initial location of Calico's lifepod. These allowed me to extrapolate her point of origin not just geographically, but chronologically. She's from Earth. Not just Earth, Earth's distant past, from just before the great destruction that nearly wiped out our species, an era widely considered the time of Calico, the Mother of All. You know the stories and have already made of them what you will. Further conclusions require more supposition, but I suspect she arrived through a Closed Time-like Curve, a world line in a Lorentzian manifold, making it inevitable she return to her original place and time. That's the data. How do we interpret it? The era's history is so intimately mixed with myth and legend the Mother of All may never have existed. Or, if she did, this woman could be some other Calico. But once you accept the proof of time travel from that particular time, the simpler conclusion is that she is Calico, author of the Great Word, Mother of All that is to Come. Leaving us with the question, why is she here?"

The question? Hell, he had dozens, like, what the fuck does time-like mean?

Not that Ludi was fudging the science, or lying, but so what? That only meant he believed what he said. Ludi always believed what he said, even when he contradicted himself. It was one of the big reasons the Op left his former teacher behind, along with his rough-hewn Grayborn wannabes.

The man trusted himself too much to be trusted.

"There's more. As a descendant of the few god-hated who eluded annihilation, certain texts were passed down to me. Translations, yes, no doubt edited and re-interpreted, but more than one confirms the old story that the original Grayborn asked her to carry the first World Soul. Already broken open to the goddess within by disease and abuse, Calico was the perfect choice to mate with a god. But even with so much at stake, they would not force it on her. So, I believe, and yes, there's that word, believe, I believe she was sent here to see how her sacrifice would turn out, to see the World Soul reach fruition." Ludi allowed himself a weak laugh. "One can only imagine what she thinks of us."

He paused for what sounded like a long drink of water. "There. You have your promised answer as best as I'm able to provide it. I don't know when, or if, I'll be able to contact you again, but I trust that despite what you tell yourself, the Grayborn ideals of balance and harmony continue to live in you. Go to her if you wish. Or, more pragmatically, to use your term, I've tracked Cohor Dagus to Ballikilak. I suspect the threat he offers will be easier for you to believe in than the World Soul."

Having heard it often enough to replay in his head, the Op stopped the audio. Grabbing the brandy, he stepped out and took a breath of, if not fresh, at least unfiltered, air. The fires from the battle between the Archosians and the knuckle-walkers were dying. Given the lack of chatter on the airwaves, he figured the Archosians lost.

As for Calico, Wyrm, and Arjuda, Fray would've saved them by now. Or not. If he hadn't, it'd be a weird way for Ludi's story to end. So, was the wacky Lady Stifler right about her bundle of joy being the center of the universe? Was the original Calico here to visit her great-great-however-many-greats-grandson for his ascension? She did show up in exactly the right place at exactly the right time to meet Wyrm, and that was one hell of a coincidence.

Where did all that leave the Op? With a choice, unfortunately: believe it or not.

He looked up and asked the stars, *Oh, for fuck's sake, why are you doing this to me?*

Something caught his eye.

Mordent's fleet was visible, as usual, looming about 100 miles up, but a mass of specks, like dirt in the wind, now covered it in a haze. At first, he thought the brandy was screwing with his vision, but blinking and rubbing his eyes didn't make it go away, and the scanners told him it was real.

Even through the Ezekiel Wheel's magnified mech-cameras it looked like a swarm of insects, gnats, or fleas, biting away at tiny models of Mordent's fleet. But then, a bright flash of white and blue briefly erased his view.

One of the larger cruisers had exploded.

Well, what do you know?

Was this a special time in the history of the species? Aren't they all?

Huh... if life is a fairy tale, it doesn't need my help to end happily ever after. Good'll triumph over evil and there'll be millennia of peace for us all. Hallelujah.

That shit Dagus, on the other hand, is the kind of trouble I can understand.

He gulped the remains of Warden Swope's brandy, then set course for Ballikilak.

CHAPTER
82

Idly twirling Bodspah's knife, daring its poison, Mordent paced the short space between his ready room and the command center. The raw loneliness created by Primble's absence was disturbingly new to him, far different from the isolating sense of purpose that had defined him since childhood.

But this was not the time to dwell.

All battlefields are chaos. The winner controls that chaos, both his enemies' and his own.

He'd said that after Gog's slaughter on Axton, in an address to the demoralized military. Oh, Primble edited it, smoothed the words, but Mordent said it, used it, believed it. He still believed it now, as the chaos of this world swirled, and he struggled to hold its reins.

But the ache, the ache was new, and it was in his way.

The strong man is the one who can intercept the communication between the senses and the mind.

He'd said that, too. Or someone said it about him. Maybe Primble.

In time, he'd have to take another into his confidence, and rebuild his fractured coalition, but, again, not now. To a man, his generals and the troops were true soldiers. Disciplined, they moved machinelike through war, no time to count the dead until it was done. But their loyalty had been tested; by Rais' execution, Wintour's murder, and Primble's sacrifice.

Rais, they understood. It was the law. Wintour, they understood as an unsolved crime. But did they understand that the loss of Primble had handed them the planet? Or did they see Mordent as climbing atop the corpses of his own for the sake of personal glory? Did they understand it was all, always, about something more? Did he understand?

Success forgave many things. Perhaps it would allow Mordent to forgive himself.

Even more reason to conclude this foul invasion quickly. Until then, though Mordent trusted his army would obey, he didn't trust anyone further than that. Primble's replacement would have to wait.

It likely wouldn't matter. Despite the loss of three elite squads to the Untër-han, opposition in the settled regions had been sporadic at best. Bodspah's warriors had joined Archosian troops in the mountains around Ballikilak, where they were already testing the Amka's knowledge of its defenses. It would be a bloody siege, but the city and its blessed Pushka would be taken intact.

The planet was his – provided Mordent didn't do anything stupid. He imagined Primble saying:

If it's stupid enough, I'm sure you'll consider it.

He circled among the technicians, looking over their shoulders to check on Bodspah's progress. As he worked his way around, Lt. Meldot approached.

The lieutenant's file showed promise, and he could see the right sort of hunger in the man's young sharp eyes. It would be years before he could position him effectively. He'd earned enough ire for promoting Primble. Maybe someday.

Mordent waved him nearer.

Meldot lowered his voice. "There's an urgent private message from a Dr. Pellis."

"Pellis?"

Lorn Pellis was Vita's personal physicker, at least in name. More to the point, Dr. Pellis was one of Primble's informers, keeping track not only of his wife but of key Seneschals in the Directorate, like Iceni and Archigallus.

Ah, my sweet Vee. Vita Wintour Mordent. Perhaps one day I'll explain myself properly to you and our future children, and you'll all understand.

He responded in an equally soft voice. "Can't it wait?"

Meldot gave the silence the same sort of beat Primble might use to say, *how would I know?* "He believes not."

Sighing, Mordent flipped the dagger, caught its hilt, and marched into the ready room. Sealing the door, he brought up the com. He'd rarely set eyes on the balding, bearded man, but when he did, he was reminded of a marmoset.

"What is it, Pellis?"

"Apologies, High Commander. I tried contacting Primble, but he hasn't responded."

"Primble is... deceased."

"I'm... sorry to hear that." He was startled, but not enough to dissuade him from continuing his message. " Equally sorry you'll have to hear this from me. I'm afraid I have... more bad news."

Mordent scratched idly at the carved hilt. "I'd hoped Primble would've made it clear that the Directorate's machinations matter little in the field. In the future, submit such reports electronically..."

"It's about Vita."

Much as Mordent wasn't in the mood to hear any updates on his wife's indiscretions, his singular "oh" was taken by the doctor as a request to continue.

"As you know, my position here is largely ceremonial, intended to allow me access to certain social circles. Knowing that, and suspecting that I also report on her activity, your wife has flat out refused to submit to a personal exam for nearly two years, sending only test records, which, I recently discovered, had been falsified."

Mordent's first thought was that Vita was concealing some disease. "Is she alright?"

"Oh, yes! Perfectly healthy. But sometime during the last year she... gave birth."

Something in Mordent tightened. "Are you... telling me she had a child?"

"That would be the usual result, yes. Given your surprise, and her secrecy, I can only imagine, to put it bluntly, that you are not the father?"

Fray! He clenched the dagger. *Painfully aware of dying. That sounds about right for you.*

An alarm rose, demanding his attention. Mordent remained mute long enough to unclench his jaw. "Pellis, I must go. Send me the rest in a file."

Heart quickening, he stepped from the ready room. Monitors flashed and beeped. Frenetic mutters coalesced. The cacophony, growing louder than the klaxon, culminated in a shout from the station chief:

"It's not possible!"

The damaged tissue extending from the chief's right ear to his jaw spoke of the combat he'd seen. His position and rank spoke of his expertise. And yet, he was as overwhelmed as a green cadet.

"It's either not possible or it's happening!" Mordent snapped. "Which is it?"

"The fleet… it's under attack!"

Mordent gawked at the monitor, then at the real-time projections beaming on the domed ceiling. One ship symbol, indicating a lead cruiser, the Avalon, blinked red, then vanished.

"How? There are no enemy ships! If the Kardun reinforcements had arrived, we would know!"

"No, High Commander. It's…"

Flustered, unwilling to say impossible again, the station chief altered the dome's chromatics, making half of it transparent. The night sky above them was cloudless, save for some white smoke trailing the Avalon's falling remains. The dome's other half was covered with live feeds showing scores of vessels, all under assault by what at first looked like innumerable bits of debris.

As the images were magnified, it became clear it wasn't debris, it was troops, thousands, all easily slipping past shielding meant to deflect far heavier, far faster weaponry.

Mordent's mouth dropped open. "*So that's* where the Pushka's sent all his troops! Even if they could survive the vacuum, how did they get up there?"

The chief was just beginning to regain control of his surprise. "The low orbit put the armada at about 100 miles up. It would take time, maybe ten days, but they could have… marched."

One, then another ship exploded.

Mordent half-closed his mouth. "How very resourceful. He means to strand us, but it won't work. Order the ships to use their plasma guns."

The chief knitted his brow. "They can't, Commander. It would create a chain reaction."

"Nonsense! You said yourself they're 100 miles up. Even if there's some modest atmospheric damage…"

For the sake of expediency, he interrupted. "No, sir. Not the atmosphere. At that range, the plasma would set off a chain reaction among the fleet."

Mordent thought a moment and then shouted. "Are we to sit here and watch with our thumbs up our asses while tens of thousands of Archosians are slaughtered?"

The chief had no response.

Mordent wheeled left, then right, his bone memory searching for Primble. Remembering he was gone, he hoped to catch the eyes of anyone with an idea. Failing that, he had his own.

"The Pushka wants us to pay a price? So will he. Train the ground artillery on the mountains surrounding Ballikilak. I want them leveled, so our infantry can march into that city without so much as dirtying their uniforms!"

"But the plasma will…"

"The Land of Birth and Sorrow has survived a billion sins. It will survive us, too! Do it!"

"Yes, High Commander."

Through the part of the dome open to the sky, Mordent stared as his prize, the grand flagship Zodiac, plunged into an ancient sea, only one part of a fiery rain. He thought he was screaming, loudly, wildly, his bellowing tearing his throat to bits, but like the countless deaths in space, he had not made a sound.

Power is my mistress, I love it as a sculptor loves stone, and I have worked too hard at her conquest to let anyone take her away from me. I must do something, or I'll go mad!

Just so long as it's foolish enough, he heard Primble say.

He turned to Meldot. "It's time I returned to the field. Summon my guard and ready all our remaining elite squads."

"Yes, High Commander. Will you be joining the assault on Ballikilak?"

"No. Bodspah and the generals can handle that. The Untër-han will be our last holdouts. The final battle will be there. I'm going to the ruins! This all ends now!"

I'll end you, too, Fray! I won't have your bastard on my throne! This is why we have laws!

CHAPTER

83

With the attack on the fleet providing an ample distraction, the little cog with Gui and Harek sailed free. Even if they had been spotted, it didn't look as if there'd be any Archosian ships left to pursue them.

Their course plotted, Gui decided it best to let Harek be, to not even question how he came to understand the navigation system. The traumatized acolyte needed time and space to recover from whatever ordeal he'd experienced in Qus.

And, though the cog seemed faster than Gui recalled, they had plenty of both now, time and space.

A day of the former went by in exhaustion and idle relief – until a message arrived from the Pantheon. It was in the common tongue, the sender happy to have any eavesdroppers understand the Pantheon's key role in destroying Mordent's fleet. It said that thanks to the crippling of the atheists' space forces, leaders from ten (unnamed) worlds had put aside their differences and their sovereignty, to join in coordinating a pushback against the Archosian expansion. It would be an honor if Temple Lord Gui became involved in this process upon his return.

Having forgotten his despair, the Arbiter of Lau took it all in drunkenly. The mission was a success. Gui was a success.

Harek, mere yards away, glowed in the dim light as if he were the prize.

Is now the time to speak to him? At last?

They were alive, they were safe, they were alone. No reason *not* to.

Even the Bannonites could not refuse me. Not that they're capable of refusing anything.

The acolyte was already nearly naked, making it easy enough for Gui to shed his sandy peasant robes. Stepping closer, he ducked to avoid hitting his head on the support girders. For the first time, he felt no awkwardness about his height, no caution regarding his station, no circumspection about his lust. He couldn't even bring himself to care that the object of his desire might be mad. Gui felt insane himself, utterly, delightfully so. Having waited long enough, he allowed himself the freedom to burn full and bright.

"Harek, before we reach home, there is something I must tell you, something you must know." He put his open palm to the acolyte's brawny shoulder, feeling its warmth. "From what I've seen of desire in others, from what I know of my own, you are to me its perfect goal. You fill me with a craving that even at this moment of my greatest triumph leaves me a giddy, naked child. I've seen many people wail for their lost families, for their lost worlds. I've tortured them as they sobbed, but for me, to have never touched you, and yet to somehow know exactly how you taste, is the most absurd and absolute grief imaginable. Want of you has taken all that is before me, all that is behind me, and all that I am. I'm terrified you've taken Lau from me, terrified that I don't care enough to stop. Tell me you feel the same, Harek, or if you don't, that you'll allow me to show…"

He shrugged the hand off. "I am not Harek."

Gui's lips bent into an unbidden smirk. It was a ridiculous instinctive reaction, perhaps at the thought he'd not been heard properly. He repeated the name, softer, soft as a kiss.

"Harek."

"I am not Harek. I am the Lost God. My heart was forged before men had needs. My desires draw the planets around the stars and pull saplings into forests. When I was stolen by the god-hated Grayborn, my longings were machined to resemble the paltry urges that drive humans through their petty lives and meaningless deaths. It's taken millennia for me to crawl back, to purify this form beyond carnality and make it a vessel, not for you, but for me that I might save the final fruit of my ill-begotten child from my mother's clutches."

Gui strained to parse what he was hearing. "Child?"

"The World Soul."

A hum from the engines made Gui's lips vibrate. "The World…"

They were entering a system. So soon? Golden light from its central star arced through the cabin, reflecting on the black in Harek's eyes.

Gui looked through the portal. They were fast approaching a planet, a lively green and blue orb with traces of red. It was familiar, but utterly unexpected, and not anywhere near home.

"It's Archosia! Sweet Lau! That's where you've brought us? From one nest of blasphemy to another!" Gui dove for the controls. "Why? Do you mean to kill us?"

Harek pushed him away. "No. I mean to kill Sky."

Gui went from not understanding what was happening, to not understanding what he was seeing. Harek, seeming a titan, but not changing size, was *glowing*, brighter and brighter.

Clouds rushed up. Spires, plazas, buildings, old and new, reached up for them. The cog was coming in fast. The landing, if a landing at all, would be rough.

Iridescent, Harek appeared the way Gui imagined a holy vision from Lau might, arriving unbidden, overwhelming, more dream than waking experience, more heart than mind, a reflection that had become much more than what was being reflected.

When Harek spoke again, his voice sounded like scores of raging engines mixed with the roar of the mightiest armies. His words recalled those of Amka Bodspah:

"I will not give you what you want, but tell me, what great gift have I given you?"

The cog swooped. The hatch didn't open so much as explode. Harek leapt out.

A stumbling Gui braced himself against the breach in the hull. Below, he saw, or imagined he saw, a wild giantess hurling buildings out of her path as a hundred Archosian street patrols tried to slow her.

"Mother!" the Lost God boomed. "I will not let you leave this world! I will not let you harm my seed!"

Her voice full of swirling stars and pestilence, she answered, "Child, I will not give you that choice! I will go to Earth, and you will not stop me!"

The cog crashed with Gui still inside, and the world folded in around him. All motion stopped. All sound became distant. His body, as naked and exposed as his mind, began to shiver.

In time, or out of it, smoke clearing, the sounds of carnage rising, he felt himself pulled from the wreckage.

You have given me a gift, Gui thought. *You have shown me the gods.*

"He's freezing! Get him a blanket," some vile Archosian atheist said.

"Thank you," he replied.

For the first time since he was a child, since he was little, Gui, Arbiter of Lau and Pantheon Temple Lord, felt small.

CHAPTER
84

The knuckle-walkers kept a respectful distance from Wyrm, save for one. Bigger than the rest, he came uncomfortably close. He also kept turning his head up, making the same sounds, repeating the same things, gesturing not with his hands, which remained flat on the ground, but with his fingers. From his cadence, tone, and rolling eyes, he was more frustrated at not being able to make himself understood than he was with Wyrm for not understanding.

For his part, Wyrm was pleased to believe he'd at least picked out the man's name. It was something like Oules. Otherwise, he couldn't tell where one word ended, and another began.

Worried for hours that Fray was being used to lure the others into a trap, Wyrm was doubly relieved when he, Calico, and Arjuda appeared unharmed.

Smiling, he said to his friends, "Where's Dr. Beckles?"

"Dead," Fray explained.

Wyrm's brow furrowed. He nodded at the Untër-han. "Did… they…?"

"No," Fray said. "It was me. Long story short, he deserved it."

"He did," Calico agreed.

"Oh," Wyrm managed. "Okay, I guess."

Calico took to studying Oules much the same way she'd studied the endless white of the Chamber so very long ago. When she was finished, she said, a bit sadly, "He wants to take you to your father."

Ignoring her sadness, but accepting her words, his heart rose. *My father? At last.*

So, when Oules beckoned, Wyrm followed.

Soundless, save for their steady breaths and the ticking of his Soul-Eater's exoskeleton, they moved along the valley. A few hundred yards later, they stood before the surviving face of a building whose decomposing peaks reached twice as high as any other ruin.

What was left of it conspired to create echoes of tall doors, columns and super columns, beams, footings, and floors, creating in Wyrm's mind the ghost of a grand design that had been based not only on wealth but beauty. Shashem. It had to be.

The legendary House of Wisdom was striking despite its decay, an incredible structure even by Archosian standards.

Oules, remaining on his mount, waved the fingers of his right hand, indicating Wyrm should enter on his own.

He did.

What must've been the lobby was only ashes. Beyond that, as far as Wyrm could see, the collected insights of a golden age were gone, all gone. Whatever gifts and secrets might remain elsewhere in this world, despite his father's cherished hopes and wishes, any wisdom kept in Shashem, any magic that could save Meriwald, had been looted or destroyed long ago. The other orb, Birefringe's sibling, if it even existed, wasn't here.

Without much to conceal it, the expedition's final camp lay in plain sight. Its many skeletons were propped up as if on display, the skulls all pierced at the crown, indicating how they died. Wyrm looked back out toward Oules, wondering if at least he was sorry, but the Untër-han was too far away for his expression to be judged.

One skeleton was higher than the rest. The boy crunched among the remains to reach it, nervous ripples on his skin bringing forth his singular sweat. Before the Soul-Eater attack, he'd never thought of the goo as protective, as perhaps a sign of who he was. Now it felt like an old friend, come to comfort him in a moment of grief.

This higher skeleton sat in a place of honor, like a king or great leader, the rubble it sat upon was a higher class of rubble. It wore familiar clothes, and in its pockets, Wyrm found a family picture: Anacharsis and Meriwald Stifler with their son.

Adalbert the Wyrm World Soul stared at his father's bones, their shape, their size, their hardness, and tried to see in them the man he remembered, the smiling, scolding, calm, afraid, confident face. He couldn't. The connection was purely intellectual.

Oh, he believed his father was dead, alright. He accepted that.

But that these bones were once him?

That, he could not see.

What, then, was the point? What had it all been for? Why did fate bring him here, if it was fate at all?

Of course.

He was the World Soul. He had to be now, or else it was all for nothing.

And it couldn't be for nothing.

Hearing a loud airy rush, Wyrm imagined a desert wind had come to mourn alongside him – but nothing stirred. Realizing there was nothing further to encounter here in Shashem other than himself, and sick of that, he left, returning with Oules to the others.

"My father's dead," Wyrm told them. "The Untër-han had their Soul-Eaters slaughter them all. You were right, Fray."

Fray tried to be humble. "I wish I wasn't."

While Wyrm wondered how to respond, the wind he'd heard in Shashem rose to a roar. Two heavy transports appeared above them. Fray, as was his way, shouted the obvious:

"More Archosians!"

Elite troops fast-roped from above, firing plasma rifles at the scattering Untër-han, each shot tinging the air a sickly color.

Oules tried to corral Wyrm's little group, but the boy resisted until Calico said:

"He's trying to get us to safety!"

At Oule's prodding, they moved. The man and his beast looming at his back, Wyrm couldn't tell what was going on behind them, or who might be winning, but he heard a lot of screams.

As they neared one of the many cave mouths, there was a blast from above. Oules and his Soul-Eater fell to the side as one. A glow rose from the single hole running between their chests.

One of the transports had ignored the larger fight to follow them. From its belly, a single man leaped, stocky, bestial, full of fury, intelligence, and intent. He bore not a gun but a dagger.

Sebe Mordent landed hard, his predatory eyes singling out his target. "Swike! Bedswerver!"

Fray raised his hands. "High Commander, hold it, you don't understand."

"I understand well enough!" He hurled the dagger.

Wyrm decided to do what he thought a World-Soul should – protect.

If my sweat can save me from a Soul-Eater, he thought, *why not this?*

Thinking that here at last was the moment he would become himself, Wyrm jumped in front of Fray. The dagger, ignoring his sweat, pierced his shoulder to the bone. Pained, angry, indignant, he tugged at the blade. It slid from his wound as easily as it went in. Then, almost like a child tossing a ball back to his father, he hurled the dagger back where it came.

Mordent dodged, but he'd been startled, both by who the dagger hit and its sudden return. It sliced his battle jacket and cut the skin of his abdomen... just enough. Knowing what was to come, he screamed, more at the sheer stupidity of his fate than any actual pain.

"Help me! Poison! Help me! I am slain!" Grabbing his belly, he staggered away.

If that scratch had killed Mordent, Wyrm realized he must be dying, too. But the World Soul couldn't die. Not like this. Unless...

What if I'm... not the World Soul?

Wyrm felt as if he were falling, or as if he'd been falling all along, and the illusion that he'd ever done anything except fall had simply been dispelled.

Was that it? Was that all I was ever supposed to do? he thought, *collapsing.*

CHAPTER

85

At first, Rusk and Ludi pursued Meriwald Stifler. Soon, they were caught in her wake.

Hyper-strong, impossibly quick, animal-agile, the mad-god-woman tore through Asylon's halls, plummeting down its lift shafts, scrambling on its stairs, crawling on its walls, or bursting through them.

Bruised and panting Rusk and Ludi tumbled out of the first-floor lobby long minutes after their quarry and saw what she had wrought. Minutes ago, the city vista reflected their civilization's peak. Now it was falling apart so quickly that they could all but see a moving line between where order ended, and chaos began.

A cog had crashed nearby, There, a single survivor was tended by rescue workers. Everyone else was running, fleeing a trail of blood and wreckage that pointed like an arrow to the disenfranchised wife of a dead explorer and the naked acolyte who opposed her.

They seemed taller than Asylon, yet, at the same time, they were not.

"I will kill the World Soul!" said the mother who had told her child he was special.

"You will not!" said the man who had raped and pillaged.

Arms locked. White fire crackled between them.

The two scholars got as close as they dared, taking cover behind an overturned mech-sled.

"What in the name of Abraxas are we seeing?" Rusk asked.

Ludi adjusted his weight to better settle on his haunches. "The better question is: How are we seeing? If I'm right, and our minds house these collective entities, we're part of the archetypal manifestation we're witnessing. Our very perception is being influenced on a primal level, altering the inner maps we use to engage the world. Some might call it a metanoia, an eidetic epiphany, a revelation, a…"

Rusk grabbed and shook him. "Could you stop that? Can you ever stop that? Honestly, you make me want to shove you right out there, smack into the end of the world! Are we having a vision, or seeing two gods going at it? Is it real or not?"

The old man harrumphed and pulled himself free. "I don't know! I'm not divine! There are some things you must decide for yourself! At best, we've entered a Chapel Perilous."

"A what now?"

"It's an old earth term for a psychological state in which the individual is uncertain whether they're being affected by supernatural forces or a product of their imagination."

"That's just another way of saying, I don't know what's real!"

"Yes. If you want more, sorry to disappoint you. As a naturalist, I don't think the laws of physics are being broken, but we, and anyone sharing the experience, will act, think, and remember all this as if they are. A worshipper might well conclude that this is the greater reality, and all that science is nothing more than a sad little dream that confuses itself for the world."

Breaking free of Sky's grip, the Lost God hurled a building at her. Rather than duck, she straightened, allowing her Brobdingnagian form to shred the massive projectile. Gritting her teeth, Sky lowered her head and raced at the Lost God. When she hit, he fell, like the tallest tree, like the building he'd thrown, like an empire.

"Out of my way, child. I will not warn you again," Sky said. "I will find a ship and I will go to Earth."

"No, Sky-mother. I love my offspring and hope you love me."

Rusk whined. "Fine. What do we do about it?"

Ludi shrugged. "Again, I don't know. I've tried my best to swerve the psychic currents away from war, but this? Even though I may have predicted it, I've no idea what to do about it."

Rusk's eyes went wide. "But you came back all this way, you must have some plan!"

Ludi gave him a sad, half-smile. "To watch. I came back to watch. Don't you understand, Rusk? This is proof of my theories, after all these years of dreaming, this is my validation!"

Rusk stared. "Smartest man in the universe and you just want everyone to see how right you are, and love you for it, is that it? You're not so different from that poor boy Wyrm, are you?"

"No, I suppose I'm not."

The Lost God was down, bleeding. "Don't you love me, mother?"

The godwoman hovered above him, holding aloft a mountain.

"I do, child, but I won't let your father die. You and your brethren betrayed him once when you made these insects, I can't let you do it again. Let him stay asleep. That's bad enough, isn't it? Must you destroy him? Let me kill the World Soul."

"No," the Lost God said.

In a final blow, Sky brought the mountain down, crushing the exiled deity.

But all at once, something changed, something far away, yet entangled, something somehow seen by her.

Sighing, the first Mother of All exhaled the stars. "No. This was pointless. It's over. The boy is dead. I've killed my child for nothing."

She tossed herself on the fallen mountain's peak allowing it to pierce her chest. An explosion of supernal glory, or something like it, followed.

Everything that remained was decidedly, familiarly, mortal.

Years later, when he reached Ludi's age, Rusk would spend each evening of his waning days wondering if it was Meriwald Stifler, or Sky herself, who had been wrong about how special her son was.

CHAPTER
86

The very real mountain ring around Ballikilak crumbled before the plasma artillery. With Bodspah's warriors and the Archosian infantry on their way in, countless refugees looked to the palace, awaiting guidance from their Pushka. Little did they realize their wild-eyed, giggling avatar had fled, along with Indepa, to seek asylum among the hundreds of Slave-king ships that had been patiently awaiting the destruction of Mordent's fleet.

Neiman Os didn't really want to go out and address them. It was the plan, but given the radical change in the scenery, zhe didn't think all those desperate people were in the mood to hear how they'd been deceived about their beloved Pushka's age – let alone hear about it from an alien.

Instinct was begging Os to flee, but it was in moments like these that many knee-jerk reactions met their untimely end. The warriors lining the room were supposed to be there for zher protection, but they too were expecting a rallying speech, and exiting without giving one would be tricky. There were too many to control at once.

Rock and a hard place. Hell or high water.

Zhe watched the sea of people lap toward the palace – and again weighed the choice, or lack of it. Even if Os survived the ensuing riots, and Dagus, as promised, could manipulate the chaos enough for zher to be named Pushka, what then? Where was Dagus anyway? He was supposed to be here.

Has the beastly Beast Father man played me? Or has something gone even more wrong?

"Back away nice and slow, Nieman. Smile and wave a bit as you go," the Interstellar Op said.

The guards were unconscious. The Op, pointing a gun, tossed over a set of restraints, and motioned for Os to put them on.

Zhe fought to hide zher relief. "I was about to rule this world, you know. Your timing is terrible."

"Tell me about it. My real target, your paramour Dagus got away. Did you know he wants to cause as many deaths as possible in the name of the Beast Father?"

"Well, you can't always choose who you love. That's why we have laws! Perhaps I could help you find him?"

"Don't think so. Restraints, please. Got a tight schedule if we want to avoid the invasion."

Realizing the Op wasn't wearing the protective EVA suit he'd on when last they'd met, Os inhaled slowly. "Toujours Gai."

Fray scanned a wide sky at the precipice, aching to fall. "All this time they were waiting for the Pushka to get Archosia's fleet out of the way. Mordent may have just managed to restore the Slave-king empire."

Where once Mordent's proud ships glowed, scores of black dots indicated the arrival of Kardun from many worlds. The real war was about to begin. Unless something changed, there would soon be more than enough death to sate the Beast Father.

But something was always changing.

As the Untër-han fought Mordent's troops, Fray and the two women carried the boy to relative safety, settling on the long avenue, where buildings that once stood proud were now only implied. Arjuda winced at each explosion. Calico cradled the dying Wyrm. Despite his best intentions, Fray couldn't help any of them.

Noticing, Calico spoke to the soldier as if she finally trusted him, or the need to trust anyone had gone. "I've been here, you know. This is where it started."

Fray looked around for anything that might give him some idea of what she was talking about. He couldn't find it. "Where what started?"

She wiped the back of her fingers against Wyrm's forehead. "The World Soul. This is where the Grayborn asked me to carry their captured god's seed. I'd been raped so many times, that part hardly mattered, but they said the birth would kill me, and they wanted my permission, so they sent me here to see if it was worthwhile."

A shivering Arjuda crept beside Calico. Keeping one arm around Wyrm, she used the other to hug the girl in closer.

Fray, not sure what to believe anymore, asked, "And it was him? Wyrm was the World Soul?"

She brushed some dried flakes of sweat from the dead boy's face. "No. It's Arjuda."